THIRTEEN STORIES FROM THIRTEEN AWARD-WINNING AUTHORS AROUND THE WORLD!

In your darkest heart, did you ever fear ...

That irrefutable DNA evidence would prove you guilty of a murder you didn't commit?
That the man of your dreams could give you nightmares?
That the wall around the ghetto might fence you in?

Have you ever found yourself ...

Stretched out upon an alien's sacrificial altar?
Battling mechanical insects who want to rob your car for body parts?
Alone at night in a room full of fairies?

Have you ever wished ...

That you could live yesterday over and over and over?
That you knew exactly which god to bet on in Friday's fight?
That you could pick out your one true love—by smell?

Award winners of the L. Ron Hubbard Writers and Illustrators of The Future Contests will take you on astonishing adventures into the imagination!

What has been said about the
L. RON HUBBARD
PRESENTS
WRITERS OF THE FUTURE
ANTHOLOGIES

"From cutting-edge high-tech to evocative fantasy, this book's got it all—it's lots of fun and I love the chance to see what tomorrow's stars are doing today."

TIM POWERS

"I recommend The Writers of The Future Contest at every writers workshop I participate in."

FREDERIK POHL

". . . an exceedingly solid collection, including SF, fantasy and horror . . ."

CHICAGO SUN TIMES

"This has become a major tributary to the new blood in fantastic fiction."

GREGORY BENFORD
AUTHOR

"It is rare to find this consistency of excellence in any series of science fiction and fantasy stories. The well deserved reputation of L. Ron Hubbard's Writers of The Future has proven itself once again."

STEPHEN V. WHALEY
PROFESSOR ENGLISH & FOREIGN LANGUAGES
CAL STATE UNIVERSITY, POMONA

"A first-rate collection of stories and illustrations."

BOOKLIST

"The untapped talents of new writers continue to astonish me and every WOTF volume provides a wellspring of the greatest energy put forth by the ambitious writers of tomorrow."

KEVIN J. ANDERSON

"This contest has changed the face of Science Fiction."

DEAN WESLEY SMITH
EDITOR OF STRANGE NEW WORLDS

"Over the long haul the 'L. Ron Hubbard Presents Writers of The Future' books have continued to support the creation of new science fiction writers and styles. Some of the best sf of the future comes from Writers of The Future and you can find it in this book."

DAVID HARTWELL

"Not only is the writing excellent . . . it is also extremely varied. There's a lot of hot new talent in it."

LOCUS MAGAZINE

"As always, this is the premier volume in the field to showcase new writers and artists. You can't go wrong here."

BARYON

"Writers of The Future is the leading SF pathway to success."

ALGIS BUDRYS

"This contest has found some of the best new writers of the last decade."

KRISTINE KATHRYN RUSCH
AUTHOR & EDITOR

SPECIAL OFFER FOR SCHOOLS AND WRITING GROUPS

The thirteen prize-winning stories in this volume, all of them selected by a panel of top professionals in the field of speculative fiction, exemplify the standards which a new writer must meet if he expects to see his work published and achieve professional success.

These stories, augmented by "how to write" articles by some of the top writers of science fiction, fantasy and horror, make this anthology virtually a textbook for use in the classroom and an invaluable resource for students, teachers and workshop instructors in the field of writing.

The materials contained in this and previous volumes have been used with outstanding results in writing courses and workshops held on college and university campuses throughout the United States—from Harvard, Duke and Rutgers to George Washington, Brigham Young and Pepperdine.

To assist and encourage creative writing programs, the **L. Ron Hubbard Presents Writers of The Future** anthologies are available at special quantity discounts when purchased in bulk by schools, universities, workshops and other related groups.

For more information, write

Specialty Sales Department
Bridge Publications, Inc.
4751 Fountain Avenue
Los Angeles, CA 90029
or call toll-free (800) 722-1733
Internet address:http://www.bridgepub.com
E-mail address: info@bridgepub.com

L. RON HUBBARD PRESENTS WRITERS OF THE FUTURE

VOLUME XIII

L. RON HUBBARD PRESENTS WRITERS OF THE FUTURE
VOLUME XIII

The Year's 13 Best Tales from the
Writers of The Future®
International Writing Program
Illustrated by the Winners in the
Illustrators of The Future®
International Illustration Program

With Essays on Writing and Art by
L. Ron Hubbard · Ron Lindahn
Ed Gorman · Janet Berliner

Edited by Dave Wolverton

Bridge Publications, Inc.

©1997 BRIDGE PUBLICATIONS, INC. All Rights Reserved.
No part of this book may be used or reproduced in any manner whatsoever without written permission except in the case of brief quotations embodied in critical articles or reviews. For information, address Bridge Publications, Inc., 4751 Fountain Ave, Los Angeles, CA 90029.

The Scent of Desire: ©1997 Bo Griffin
Recursion: ©1997 S. Seaport
Altar: ©1997 Malcolm Twigg
White Jade: ©1997 Janet Martin
Orange: ©1997 Sara Backer
Black on Black: ©1997 Kyle David Jelle
The Art of Love: ©1997 Ron Lindahn
A Prayer for the Insect Gods: ©1997 Morgan Burke
The Winds: ©1997 Heidi Stallman
The Garden: ©1997 Cati Coe
Only Half the Equation: ©1997 Ed Gorman
Wings: ©1997 Alan Smale
The Gods Perspire: ©1997 Ken Rand
The Biggest Little Job in Fiction: ©1997 Janet Berliner
Troder: ©1997 David L. Felts
For The Strength of the Hills: ©1997 Lee Allred
Illustration on page: 25 David T. Hubbard ©1997
Illustration on page: 54 Patrick Haslow ©1997
Illustration on page: 90 Mia Hopper ©1997
Illustration on page: 126 Igor Baranko ©1997
Illustration on page: 178 Ulia Semenenko ©1997
Illustration on page: 195 Jack Hines ©1997
Illustration on page: 246 Karen Pollitt ©1997
Illustration on page: 255 Nathan Hale ©1997
Illustration on page: 329 Eric Williams ©1997
Illustration on page: 338 Arthur Roberg ©1997
Illustration on page: 371 Viktoria Dunayeva ©1997
Illustration on page: 405 Eric Williams ©1997
Illustration on page: 444 Steve Turner ©1997
Cover Artwork: "A Fighting Man of Mars" ©1997 Frank Frazetta

This anthology contains works of fiction. Names, characters, places and incidents are either the product of the author's imagination or are used fictitiously. Any resemblance to actual events or locales or persons, living or dead, is entirely coincidental. Opinions expressed by nonfiction essayists are their own.

ISBN 1-57318-064-5
Library of Congress Catalog Card Number: 84-73270
First Edition Paperback 10 9 8 7 6 5 4 3 2 1
Printed in the United States of America
Cover Artwork "A Fighting Man of Mars" by Frank Frazetta
Cover design by Peter Green Design

WRITERS OF THE FUTURE and its logo and ILLUSTRATORS OF THE FUTURE and its logo are trademarks owned by L. Ron Hubbard Library.

CONTENTS

WELCOME TO THE FUTURE by *Dave Wolverton* 1

THE SCENT OF DESIRE *Bo Griffin*
    Illustrated by David T. Hubbard.......... 3

RECURSION *S. Seaport*
    Illustrated by Patrick Haslow........... 44

ALTAR *Malcolm Twigg*
    Illustrated by Mia Hopper 58

THE FAST PRODUCTION WRITER
    by L. Ron Hubbard 101

WHITE JADE *Janet Martin*
    Illustrated by Igor Baranko 107

ORANGE *Sara Backer*
    Illustrated by Ulia Semenenko......... 128

BLACK ON BLACK *Kyle David Jelle*
    Illustrated by Jack Hines 180

THE ART OF LOVE
    by Ron Lindahn 215

A PRAYER FOR THE INSECT GODS *Morgan Burke*
    Illustrated by Karen Pollitt.............. 223

THE WINDS *Heidi Stallman*
    Illustrated by Nathan Hale 251

THE GARDEN *Cati Coe*
    Illustrated by Eric Williams 281

ONLY HALF THE EQUATION
    by Ed Gorman 331

WINGS *Alan Smale*
    Illustrated by Arthur Roberg 335

THE GODS PERSPIRE *Ken Rand*
    Illustrated by Viktoria Dunayeva 354

THE BIGGEST LITTLE JOB IN FICTION
    by Janet Berliner. 373

TRODER *David L. Felts*
    Illustrated by Eric Williams. 379

FOR THE STRENGTH OF THE HILLS *Lee Allred*
    Illustrated by Steve Turner 414

ABOUT WRITERS OF THE FUTURE
    by Dave Wolverton. 486

CONTEST INFORMATION 493

WELCOME TO THE FUTURE

Written by

Dave Wolverton

The book you are holding is the thirteenth volume of prize-winning stories and art from the winners of the L. Ron Hubbard Writers and Illustrators of The Future Contests. Together, these two contests make up the world's most aggressive talent hunt for new writers and illustrators of fantasy, science fiction and horror.

If you've read previous volumes, welcome back. If this is your first glance at the anthology, welcome.

In the past thirteen years, we've published stories from 180 authors and we've published artwork by over a hundred illustrators. In addition, we've published some fifty articles on writing and illustration, articles written by some of the premier professionals in the field.

Surveys show that most of the authors in previous anthologies have gone on to publish many fine novels, short stories and screenplays, and to win various literary awards. The illustrators also tend to excel.

It's sometimes interesting to note trends in the Contest. Last year, it seemed that stories by female authors were in. Over the past several years, more and more women have been winning the contest. But, of course, as soon as you spot a trend, it seems to disappear. This year, only four of our prizewinners are women.

Also this year, I've noticed that we had a tremendous influx of horror stories or tales that otherwise had dark endings—in spite of the fact that our judges often pick the lighter tales as winners. I could make up an extremely fine horror anthology from stories that didn't win a first, second, or third-place prize in their quarter. This may have to do with a collapse of some markets in horror fiction rather than an increased number of people writing in those genres.

As a Contest judge, I am often surprised at our mix. People often ask, "How can I win the Contest?" And the answer is simple. Write an excellent story.

But of course the next question is often, "Well, what are you looking for?" The answer seems kind of flip, but the answer is that we often don't know until we see it. Once again, we're looking for stories that stand out.

But here are some hints that might help you stand out from the crowd. We seldom get as much humor as we'd like, and we don't get a great many stories with upbeat endings. Perhaps that's because when an author is trying to win a contest, he tends to get a little serious in tone. We also don't get as much high fantasy as we'd like. You'd think that with the popularity of the genre, we'd have plenty.

So, for those who'd like tips on how to win the Contest, I hope those help. For those of you who have just come for entertainment, enjoy. . . .

THE SCENT OF DESIRE

Written by
BO GRIFFIN

Illustrated by
David T. Hubbard

About the Author

Bo Griffin was born in 1966 into a family that owned a large floral and nursery business in Salt Lake City, Utah, so that he was raised amidst the scent of pesticides, endless bags of manure and buckets of cut carnations.

He has a long-standing interest in art and a much more recent interest in writing.

He first met his wife, Nellie Johnson, while serving as a missionary in the Netherlands, where neither one of them was much impressed by the other. A few years later, after their second date, Bo says that he felt he had about as much chance of escaping marrying Nellie as a cow on her father's ranch had of escaping the branding chute. She accepted his proposal, but wore a black wedding dress.

In college, Bo caught the creative writing bug after reading T. Coraghessan Boyle's short stories and Orson Scott Card's novels, and attending readings by the fine Welsh poet Leslie Norris. For several years he took creative writing classes, feeling that he wasn't getting the "big picture," until he *attended a shortened form of the* Writers of The Future *seminar given to the public, where Dave Wolverton and Shayne Bell served as instructors.*

The story that follows grew from using two idea-generating techniques Bo learned at that seminar.

About the Illustrator

David T. Hubbard has lived in Elkhart, Indiana, all his life. He first began sketching regularly at the age of three, when his father brought home a bag of plastic dinosaurs that gave him the creative spark.

As he grew, he divided his time equally between drawing and catching snakes. His love for creatures—whether alive, extinct or mythical—has constantly fueled his work.

In 1983, David obtained his B.A. in art and education from Goshen College. Since graduating, he has worked as a teacher, in factories, print shops and craft studios. He is currently employed by Goshen Rubber Company, where he runs a press.

David has won awards in some local art shows, and says he spends time pondering where next to push his wandering imagination.

Ronald Wolf knew his deceased lovers had come back to make trouble when a large mallard tumbled like a drunkard out of a blue sky and smashed onto his porch. He could read the signs: He knew that the women had begun hiding out in the woods again when a family of skunks fumigated his front door. He knew at least that Polly, his first lover, had resurfaced when he found "Adulterer" and "Death" written on all his windows with some substance that evaporated with the afternoon sun.

Polly—thank the Lord that she hadn't survived—had done such things before. But for two days Ronald had pushed the thought of his dead lovers aside.

In the back of his mind, yes, he heard alarms. But the fact was that the living Emma Dixon occupied most of his thoughts—Emma Dixon and the meadowlarks they'd heard together on an innocent stroll out past Old Man Buckey's place. Emma Dixon, who knew that the secret to a good, hard ice cream was at least five hearty laughs. She'd showed him that secret just last night on his porch while she cranked the old ice cream maker with arms that were naked and strong. He knew that he'd always remember those rosy, naked arms and the opening to her blouse that revealed her lacy bra. He would remember that night for years. Not that he had many left. But for the few that remained, Emma Dixon would occupy an unfair share of his time.

Ronald had felt this way six times before. And in every case the relationship had ended in death. But the women couldn't help themselves. Not even from forty miles away they couldn't. In fact, it was usually women from out of town whose noses began to pick up his scent. They'd smell something on the breeze each time they opened their windows to air the house. They'd recall obscure, happy incidents and moments from their past. They'd smell gardenias or rhubarb pie or—as in the case of Evonne Richards—fresh leather-bound books. They'd catch whiffs just before entering the post office, library or Bye Ryte Market.

Sooner or later they'd home in on Glover's Pond and bloodhound the streets that led in and out and through the town. Sooner or later they'd end up standing at Ronald's gate with their eyes closed, luxuriating in a most powerful scent.

Then Ronald would come out to be friendly, and they'd discover that what they smelled was Ronald Wolf himself. Grace had told him he was delicious. Brenda had said it was all spring and lilacs. Polly had flared her nostrils and said, "Horses and hay, Brother Wolf. Horses and hay."

They all succumbed to his scent, his aura, his whatever the hell it was. They all looked at him with fire in their eyes. They all decided to give themselves to him out there, on the spot, in his waist-high garden of whispering grasses and wildflowers.

Color, beauty, height, size—none of that mattered to Ronald. He had welcomed them all. He was a sensitive lover of women, and it was only a matter of time before they woke his passion. Only a matter of time before he burned them up.

• • •

Emma stood at the sink in a peony print dress washing pancake batter out of an enormous ceramic mixing bowl. "I know men when the lights go out." She didn't want Ronald getting any wrong ideas. This wasn't going to be a love-in.

"On my honor, I won't touch you," Ronald said. "You can turn off the light. Lock the door, if that will make you feel better."

She had principles. Just because a man made her feel like cream puffs inside, didn't mean she had to go all to pieces. But it was more than cream puffs with Ronald. She was wired and loose. Muddled and sharp. She was like a car racing about on two wheels. She looked out the window. "The moon's going to come up over there. You can see it like headlights on the other side of a hill."

"Emma."

"Don't you 'Emma' me." She didn't trust herself, that's what it was. She was feeling like a girl so caught up with a man she might do anything at all. And maybe for Ronald, maybe for all the enlightened women of the day, it was nothing to stay a chaste night in her boyfriend's bed, but, for Emma, staying went against everything she'd been raised to believe was appropriate when a man and a woman courted. No matter that Ronald had offered to sleep in the kitchen. For Emma, staying was like living on the edge, and tonight she felt especially susceptible to temptation.

"Maybe you'd like to see the moon rise? Twenty minutes and we can be up on Blue Ridge."

"Fresh air would do me good," she said. Anything to clear her mind. But her mind was clear—she wanted Ronald. But she just couldn't believe the intensity of her emotions. This wasn't love, that was for sure: love percolated over time.

And this wasn't infatuation. She'd been infatuated before and never had an appetite like this. Ronald was a perfect watermelon. She could eat up pounds of his watery sweetness. She could eat until she was digging rind and she'd still want more. Something faint told her it was dangerous to be so doped up with a man. But she ignored it. Instead she turned to Ronald in his overalls and said, "What you got for the bugs?"

They walked at a brisk pace through the woods, Emma not wanting Ronald to think he had a wimp in tow, and Ronald just trying to keep up. He said it was easier to see with the light, but she grabbed it out of his hands and turned it off. Ronald made her bold. "No flashlight," she said. "There's no adventure unless it's dark." The path was easy to follow, a clearly blacker strip running through grass and bush. Besides, the light was mucking up her night vision and she wanted to see the woods in the dark.

At one point Ronald asked for the light back. "I'm missing the view," he said.

"What view?"

"The backside of Mother Nature," he said.

"My, my, my," she said, never having imagined herself attractive in that way at forty-seven.

Another few steps and she took his hand. Dangerous and bold. A far cry from anything anyone would expect from the woman who'd raised five kids and managed the Dixon dairy. A far cry from anything Emma had ever expected herself. The crickets and cicada's filled the night with a thrumming song.

Maybe she'd stay the night. Just because she slept in a man's bed didn't mean she wanted him in there with her. She was a big girl. She could hold a little romance in her heart and not act on it. Her hand felt hopelessly small in his, but she gave him a squeeze, and he squeezed back. Emma considered that given time and no awful surprises, this just might be the second man she'd marry. She wondered if her feelings were just the reaction of a woman too long without love. Then she decided she didn't care. The moon was just about to break over the mountains.

Emma said, "I'm feeling as loose as one of those scruffy Nevada mustangs."

•••

The moon did rise up the back of Blue Ridge, but so did the ghosts of six women. Ronald stood on an outcropping of rock that stuck up like the bow of a sinking ship. Emma had stopped ten feet below him to gather her skirts. She wasn't one to wear panty hose. He didn't blame her. He could never figure why women had started wearing them in the first place. He looked back at her. He'd have to control himself this time. He'd almost made it a year with Brenda, but then one time he'd slipped. One time and she went up in a lemon-scented smoke. Since Brenda's death he'd lived for weeks at a time in a numbing, gray fog. There was neither hope nor despair, joy nor pain, only a series of tasks that needed to be done.

When the desire began to bubble and cook in his gut, he planned to send Emma away. And if she wouldn't go, then he'd get in his truck and drive like hell. He knew how his desire ebbed and flowed. He knew when a touch would ignite a woman like flash paper. He refused to do it this time with Emma. This time he'd grow old in love.

Ronald felt hope for the first time in many months. Not long ago he had gone out and bought a roll of duct tape. He figured that was the best way to rig up a section of garden hose from his truck's exhaust to the passenger window. But Ronald couldn't follow through. He sat in the kitchen holding the roll of tape into the wee hours of the morning. And when dawn finally broke, Ronald knew it was too late. His mood had lifted a bit. He had work to do. So the tape went out into the garage, and now with Emma around, that tape would stay there.

"Emma," he said, "the moon's as big as it's going to get."

"I'm coming," she said and stepped up onto a generous ledge.

Ronald couldn't help but notice how shadowy and pale the moonlight made her legs. Strong legs, and as she climbed closer, he could see that they were hairy as well. He liked that. He liked her brown shoes with waffle-iron soles. Emma was animal, and proud of it.

"When I was a girl," she said, still climbing, "I used to think God lived on the moon."

"Maybe he still does."

"I could go out any time of night as long as the moon was looking down on me, and I'd feel safe."

Ronald caught a flash in the corner of his eye.

"I thought moonlight was the color of angels, and when I died I'd go there, 'cause that's where heaven was, and I would ride the moon like some Ferris wheel around the earth."

He looked into the woods past Emma. A flicker of gray between two pines. Another at the base of the rock.

Damn.

He could see Isabel halfway up a birch, waving at him, flickering like an old black-and-white movie. He could see Brenda, decidedly skinnier than she had been in life, landing on the rock. Evonne, Grace and Maria clustered on the trail.

Polly. Polly was nowhere to be seen, which was more dangerous than he'd wanted things at the moment. The ghosts of jealous women couldn't be trusted.

It's a fact that ghosts can't fly, and they certainly can't pass through walls, which shows just how far you can trust fairy tales. It seemed they could affect things in Ronald's world, but not consistently. His dead lovers had orchestrated a microburst once, abusing his garbage can on the driveway, then whipping it a hundred yards above Doug Yule's house to spin like some UFO, but such an event must have drained them, because Ronald hadn't seen even a glimmer of his lovers for almost a year afterward.

Still, ghosts can jump like moon men. They have bodies. And Ronald figured that made them mortal. He'd never killed one, but he'd grabbed hold of Polly once and given her a good shaking. He hadn't been able to hold on though. She slipped out of his grasp like a fish, jumped out of his window and up on his neighbor's roof where she gestured every obscenity she knew until the dawn washed her out. So if these women decided to block his way, he could karate chop a path through them.

But he didn't want the situation to develop that far. He didn't want Emma to learn about them, not yet. After sending the dead mallard and the skunks, these ghosts probably couldn't do much but talk. But talking was far too much. They'd poison Emma against him, as sure as cows ate grass.

Emma straightened next to him. "Wow. I can see the ponds."

"We've got to go," he said.

"What?"

"It isn't safe out here."

Emma looked at him.

"Please," he said. He could go down first and boot Brenda off the rock.

"If you're worried about falling," Emma said, "why'd you climb up in the first place?"

"I just remembered that this place is infested with spiders," Ronald said. "Honest. A guy got bit last week and his hand swelled up and turned brown. They might have to cut it off."

Emma looked at her feet.

"They're pouncers. These spiders can jump . . . ten feet maybe. They don't need webs."

"Ronald, you are so full of crap."

"Please."

She looked back at the moon, the valley. "All right. Whatever."

But it was too late. Ronald could see Polly descending toward them. Who knows which tree she'd jumped out of. Emma turned to follow Ronald, but instead got Polly in her face.

Emma started. "Whoa," she said and batted at the ghost.

"Girl," Polly said in her faint voice, taking Emma by the ears. "You're an idiot. He'll burn—"

Ronald grabbed Polly by a leg and flung her with all his might off the side of the ridge. He knew that she'd float the two hundred feet to the bottom and come back to torment him, but at least he'd got her out of the way for now.

Emma watched Polly's ghost float out into the night. "What the heck was that?"

"Plastic bag," Ronald said.

"I thought it said, 'You're an idiot.' A faint voice. I'm sure of it."

"Right," Ronald said.

Brenda sprung and jumped. She zoomed up the rock and when her head was level with Ronald's boot, he punted her out toward Polly. "Damn litterbugs," he said.

"It's the hooligan beer drinkers," Emma offered. "All I ever see in the woods is empty beer cans."

At the bottom of the rock Emma untied her skirts. Isabel was no longer in the tree. The others blocked the path ten feet ahead. Ronald wasn't fast enough to take out all three. He had to get them to move. "I just remembered there's a short cut," Ronald said and pointed down the hill.

It worked. Evonne, Grace and Maria jumped over the ledge.

"But it's a little too treacherous at night." He grabbed Emma's hand and walked underneath the three ghosts who were still rising to the apex of their arch.

Of course, the women didn't give up the chase. They almost caught him stone-stepping across Talbot Creek, but Ronald was too smart to be outmaneuvered by a pack of ghosts. When he reached the house, he shut all the windows, locked the door, and closed the flue. They weren't going to take Emma away from him. Not tonight.

• • •

Emma had expected Ronald's bed to stink. But the sheets were crisp, and the quilt smelled of a flower she couldn't put her finger on. The smell reminded her of sunlight and lying in the grass under apple blossoms. She couldn't remember how it had felt to fall in love with her first husband, Bill, but it must have been like this. He had been the most dependable man a woman could ever find. Dependable in love. Dependable in life. He'd died from cigarettes, may the tobacco industry rot.

Her mind told her she should leave but in her heart she felt peace. Peace and something similar to the weirdness she'd felt when her son had thought to make a joke and bake hashish into his sister's birthday cake.

Ronald had a cheap dresser with bright red knobs. He hung his pants on the bedposts. He lined his shoes up underneath the foot of the bed. She had never liked a man in overalls, not until yesterday. And it had been a tender gesture for him to pull the blinds and tuck her in before he went to sleep in the kitchen on a cot he'd bought years ago down at Jack's Army Surplus. She had almost told him the cot wasn't necessary. But Ronald had seen the look in her eyes and said, "We're going to take this relationship slow. I'll be just fine in the kitchen."

"God," she whispered to the ceiling. "Let this be right." Maybe it wasn't her lot to die a lonely woman. She imagined sleeping with Ronald in this bed. To have a man warm and scratchy at her back. She could learn to enjoy that again. She looked at the window. However, he'd have to learn to sleep with the blinds open. She threw back the covers and sat up, and that's when the ghost came crawling out from underneath the bed.

Emma almost screamed, but before she could catch her breath, the ghost knelt down at her knees, in a pose of pleading, almost praying, and she was so beautiful that Emma couldn't help bending over for a closer look. That's when she heard the ghost say in an almost inaudible voice, "He's a royal idiot, that one." The ghost jerked a chin toward the kitchen. "Can you hear me?"

Emma's eyes widened.

"So, you're not deaf." The ghost stood up. "Listen to me: I ran the whole way here as soon as Polly jumped at you. That stuff up on the ridge was just a diversion. I'm lover number four. Isabel."

"What?"

"Isabel."

What kind of man kept ghosts under his bed?

"Hey!" Isabel clapped her hands in front of Emma's face. "Don't go wimping out on me, girl."

Emma closed her eyes, took a deep breath, counted to three. The ghost was still there. "Ah, hell," Emma said.

"That's right," Isabel said. "Now listen. Ronald had six lovers and burned every one of them up." She laid a hand on Emma's arm that was soft as sunlight on a spring day. "You've got a choice. Leave him. Die in ecstasy. Or kill him. We'd actually prefer the latter because we still pick up his scent when he goes into heat or whatever it is, and if he were here with us dead, well, then we could do something about him."

"Ronald burned you up?" Ronald was too sweet to commit such horror.

"It's not what you think," she said. "It was the burning heat of his desire."

"Ronald?" He'd never mentioned anyone named Isabel.

"He's a loving man. And you can't slake him. Not as you are."

Ronald had never once gone beyond the limits of decorum. He didn't cuss. He didn't lie. Her Ronald?

"Look. You've only known him two days."

"But—"

"Wake up. Ronald Wolf is a serial killer." Isabel pointed at the window. "Pull the blinds."

Emma did. And crowding the pane were the flickering faces of one, two, three, four, five women.

At that moment Emma heard Ronald creaking down the hallway to the bedroom.

"Quick," Isabel said and pointed at the window. "Let me out."

Ronald tapped the door. "Emma?"

Emma opened the window. "Yes?"

Isabel said something almost audible and the ghosts scattered.

"You okay?" he asked through the door.

"Come in. I'm decent."

Ronald swung the door in and looked at the window. Emma followed his gaze. Nothing but moonlight.

"What are you thinking?" Ronald said. "I haven't got any screens."

"It was too beautiful."

"You'll think 'too beautiful' when the mosquitoes home in on your face." He walked to the window, cautiously scanned his backyard, then shut the window.

"Not the blinds," Emma said. "I'll feel like I'm in a cave."

Ronald peered through the glass. When the silence had gone on too long, he said, "I came to tell you that there's an extra blanket on top in the closet."

Not my Ronald, she thought. How considerate.

"Anyway, good night."

As he left, he shut the bedroom door behind him, but he didn't go to his room. She heard the front screen door slam. Heard his footsteps grind the gravel out front and stop somewhere near the shed.

Nobody said ghosts couldn't lie. Emma lay back down on the bed. She'd always trusted her heart. She suspected that she'd know it if she were in danger; she had that sense.

Of all the things . . . ghosts wanting her to murder a man!

Still, they could be right. And if they were? Running wouldn't help. Leaving Ronald would be like fasting. She'd have to come back eventually. She might die if she stayed, but she doubted it. Everything about this felt right . . . except for the ghosts, and they could be ignored.

What was she thinking? She's just talked to a ghost! You don't ignore ghosts.

Ronald had turned her brains into pudding.

Emma lay on the bed, wondering if she wanted to flee, and trying to feel shocked that she'd even consider staying.

But she couldn't feel shocked. It simply wasn't in her. And she wouldn't flee, so if she was going to die, she wanted to know it. And if the ghosts were imaginings, she wanted to know that, as well.

Emma was not one for anxiety. She and Ronald were going to have a chat. And if he wanted to stab her to death, then let him do it like an honest man. She had lived a good life, and Bill was waiting on the other side. Besides, she'd heard that willing victims turned wackos off.

She put on her slippers and walked out into the hallway. "Ronald, get in here. You and I need to talk." She opened the front door and stepped out onto the porch.

"Ronald?" That, of course, brought him running.

• • •

Ronald sat at the table hanging his head. Emma sat across from him and pushed a thick strand of dark hair behind her ear. "What do you mean it comes and goes?"

"It comes and goes." He looked at Emma with honest eyes. "I never wanted to kill them. I loved them."

"But you didn't tell them of the danger."

"I didn't know what the hell happened the first two times. And I did warn Evonne that I'd burn her up with my loving. She'd heat up with desire and—poof. But all she would do is kiss my hand and say things like, 'You're my backwoods Byron,' and 'There you go with your metaphors of love.' With the others . . ." He hung his head again. "With the others I was lonely and weak. But I almost made it with Brenda. This time it's going to work, Emma."

He had been completely forthright. She sensed no insincerity. It must be horrible to see your lovers go up in smoke.

"I thought that maybe with you I could hold back. I thought that maybe you and I could grow old together."

She could see by the set of his jaw that he was going to pack her off. But she didn't want to go. It was that smell of desire. That smell pulled at her now, and she realized that it had come and gone these last two days. What she wanted now was for him to look at her, see how she ached for him to touch her, see that she trusted him. She'd been alone for so long.

Emma knew men. She knew how deep her desire could go.

"Maybe those other women shorted out." She took his hand and pulled him up. "Maybe they didn't give enough back." She kissed him. The first kiss she'd allowed.

Ronald said, "I'm cursed."

"It's just the smell of your good soul," she said. "And it's delicious."

They kissed again, and she recognized the smell.

"Grass," she said. "Fresh cut grass and autumn leaves." And then the heat began working like tendrils through her.

He took her hand and led her to the bedroom. The heat softened every muscle. She sat on the edge of the bed and caressed his hand and arm. He cupped the back of her head and sent goose bumps down her arms.

"Are you sure you want to stay?"

"Positive," she said and looked up at him. He did not have a pretty or dignified face. His face was weathered and hard and kind, and she knew she had made the right choice to stay with him.

He slipped her nightgown off one shoulder, traced a line along her neck, and kissed her back. "You're warm," he said.

"I feel like I'm floating in a summer sea." She didn't want to consummate a marriage that hadn't happened, but she could make love like this for hours. It had been a long time since she had necked. Besides, she and Ronald had discussed morality their first evening, and Ronald agreed with her views. So when he kissed her collarbone, she didn't flinch. He wasn't going anywhere with this.

She tipped her head back so he could more easily kiss her neck. And when he slid his hand underneath her nightgown and stroked her thigh, she nibbled on his ear. However, the heat kept building, and with that building, her desire bunched and tightened in her loins, her breasts, her skin.

They kissed and caressed, dallying on the edge of chastity until Emma no longer wanted to stop herself. She opened his shirt. When she stroked his chest, she noticed for the first time that he glowed soft as a lightning bug.

"No," he said. "Emma, please." And tried to close his shirt.

But she held his hands, took one nipple into her mouth, and gently tugged.

"Oh, Lord," he said. "No." Then he backed away from her and ran.

She sat on the edge of the bed, reveling in the warmth, the tingle on her lips, and the earthy smell of rich loam. A fine man Ronald Wolf was, respecting her limits when she'd been ready to let herself go too far. She lay back, and then everything turned yellow-green and the color took her.

•••

Emma was still in her nightgown the next afternoon when Ronald walked into the house with muddied boots. She stood by the oven with flour on her jaw.

He sniffed, looked at her mixing bowl. "What is that?"

"Gingersnaps," she said.

He sat at the table. This was not going to work. He'd driven five hours last night before the desire ebbed. He grabbed a glass of water that stood on the counter, drank a sip, and spit it out. "What the hell is in here?"

Emma hooted. "It's baking soda," she said. "I felt a little nauseated this morning when I woke up."

Brenda had done that. A bad sign, a very bad sign. "It's no good between us," Ronald warned. "Next time, I'm not going to be able to pull back like I did last night."

"I'm okay," Emma said.

"No you're not. Hell, with Grace we were just reading in the parlor. I reached over and held her hand, and the next minute she flashed and took all the hair off my arm."

I'm dangerous and selfish, he thought. Couldn't Emma see that? She was going to die unless he did what should have been done long ago.

"I can't leave you," Emma said.

"I never wanted you to." He poured her some apple juice out of the jug and stared out the window at the sun shining off his flagstone path.

A bullet to the head would make things quick and clean. He was a decent man, and decent men didn't have a right to kill women, even if they came willingly.

"There's got to be somebody who knows about this stuff," Emma said. "Don't you know some Indian or crazy prophet?"

"Emma, nobody knows what I've got. I don't even know how I do it myself. I just start thinking that I need someone. I start feeling hollow inside, and somebody shows up."

"I don't care if I die."

"You would care—if you're brains weren't stewed with my scent." He could see that's what she'd wanted him to say.

"But I am stewed," she said. "That's the point."

"I'm going back to work," he said. "Doug Bills needs some help with his sheep."

"I'll be here when you get back."

"No," he said. "You won't," wanting her to leave.

She was too confident, Emma was. She thought they'd overcome this together, as if lover burning was just one of those obstacles couples faced. But she'd end up tempting him longer than he had power to resist.

Except, he reminded himself, this time he'd decided to remove himself from the situation—permanently.

• • •

That evening, with a pot of her own beef goulash and a pan of corn bread covered to keep warm, Emma waited for Ronald like she waited for cows to calf—no rushing about. She figured he'd come when he was good and ready. She waited until sundown, sat on the porch in Ronald's rocker, and waited until it occurred to her that Ronald wasn't coming back.

She called Doug Bills, who said they'd finished work early that afternoon. She called Ida's Cafe—which served the best chicken-fried steak Ronald said he'd ever eaten—and found he hadn't been in for days. Finally, she called the sheriff's office, and the deputy there said in her undeputylike voice that Ronald was probably out somewhere fixing somebody's something, but that they'd be on the lookout.

The bugs made a racket in the darkness, screeching, droning, trilling. Moths fluttered and careened about Ronald's porch light. She could smell him out there. She could almost point in his direction. She didn't need any sheriff or bimbo deputy to bring him home.

Emma kept her pickup in second and drove with the windows rolled down. South of Glover's Pond she followed him. South and then east along a smooth dirt road that would take her to Whitney if she let it. Maybe a mile down the road she saw his truck in a clearing, next to a campfire. She drove up and shined him with her high beams.

He lay on the ground and didn't move.

Something white leaned in her window.

Isabel.

Emma stepped out of the truck. "What's going on?" Emma asked. She could see the other ghosts vanishing and reappearing as they waltzed in and out of her high beams. The smell of Ronald washed over her.

Dancing?

"You did it!" Isabel said joyously.

Emma could barely hear her over the truck's engine. She turned the ignition off. "What?"

"He's dying—as we speak."

"What?"

"A bullet through his heart."

"No!"

Emma flung the door open and ran to him. Ronald wheezed and rattled and gurgled in short breaths. A .22 rifle lay askew on the ground.

"Ronald!" She kneeled next to him. A neat circle of blood soaked his T-shirt. Could ghosts do this? Lure him into the woods and shoot him?

He moved his head toward her, almost opened one of his eyes, then began to cough and spasm, trying to get air.

Get him to the clinic, that's what she needed to do—take him in the back of the truck.

She tried to help him up, but he couldn't stand. He didn't know what was going on. Drowning in blood. She tried to pick him up, tried to drag him and failed.

The ghosts flickered around her. "Emma," Isabel called.

"What!" Emma said and turned on her. "Stay away!" She waved her arm to clear the ghosts away from her,

Illustrated by David T. Hubbard

and knocked Isabel back. That surprised Emma. She'd never known it was possible to smack a ghost. Then she got an idea. Maybe if she dragged Ronald on her back—pulled his arms over her shoulders.

She hunkered down, set his wrists on her shoulders, and heaved upward. He moved. She could do this. But five steps later he began hacking and shuddering with such violence it scared her.

She let him back down. There was no use in this. She wouldn't be able to lift him into the pickup bed anyway.

A pebble struck her arm. Another struck her head. She looked up and saw the ghosts brighter than she'd ever seen them, shining like white china. They looked as tangible and smooth as figurines. A rock bounced into the turf next to her. Isabel came with a smoking branch from the campfire.

Emma dodged aside and watched Isabel turn hot white and vanish. The branch fell into the grass and glowed red at its tip. Emma looked up at the other ghosts and watched them wink out one by one.

At first she worried that this was some disappearing trick, that suddenly a ghost would appear behind her with a knife in its hands. But the ghosts didn't reappear. Maybe they'd burned themselves out like Ronald said they could, trying to project themselves into a dimension in which they didn't belong. Who knew the physical laws ghosts were bound by?

Ronald had said the dead Isabel once laid a strangled chicken at his doorstep. Why hadn't his lovers killed him before now? Could they? Emma couldn't shake the feeling that those dead women stood right behind her. The campfire popped. Emma turned around once, twice. Ronald wheezed and lay still. To hell with the ghosts, she thought. Either they kill me or they don't.

Emma stroked his hair. "Ronald, don't you die on me."

He coughed. If he'd shot himself in the heart, he'd be dead by now. Lying ghosts. He must have blown a hole in a lung.

"I'm not like those others," she said. "I've got fire in me you can't imagine." She sat him up straight. "Ronald! Dammit. Help me get you to the truck." To her surprise Ronald grabbed her shoulder and struggled to get to his knees.

• • •

They made it to the hospital in Thurston. A doctor drained the fluid and inserted a chest tube to help Ronald's lung reinflate. Miraculously, the bullet hadn't created a hole big enough to require surgery. Emma held his hand the whole time and smelled her grandmother's spicy geraniums.

She'd been selfish. She'd been just like all the others. Ronald hadn't killed those women. They'd killed themselves because they had wanted the ecstasy Ronald could give them more than they had wanted Ronald. What they'd felt was desire, not love. They didn't give anything in return. They didn't have anything to give.

Parasites is what they were, parasites trying to freeload off a miracle. And Emma felt she wasn't any better than the rest.

Early the next morning a nurse wheeled Ronald to a room, and after watching the nurse fuss with his IV and chest tube apparatus, Emma fell asleep on a wide orange chair next to Ronald's bed. She awoke to the murmur of women in the hallway and found Ronald watching her.

"I tried," he said.

Emma shook her head. "You shouldn't have. I was selfish."

Ronald looked away.

Would he try suicide again? Yes.

He didn't want to die—Emma could see that—but Emma knew Ronald would try again. The certainty sat in her as calm and solid as a stone. And the next time Ronald would do a good job of it.

"I'm leaving," Emma said and stood.

"Somebody else will show up."

"I can't help that. I won't be like the others. God has worked something strange with you."

Ronald put a hand to his chest. "God? What makes you so sure this ain't some recessive monkey gene? What makes you think this isn't something like moths? Hell, they can smell each other out miles apart."

Emma leaned over him and kissed his forehead. His bangs were matted with sweat. "And who created the moths?" She trembled. "I've got to go now, Ronald."

"I love you," Ronald whispered.

She traced his eyebrow and cheek with the back of one finger.

Then the room began to whirl and Emma fled.

•••

She didn't completely shake Ronald's feel until three days later when she stepped off a plane hundreds of miles west in Seattle, and even then a pang of desire would shoot up her thighs every now and again and make her stumble. She'd given Hector, her hired help, the reins at the dairy, and then called her oldest to tell him she was coming to stay for a while. It had been two years since she'd seen him and his wife, and they could sure as hell tolerate her in their spare bedroom. They wouldn't even know she was there.

For the first few days Emma thought she'd beaten the desire. She ate like she'd just stepped off the boat from Africa. She walked for miles. She even clapped her hands and danced for two young street musicians playing a clarinet and guitar and looking for all the world like they were wearing their fathers' pants. And much to her surprise, she found that her daughter-in-law had a winning sense of humor.

But it didn't last. She missed Ronald. She craved Ronald.

"Mother," her son said one evening well into the second week. "What is it with your hands?" The TV showed some scientist talking about pollution levels around Bainbridge Island.

"What?" she said.

"You're fidgeting like some druggie."

"I don't know."

"Well, knock it off. All I can do is watch your freaking hands."

Emma tried to hold her hands, tried to concentrate on what the woman on TV was saying, but couldn't. She couldn't stop thinking of how it had felt to have Ronald's hand on her thigh. She couldn't stop herself from imagining how the touch of Ronald's lips and hands could satisfy the craving she felt from her thighs to her neck. So she left the house and walked until she could think of something besides Ronald. Around eleven o'clock the craving subsided.

Dear God, she thought, that craving had been as tiring as contractions. Then it occurred to her that if she could endure three births without painkillers, she could endure Ronald Wolf.

Emma believed that in most things you needed to stand up and fight first. She had seen her orange tomcat face down all kinds of dogs, but if that cat ever ran, ever looked away, that's all it took, and those dogs would harry him to the trees. She had planned on visiting each of her three children and then spending a month with her parents. But all visiting did was give her mind time to wander. All she was really doing was running, not fighting.

She could detox better at home, she decided. At least there she'd have something to occupy her thoughts.

Having decided to face her problems, Emma realized she'd been walking dark sidewalks in a big city at night. Her heart jumped. Fool woman. Well, there was nothing to do but move, so she set off for her son's place, hips swinging in what would be one of her fastest speed walks since she stopped exercising with Louise Kelley.

Two days later she boarded a red-eye to Louisville.

She found Hector halfway down the row of milking stalls, hooking a heifer up to the milk pump. She tapped him on the shoulder. "Play," she said. "Go enjoy your wife and kids. It's time you had a paid vacation." If she was going to fight her desire, Emma was going to need all the work she could find.

• • •

Emma stood over her gas stove, fluffing the rice for a rice pudding which she would have for dinner because she wasn't in the mood to eat anything else. She'd smelled Ronald twice today. Once when she had to get up on top of the haystack to tip a stubborn column of bales. And just now. It was autumn leaves again.

She wondered how Ronald had healed, if he was back home right now. She could call him just to make sure everything was all right.

But calling would make staying away that much harder. No. She wouldn't call. She'd bake her pudding, eat it, and sleep. So she walked into her front room and began playing the *Fiddler on the Roof* CD her daughter had sent her last Christmas. And thank the Lord she'd done the work of three men today, because while she waited for the pudding to bake, she could think of nothing but Ronald. Only exhaustion held her in Bill's recliner chair until the timer dinged.

She ate the pudding hot with milk and bottled peaches. There had to be some way they could love one another without her dying.

There was a trick to everything, wasn't there? It was just a matter of figuring it out.

However, Emma didn't get much time to think. After finishing two bowls of pudding she felt too tired to brush her teeth and went straight to bed. She set her alarm, then pulled that soft Wal-Mart blanket up to her nose.

Emma dreamed of her and Ronald riding two roans whose tails and manes flowed black and smooth as ink.

She dreamed of an electrical storm whose lightning split and scorched seven trees.

She dreamed of Ronald singing on the Lawrence Welk show, wearing long green and yellow scarves, and tap-dancing like Gene Kelly.

Then the buzzer on her alarm woke her. Five a.m. Time for the first milking.

She had to squint to keep her eyes open, but she pulled on the jeans she'd worn yesterday and headed out into the dark. The screen door squeaked and slammed behind her. The cows mooed. The stars shone clear and quiet. She walked to the barn with a slice of jack cheese in one hand, a coke in the other, and Ronald on the wind.

•••

Ronald watched the tall woman in her cream suit jacket and sunglasses walk past his house three times. Then she opened his gate and marched up the walk. Her red fingernails flashed in the sunlight.

When she rang the doorbell, Ronald ripped the door open and said, "What the hell do you want?" He kept the screen door latched.

The woman put a hand to her chest and said, "Why, I'm sorry. I hope I didn't disturb you." She set her sunglasses on her head.

Ronald could see it in her eyes. She was blind with the scent. He could have been a dog for all she cared.

"Well, you did disturb me. Now get."

"But don't you smell it?" she said.

Ronald said nothing.

She looked down. "Of course you don't," she said and fingered her bracelet.

"You get off my porch," Ronald said. "I don't want no druggies on my porch."

"No," the woman said. "Sorry." She slid her glasses back down over her eyes and walked to the front gate. An hour she loitered in front of Ronald's house and then drove off in some Japanese outfit.

She came back a few days later. And again a few days after that. Each time Ronald stood behind the screen door and brusquely shooed her away.

Five more women showed up over the course of the next year, and Ronald treated each the same as the first.

Ronald almost opened the door for the last. She had skin the color of the good earth and hair braided in cornrows that fell to her shoulders. He found her sitting barefoot on his porch swing when he came home from delivering Mrs. Early a load of coal.

"Good evening," she had said.

"No it's not," Ronald said and stomped past her. She sat on his porch swing all through dinner and the news. And Ronald had almost let her in, but then remembered Emma. He remembered how hard it had been to pull away from her that evening in his bedroom, and so he called the sheriff.

When the woman left, the sheriff stood with Ronald in his driveway and said, "What is it with you, Ronald?"

"I don't know, Dennis. Bad genes, I guess."

"Hell," the sheriff said. "I'd give an arm and a leg for some bad genes."

"No," Ronald said. "You'd have to give up far more than that."

"Who? Meg?" The sheriff laughed. "My wife ain't worth that much."

Ronald said nothing. He wondered how long he could live like this.

The sheriff lit up a cigarette and said, "I'm calling it a night." He pulled out of the driveway in his Ford Bronco, gave his lights a whirl, then sped off for town like somebody had just robbed the bank.

That night Ronald lay in bed, thinking about Emma, and saw a flicker of light outside. The light flickered again. He got out of bed to look out his window.

Nothing. He walked into his front room and saw his lovers outside his kitchen.

He realized now that he'd never really loved those women—not like he loved Emma. He'd been juiced up with them. Desired them. His relationships with them had been like running rivers out west. He'd never made it past the rapids with these women, never made it to the other side of the white water. But with Emma it was different. The desire for her body had been overshadowed by a desire for her welfare.

He opened the drapes to his front window and watched his lovers gather in his flowers. The tall delphiniums and orange poppies swayed as the ghosts brushed past. Then his lovers began to call to him.

Polly was not herself; there were no threats. Instead she mouthed over and over, "I love you, Ronald. I miss you."

Ronald missed something. He tried to tell himself that this emotional hunger was all biology, like chimpanzees needing grooming, but that didn't help. He still ached inside. He ached for all these women, even Polly.

Maybe Ronald should buy himself a dog. But Ronald didn't want to care for a dog. He didn't have time for walks and feedings. And he sure as heck wasn't going to buy a fine animal to lock it up in a run in the back.

Brenda put her shining hands to the window. She wasn't mouthing anything. She simply looked at Ronald with her large eyes. In life they had been blue, like cornflowers.

He had got these poor women all caught in some lover's afterworld limbo. "I used you," he shouted through the glass. "I used you all!"

They continued to speak to him. Maybe they had something to say, a plan. Maybe as ghosts they knew more about the spiritual side of existence. So Ronald went to the front door and opened it wide.

They walked slowly toward him until they stood around him in a circle. Their warm, white hands touched his face, his hair, his arms. They whispered love. Evonne embraced him and then caressed his face with her waist-length hair, like she had done when they first met. It felt like the slightest brush of silk.

Then Polly stood in front of him. She leaned up to his ear and said, "Ronald, this is no life for you. Come with us. We've learned to make peace."

"You can break this curse?"

"No," she said. "Only you can break it."

He could end it now with his lovers around him. Or he could wait until he died some other way. What did a few years of loneliness matter?

"Did you ever love me?" he asked.

"We need you," Isabel said. The others murmured their agreement.

"How do I break this?" he asked.

Grace put her mouth to his ear. "It's passion," she said. "You wait it out, or you feed it until you're satiated."

"I tried that already."

"Then shed your body, Ronald," Isabel said. "Ghosts can't die. Perhaps you can feed it on this side of life—with us."

Did Ronald want to be a ghost? Would he even become a ghost when he died? Was there some qualification for ghosthood? Or would he just cease to exist like those two Jehovah Witness ladies had told him he would? He had no idea how things worked after death.

"How do you know this will work?" he asked.

"We don't," Brenda said.

"We're ghosts," Evonne said at the same time.

Ronald saw Brenda glance at Polly, and when he followed Brenda's gaze he could have sworn that Polly had been glaring at her. She'd shushed Brenda. Ronald had caught it.

"What?" he demanded.

Brenda looked at Ronald's other lovers and then folded her arms. "Lying to him won't help," Brenda said to his other lovers. "We're desperate women, Ronald."

"Here we go," Isabel said.

"Ronald," Brenda said. "I'm speaking honestly. Death may not help, but it's your only alternative. Ghosts can't die—we've shed the corruptible. Maybe it's only true spirit that can connect with true spirit. Maybe there's no other way for this passion, this energy, to conduct."

They had come here to trick him, come to push him over the edge when things looked bleakest. And Brenda with her college education and big words was simply acting her part in a well-calculated play.

"Think about it, Ronald," Grace said. "Death is only a doorway."

"Maybe you should leave," he said.

His lovers stole glances at each other and didn't move.

"I don't plan on dying any time soon," he said. "Obviously you can't do much about that, or you already would have. So move it."

They left him in a bright rush of touches and whispers. Ronald watched them until their pale light faded in the trees on the other side of the road.

Ghosts. Wiley women. What a life.

Then he thought about what Brenda had said. "Energy to conduct." Maybe it was electricity. Maybe he was just a live wire that needed grounding, he wondered. Maybe all this time what he needed was to ground his desire in something bigger than himself.

●●●

After the first month away from Ronald, Emma decided Ronald's scent was like arthritis. There was nothing you could do when it flared up. You just had to treat the symptoms and ride it out. Knowing that the scent would eventually leave her made it bearable.

She'd found that working as part of Hector's crew and campaigning for LeAnne Snow's bid for county commissioner kept her too tired to do much about Ronald.

Four or five months after leaving Ronald, Emma thought she had his craziness beat. Then almost a year to the day after she had left Ronald in that hospital bed, she was fishing for a bag of fencing clips in the bottom of a five-gallon bucket when Ronald's scent washed over her and made her shiver. It hadn't been that strong for quite some time.

She found the clips and stood up, and another wave of the scent rolled over her; she lost her legs and sat with a thud in the dust. Ronald was coming. Her head buzzed, but she knew that much.

When her mind cleared, she made her way out of the barn. Emma stood in the middle of the road with her arms crossed when he came barreling up the road in his rust-dotted, baby-blue Ford pickup.

That damn man. She'd had this thing beat, and he had to get weak on her.

Ronald turned off the road in a cloud of dust. "Emma," he said and swung the door open. "Emma, I've got it!"

She had to close her eyes, keep herself from running to him.

"Emma, it's all electrons and wires."

Emma opened her eyes and watched him approach. She couldn't really understand him. All she knew was that the world smelled of grass. She could not remember the scent ever being this strong.

He stood right in front of her, grinning like he'd just won first prize at the pie bake-off. "Emma," he said and touched her shoulder.

The heat didn't hurt. That surprised her. She felt it spread like an itch. So this is how it ends, she thought.

"Ronald," she said. She'd miss him. She wondered if Bill or Ronald's dead lovers would greet her on the other side.

Ronald's eyes went wide and he took a step back. "No," he said. "No!"

There was a bright flash and a cloud of yellow smoke that started her coughing. When the smoke cleared she saw Ronald on his knees in anguish. She held her arms up before her. They glowed with a bluish, white light. She looked down at her legs, belly and chest. They too glowed with the same clear light. At first Emma thought she was a ghost. Then the light began to dim and change color from white to yellow to a dull orange. Then the light and heat left her altogether. She felt exhilarated, clean like she'd just washed at Kenny Falls.

Ronald began to wail, then he opened his eyes and stared at her.

"Your clothes," he said.

Indeed. Emma had none. All that was left was a white ash that began to flow and swirl toward the barn in a light breeze. Her skin had returned to its normal color. She squeezed her arm and felt her chest. The breeze goose-pimpled the skin all down her sides. She wasn't a ghost. She was alive!

"Go," she said. "And find us a preacher."

● ● ●

Everybody balked—there was paperwork to be done, tests to run. You couldn't just marry someone on a whim. Emma was going to talk to LeAnne about changing that. Then they found a Baptist minister in Greenville who said, "I'll marry you before God tonight, if you promise to come back tomorrow and let me marry you before the State."

Emma was afraid anything Ronald touched would ignite, but she couldn't go to the preacher buck naked. So she put on the old batik dress she'd never wanted to wear.

It would never do. She looked like one of those arts festival types. You only lived once, and if your dress burned, it burned. Emma threw that batik thing in her trash and slipped on the mauve dress with the fine lacework down the front. She smoothed the front and looked in the full-length mirror. Who would have thought she'd marry twice?

Ronald had gelled his hair back and shaved. He wore a suit that made him look like he belonged on Wall Street.

"Cuff links?" Emma asked.

"Evonne bought it for me," he said. He smoothed the front of his suit. "I don't know. I thought it was kinda nice."

"Humm," she said. What would she do with those ghosts?

The minister met them at the church. He unlocked the doors and Ronald said, "Nothing fancy. Okay?"

"Okay," the minister said. "You may call me Brother Paul."

They promised for life, through sickness and health, and then Brother Paul said, "You may kiss the bride."

Ronald held his hands up. "Not tonight, Brother. We'll wait."

Emma suppressed a smile.

Then Ronald stuffed three twenties into Brother Paul's hand.

"You're a true Christian," Ronald said.

"Tomorrow," Brother Paul said.

"We won't miss it," Emma said.

•••

They sat on Ronald's porch, listening to the evening breathe with the sounds of insects, not daring to touch each other yet. Moths fluttered in and out of the porch light. "First thing we're going to do," Emma said, "is screen off this porch and put in a yellow bulb in that light."

"First thing," Ronald said.

They sat in silence for a while and then Ronald said, "May I hold your hand?"

"Are we ready?" Emma said.

She hadn't flashed out by her house. And he was trying to think of her, trying to be one. "We'll never know until we try," he said.

"Maybe all we needed was some personal sacrifice," she said. "It sounds trite, but maybe that was the trick."

"Or maybe it's like Thomas Edison finding the right material for a filament. At least I didn't have to go through as many as he did."

"Ronald!" she said.

"Or maybe nothing is fixed."

Emma stood up and began to unbutton her dress. "Well, I'm not going to ruin this dress finding out," she said.

Ronald looked out to the road and down to Doug Yule's house. "Emma," he said. "For heaven's sake. Go inside."

He watched her undress in the moonlight that washed through his bedroom window. And when she stood proud and naked before him, he said, "I'd believe in a God who made such a thing as you."

Emma smiled, then took his hand and led him to the bed. Ronald traced the curve of her body from her shoulder to her knee. Then he sniffed. "So this is how it works," he said. "I just remembered one day when I was a boy. My grandpa deWaal and I had just tilled his garden. He sat on a bucket in the shade of a cherry tree drinking a can of apple beer. And I ran through the soil in my bare feet. The soil was so light, I'd sink up above my ankle with each step. I loved that man."

Ronald sniffed again and looked into Emma's eyes. "Is this what you've been smelling?" he said. He took a deep breath through his nose. "Grass."

"At last," Emma said, "you've finally got a taste of your own medicine." She kissed him lightly on the lips. "Maybe we're ready."

They kissed and stroked each other until their bodies shone like the moon. When Emma climaxed, everything went white. There was neither house nor bed, only the stars and the scent of the forest, of green things living and dying. Emma thought she had died and ridden that Ferris wheel around the earth, but when their bodies cooled, Emma and Ronald found themselves naked on a field of white ash.

•••

The sheriff finally found Ronald out at Emma's place. "Haven't you heard?" he said over the telephone.

"What?" Ronald asked the sheriff.

"Doug Yule swears it was some damn UFO. Ronald, there's nothing left of your place. It all burned."

"What?" Ronald said.

Emma whispered, "Who is it?"

Ronald mouthed back, "Dennis Brown."

"Gone," the sheriff said. "I mean gone."

Ronald said, "Couldn't have been a UFO. I don't believe in UFOs."

Emma covered her mouth and began to laugh.

The sheriff said, "Doug says a light bright as the sun woke him up."

"Well, you know Doug," Ronald said.

"I don't know," the sheriff said. "There's a white ash out here, fine as flour. About an acre's been burnt. And you tell me: What would make a perfect circle like this?"

"I don't know," Ronald said.

"Well, I'm sure the insurance adjuster is going to want to ask you some questions. You'd best get down here."

"I'd best," Ronald said.

•••

Nobody could explain the burning at Ronald Wolf's place. Nor could they explain the similar circles that began to appear in the woods and fields around Glover's Pond. UFO crazies began to flock to the town. A few big-time reporters even came to ferret out the truth, but all they turned up was nonsense.

Doug Yule swore by all that was holy that he once saw ghosts dancing on the spot where Ronald's house had stood.

Robert Pexton and his gal Kristi claimed that they were necking in his Camaro out by the Johnson farm when they saw a bright light. And when they went to investigate, they saw a couple run stark naked into the trees.

The circles became a stop for local tourists. The strange thing was that every once in a while, Dennis Brown would have to go haul some man or woman off one of those sites. Everyone of them had gone crazy, blabbering about the scent of the place.

Dennis sent some of the ash to be tested, thinking maybe someone was running a new drug lab in his area. But every sample came back certified carbon.

And all the while, Ronald and Emma worked on her dairy, the scent of their desires blending and mellowing with age.

RECURSION

Written by
S. Seaport

Illustrated by
Patrick Haslow

About the Author

In 1972 S. Seaport had the misfortune of being born twelve hours before Halloween. As she grew, she always felt herself attracted to science and books and at age thirteen a friend introduced her to speculative fiction through an Arthur C. Clarke novel, Childhood's End.

In the years since, she's collected an extensive library, and somewhere along the line decided that she could tell her own stories.

Recently she married her significant other of six years, and somewhere found the time to pen this fine tale.

About the Illustrator

Patrick Haslow has been interested in the art of science fiction and fantasy for as long as he can remember, His biggest inspiration has been Star Wars and the paintings of Ralph McQuarrie. Seeing his work really showed him that his two favorite hobbies, drawing and fantasizing, could be put to good use.

Patrick grew up in small towns in the Adirondack mountains. As a child in school his mind spent a great deal more time in the margins of his notebooks than it did in the classroom. He was even called space cadet. He attended college at Rochester Institute of Technology where he learned that good drawing skills were a must in any genre of illustration. While at RIT, he became completely involved in the "business" of being an artist and somehow forgot that fantasy art was his initial impetus for wanting to be an artist. After graduating RIT he enrolled at the Savannah College of Art and Design in a graduate illustration program to rediscover what it was that he had loved so much. The fantasy art that he is now creating is the rediscovery of his imagination.

The date was Thursday, November 18th, 1928, 7:06 p.m., when Harold Fitzpatrick first undid time.

Like many, perhaps most, discoveries, serendipity in the form of sheer chance played the crucial role: If Mrs. Fitzpatrick hadn't just acquired the porcelain Ming horse, if she hadn't placed it on the precarious glass sidetable, if Harold hadn't been running down the hall late for a dinner always served precisely at 7:00 p.m. and if he hadn't been wearing his new and treacherously slick dress shoes, the incident may never have occurred. However, chance conspired, and thus at 7:03 p.m. plus 26 seconds, Harold found himself sprawled on his back across the hallway amid shards of horse and table. At 7:04 p.m., Mrs. Fitzpatrick arrived on the scene of her son's distress, and promptly increased said distress tenfold.

Not that Mrs. Fitzpatrick would ever do anything so uncouth as throw a temper tantrum. No, certainly not. Instead, she lamented the trials of motherhood in that anguished yet utterly refined tone she had spent the last sixteen years, ten months and four days perfecting. At least Harold had been spared the first nine months of her practice.

Harold squirmed under the flow of quietly cutting words, then froze as glass crunched, wondering if he'd invite more trouble by interrupting her or leaving bloodstains on her redwood floor. Not for the first time, he began to believe that bleeding to death would be a far kinder fate than listening to another of his mother's chastisements. He closed his eyes and wished desperately that the last few minutes had never happened.

Exasperation crept into her voice, "Young man, you will look at me when I speak to—" Mrs. Fitzpatrick's voice was silenced as abruptly as a radio turned off.

Harold blinked in amazement. He was standing at the end of the hallway once more and both horse and table were intact. For a moment panic threatened to overwhelm him, and he clapped a hand over his mouth just in time to muffle the whimper that was rapidly building to a full-blown shriek. He blinked several more times, expecting the scene to return to its former state of chaos. Then his scattered thoughts were focused by the imperious summons of his mother's bell. Deciding to ignore the enigma for the present, he hurried cautiously toward the dining room, edging past the horse on the far side of the hall as if it were a live, and much more lethal, animal.

He arrived just as Mrs. Fitzpatrick's carefully manicured hand reached once more for her small silver bell. The bell was something of a mystery: how she managed to make this five-ounce object sound like its hundred-pound cousins in the Hagia Sophia, no one in the household was quite sure. But then no one was quite sure how she, born Nell Jones of Middleton, Oklahoma, managed to fill the role of Mrs. Reginald Fitzpatrick, mistress of one of Virginia's oldest and richest families and high-society hostess, to such glittering perfection.

For once, her icy glare of disapproval failed to penetrate as he mumbled his apologies and took his seat at the table.

Three weeks and six days passed, and Harold was beginning to believe the first episode nothing more than a hallucination when the next incident occurred.

His private and exclusive preparatory school for boys, the Robert E. Lee Seminary, was hosting a recital of Christmas music, a fine opportunity for the orchestra to demonstrate its skills and, more particularly, for the parents to compare their sons' abilities.

Attacked by an acute case of stage fright, Harold retreated to the lavatory, failing to emerge until just before the recital began. Seated in the front row, he clutched his saxophone like a talisman and waited for the starting point of his solo in "Silent Night." But the music, surprisingly good for a group of adolescents and preadolescents, worked its soothing magic. Harold felt quite confident and relaxed as he lifted his sax.

The sound that emerged was the painful, dissonant squawk of a strangled goose. Horrified by his instrument's betrayal, he dropped it and gazed in crimson-hued humiliation at the gaping sea of faces. One face, most certainly not uncouthly gaping, snapped into focus: Mrs. Fitzpatrick raised a delicate and long-suffering hand to her temples, silently declaring that she expected nothing else of her hopeless son. Then a quiet snicker behind him broke the stunned silence, and he swung around to confront the smug, victorious smirk of Alexander Fullbright as the entire auditorium began laughing.

Desperation triumphed over skepticism; Harold closed his eyes and wished. The laughter was abruptly replaced by the relative quiet of the backstage. Opening his eyes, he found that he had just put down his saxophone case to hang up his coat.

It worked! he silently rejoiced.

Wasting no more time, he opened the case, replaced the brand-new reed with an older spare, and slid the new one into his pocket. Won't Alexander be surprised, he thought with great anticipation.

Then suddenly it was no longer enough to merely avoid Alexander's torment. He wanted to turn the tables, to pay back years of embarrassment, to be the downfall of Mr. Alexander "Perfect" Fullbright, who had never accepted that awkward, hapless Harold sat as first chair saxophone while he was but second, who was his mother's favorite example of all that an exemplary son should be. . . .

And so it was that fifteen minutes later, Alexander Fullbright's saxophone made an ungodly noise as the second chair began to play. Fully prepared for the ghastly sound, Harold played blissfully on and earned his first standing ovation.

Still floating through a golden haze, saxophone cradled to his side, Harold slipped behind some curtains to press his face against an icy windowpane. Throughout the reception people had been complimenting him, both for his actual playing skill as well as his ability to carry on. He had even received several acknowledgments from some other boys, other victims of Mr. Alexander "Squawk" Fullbright, who had not been seen since slinking off the stage at the recital's end.

Just as he was about to reemerge, he heard footsteps approach, bringing two familiar voices. The first was Mr. Cartwright's, his music teacher's, earnestly commenting, ". . . Harold has always been quite the musician. I'd like to give him some extra lessons. He's talented enough to play for a professional orchestra with a few more years' practice."

The second voice, genteel, but with the slightly bored tones Mrs. Fitzpatrick had cultivated for use with those whom she considered underlings, replied, "One should hope he'd be talented at *something*, considering all his other deficiencies. Very well. When . . ."

Her voice faded into the background hum. Harold scrabbled free from the curtains and stumbled in the opposite direction, victory suddenly stale and tasteless.

•••

Nonetheless, for the next five days Harold's life was unusually good. The second incident had stripped him of all inhibitions in applying his ability. In the course of experimenting, he discovered that while he could not undo the actions of others, he could change any of his own, as many times as he liked. Foreknowledge was an admirably potent weapon.

Thus did Alexander's two attempts at revenge fail miserably and Harold's test scores begin to demonstrate a slow but cumulative improvement.

His joy, however, was to prove ephemeral. Upon his return home after the last day of school Mrs. Fitzpatrick informed him that the Penhursts would be arriving the next morning to spend the holidays in America, a benison Harold would gladly have forfeited. The Penhursts consisted of Uncle Thomas, Aunt Regina and the terror (Harold's own private prefix) twins Arabel and Anabel.

During her tour of the Continent, Regina Penhurst, née Fitzpatrick, had managed to marry a British lord, an accomplishment which Mrs. Fitzpatrick regarded with both pride and envy. Certainly it was good to have semi-royal connections, but life had never presented Nell

Jones with the opportunity to snare a member of the nobility. A widowed, still lovely, and fabulously rich Mrs. Fitzpatrick, on the other hand, would have had better prospects . . . but once again fate had conspired against her, leaving her with a crippled but still-living husband. Thus, she faced the coming call with an odd mixture of elation and dread. The former emotion inspired by the opportunity to associate with true blue-bloods and the latter by the deeply buried insecurity that all her accomplishments could not replace lineage. Even the fact that the Fitzpatrick fortunes had certainly not suffered from the loss of Reginald (if anything, the family finances flourished under the precise ministrations of Mrs. Fitzpatrick) did not dispel her nagging worries; her very success could be perceived as a sign of her lower-class origins. For what would a real lady know of business?

Harold's reaction, on the other hand, was far simpler: he anticipated the Penhursts' arrival with all the eagerness of the Romans awaiting the Visigoths. He would have far preferred a visit from the maternal side of the family. Although the single visit courtesy the Jones family had been an unmitigated disaster according to Mrs. Fitzpatrick, Harold remembered it fondly. His five cousins had enjoyed endless active games and had not been the least shy about either involving him or getting into trouble.

The following morning, with all due fanfare, the Penhursts descended upon the Fitzpatrick manor. Reginald had even been wheeled downstairs to be present at the greetings. Stiff and uncomfortable in his Sunday best, Harold suffered through the welcome. It was for moments like these that he wished he could skip forward in time; experimentation had proved otherwise. He stoically ignored the face Anabel—or was it

Arabel?—was making at him behind the adults' backs. Fortunately, the travelers needed to refresh themselves and unpack, bringing the proceedings to a rather more rapid close than otherwise. Harold faded into the opulent furnishings as the group dispersed.

Unfortunately, the trial by ordeal that Mrs. Fitzpatrick named "a casual luncheon" also arrived with undue promptness. Harold sat uneasily, a politely attentive expression plastered onto his face. Carefully adhering to the principle of attention-incurs-risk-and-should-therefore-be-avoided, he spoke only when spoken to and then replied briefly but courteously. The strategy appeared to be succeeding; lunch was more than half completed and no major catastrophes had occurred. Then Arabel spilled her tea.

Blushing prettily, she apologized. Mrs. Fitzpatrick comforted her indulgently. Then to further soothe the girl's feeling, she embarked upon a tale of one of Harold's more humiliating misadventures. It was Harold's turn to blush—not at all attractively—as his mother recounted the time when he had caught his bathing suit on a nail that projected from a jetty, then plunged sans suit into the ocean. The beach had been quite crowded that pleasant summer's day and Harold's fall had provided entertainment for a sizable audience. The episode was no less amusing now, under Mrs. Fitzpatrick's clever narration, and the Penhursts also laughed most appreciatively. Harold withered under the twins' combined smirk.

He closed his eyes. They flew open again at a blinding glare; he then became aware of a wet salty smell, the cries of gulls, and rough wood and gritty sand under his feet. Eyes now adjusted to the brightness, Harold silently ran though his vocabulary of profanity—not a particularly impressive list nor anywhere near sufficient to vent his emotions—as he gazed down in dismay at his suddenly ten-year-old body.

•••

Four months, two days later, Harold was still overcoming his residual horror at having to relive the next six years of his life. The fact that he could now better those years was of scant comfort, as he had to be careful to not perform *too* well. A child changes quite substantially through adolescence, and having a mind six years in advance of his body did not permit comfortable cohesion. A little on the late side—or would the correct term be early?—Harold came to appreciate that his talent was not an unmixed blessing and resolved to treat it with much greater caution.

One afternoon, bored to distraction by the books and puzzles which had entertained his younger self, Harold wandered into the library. There he found a copy of *Tom Sawyer*, a book he had read several years later as a school assignment and, to his surprise, greatly enjoyed. Curling up in a window seat, the only comfortable piece of "furniture" left by Mrs. Fitzpatrick in her redecoration of the manor, Harold lost himself for several hours in the adventures of a river boy.

As dusk fell he decided against turning on a light, too clear an announcement of his presence. On his way out of the library, he knocked a large leather-bound book off a pedestal. Retrieving it, he discovered the volume to be the Fitzpatrick family photo album, a valuable resource indeed for a person who was attempting to play a role six years in his past. Lips curved in a slight smile, an expression too old for his current face, Harold flipped open the album to confront a photograph of a

Illustrated by Patrick Haslow

yet younger self staring popeyed into the camera and clutching a dark fuzzy teddy bear.

"Teddy R," he breathed.

Eleven years had not fully soothed the desolation. The last gift from his father, right before Mr. Fitzpatrick boarded the ship that would take him to Europe and the Great War, which cost him his health and his mind, Harold had treasured Theodore Roosevelt—or Teddy R to his five-year-old enunciation abilities. Mrs. Fitzpatrick had been ambivalent about the toy; certainly the stuffed bears were fashionable and patriotic, but they were not at all traditional and her son seemed far too attached to his.

The issue reached its crisis point one day when Mrs. Fitzpatrick had removed Teddy R from Harold's frantic grasp and placed it high up on a display case. Teddy R was to remain there for the next several hours as punishment for some minor infraction on Harold's part.

He had been sent to his room, but he soon eluded the servants and crept back to the parlor, around which he skulked until Mrs. Fitzpatrick and her guests vacated it. He had then sneaked into the room, gazing at the out of reach Teddy R with frustration, longing churning his soul. Unfortunately, five-year-old Harold's next move was not well considered: he had tried to climb directly up the display case, with disastrous results—the least of which were a concussion and a broken arm. Alerted by the crash, Mrs. Fitzpatrick arrived on the scene and in extreme irritation thrust Teddy R into the hands of a maid, commanding the girl to dispose of it. She ignored Harold's screams and tears, which were far more for the removal of his bear than any mere physical pain.

Standing in the dark library, blinking away a haze of tears, Harold found himself stretching involuntarily, reflexively, and desperately once more for the forever out of reach Teddy R.

Or perhaps not forever.

A suddenly much shorter Harold discovered himself standing in the parlor at the foot of the display case, on top of which reposed a stuffed bear. For a moment he was appalled. He had just reversed another five years of his life. Then regrets were swept aside in a flurry of action.

Harold wrapped his arms around Teddy R and buried his face in the tattered fur, wholly secure and at peace for the first time in more than a decade.

• • •

Despite immense chagrin at this further reduction of his state in life, Harold was nonetheless a fairly happy boy. The restoration of one's best friend after eleven years of absence can assuage many losses.

Harold drifted circumspectly through his days. The demands of a five-year-old's existence were not onerous. His main difficulty lay in avoiding other people. Unhappily, Mrs. Fitzpatrick planned a lawn party which Harold would be required to attend.

An hour into the party, Harold was managing to play his role deftly, running about with the other children and begging for treats. Then Mrs. Fitzpatrick called for him. He scampered over to her, performing his best young-and-obedient-son appearance. He smiled inanely as she introduced him to several guests. One of the ladies, a large and matronly woman, leaned over to pinch his cheek and coo baby-talk at him. His smile slipping, Harold attempted to unobtrusively back away and he tripped.

He desperately tried to catch his balance, but the coordination of his five-year-old body was not up to the task, and one of his flying hands—the one holding the chocolate ice cream cone—smacked into Mrs. Fitzpatrick.

From his perspective on the ground, Harold noted that he had left a long chocolate smear down the side of his mother's new white silk dress. He was not allowed to ponder the view for long as Mrs. Fitzpatrick snatched him up, made some stilted excuses to her guests, and dragged him off in the direction of the house.

"Clumsy, dreadful child," Mrs. Fitzpatrick seethed once they were out of hearing range. "I wish you had never been born!"

Harold closed his eyes and . . .

Dedicated to my mother: I still have my teddy bear.

ALTAR

Written by
Malcolm Twigg

Illustrated by
Mia Hopper

About the Author

Malcolm Twigg lives with his wife and son in Torquay, Devonshire, in the south of England. There, he is currently studying part time for his master's degree in creative writing from Plymouth University. He helps run a writing circle in nearby Newton Abbot and also teaches creative writing.

Malcolm's career is beginning to take off. He has published numerous nonfiction articles and has had some of his short stories broadcast over radio. He has won national awards in the UK for humor writing, including the Peter Pook Humorous Novel Competition. By the time you read this, his first novel, a humorous science fantasy tale called To Hell with the Harp! *will be in print in the UK through Emissary Publications. A further novel,* Slippered! *is under discussion with his publishers.*

He is also a member of the Agatha Christie Society. Agatha Christie was born in his home town and once worked in the same building where Malcolm is now employed.

Malcolm likes to think he plays the blues guitar, used to fence, and plays badminton and tennis. Despite the fact that he has won awards for his humorous tales, you'll find little humor in the marvelously grim horror story that follows....

About the Illustrator

Mia Hopper grew up in Phoenix, Arizona, and says she took classes in life drawing at colleges so many times that they had to put her on independent study to let her keep taking them.

She's done a number of comic-book sketches at comic conventions and hopes someday to illustrate book covers.

Her inspiration comes from such illustrators as Bernie Wrightson, Simon Bisley and Frank Frazetta.

"All sacrificial civilizations are much the same, Anson," Sharman said. "Blood was always reckoned to be a potent force in appeasing the godhead—whatever that is. Of course, this lot takes it to its limits. Almost anything that squawks, flies, flutters or crawls makes it to the altar. I sometimes think there's no natural death here at all—hence all the livestock." Sharman indicated the pens around the perimeter of the compound, where an incessant lowing and bleating formed a backdrop to the village life. He waved a hand languidly to the Silassian manservant waiting patiently in the corner, and another drink appeared, as if by magic, at his elbow. The compliant native melted quietly back to his post. Sharman eased the neck of his shirt, already wringing wet in the spongy atmosphere of the Silassian tropics, even so early in the morning.

He took a sip of the pungent liquid and grimaced. "Believe it or not," Sharman said, gesturing distastefully toward the drink, "this stuff is a lifeline to the likes of you and me. Tastes like shit, but it's so stuffed with spice and natural antibiotics that bugs don't get a chance to breed—it actually cools your blood for a time. Just enough to make life bearable—that, and the women, of course." He nodded across the compound to the women's quarters set at a respectable distance from the men's living complex. "I would probably have gone mad by now but for the women. The Silassians share everything with their guests—but I mean, everything."

Anson sipped his own drink and gasped as the spice caught at his throat.

Sharman laughed, mirthlessly. "Don't worry, the first few gallons are the worst. You'll kill for it eventually." He shifted his gaze toward the clearing. "Here comes old Tala, to pay his morning respects."

Anson looked out across the clearing to see the old Silassian gliding smoothly over the compound, his robe barely showing signs of movement. Behind him the trees of the Silassian forest swayed only slightly in the morning breeze, the bluish tinge of the vegetation jarring Anson's senses, more used to the vibrant greens of Earth. The scents, too, were heavier than he was used to, more cloying and tending to linger, almost as if the humidity of the Silassian jungle had trapped the oppressive morbidity of its plant life, unwilling to let it dissipate into the atmosphere. The same applied to the Silassians themselves. They had a faint, clinging odor, impossible to describe, but reminding Anson of mildew. He wondered that Sharman had been able to stick to the Company Agent post for so long—the women must be something else.

Tala approached in the deliberate, almost haughty, way that the people had. The naturally disdainful cast of the Silassian features added to the air of hauteur, and the way in which he stopped in front of Sharman and bowed stiffly from the waist, hands thrust by his sides, put Anson in mind of an old-fashioned butler, reinforcing his sense of something long shut away inside a musty wardrobe.

"My Lord Sharman lives this morning?" the old Silassian enquired politely.

Sharman bowed back. "Lord Sharman lives, Tala, and has the graciousness to receive you."

"The honor must be delayed, Lord Sharman. Tala has business elsewhere." The Silassian bowed again and glided past, throwing a half-bow to Anson as he moved off in the direction of the Priests' quarters, set diametrically opposite those of the women.

"What was that about?" Anson asked, wiping his brow.

Sharman pushed Anson's drink toward him, urging him to take a draught. "Ritual greeting. Doesn't mean a thing, really, but these people have an enormous respect for the life-death cycle. You might find that surprising given what I just said about the chickens and things, but practically everything about Silassia is surprising. And don't let that dour expression fool you either. Tala's one of the best."

Anson raised his eyebrows. "He looks a riot."

Sharman levered himself from his chair and gestured his companion to follow. "One thing you will find hard to start with is meal times. But never forget, we're guests of these people—at least for the time being—so stick with it. It gets easier to handle. Believe me. If you like to eat sometimes, it gets easier to handle."

Anson followed the Company Agent from the room, wondering at the last statement. Ever since the shuttle had dropped him into the clearing in the early hours, he had been uncomfortably aware of the slightly sardonic feel to Sharman's conversation. But, after ten years as the sole representative of the Terran Federation on Silassia, it was only natural that Sharman should be somewhat circumspect about welcoming a newcomer. Company Agents chose their solitude purposely.

The dimness of the shack's interior gave only the illusion of coolness, but at the appearance of the two foreigners, the young Silassian at the foot of the table began foot-cranking the huge overhead fan. As it gathered speed, the fug started to shift around until, on occasion, there was almost a cool breeze. It did little but deflect the sweat slightly from its inexorable descent, and Anson felt glad of the Silassian brew which he quaffed with every evidence of increasing relish.

Sharman clapped his hands. Silassians appeared, standing silently in the shadows of the room, holding dishes of steaming food. He clapped his hands again and stood, nodding at Anson to do likewise. Two more Silassians appeared, one of whom approached the other side of the table and placed a large bowl in front of him. The larger Silassian, Anson could now see, held some species of animal in his arms, struggling silently. A low murmur rose from the ranked servants at the back of the hall, gradually increasing in tempo. As it reached a crescendo, the tall Silassian joined his companion at table, hoisted the animal aloft with a cry, and with a deft flick of an evil-looking knife, the smaller man slit the helpless animal from gizzard to loin. The entrails and blood cascaded into the bowl below. The Silassians fell silent. The taller man dipped his finger in the steaming slurry and made The Sign of the Claw in the air toward Sharman and Anson in turn, then withdrew, leaving the bowl of entrails on the table. The animal lay beside it, still twitching.

Immediately, the Silassian food bearers laid dishes on the table and withdrew. Sharman sat down and pulled the nearest dish toward him. Anson remained standing, clutching at the table for support, and gagging. Sharman regarded him with wry amusement. "Get used to it, Anson. That is dinner tonight," he said, nodding at the now-still animal. "They're a methodical lot. Every meal needs a sacrifice to be offered, so they use it for the next meal. It's a bloody practical solution, really." He pulled out a handful of doughy mixture and began to chew on it.

Anson sank to his chair, ashen-faced. "I am going to be sick," he said, faintly.

"Well, take it outside then," Sharman responded laconically around a mouthful of stringy-looking meat. "It's a shame to ruin a good breakfast. They've really pushed the boat out in your honor, you know. We don't eat like this every morning."

Anson catapulted from his chair and dashed onto the verandah, doubled over the rail, and retched. A Silassian spirited out of nowhere and began to clean up.

•••

After breakfast, Sharman joined Anson in the living quarters. Anson had not felt able to rejoin the breakfast table. "Why didn't you at least warn me?" he asked hollowly as Sharman slumped his length onto the verandah chair.

"There's no way to prepare anyone for that, Anson. It doesn't get much better, so initiation by fire is probably the best way." He pulled a couple of fruits out of his tunic pocket and tossed them to his companion. Anson caught them awkwardly. "Here. Get these inside you. There'll be nothing else until dinner. Silassians don't snack, as a general rule—it's the sacrifice thing. You can't go around sacrificing something every time you feel like a quick bite. The fundamentalists won't even touch fruit, but some of them don't hold it against us, except on fast days, feast days, holy days and on alternate weekdays when the moons are at the full, or so it seems. Which is why I don't bother—you never know when you're going to offend someone. These Silassians are very touchy about religion."

Anson took a tentative bite from one of the fruits, then consumed it voraciously. "How the hell do you know if you've offended someone?" he asked, wiping his mouth. "They all look as miserable as sin to start with."

Sharman barked a short laugh. "Hah! They smile at you, Anson. You see a Silassian smiling at you, get something solid between you and him and keep it there until he looks as though he'd slit his own throat if someone said 'Boo'—you know you're on safe ground then. You've got to read emotions back to front on Silassia. Not that they'll do you any physical harm, of course. They'd just make it pretty plain you'd offended their principles, that's all. I tell you, after a few days like that stuck here on your own, you soon learn not to do it again. But they're okay." He swung his feet off the chair and leaned on the verandah rail, looking out into the steaming Silassian jungle. "What beats me is why you had to come out here at all. You could have got everything you wanted from my reports."

Anson joined him at the rail. "Not everything, Sharman. I couldn't get the feel. Your reports say what it's *like* to be on Silassia. They don't say what Silassian life is *like*. There's a difference. The Company wants to know. What's the problem? Feel threatened? I'm not here to take your place, you know."

Sharman shook his head. "You couldn't take my place, Anson. I know these people too well. I'm just worried you're going to screw up the rapport I got with them. It's taken me years to do this. I don't want it all down the tubes because of some snot-nosed sociologist straight out of Company school who doesn't have the sense yet to wipe his arse before he pulls his britches up. Company Agents aren't made, Anson, they grow."

"Maybe that's the problem, Sharman. You've gone too native to be purely objective. But that doesn't concern me," he said, hurriedly, as he caught a glint in Sharman's eye. "Believe me. I'm not on any witch hunt here. So long as you keep our friends here sweet and hold the channels open, the Company doesn't care if you wear grass skirts and stick a bone through your nose. Keep the profits rolling and the Board is happy." Anson took a draught of the Silassian spice punch and gasped. "But they need a better P.R. job. There's a lot of flack back home from the Native Rights Lobby. 'Exploitation' is a dirty word right now. It surfaces now and then, and someone who matters has got a bee in their bonnet about it at the moment."

"So they send you out here to cover up," Sharman finished. "Don't bother denying it. Personally I don't give a shit. You couldn't exploit these people if you tried. They cooperate because they actually want to—can you believe that? You've seen the way they fall over themselves to help you. It was the same as soon as the Company set up base here. They send a whole marine unit, armed to the teeth, ready to slaughter half the planet if they have to, and what happens? They end up being smothered with kindness. The Silassians can't do enough for them. Treat them like gods or something. Had to ship them back home in the end because they were going too soft. That's when I came. The rest you know." Sharman sat down again and mopped his brow. "Shit, it's too hot to spout off, Anson. You know all this. You've been reading the reports."

Anson stayed gazing out over the clearing. Silassians moved in a steady stream in and out of the jungle, dumping hopperfuls of ore into the Company Ex-Port. The thin whine thickened as the machine processed each load and shot the molecular matrix to the Stellar-Port orbiting above. From there, Anson knew, it was then shot in a series of hops back to the main processing station, where the material was reconstituted into the luminescent Silassian blue gold that was the envy of everyone who had any pretensions to being anyone. They couldn't get enough of it. The whole process was so damn easy it reeked of exploitation—according to the Lobby. And the Company couldn't afford to alienate the Lobby: there were some very influential people aboard.

Tala crossed the clearing and bowed from the waist toward Anson. "My Lord Anson lives," the Silassian said softly, and went on his way.

Anson sat down opposite Sharman. "What is this greeting?" he asked. "It sounds so matter-of-fact, it's almost sinister."

Sharman shrugged. "You won't begin to understand until you've been here as long as I have. I'm not sure I know even now. Yin-Yang? Good and Bad? Life and Death? Sacrificial. The whole lifestyle is based on sacrifice. You found that out this morning. Hell, they've even got a caste system of sacrificial animals. Their major religious ceremony is like an abattoir. The greeting?" Sharman shrugged again. "Veneration of life because death is just around the corner? Polite surprise that no one has had the foresight to slit your gizzard and serve you up for breakfast? Who knows? Isn't that what you've come to find out? Me? I just go with it. If you're really interested, ask Tala. He's the closest thing to a lexicon on Silassian life that I know." Sharman got up. "But not for the next four hours. Everyone sleeps for the next four hours. It's too damn hot to do anything else. I suggest you do the same." He paused on his way out. "Oh, and the sacrifice tonight will be a creature something like a chicken. The insides don't come out of that. The head comes off. Just so's you know."

• • •

Anson dozed only fitfully. Each time he woke, he found his pitcher of spiced punch replenished. It was almost as if the Silassian servants had materialized out of nowhere and just as mysteriously faded away again. Sharman's reports had mentioned their uncanny ability to be just where they were expected at the exact moment they were required, without any order having been given, but nothing could have prepared Anson for the reality. It was distinctly unnerving.

He downed the contents of the pitcher in one go, feeling the spike of its passage down his gullet and the temporary shriveling of the sweat on his brow. His shirt clung to him like a second skin, and he peeled it off distastefully, tossing it into a corner. It thudded wetly onto the floor like an over-ripe melon.

The Ex-Porter had fallen silent. Even for Silassians, Sharman had said, the middle of the day was too hot to work—except, apparently, for the ubiquitous servants. Anson saw groups of the natives sitting in the shade of the trees at the forest's fringe, some dozing, others playing a form of four-handed chess complicated by the act of pulling additional pieces out of the box with great verve at seemingly random intervals. Judging by the solemnity with which it was played, the participants were having a whale of a time.

"Inshalaka."

Anson jumped.

Tala had appeared at his side like a whisper. "The Game of the Gods. My Lord Anson would like to learn?" The old Silassian stood, hands clasped on his stomach, head bowed slightly with the small smiling rictus of Silassian subservience hovering on his lips.

"It looks complicated, Tala." Anson recovered his composure. "You gave me a start. Shar . . . My Lord Sharman . . . warned me how silently you moved. I was not expecting to see anyone in the rest time."

"My Lord Anson will forgive Tala. It is the Silassian way." He reached out and passed Anson his pitcher. It was full again. "It takes many months for an Outsider to become used to the climate, and our ways. My Lord Sharman is almost Silassian himself, now."

Anson drank from the pitcher. "I can't dispute that, Tala." He motioned the Silassian to sit and offered him a draught from the pitcher. Tala raised a hand in negation.

"The drink is for Outsiders only, My Lord Anson. The Silassian body has no need of it." He waved a hand outside. "The midday rest is all that we require." He folded his hands in his lap again. "There is something that My Lord Anson requires."

The words were phrased not as a question. Anson looked narrowly at Tala. "What makes you say that, Tala?"

"Forgive me, My Lord Anson. It is ten years since My Lord Sharman came, and since then no other of your race. It would be unthinkable that one should come now with no reason. My Lord Sharman is content and has no need of company."

Anson must have looked uncomfortable, for Tala raised a hand. "It is of no consequence. Our people are here to serve. My Lord Anson is our guest as much as My Lord Sharman."

Anson latched onto the point. "What you can do, Tala, is tell me why it is that your people are so accommodating. After all, you owe Sharman and me nothing. You owe the Company even less. We take your minerals and give nothing in return."

Tala's eyes locked with Anson's in an uncomprehending stare. "My Lord Sharman has made the point before. It is not one that translates. It is our way. You are our guests. The meanest kitchen menial would lay down his life for you, and exult in it."

Anson shook his head slowly and watched as Tala exhaled and dropped his head to his chest, the Silassian equivalent of the shrug, so Sharman had explained to him on his arrival. "It is simply our way, My Lord Anson. Words cannot explain a difference in culture. Just accept."

Tala's eyes fell upon the discarded stones from the fruit Sharman had brought, and Anson thought he detected a glint in them, barely suppressed. "My Lord Anson was unable to honor the killing ceremony this morning." Again it was a statement.

Anson looked uncomfortable. "Forgive me, Tala. But our food on Earth is no longer . . ."

Tala shook his head. "It is understandable, My Lord Anson. My Lord Sharman should have spoken." He eyed the fruit again. A smile of annoyance flickered across his features. "But, please understand, it is coming to the Time of The Slaughter. Such lapses may not be lightly excused by some."

"I understand that, Tala. My Lord Sharman has explained."

Tala shook his head in satisfaction. "It is well. We hope to see My Lord Anson at the dinner table." With that he rose, bowed from the waist in the Silassian manner, and glided out of the room. Sharman was just entering and stepped aside to let him pass, then helped himself to some of Anson's brew.

"Been pumping Tala?"

"I think I've just been warned off, Sharman."

"Tala? No. Pointed in the right direction, Anson. On Earth old Tala would've been a diplomat."

"Nevertheless . . ."

Sharman's eyes took in the stones on the table. "Silly. It wouldn't have taken much to clear those away. I expect that did get just slightly up Tala's nose, what with The Slaughter. . . ."

Anson broke in. "Yes, I heard. I wish I hadn't."

"Nothing that should worry you, Anson. Strictly a native do. You don't even have to watch if you don't want." Sharman sat down and the Ex-Porter outside started up again.

"Just what is Tala's role here?" Anson wandered over to the verandah again. "He doesn't seem to do anything except float around from one place to the next, while everyone else works their guts out."

"Tala is a very important man around here, Anson. You'd do well not to forget it. Apart from which he's Mr. Fixer. You've heard his English. Impeccable. He picked that up in a month flat, and taught the rest. God knows I've tried the local language, but it's impenetrable. Full of glottal stops, curlicues and heavy, pregnant pauses. They're full of meaning to the locals, those pauses, but I'm damned if I can fathom it. Besides, they don't speak that much. If it wasn't for Tala, I doubt that this operation would run quite as smoothly as it does."

"That doesn't explain where he gets to."

Sharman shrugged. "That's Tala's business, I would say. Dinner tonight will be a low-key affair," he said. "Try not to miss it. I'd rather not offend anyone with The Slaughter coming up. Tala would be grateful, too. That's all I came to say. I have to go to the quarry now to check out a new vein. I'd ask you to come, but you haven't served out your time yet. Just stick around the compound and ask for anything you want. You'll find these people more than accommodating. But you know that."

Anson watched Sharman leave the room and walk across the clearing to the path, along which gangs of Silassian laborers were toiling, and disappear into the forest. Suddenly he felt himself staring into a sea of impassive faces, but then just as suddenly the Silassians resumed their tasks. Despite the heat, Anson felt a shiver thrill down his spine.

• • •

The head came off, just as Sharman had said it would, and after the shock of the morning sacrifice it came as a relief to find that there was little blood. The bird, Sharman explained, was a lethargic creature with a heart barely equal to the task of pumping its life stuff around its body. Neither part of the bird believed it was dead however, and Anson spent the meal uncomfortably aware of the twitching body trying to free its pinioned legs whilst the head opened and closed its gape in a vain attempt to suck air into lungs. He managed to do halfhearted justice to the meal, and was grateful when the servants cleared the table and melted away.

"I've fixed up for Tala to give you a rundown on Silassian society tomorrow," Sharman announced when the two were alone. "It'll save you time. And it's a bigger favor than you realize, with The Slaughter coming up."

Anson felt himself reaching for the spice-punch unconsciously. By now it had become a habit. He waited for the tingle to spread out from his stomach, and caught his breath as it punched through his lungs. "That's good of you, Sharman," he gasped.

"Practical. You can't move out of the compound for four days yet. You may as well do something useful."

"What's the origin of this four-day seclusion? I feel as if I'm in quarantine."

"Maybe you are. Ask Tala. It's just one more ritual. Everyone has to go through it, even visiting Silassians."

Anson paused. "You know, Sharman, I get the distinct impression I'm not wanted here."

Sharman shrugged. "I don't know where you get that idea, Anson. I don't give a tuppenny tit one way or the other. If the Company says you come, you come. There's nothing I can do about it. Oh, I won't deny I'll be glad when you're through, and things get back to normal. It upsets the equilibrium having you here. And you could have chosen a better time."

"It's not just that, Sharman. I could've sworn that the laborers looked at me this morning."

"That's hardly surprising, Anson. You're the first Outsider they've seen in ten years, apart from me."

Anson remembered that gaze, and shivered again. "It was no ordinary look, Sharman."

"How the hell would you know, Anson? I told you before, these guys have as much expression as that table over there. Did they smile? Then you should worry."

Anson shook his head.

"Anyway, you ask Tala," Sharman said, excusing himself. "You'll breakfast alone tomorrow. I've got dispensation from Tala to leave early and start them off in the quarry—they need new settings on the cutter. The vein they uncovered yesterday afternoon will keep the Company in clover for the next two years, at least. Maybe we should 'port some direct to your Native

Rights Lobby, huh? It might buy them a few placards. I've got to go."

"Yes, but what about—"

"Ask Tala! Tala knows everything." Sharman hurried out.

Anson was left staring at the swinging door and thinking over what Sharman had just said. Dispensation?

"My Lord Anson must understand the Silassian way." Anson jumped and turned around. Tala had appeared behind him quietly. The Silassian bowed reverently. "The Seclusion is required, My Lord Anson. The time approaching The Slaughter is revered amongst my people. To have the ground defiled by strangers is impious. I am sure My Lord Anson will wish to honor the Silassian way. My Lord Sharman, of course, has exemption." He offered the pitcher. Anson took it automatically.

"Sha . . . My Lord Sharman said that you would speak with me this morning, Tala."

Tala inclined his head and waited for Anson to sit, then perched himself carefully on a chair. "The Silassians are a simple people, My Lord Anson. Before the Company came, we lived our lives quietly. We had our rituals, but we had little direction. As you will have observed, we live to serve."

Anson nodded as the old Silassian gathered his thoughts. "Our whole life is in service. We serve the earth. We serve the air. We serve the trees. We serve life itself. It is the Silassian way." He closed his eyes and adopted a haranguing tone. "'In the Beginning the first Priest was born from the blood of The Slaughtered Beast. And He said, 'Henceforth, let all beasts of the earth be honored and their blood become my People.'

And He slaughtered the beasts, and it was so. And the People were born and spread about the World like unto the beasts of the earth, that were many. And the more it was, so it was, and so shall be until the time that The Beast shall live again. Holy shall be The Slaughter.'"

Tala paused and opened his eyes, fixing Anson with a visionary stare. *"The Book of Priests."* He clutched at a medallion of a curved blade at his throat and continued in more measured tones. "In the giving of their lives to feed the people, the beasts of the earth become the people." He dipped his head in a shrug. "It is symbolic. I know this. But my people are a simple people, not like yours. They accept the teaching as fact. It is the Silassian way."

Anson said nothing. Listening to Tala proclaim his faith had raised goose bumps. It was the nearest thing to emotion that he had seen since his arrival.

Tala shrugged again. "Many rituals govern our lives, My Lord Anson. In the past we are told that men dishonored the Blood of The Beast and killed without ritual. We are told even that men killed men in anger, so The Priest caused a great pestilence to be visited on the people, and The Rebirth of The Beast was not—for the people became as the beasts of the earth, with no one to give the sacrificial rite." He fixed Anson with a level and inscrutable stare. "My Lord Sharman has told me that men still kill men in anger on your world. It is no longer so on Silassia."

Anson sat, hypnotized by Tala's eloquence.

"I tell you these things, My Lord Anson, so that you will understand the importance of these next few days. The Slaughter is the most honored of our rituals. It is the end of life and the start of life. The presence of outsiders on Holy Ground taints the blood, so The Rebirth cannot take place. Within the compound, My Lord Anson is welcome."

"And without?"

Tala flashed him the briefest flicker of a smile. "Without, My Lord Anson would offend my people deeply. It is, I think, something My Lord Anson would not wish to do."

"No, of course not, Tala."

"It is well, and I am grateful for my Lord Anson's understanding. My Lord Anson lives in Silassian spirit."

"You mentioned Holy Ground, Tala. Where is this?"

Tala regarded him blankly. "The world, My Lord Anson. Where else? The sin of man surrounds him where he sleeps, so the compound cannot be considered Holy, but everywhere else is. There are some places where only Silassians of the highest order may go, but that will not concern you."

"The pendant at your neck, Tala . . ."

Tala put his hand to it again. "The shuringa, My Lord Anson."

"I have seen that a few of your people wear it."

Tala drew a full-sized blade from his belt. It was razor-thin and glistened with the patina of thousands of embossed miniatures of the weapon itself. "Every Silassian has a shuringa, My Lord Anson. The ceremonial dagger." He handed it to Anson, who turned it over in his hands. It was heavier than it looked. The embossed pattern, Anson saw, was chased with luminescent blue-gold lines, and the hilt itself was wound with the same blue-gold wire, finishing with a pommel fashioned in the form of a burst of scimitarlike objects, each razor-sharp. Anson shuddered and handed it back. He had always had a fear of knives. "A fine blade, Tala."

"It suffices, My Lord Anson."

"Are all as fine as that?"

"Some are finer, My Lord Anson. There are varying degrees."

"And where does yours come on the scale, Tala?"

Tala returned the knife to his belt and gazed levelly at Anson again. "My Lord Anson was pleased to take supper last night," he said. "It pleased Tala also. My Lord Anson was asking about the quarry."

"I was about to, Tala," said Anson, noting the change of subject and the direction of the Silassian's thoughts with some surprise. "Tell me."

"The blue gold is much valued amongst your people, My Lord Anson."

Again Anson noted that the Silassian phrased his questions with such certainty that there could be no argument. He nodded and looked to where the team of Silassians were still busy dumping it into the Ex-Port.

"It pleases us that we are able to supply it," Tala continued. "It is much valued on Silassia, too—it is of great significance to us. The Company is tireless in its demand. Its machines make the working easier—it is well that My Lord Sharman has the knowledge to cut rock much quicker than at any time in Silassian history. Already the quarry is as deep as The Beast's lair. That is a cause for much rejoicing amongst our people."

"Can I see it—the quarry—when The Slaughter is over?" Anson asked. "After all, my purpose in being here is to make sure that your people are not taken advantage of. To see them at work would be invaluable."

"Alas, no, My Lord Anson. The quarry is a sacred place."

"But, Shar . . . My Lord Sharman is allowed."

"It has been a cause of much debate, but My Lord Sharman has the knowledge to extract the blue gold.

Religious principle must be set on one side for the wider purpose."

Tala looked across the clearing. Anson followed his gaze. One of the younger Silassians from Sharman's quarry team was hurrying out of the jungle. The other Silassians stood aside to let him pass. Tala rose and glided to the verandah to meet the younger man, who spoke quietly but urgently into his ear. The young man bowed to Anson and left for the jungle again, passing Sharman, who was striding out along the path. The young man allowed him to pass, bowed briefly to him, and hurried on. Tala watched Sharman approach impassively as the whine of the Ex-Port suddenly died away. Sharman turned at the dying whine and watched the last of his Silassian team disappear along the jungle path. He vaulted over the verandah rail and faced Tala angrily.

"Tala, I've been thrown off site! And what's the problem with the Ex-Port team? It's nowhere near time for the midday rest."

"The settings are made?" Tala asked.

"Yes, the settings are done. But I always start off the first cut, Tala, you know that. If the intensity of the beam isn't just right, it could damage the quality of the ore. I have the dispensation."

Tala bowed. "My Lord Sharman will forgive me, but the dispensation is not absolute right, and The Slaughter approaches." He bowed to both men. "My Lords Sharman and Anson, live well in harmony and in close comfort until I return. Tala must excuse himself." He clapped his hands softly and, as he left, a bevy of Silassian servants glided in from the next room, bearing drinks.

Sharman let loose an exasperated snort and flung himself into a chair. Irritated, he waved away a proffered drink. "There's something up, Anson," he rasped.

"I need access to that new vein, to assay it. I've never seen anything like it before. But as soon as I start to program in the coordinates, Tala's overseer at the quarry very politely escorts me off the premises! That first cut can be crucial. They know that. One false move and they could ruin the entire molecular structure of the stuff. It'll be worth less than the guts of a breakfast-pig. And to top that, the Ex-Port crew have downed tools!" He flipped his fingers and snatched at a drink.

"Maybe you found the lair of The Beast?" Anson asked, lightheartedly.

Sharman glared at him. "Tala been spinning you that old yarn, has he? The quarry is a sacred place to them, certainly, and the gold does have some religious significance, which is why I wonder that they're so accommodating about letting us have it. But the fervor seems more to do with the act of cutting it out of the ground than in its retention. They keep very little for themselves. A few trinkets, that's all. As for The Beast, that's just mythology. They're riddled with it."

"It sounds more than just mythology to me, Sharman. It comes over as a deeply held conviction."

"Tala is a convincing sort of person, Anson," Sharman said. He tossed his drink back. "You heard what the man said, 'Live in close comfort'? You know what that means? Out of bounds. After ten years, out of bounds! Confined to quarters! The Slaughter's never been like this before. It has to be the new vein." He turned to Anson. "You should see it, Anson," he said enthusiastically. "You know how the blue gold shimmers? This stuff throbs, even without refinement! To push that the Company's way would see me made, Anson. Instead," he barked bitterly, ". . . confined to quarters! How's that for exploited, underprivileged natives? That Ex-Porter hasn't stopped running for ten years, apart from the odd maintenance."

Anson followed Sharman's gaze to where the Ex-Porter stood, angling its now-idle nose to the sky. Faintly, the sound of chanting muted by the lush foliage of the Silassian jungle could be heard, tinged, so it seemed to Anson, with a subtle note of expectancy. If it was so, then that did not seem to transmit itself to the servants, still hanging around in the shadows. They stood, impassive as ever, awaiting the whim of their masters.

"Don't you feel anything, Sharman?" Anson asked.

The older man roused himself. "Feel? The atmosphere you mean? Every year. Their emotions don't register on our scale of perception but you can somehow tell they're working themselves into a frenzy for The Slaughter. I know what you mean, though. It's unnerving, isn't it? Four days this will go on. Not, " he added, "that we'll see much of it from in here."

"Sharman!" Anson pointed and Sharman looked up just in time to catch the dying flicker of blue flame that outlined the foliage of the jungle. He drew in his breath and waited for the sound that would surely follow. "Shit, I knew it. They've blown the cutter!"

They stood, awaiting the inevitable clatter of shattered metal, but it never came. Instead Tala appeared on the forest path. If anything his face was even more composed than usual. Quickly he moved to the centre of the clearing and raised his arms. Almost immediately Silassians appeared, as if from nowhere, and stood in a circle around him.

"It's started," Sharman grunted. "Earlier than usual. I hope to God you're not too squeamish, Anson. The meal killing's got nothing on this."

Tala dropped his arms and the Silassians in charge of the livestock pens started to dismantle them. The animals milled about in fright, then spilled into the clearing. The ring of Silassians awaited their approach in silence, then, as one man, they drew their shuringas and with a united roar threw themselves on the animals, cutting, stabbing and slicing until the clearing became a steaming slurry of blood, guts and twitching meat. Tala stood in the middle watching, eyes darting ferally in his head as he followed every murderous move.

It seemed to Anson that it went on for hours. He stood frozen to the spot, appalled at what he was witnessing, yet fascinated at the mad frenzy that had gripped his Silassian hosts. One animal, quicker or more intelligent than its fellows, escaped squealing into the jungle. It was as though it were a signal, and the blood-soaked Silassians drew around Tala again, who once more raised his arms, holding his own shuringa aloft. Light glanced from its blade, casting dancing motes of reflection in the dimness of the shack's interior. Each Silassian raised his own blood-dripped dagger similarly, and the clearing rang with a howling ululation as they threw back their heads and gave voice. Then it was over. Tala dropped his arms, and they dispersed, leaving him amidst a sea of twitching bodies.

Anson turned his back on the carnage, gagging. Sharman appeared shaken, too. "For such a mild-mannered bunch, they've got one hell of a murderous streak, Anson. It's a good job it's all symbolic."

"Tell that to the animals."

"Shit, they were for the chop one way or another. But that was extreme, Anson, that was extreme." He reached for a drink and threw it back. "And that was just the start."

Anson groped for a drink too, but the tray was empty. He clicked his fingers, but no servant appeared. They had all silently disappeared. A noise that reminded him sickeningly of an axe being driven into a corpse made him glance around to see that it was just that—the servants were all butchering the carcasses with huge cleavers. Tala had gone.

• • •

Sharman was unusually quiet for the rest of the day, prowling restlessly around the confines of the living quarters. Anson hardly noticed. He was still in a mild state of shock. Although the servants had returned some time ago and had resumed their normal duties, there was still an air of subdued excitement. Neither man felt like eating, but endured the usual killing ceremony at the evening meal with a grim fortitude. There was an urgent, hurried air about the servants. Both men were glad to release them as soon as possible. All day there had been a constant, distant chanting from the direction of the Priests' compound, interspersed with shouting and trumpeting, as the aftermath of The Slaughter was celebrated.

Sharman had explained this to Anson with his usual lassitude. "All year long they hardly visit the Priests' quarters. Then, for the four days of The Slaughter, they practically live there. It's strictly out of bounds for you and me, though. It tops the quarry for sanctity. The curious thing is, you never get to see the Priests, but they live like kings. Top-class food and drink. Women. A constant supply of women. I asked Tala about them once, but all I could get out of him was 'They are The Chosen. They learn Silassian lore,' you know, in that deadpan way of his. I believe him."

"Where is Tala?" Anson asked dully, then started back at the quietly spoken "My Lords Anson and Sharman."

Tala stood in the doorway. "You have honored The Ritual, My Lords. It is well." He bowed and glided into the room. Sherman leapt to his feet.

"Tala! What the devil is all this nonsense? And what the hell was that flash this afternoon? Have you ruined the cutter? How much longer is this going on? Anson here I can understand, but I've been exempt from seclusion ever since I came. I have things I need to do outside."

Tala bowed again. "My Lord Sharman will be patient. The Beast stirs."

Sharman snorted. "Listen, Tala . . ." Tala turned a mild face to him, and the corners of his mouth twitched. Sharman tailed off and sat down.

"My Lord Anson lives?" Tala asked, still looking at Sharman. "The Slaughter will have come as a shock to him, I think? But glory with Silassia in the stirring of The Beast. It is not given to all Outsiders. It is the tenth year of the Priesthood and this . . ." he pulled out a small lump of ore from the folds of his robe, setting it on the table ". . . is The Sign." He turned to Sharman again. "The Silassians thank My Lord Sharman."

As Sharman had said, the ore throbbed. Light chased up and down the blue quartz veins that latticed the rock, making it seem as though a pulse beat deep inside it. Sharman ogled it and reached out a hand, but Tala gently restrained it. "This blue gold is for Silassian touch only, My Lord Anson. I show it simply that you will understand. It is the Breath of The Beast." He pocketed it again.

"The Ex-Port, Tala . . ." Sharman said in exasperation " . . . when will you start to operate again?"

Tala looked levelly at Sharman and made The Sign of the Claw toward him and Anson. "Live well, My Lords, and let the servants tend you close." The door swung to gently behind him.

Anson felt an unease beginning to grow. "That's the second direct question Tala's declined to answer," he said. "I asked him how his shuringa rated on the scale and he changed the subject, and now the same with the Ex-Port."

Sharman scowled. "It's The Slaughter. Don't expect anything to make sense for the next few days."

Nothing did. On the face of it, life carried on as normal. The servants served. The meal-killing ceremony proceeded inexorably. The heat still beat everything down. Tala still drifted in and out of the clearing, bowing occasionally to Sharman and Anson as they stood on the verandah. The only thing missing was the gang of men toiling on the Ex-Port, which still stood idle. In the trees, though, Anson and Sharman glimpsed the movement of scores of bodies laboring from the direction of the quarry deeper in the jungle. Laying over all this was the, by now, insidious chanting from the Priests' compound.

Sharman sat fretting on the verandah, shredding the bark from the rail with his fingernails. "I shall be glad when this Slaughter is over, Anson. Perhaps this'll teach the Company not to poke its nose in where it's not wanted."

"Mmm," Anson mused. "Who's exploiting whom?"

Sharman looked round sharply. What do you mean?"

"I've been thinking this over for the past four days. Haven't you worked it out yet, Sharman? Tala's just been using you to dig out his pit for him, for whatever arcane purposes they've got in mind. The gold was just a sop, until they got what they wanted. You think there's going to be any more after this is over?"

Sharman fell silent, then shook his head. "No. You've got that wrong. I know Tala. Fanatic he may be. Two-faced he's not. He knows what the blue gold means to the Company—to me. He wouldn't see anything jeopardize that."

"I wish I had your certitude, Sharman."

"You forget, Anson, I've lived amongst these people for ten years. Okay, I've got a laconic view. It's what comes of being nothing short of a godlike figure for all that time. But these people are as straight as they come."

"And what about the new vein?"

"Like Tala said, that's for the Silassians. There'll be other veins."

"And what are they doing with it? Did you ever think about that?"

"Hell, I don't know, Anson. That's their business. You don't ask a Silassian what he does with his praying time. That isn't the done thing."

"And what if you did? What would be the consequence?"

Sharman looked blank. "The case doesn't arise, Anson. You just don't do it . . ."

"Or Tala slits your gizzard?" Anson finished off.

Sharman scoffed. "Good god, no! These boys might have some fancy wrist work with a knife, but they don't—repeat don't—take human life."

"You know that for a fact?"

"I know that for a certainty, Anson. It's not their creed. I'll stake my life on it."

Anson dropped his head. "I hope you don't have to."

Sharman started fingering the verandah rail again.

Anson laughed softly. "The Native Rights Lobby should be pleased, anyhow. Tala could give lessons." A line of Silassian women filed out from the Priests' compound and made their way to their own on the other side of the clearing. Anson watched until they were inside. "The more I see of this society, the less I like it, Sharman. It's too strictured to be healthy."

"Don't judge things by your standards, Anson. Earth is a long way away. The Silassians have a lot of qualities anyone would be glad of. Humility is only one of them. And I'll tell you something else I've thought for a long time now: they've got an ability that borders on telepathy."

"That's an assertion you'll find difficult to prove, Sharman."

"I don't need to prove anything. How else do they know what you want before you even know yourself?"

Anson thought about it. "Order," he said, shortly. "Theirs is a very ordered life. And yours with it, as a consequence. Order brings its own logic. Order, forethought and sheer, downright professionalism—that amounts almost to prescience."

Sharman shook his head. "You've never played Inshalaka, Anson. Play that, and then tell me there's no telepathy involved. Maybe not on the conscious level but, believe me, it's there."

"'The Game of The Gods' Tala called it," Anson said. "Even their leisure pursuits have a theistic element."

"Not overtly. What're you driving at?"

"I'm not entirely sure myself."

"Well, do me a favor and keep it to yourself!" Sharman bridled. "I'm getting a little tired of being on the defensive with you. Tala's all right. The Silassians are all right. In fact everything was all right until you showed up."

"You think this is something to do with me, Sharman?"

"I would be surprised if it wasn't."

Both men subsided, their anger spent in the enervating heat. At last Sharman spoke. "Ten years on your own makes it difficult to share space, Anson. I'm sorry. But you're wrong about Tala."

Anson shrugged. "I'm out of here anyway, as soon as the shuttle drops back. I've got all I want. You and the Silassians can snuggle up as close as you want after that. The N.R.L. won't be pressing any further investigation after my report."

"The N.R.L. may not be, but the Company will if the Ex-Port is out of action much longer," Sharman fumed. "The sooner Tala gets this Slaughter over, the better."

Anson pointed past Sharman's shoulder at the Priests' compound. Silassians were filing out of it. They formed a hollow, double line and commenced a rhythmic chanting, keeping time with their feet. Slowly, a further file of scarlet-robed and cowled figures formed up in the middle of the chanting men.

"The Priests!" Sharman breathed.

There was a sudden commotion at the fringe of the jungle and a huge buffalolike animal burst out, goaded by a half-dozen Silassians wielding long spears.

It stood bewildered, snorting and pawing the ground in frustration, its retreat blocked by its tormentors. The only escape was forward. It broke into a lumbering trot toward the chanting line of Silassians and the silent Priests. It stopped uncertainly, then started pawing the ground more frantically, steeling itself for the final charge.

The leading Priest stepped forward and blocked its path, unmoving. The Silassians fell silent. As if enraged at this, the animal gave a heart-stopping bellow and clattered straight toward the still figure.

When it was scant yards from him, the Priest shot out his hand in The Sign of the Claw. The animal skidded to a stop, panting. It stood there, splay-legged and salivating with a huge tongue lolling from the side of its mouth. Then, in one fluid movement, the Priest suddenly stepped forward, lifted the huge head by its beard with one hand until the snub snout was nosing at the sky. The other hand swept down and out in a glittering arc, tearing the animal's throat apart. Blood fountained out and the animal collapsed like a sack.

The cowled Priest turned triumphantly to the others, with his shuringa held aloft. It was a signal for the chanting to break out again. The group moved off into the jungle, following the Priest's lead, each man, except the red-cloaked Priests, dipping a hand in the gouting blood of the animal as he passed.

Sharman turned to Anson. "This is different. This is something special," he said, in awe. "The Priests usually only come out of the compound when they're carried out feet first. They spend their lives in there, just soaking up Silassian lore."

Anson reached for a drink and found the tray empty again. He flipped his fingers for more, but there was no response. Then, one by one, Silassians trickled out from all quarters of the compound, making for the jungle in pursuit of the priestly procession.

Soon, the two men were alone.

• • •

The silence screamed. Anson sat down in his chair for the umpteenth time and as quickly stood up again

Illustrated by Mia Hopper

to pace around the room. "Anson, if you don't settle down, you're going to collapse from exhaustion." Sharman sat on the verandah quietly fanning himself.

"You can't tell me you're completely at ease, Sharman. You may fool yourself, but you don't fool me. There's something strange going on here."

"It's The Slaughter, Anson. Things are always strange at The Slaughter."

"You said yourself it was different this time."

Sharman grunted. "Things will be back to normal tomorrow, Anson. I guarantee it. Let them get this out of their system and there's no problem. You above all people should know you can't buck religion. And there's damn-all you can do anyway. We're confined here, remember?"

Anson looked at him. "I don't see any fences, Sharman."

"What d'you mean?"

"I mean, where is everyone? You've had Silassians dogging your every footstep somewhere in the background for the past ten years. Suddenly, nothing."

"It's The—"

"Slaughter. I know. Everything stops for The Slaughter. I've got a bad feeling about this, and I'm not going to rest until I've satisfied myself. Forewarned is forearmed."

"What are you talking about?" Sharman swung his feet off the verandah rail.

"You can come, or you can stay," Anson said, levering his own legs over the rail and dropping lightly to the ground outside. "But I'm going to find out what's going on. I can't live on this knife edge any longer."

"Anson, are you crazy?" Sharman yelled after him, as he walked quickly up toward the track. "You're breaking faith."

Anson paused at the Ex-Port and turned back to face the hut. "Our friends have been breaking more than that, Sharman. This machine is never going to work again."

"Shit!" Sharman swore, then, glancing nervously around, he shinned over the verandah rail and ran, doubled up, to join Anson. The inspection panel had been torn open and coils of fine wire hung like disemboweled intestines, trailing on the still-bloodstained ground.

"Now do you believe things will get back to normal?"

Sharman ran the wires helplessly through his fingers. "I don't understand."

"You'd better start! Where do you keep your guns?"

"Guns? What do I want with guns?" Sharman threw the tangled mess of wires from him angrily.

"You mean you haven't got any?" Anson asked incredulously.

"No! Hell, do you keep guns in a friggin' monastery? That's what we've got here, Anson."

Anson swore quietly and considered. "Come on, then. Take me to the quarry."

"What?"

"The quarry, man! Don't argue!"

Dazed, Sharman allowed himself to be led in the direction of the jungle.

•••

The quarry was a cavernous gouge in an outcrop of igneous rock, festooned at the entrance with trailing creepers and choked by climbing greenery. Inside, it widened out and opened to the sky. Trees hung over the top, waving very slightly in the almost nonexistent breeze. The rock showed signs of having been neatly sliced and vitrified—Sharman certainly knew his job. At the steeply shelving bottom, a shimmer of blue showed the working vein. Anson had no time to take in the sights, however, for the laser cutter stood abandoned at the base of the quarry. He scrambled down the sides, scraping his legs on the vitrified rock residue, with Sharman close behind.

"Anson, this is blasphemy," he gasped.

"Bollocks, Sharman," Anson replied, wrenching the cutter from its mounting. "Where's the thunder and lightning? Where's the hand of God? You don't even believe in the crap."

"No, but Tala does."

"Tala's got you by the balls, my friend." Anson scrabbled past Sharman with the cutter cradled in his arm. "The sooner we can persuade him to relax his grip, the sooner your testosterone kicks back in. You've gone soft, Sharman."

Sharman pulled him back by the shoulder, spinning him around. "What the hell is it with you? What're you afraid of?"

Anson pushed his hand away and stared vehemently at him. "At this precise moment, Sharman, you. You scare the shit out of me. You can't see any further than the next load of gold. Now help me out of the quarry with the cutter." He threw the butt end into Sharman's hands and took hold of the barrel. Sharman hesitated, then followed Anson's lead up the steep slope to the jungle path.

At the top, the two men collapsed, breath rasping in the stifling atmosphere. The cutter, although lightweight, was still heavy. Sharman sat with his head hung low, gasping for breath. "I don't believe I'm doing this, Anson. Tala may just forgive you. I don't know about the rest."

Anson leaned back on his hands, drawing in searing lungfuls of air. "And what sanction are they going to apply, Sharman. Slap your wrists?"

"They can withdraw their labor for a start. That's not going to sit too well with the Company."

"They've already done that, Sharman. Come on, back to the shack before they return from wherever they've all gone. I want to get this set up where it'll do the most damage, if it's needed."

"Anson, I don't know what's going on anymore. You've taken leave of your senses!"

"I don't think so, Sharman. Now, move it!" Anson struggled to his feet and staggered off down the rising track, with Sharman stumbling along in the rear. Suddenly, Anson stopped and crouched, motioning Sharman to do likewise. Below them, glimpsed through the foliage, a red-cloaked figure was moving steadily up the winding track.

"Shit! Back!" hissed Anson. Both men backed up, then broke into a crouching run, keeping hidden from the approaching figure around the twisting turns of the jungle path. Birds flapped in sudden panic at their passage, crashing through the upper branches of the trees in raucous flight. The track continued to rise.

"Where does this go?" Anson asked urgently.

"To the top of the mountain, I suppose. I don't know. I've never been this far. I usually hang out around the other side of the compound, by the river."

"Is there another track anywhere?"

Sharman stumbled, then recovered. "There's one that comes down on the other side of the women's compound. I don't know where it goes."

"It's a safe bet it joins up with this somewhere, then. Keep your eyes peeled." He relieved Sharman of his part of the burden and, tucking the cutter under his arm, struggled upward. The red-cloaked figure behind climbed on, still seemingly oblivious to the two fugitives in front, but closing the gap all the time. A little farther on, Sharman's legs gave out and he collapsed on the ground with a despairing groan.

"I'll take my chances, Anson," he gasped. "You go on. Make it back to the shack, and I'll say nothing about it. I stand more chance of being excused than you."

Anson hesitated, but any prospect of proceeding was removed at the next instant by the sudden onset of hundreds of voices chanting immediately ahead. He swore and dived into the undergrowth at the side of the track, dragging Sharman with him. They wormed their way deeper into the cover, climbing all the time, until they were hidden as well as could be from anyone passing. Anson struggled with the cutter. "How do you arm this thing?" he whispered.

Sharman showed him, exhausted. "For God's sake, watch what you're doing with it."

There was no need to do anything with it. The figure drew level with their position and moved on without a sideways look. Sharman let out a sigh, and disarmed the cutter again, pocketing the mechanism. Both men leaned back against the slope of the ground in relief. "Anson, if I get out of this in one piece, I'm going to make your life hell. You won't ride another Company ship again."

"I hope you have the opportunity. Right now, all I want is the other ship. Off this planet. And if you're wise, you'll take it with me." He roused himself. "Come on. If we leave it much longer, it'll be too hot to move at all."

Sharman had already struggled to his feet and was supporting himself on a natural rock wall that surmounted the mound up which they had climbed. Clear sky showed above the craggy parapet, where a bare rock face some distance behind the wall was just visible. The chanting, which had earlier prevented them from carrying on up the track, had stopped when the figure in red had passed. Now it started again, much closer to hand.

Not only that, but a pulsing blue light began to throb, reflecting ominously from the bare rock face, in synchronization with the chanting. Sharman raised his head tentatively above the parapet and almost immediately drew in a hissing breath of astonishment. "Anson! Look here!"

Anson drew himself up to Sharman's side and peered over the parapet. The mountain opened out before him into a natural amphitheater. Fingers and slabs of bare rock reached up to the sky on all sides as though in supplication, alternately washed in an electric-blue light from below and then plunged back into their anonymous neutral hues. And all the time it was orchestrated by the sound of a thousand throats. Anson let his gaze travel downward. Line after line of Silassians thronged the sides of the amphitheater, far more than could ever have come from the village—they must have come in from miles around. As he watched, more marched in from a gully on the far side, another double file escorting a line of red-cloaked and hooded priests. But it was more than the spectacle of so many Silassians in one place that took his breath.

Sharman gripped his arm. "Shit, Anson. The Beast!"

• • •

It could be nothing else. On the floor of the amphitheater, alternately glowing blue and then throbbing back to a dull gold, was the effigy of what appeared to be an animal's head pointed to the sky, with a single enormous and impossibly thin forward-pointing horn reaching vertically upward to meet four platforms set at the points of the compass and cantilevered from the sides of the rock. The blue light emanated from the effigy's slitted eyes, which, when lit, gave it a startling malevolent look and, when dimmed, transformed it into a sightless, staring death mask.

The head itself angled back into the ground where the rest of the idol was buried. The acrid tang of ozone-charged air rose up to the parapet, laced with the stench of thousands of sweat-stained bodies.

As Anson and Sharman watched, a figure made diminutive by distance and the size of the artifact emerged from a hole in its base. The intensity of the blue light increased immediately, throbbing imperceptibly up the scale until it became an almost audible, sickening vibration. The chanting kept pace with the changing frequency until the amphitheater rang and echoed with the sound.

"I should've known about this," Sharman breathed. "They couldn't have kept something like this quiet for ten years."

"Sharman, they've covered you in cotton wool for ten years," Anson replied, barely able to take his eyes off the spectacle below. "This is the real place of The Slaughter. Look there." He pointed out what he had been trying to come to terms with over the past few minutes.

What he had previously taken as ground into which the idol was buried was, in fact, a carpet of bones. Not just strewn, but piled thickly to an unjudgeable depth.

The reason soon became apparent. During the time they had been watching, the files of red-cloaked priests had been climbing the wooden scaffolding built around the horn. They now shuffled out onto the cantilevered platforms in tightly-packed lines. The chants from the watching crowds rose to an ear-shattering crescendo and then immediately cut off.

The silence that followed was bowel-clutching. Then, with a yell of rapture, the first of the priests on one of the platforms threw himself off, with arms and legs spread-eagled, to impale himself on the gleaming spike that pierced the sky.

The body spun about the centre as it gyrated to the ground, screaming in blissful agony. Without hesitation, the rest of the waiting priests in turn threw themselves after the first, each making the same shriek of adulation as they fell, impaled upon the spike.

Both men watched the scene in horror. Then, Sharman stiffened, and turned to his companion with awe in his eyes. "Anson. I know what this is. That," he said, pointing to the effigy "is the Inshalaka. I mean, the real Inshalaka. It's the spitting image of the kingpin in that interminable game of theirs. The Game of the Gods. I've never been able to get the hang of it, but it's a mixture of strategy, divination and story. The point seems to be to surround the Inshalaka, make a sacrifice, and the gods breathe life into it and take it into their kingdom. The damn thing is a ship, Anson. An ancient space ship."

"And this new vein of blue gold . . ."

"Gives it the power? 'The Breath of The Beast!' That's why Tala was so cagey about it."

"My Lord Sharman is right."

The words sent shivers down both men's backs. Slowly they turned. The red-cloaked figure standing behind them reached up to its cowl and slowly turned it down. Tala!

He was smiling.

"My Lords will forgive me. They were so engrossed in *desecrating* our ceremony that they did not hear me." The word was spat out with a venom that belied the benign appearance of Tala's face.

"But why, Tala? Why all this?" Sharman gestured over his shoulder, bewildered. "All your priests. All that knowledge—gone."

Tala's smile didn't slacken. "Not lost, My Lord Sharman. Harnessed. It is written in The Book of The Beast, 'And they shall come, they that have learning, and shall apply it, and shall breathe life into The Beast. And The Beast shall rise up . . .'"

Anson raised the cutter. "Tala. Stand back."

Tala nodded his head sadly. "Alas, it will avail you little, My Lord Anson. The arming mechanism is in My Lord Sharman's pocket." He suddenly raised a clawed hand into their faces and both men felt their will slowly drain away. The cutter fell out of Anson's grasp and slithered away into the vegetation.

"Come, My Lords Sharman and Anson. Come. The Beast hungers."

And, knowing, they went, unable to do anything about it.

Anson caught Sharman's eye as they stumbled down the slope toward the jungle path. An awful glimmer of understanding shone there, and the helpless glance exchanged between them drew them together, but too late.

Breasting the ridge at the top of the path, the Inshalaka, with its gruesome burden, came into full view. At their appearance, the chanting grew in volume as Tala led them down toward the scaffold like little lambs. Lambs, to The Slaughter, Anson thought as his eyes took in the writhing mass of impaled Silassians. His mind refused to accept the inevitable conclusion.

The Beast had risen . . . and the shuttle was due soon. Now The Slaughter would really begin.

THE FAST PRODUCTION WRITER

Written by
L. Ron Hubbard

About the Author

L. Ron Hubbard's remarkably productive writing career spanned more than half a century of literary achievement and enduring creative influence. Its scope and diversity eventually embraced more than 550 works—over 60 million words—of published fiction and nonfiction. And though always, quintessentially, a writer's writer, his zest for adventure, his inexhaustible curiosity and his catalyzing personal belief that one should live life as a professional led him to impressive accomplishments in other fields—as an explorer and prospector, mariner and aviator, filmmaker and photographer, educator and artist, composer and musician.

Growing up in the still-unsparingly rugged frontier country of Montana, he was riding horses by the time he was three, and had been initiated as a blood brother of the Blackfeet Indian tribe by the age of six. While still a teenager, before the advent of commercial air transportation as we know it, he journeyed more than a quarter of a million miles by sea and land into remote areas of the Far East rarely traveled by

Westerners, intensively broadening his knowledge of other peoples and cultures.

In later years, as a master mariner and helmsman, he led three separate voyages of discovery and exploration under the flag of the prestigious Explorers' Club.

Returning to the United States from the Far East in 1929, Mr. Hubbard studied at George Washington University where he became president of both the Engineering Society and Flying Club, and wrote articles, stories, and a prizewinning play for the school's newspaper and literary magazine.

A daredevil pilot, he barnstormed across the United States in gliders and early powered aircraft, became a correspondent and photographer for the Sportsman Pilot, *the most popular national aviation magazine of its day, subsequently worked as a successful screenwriter in Hollywood, and, when only 25, was elected president of the New York Chapter of the American Fiction Guild, whose membership at the time included Dashiell Hammet, Raymond Chandler and Edgar Rice Burroughs.*

All of this—and much more—over the breadth and range of his professional career found its way into his writing and gave his stories a memorable authenticity, and a compelling sense of the way things credibly might be in some possible future or alternative dimension, that continues to attract and engross readers everywhere.

Beginning with the publication in 1934 of The Green God, *his first adventure, in one of the hugely popular all-fiction "pulp" magazines of the day, L. Ron Hubbard's outpouring of fiction was prodigious—often exceeding a million words a year. Ultimately, it encompassed more than 260 published novels, novelettes, short stories and screenplays in virtually every major genre, from action and adventure, western and romance, to mystery and, suspense and of course, science fiction and fantasy.*

Mr. Hubbard had, in fact, already achieved broad popularity and acclaim in other genres when he burst onto the landscape of speculative literature with his first published science fiction story, The Dangerous Dimension, *in 1938. But it was his trendsetting work in this field, particularly, that not only helped expand the imaginative boundaries of the genre, but established him as one of the founders and principal architects of what remains its most celebrated—and legendary—period of productivity and literary invention, the "Golden Age of Science Fiction" of the 1930s and 1940s.*

Such timeless L. Ron Hubbard classics of speculative fiction as Final Blackout, Fear, Ole Doc Methuselah, *and* Typewriter in the Sky, *as well as his powerful capstone novels, the ultimate alien invasion story,* Battlefield Earth *and the sweeping* Mission Earth *10 volume dekalogy, continue, meanwhile, to appear perennially on bestseller lists and to garner critical accolades in countries around the world.*

L. Ron Hubbard's extraordinary 56-year career as a professional writer was distinguished, equally, by his deeply felt and lifelong commitment to helping other writers, especially beginners, become better, more productive and more successful at their craft. This culminated in 1983 in his establishment of both the Writers of The Future Contest—now the largest and most successful merit competition of its kind in the world—and the annual anthology of the winning best new, original stories of science fiction and fantasy.

The companion contest for Illustrators of The Future, for whose winners this anthology also provides an important international showcase, was inaugurated five years later.

Mr. Hubbard's initial work with fledging writers, however—undertaken even as he himself, still in his 20s, was rising to prominence—found salient expression in lectures at such schools as Harvard and George Washington University on how to get started.

He also began, as early as 1935, to publish candidly practical "how to" articles about writing as a craft and profession which appeared in major writers' magazines for many years and continue to be used today in writing courses and seminars and as the basis for the Writers' Workshops held each year for the winners and published finalists of the Writers of The Future Contest.

*The article that follows—*The Fast Production Writer*— originally appeared in the letters to the editor section of* Argosy, *arguably the most celebrated and longest-lived of the all-story magazines and one which at the time, had only recently finished publishing L. Ron Hubbard's "Hell Job" stories. This was a series of 17 tales based on some of the world's most dangerous occupations that appeared in the magazine rapidly, one after the other, over a period of little more than a year. They, in fact, speak tellingly to the theme of* The Fast Production Writer—*that quantity and quality are dynamically compatible, and that over the long course of literary history words like "prolific," "creativity" and "artistic craftsmanship" have classically gone hand in hand.*

I like the new make-up very much. You have considerably increased the appearance of the magazine. I also enjoyed the Argonotes of the June 26th issue. Whoever wrote it did a good job on it.

There was also a comment in there by Ralph Lake. In part, he says, "This Brand, while a prolific writer, is a genius nonetheless."

I think Mr. Lake would be greatly amused or perhaps astounded if he knew Max Brand, Fred Faust's or whose have you, literary history.

Just why is it, pray tell, that John Public (and Hollywood) dwells in the dark about a fast production writer? If a man writes one story a year, everybody says, "Ah! He must be an *artist!*"

No merit to a man who works himself bald and into an early grave putting out repeated bits of the marvelous.

O. Henry's production speed would put most of us to shame. Dickens wrote like a whirlwind, was practically an H. Bedford-Jones. And so on down the list of those stories we have come to regard as classic. And don't forget Scott! Gadzooks, but the man rolled out the wordage!

The difference, I think, between the "artist" and the fast production writer is that the latter has a more nimble brain, is a better writer, has more unconscious technique.

If I write less than fifty thousand a month, my idea-machine practically breaks down, I don't think of anything to write. Of course I'm no Brand or Jones but like most of my brethren, when it has to be rolled, I can roll it—and strangely, the best stories I ever did were done spontaneously at a composition speed of between two and three thousand words an hour—which includes getting up, walking around the chair, lighting the pipe and wishing they'd turn off the radio next door.

As a matter of fact this was the reason I wanted to write this letter.

Let me make the flat statement that most of the greatest literary lights in the world and certainly those in our present field, wrote and write at a speed which would make a layman faint from shock.

Toss that into Argonotes and listen to the howl.

Enough stalling. I've got to finish this shooting script.

Hollywood, Calif.

WHITE JADE

Written by
Janet Martin

Illustrated by
Igor Baranko

About the Author

Janet Martin has always been a reader. Her family moved frequently during her early school years as they followed her father around the country from one Air Force base to another. In between assignments, Janet spent time on a farm in Iowa, and returned there when she was in fifth grade. Both lifestyles led her to look on books as her most reliable friends. Very early she discovered a preference for fantasy, devouring the works of Andrew Lang, George MacDonald and C.S. Lewis.

On the farm, books were sometimes in short supply, so Janet expanded her reading to include the complete works of Dickens, which she found in the attic, and Zane Gray westerns which she borrowed from a cousin. A year or so later Janet wrote her first "novel" in a desperate attempt to find something new to read.

During her high school years, access to a public library allowed her to indulge herself with more fantasy. Janet's favorite writers at that time were Bradbury, Lovecraft, James Stephens and again, George MacDonald.

At the University of Florida, she majored in anthropology, but marriage and the immediate arrival of a family interrupted any plans of a career in that field. The next few years were busy ones, raising three children, working in education and following her husband around the world—they spent five years in Saudi Arabia. At the same time, Janet drifted toward libraries, not only as a place of refuge and source of supply for her serious reading habit, but a job. She worked as a librarian in Dhahran. Her husband declared it a case of throwing the fox in with the chickens, as during her after-work hours, she was able to indulge her reading habits as never before.

When Janet returned to the US about ten years ago, she settled in Austin, Texas. She began writing fantasy as well as continuing to read it, using her spare time to work for the University of Texas libraries and acquired a master's degree in library science. Janet is currently a school librarian in Del Valle, Texas.

About the Illustrator

Igor Baranko was born in Kiev in 1970. He spent a couple of years doing comics for a French newspaper. Since then, art for comics became his ambition.

In 1988, Igor graduated from Kiev's Art School. After spending two years in the Soviet army, he returned home and began working as an artist.

His artwork has been influenced by Kasusika Hokusai, Albert Duzer, Holbein, Hugo Pratt, Gregory Narbut, Wilfred Vance and Nilo Manara. Igor also loves the traditional graphic art of ancient Egypt, Greece, China and Japan as well as the primitive art of Africa, American Indians and the cavemen.

A slender, erect figure swathed in peacock silks, Lu Chin waited quietly in the shadows as the procession formed. Only the glints of silver in her elaborately braided hair hinted at her venerability. She stood a bit apart from the rest of the concubines who twittered as nervously as a flock of songbirds at their unexpected release from the security of the women's quarters. None of them had ever seen the Grand Courtyard before this day, and their awe united them, the convoluted politics of their female world for the moment put aside.

But Lu Chin had been here before, and, comfortingly, it had changed little in the thirty years since she had last seen it. The sense of familiarity assisted her as she struggled to maintain her mask of serenity.

The emperor, center of the universe and, until a handful of days past, master of the lives of all who congregated in the brightness of the funeral dawn, was invisible beneath the scarlet brocades draped from the tall canopies of his bier. Forty oxen with gilded yokes would pull it from the city to the tomb that had been hollowed under the mountain a day's journey away.

He would have hated it, she thought, being hidden from view. Although not heavy-handed with his power, he had always loved being seen, being worshiped by his subjects, and had enjoyed all the panoply that had accompanied his every move. His death had crept upon him, unexpected by all but the gods who had ordained it, springing silently and snatching him before Lu Chin had prepared herself.

Few of those who attended the emperor would return, for most who stood in the courtyard had been selected to serve him for eternity. Lu Chin herself had chosen from among the women the prettiest and most talented, those who danced lightly on their feet or played the music he had always loved, and those most skilled in the arts of love. Of course they were all young; there were few women of Lu Chin's seniority among the emperor's concubines. She had killed any who might have challenged her position.

Only Pau Li, Wife Number Three, outranked her. Unlovely, but the well-connected daughter of a powerful warlord, she was late to join the throng and bid her lord farewell. Lu Chin plotted even now that such rank be rewarded with the place of honor beside the emperor, for Lu Chin herself had no intention of leaving the comforts of life prematurely.

Priests in their saffron robes assumed places at the corners of the bier, beginning the ceremonies that would culminate with the departure of the funeral procession from the palace. Pau Li hurried to take a place at the front of the gathering of women. *So like her*, thought Lu Chin, *to wait until the last*. As always, Pau Li appeared untidy, unprepared, yet eager to make a show of her apparent grief.

In this instance, Lu Chin would not challenge Pau Li's right to stand foremost. Instead, she edged up behind the warlord's daughter, speaking softly so that only Pau Li might hear.

"Will you accompany our lord, Third Wife?" she asked.

"It has been decided," Pau Li stated. "I am to remain here to see to the needs of my son, the new emperor."

Lu Chin nodded, seemingly in agreement. "Of course," she said. "But it is strange, is it not, that the Son of the Morning Star would let a mere concubine take the exalted place beside his imperial father."

Lu Chin held her silence a while, permitting her words to fester. Incense wafted upward in smoky spirals, and the chanting grew loud enough to overwhelm any who might have sought to overhear the conversation.

"They say all is quite magnificent," Lu Chin said.

Pau Li turned to look. "Of course it's magnificent. What are you talking about?"

"Why, our lord's new palace. There are scarcely any jewels left in the kingdom, so many have been used to decorate his tomb. They say that he and his consort will lie preserved for all time, their spirits dwelling with the gods as their bodies repose fragrant and uncorrupted."

Pau Li seemed curious, even a bit puzzled. Lu Chin began to feel pleased with herself. The seeds she had planted would take some nurturing to sprout, but she was not without additional powers. The work of the priests as they invoked the guidance of the ancestors' spirits might well enhance Lu Chin's spellmaking. She moved her fingers, hidden as they were by her flowing sleeves, in a spell of compulsion. But then, with a subject as vain and stupid as Pau Li, little sorcery would be needed, certainly none strong enough to attract unwanted attention from the priests. Even now, Lu Chin feared the priests and their monopolies on magic.

"Perhaps you should accompany the cortege so you may assure yourself that all is as it should be and that our lord will have all his desires attended," she suggested. "And you will want to see the white jade, of course."

"White jade? What white jade?" Pau Li fingered a clouded jade amulet, as green as a stagnant pond, resting over her own generous bosom. It was of inferior quality to Lu Chin's mind, but ancient and probably of power nonetheless.

"You didn't know of it?" Lu Chin inquired innocently. I'm surprised he never told you. But then it is very rare, and there was only enough for two. If he didn't wish you to be with him in eternity, he would not have wanted to hurt you."

"Of course he wanted me," Pau Li snapped. "It was undoubtedly to be a surprise. He often gave me surprises."

Well pleased, Lu Chin bowed her head. It had been wise after all to let this one live. But Third Wife had never been a threat to Lu Chin's position. In addition to her pride and stupidity, she had never been pretty enough to have held the emperor's attention past the obligatory impregnation that had given Pau Li the unexpected position as mother of the heir. A fever had carried off the oldest son, then a fall from a horse had dispatched the next. Son number three had drowned, and number four had drunk himself to death—leaving number five to assume the throne, the offspring of the stupidest of wives, but grandson of a warlord powerful enough to ensure the boy's inheritance.

Lu Chin took no responsibility for the expiration of the princes. Barren herself, she had taken little interest in the succession, seeking only to maintain her position with the emperor himself. She had, in her way, cared for him.

Born in the women's quarters of the palace itself, Lu Chin had been only the worthless female child of a dancing girl, dead in childbed. Showing no promise of the beauty she would become, she was deemed unfit to be trained as a courtesan. She had been sent instead to the imperial forces where she had been selected to become an assassin.

A skilled warrior, she learned to use her physical charms as a lure, her cleverness as a tool, and her hands as weapons. Had her rudimentary skill at magic been discovered, she would have been snatched away and made a priestess, but the life of an assassin had been much to her liking. Even the discipline within its corps was to her a freedom she had never imagined.

But fate, or more likely, duty, had returned Lu Chin to the royal circle when she had been assigned to the imperial guards. A pleasure outing near a favorite hunting lodge had turned into an ambush. The lovely killer had found herself in a position to save the life of the young prince, but, sadly, not that of his father.

Certain that the gods had provided her as his savior, the prince took her as his handmaid, his advisor, and soon thereafter, as his concubine. She held his counsel as did no other and he never once suspected that the accidents that carried off one after another of his women might have been the actions of Lu Chin.

For she was always discreet, and never used a method more than once. A princess garroted was later found hanging from her own hair. An exquisite dancer fell prey to wild mushrooms, and the cook thought to have been careless was boiled in his own stewpot. Second Wife, clever herself and mother to the two middle princes, was found within a failed pentagram with a look of such horror frozen on her visage that all were certain she had been struck down by some demon she had raised. One after another, each of the emperor's favorites, save Lu Chin herself, had perished.

"I fear for you, beloved," he would say as she comforted him for yet another loss. "Promise me you will take care, for I could not bear to live without you."

As years had passed, he had sent less often for any of the women who might have warmed his couch, letting Lu Chin choose for him on the rare occasions when she wished to be released from his attentions.

And now it had fallen to Lu Chin to select those who would serve him for all eternity, even one who would be empress at last. But Lu Chin would not permit herself to take satisfaction in that deed until Pau Li was safely and permanently ensconced in her very own white jade shroud.

The chanting grew louder as the young emperor entered the courtyard. He had chosen the role of High Priest for this, his first official appearance. Draped in his simple robes, he could have almost been taken for a monk. To his right was his grandfather, the warlord, in his arrogance outshining the ruler with the magnificence of his bronze armor and the pride of his stance. Lu Chin smiled to herself at the conflicts to come, for she knew that the serene countenance of the boy hid a will as strong as that of his grandfather. Life in the palace could again become interesting. She anticipated the challenges with pleasure.

But to the left of the ruler was one whom Lu Chin had not seen for many years. Soong, once a senior assassin, now garbed in the plain dun uniform of a guardsman, appeared with the jewel-encrusted amulet displayed on his chest that identified him as chief of the emperor's forces. He was as lean of body, as fierce of expression as when last she had known him. She felt her breath catch in her throat, and the years seemed to drop from her memory as she felt again the power of his presence.

Surprisingly, given the passage of time, Lu Chin had not escaped Soong's notice. His sharp black eyes caught hers, and his lips curved in the slightest smile. She raised an eyebrow in response, then turned away, strangely fearful that he might guess her purpose as he had always done while she had served as a junior in his command. She told herself she acted only to prevent Pau Li from being recognized by her son or father.

The ruler's presence enlivened the priests. Their dancing became more frenzied, their chants a cacophony. Smoke poured out of the whirling censers to spiral upward in the morning sky. Then oxen were led into the courtyard, well fed and quiet as they were harnessed to the bier. With the arrival of the animals, the priests left off their ritual, and lined up at the sides of the bier.

Lu Chin motioned to the bearers of the palanquin that was to have carried her in luxurious seclusion.

"Third Wife," she said, "may I offer you transportation for your convenience on our journey? Despite your wish to pay respects to our lord, one of your rank ought not to be gawked at." Nor noted by relatives who might choose to detain her at the palace.

"I'm only going to look at it, the white jade that is, and to be sure that it is fine enough for my husband," Pau Li replied as she gracefully clambered inside to recline on the satin cushions.

The curtains twitched into place. Lu Chin smiled, just a little, at the progression of her plan. Would that she could take this opportunity to slip away to her apartments in the women's quarter, to the retirement she had planned and the freedom to come and go from the palace at will, no longer confined as the property of her lord.

But she could not yet permit herself to breathe easily. Instead, she turned to the concubines. Widening her smile to reassure them, she motioned them to follow her to the great covered wagon that was to be their own transport. The women were barely settled inside when it began to move on its huge wheels, each half again as tall as the guardsmen who trudged alongside.

Still ignorant of their fate, the girls chattered and pointed at the wonders of a world fresh and new to their eyes, the fields of grain stretching in undulating green at the sides of the road, the vistas of mountains shimmering blue in the distance. Uncharacteristically, Lu Chin felt a pang of regret at their delight, that it should come with such a price. She brushed the thought aside. To die in youth was a blessed escape from the tyranny of the palace. Besides, all subjects of the empire existed only to gratify the whims of the emperors. Lu Chin's own freedom was one she had long planned and carefully plotted.

The caravan stopped briefly at midday to rest the animals and the weary bearers, but was soon on its way again, the terrain climbing steeply as the travelers approached the mountain tomb. Occupied as she was with distracting her charges, Lu Chin had little time to formulate her final plans. Yet she felt a sadness at being forced to spend the journey closed in the wagon instead of riding an armored steed and feeling again the weight of weapons in her hand. Her life at the palace seemed to have passed so quickly, yet so uneventfully, each day filled with the small bits of living that now left her barren of meaningful memory, empty of satisfaction.

The sun was dropping in the sky when the wagon lumbered to its final halt. Time was so short. Her actions must be precise. The business of Third Wife was by no means settled. Without even waiting for the stairway down from the wagon to be fastened in place, Lu Chin slid easily to the ground and hurried forward to the palanquin.

Soong was there before her, bowing deeply to Pau Li who struggled alone to rise from the pillows, his manners not permitting him to touch a woman of such high birth, even to assist her. It fell to Lu Chin to bend to the task, ignoring her own stiffness to show her solicitude to the larger woman.

"Third Wife has accompanied her lord to see for herself that all is well," she said softly to the man. She had wished not to confront him, but it was not so difficult after all. The years in the women's quarter had honed her skills of deception, and she could see nothing in his countenance to challenge her purpose.

Soong bowed silently in reply.

"Perhaps the ladies can be entertained in one of the outer chambers," she suggested. "They are weary from the journey, and should be refreshed before they take their final places."

Soong bent again in acquiescence and Lu Chin knew that he had responded to her unspoken request to let the younger concubines postpone their fear a while longer.

"Third Wife," she said, "it is now our duty to see to our husband." Turning she led the way into the tomb, her fingers hidden in the folds of her sleeve as she worked her magic once again, this time a spell of concealment to let the two women pass unnoticed by the priests.

Although the tunnel that led inward from the opening to the tomb was somewhat narrow and circuitous, they soon reached the first open chamber, as large and fine as the throne room of the palace they had left behind. Lu Chin could discern, however, that the suddenness of the emperor's death had taken the work by surprise, for many of the furnishings were not yet fully prepared.

Torches flickered everywhere, from the sconces on the walls and from pillars set in the floor. The light was strong enough for Lu Chin to see the last of the priests disappear into an opening on the far side of the cavern. She set off in pursuit. Pau Li was clearly uncomfortable, a worried frown marring the smoothness of her forehead as she hurried to keep up.

The central chamber was unbelievably large, so high that paintings on the ceiling were indistinct in the darkness. A full-sized replica of the emperor's favorite summer lodge sat in a garden of stone. A legion of effigies guarded the perimeters, and colorful images of demons spanned the roofs.

Pau Li was puffing with exhaustion by the time the two women climbed the stairs of the building together. Lu Chin took Pau Li's hand, unwilling to let any control slip away at the crucial moment. They passed through rooms hung with silken tapestries and furnished with chests of carved sandalwood. Gold leaf covered the walls, the wealth of the empire gathered here only to be hidden in eternal darkness.

The emperor's inner sepulcher was rich beyond any of the antechambers. Lu Chin spared not a moment to admire it, but walked to the great alabaster sarcophagus, open to await its owner. It was lined with gold, and the carved plates of white jade that would be his final armor were laid out to receive him, the crown of gold, and jade sitting at the head. The coffin of the empress was just behind, small enough that Lu Chin had not seen it until she pulled Pau Li around to the back.

"Have you ever seen anything so grand?" Lu Chin asked, her voice reverent. "Did you ever imagine the clarity, the translucence of the jade?"

Pau Li shook her head.

"Its magic will keep him safe, uncorrupted for all time as the rest of us molder into nothingness," Lu Chin went on, "and as long as the body shall last, our lord shall know comfort." Then, more slyly, she added, "His consort as well. I was so certain he would have mentioned it. But, then, you were never actually crowned empress."

"It was to be," Pau Li exclaimed, Lu Chin's slights more than she could tolerate. "He died too soon."

"The empress's crown is here too," Lu Chin went on, picking it up from the smaller coffin. She started to set it on her own head, but stopped when she saw the look of outrage on Pau Li's face.

"Sacrilege!" Pau Li hissed. "Only an emperor's wife can wear an empress's crown."

Lu Chin shrugged, and handed it to Pau Li, who jammed it on top of her braids.

"Would you like to try the jade armor?" Lu Chin asked. "Just to see if you can feel the magic it holds, of course." She brushed her hand over the cold stones. "There is such power here, Third Wife. Surely you feel it. Even as I touch it, I can see beyond the tomb, and float above the mountain like a cloud."

Pau Li looked dubious, but nodded, and Lu Chin helped her don the heavy plates. Third Wife looked ridiculous; the armor had been fabricated for the slighter form of Lu Chin herself. Even so, it was so heavy that Pau Li could barely move. But she smiled at last, as satisfied with herself as a lizard sunning on a black rock. "I can feel its power," she said. "It's like nothing else."

She preened. Lu Chin came closer to help arrange her hair around the crown, and to lift Pau Li's jade amulet over the armor.

"The coffin is a vortex and has been created to amplify the magic," Lu Chin suggested. "The priests are not here yet. Perhaps you would like to lie down and see for yourself. There is time."

Again Pau Li hesitated until Lu Chin started to step in herself. "I will test it," Pau Li said, pushing Lu Chin aside. But weighed down as she was by the heavy plates of jade, she accepted Lu Chin's able assistance.

Settling Third Wife in the close quarters of the coffin took precious moments, and Lu Chin kept up a steady stream of comments to distract her. "You must close your eyes and concentrate," she instructed Third Wife. "I'm convinced you will be able to see as far as the city with so much power around you."

Obediently, Pau Li shut her eyes. Lu Chin snatched her chance. Reaching down, she gripped the chain that held Pau Li's amulet. Praying silently to the goddess of death, she pulled it tight, twisting and jerking it with all the unexpected strength of her aged assassin's arms.

Pau Li struggled. She clutched at her murderer's hands, snapping off her long ceremonial fingernails as she tried to gain purchase against the relentless grip. She tried to call out, but the makeshift garotte stopped the air she needed, and she moved her mouth in words that carried no sound, but pierced Lu Chin's consciousness with their accusations. Third Wife kicked uselessly, banging her heels against the cold stone. A sandal, knocked loose by the struggle, clattered on the pavement. But she was too confined in the coffin, too encumbered by the jade armor, to prevent her fate.

Lu Chin fought to hold her grip, relying on the strength of her resolve to reinforce the now failing power of her arms, turning her face from the bulging stare of her victim, and from the silent screams that echoed in her head. When she felt certain her victim was dead, Lu Chin took a moment to compose herself. When her breath was once more even, her heartbeat slowed to its normal rate, she bent to rearrange Pau

Li, straightening her gown and the armor, even restoring order to the tangled braids. She regretted leaving the white jade for Pau Li's shroud, for Lu Chin had not lied about it; she had felt its power beginning to stir beneath her touch.

Soong met Lu Chin at the door. She stood aside to let him enter.

"Why are you here?" he asked, his rough voice washing away all the years that had passed since they'd last spoken. She was reminded that she had always been subordinate to him, yet there was a gentleness underlying his tone that seemed new to her.

"Third Wife wished my assistance as she prepared to serve our lord," she answered, gathering her decorum like a cloak. "She was afraid that because she was not yet empress, she would be denied her place."

Soong nodded abruptly, then went to look in the coffin. He was as good at hiding his thoughts as she, and Lu Chin could not determine whether or not he guessed the truth. "Poison would have been easier," he said at last. "But it is good that she has accepted her destiny, regardless of your method."

The entrance of the priests with the body of the emperor permitted Lu Chin to leave the chamber without speaking to Soong again. But she knew there had been no need for words between them, after all. He had always known her as she was, and even now had no complaint of her, nor she of him.

Lu Chin found the rest of the women in a lower room of the eternal palace, one lined with marble benches and furnished as a bower. Knowing its purpose as the resting place of the maidens, she made them gather some instruments and step out into the stone garden, among the jeweled plants that parodied the flowers that grew above on the mountain.

"Let our emperor pass from us hearing your sweet voices, the sound of the flute, and the beat of a drum," she said.

Tremulous at first, the song grew to fill the cavern. When Soong appeared, Lu Chin knew it was time. She set down her viol and rose to meet him.

"They are still innocent of what will come," she told him. "If you will await us inside, I will call them in one at a time, so as not to frighten them."

He hesitated.

"There is no need to make their deaths difficult," she argued, unsure why it had become important to her to protect the others. As an assassin she had never thought of the lives that were ended by her hand, only the need to kill quickly, with the least risk to herself. And after all, the decisions of life and death had rarely been hers alone to make. Even the murders of the emperor's wives and favorites had seemed preordained, a requirement of her survival instead of the acts of treachery others might have considered them.

"They will do their duty," she said. There was always duty. "So perform yours gently," she continued, "to make the luck good. Their ghosts will not be angry."

One by one, Lu Chin led the concubines to their doom. Holding their hands, talking of silly things as Soong dealt the blow to the back of the head that ended life instantly. With only a soft explosion of breath to mark the passing of the spirit, one by one they wilted like parched roses in Lu Chin's embrace, and Soong carried them to their places on the marble benches. With each death, Lu Chin felt a blackness well up in her soul, a darkness that seemed to eclipse the torchlight flickering in the room. She sensed that Soong knew no more joy of the executions than did she.

At last the killing was done, the benches covered with the brightly garbed corpses. Wordlessly, she and Soong left the room. Outside the torches still burned, guttering low in their sconces. The priests were absent, their spells silent. Lu Chin sensed that she and Soong were the only living beings to remain inside. She felt an urgency to escape the weight of the mountain that arched above the roof of the cavern, to see the clear night sky stretching endlessly over her.

"We must hasten," she said. "The workers will want to close the tomb."

Soong looked down at her for a long moment. "I thought of you often," he said at last. "After that ambush when the old emperor was slain, I was told you had been taken to the women's quarter to serve the new emperor, the one who lies here now. Even though you were safe, at that moment I knew that you were dead to me, that I would never see your face pillowed beside mine, never feel the soft wind of your breath."

"You should have asked for me earlier," she said, startled by his confession, startled too by the flush of warmth his words brought to her face. "My training with you was long finished when I joined the imperial guard. It was yet a while after that before I came to the attention of our lord."

"But now, we have time for a glass of wine." Changing the subject yet again, Soong offered his arm and escorted her to a table near the entrance to the garden.

Lu Chin was puzzled by his strange behavior, and his willingness to partake of the wine left for the use of the emperor's spirit. With an apology to the gods, she let Soong fill two alabaster cups, and accepted the one he offered to her. It was delicious, cool and sweet; it reminded her that she had been all this long day without food.

"I would like to go," she said when she had finished. "Our lord has begun his long sleep. His wife and servants rest quietly near him. I have done all that I came to do."

"No," Soong said, a trace of sadness in his voice.

"What do you mean?" she asked, dread filling her soul. "Third Wife has taken the place next to my lord, and the room of the maidens is filled."

"Your purpose was never to lie beside him, never to lie with the ladies of joy. You are here to be an assassin, you the cleverest of all assassins. I have brought you to your post, and together we are to guard the gate, protecting our charges for all eternity. The emperor was carried in at the very last. The tomb is sealed behind him."

Sensing her shock, he reached toward her, but she stepped back, her spine rigid in protest against the fate Soong pronounced.

"None who entered the tunnel were permitted to leave," he told her. "Each of us has spent long years bowing to the will of the emperor. Now it remains to us to do our duty in death as we did in life."

Lu Chin looked up into his eyes, and saw love and regret etched as pain on his face. For a brief moment she glimpsed a life she had never imagined, a life of shared purpose, shared joys. Beside that possibility, the reality of the spacious rooms of her widow's quarters, even the freedom to leave the palace and return at her own will, paled.

It was too late for another path. There had never really been a choice, for her life had been ordained. Soong had spoken of duty, and that was all there had

Illustrated by Igor Baranko

ever been. As an assassin, she had disposed of enemies who had threatened the empire; as a concubine, she had disposed of those who might have threatened the peace of the emperor.

Soong took her hand and gave her an object, smooth and warm from his grasp, pressing her fingers close around it. She gripped it so tightly a sharp corner bit into her palm. Looking down, she saw that it was one of the plates from the emperor's armor, his white jade shroud. She lifted it against her heart, feeling the stone start to warm her, fill her with its enchantment.

When she raised her eyes, her gaze met that of Soong looking down at her, embracing her spirit. He offered her the promise that he would be with her forever. As had been the way between them, there were now no words, but she knew he would sacrifice, remaining alone at the end to ease her own passing to eternity. Holding tight to the white jade, she turned from her executioner and bowed her head for his blow.

ORANGE

Written by
Sara Backer

Illustrated by
Ulia Semenenko

About the Author

Sara Backer received her B.A. in music at Oregon State University and her M.A. in English at the University of California at Davis. She has published poetry regularly over the years, sold short stories outside of the science fiction genre to BitterSweet and Playgirl, and written play reviews and a treatment for a computer adventure game.

For three years, she taught English at Shizuoka University in Japan, where she spent some time working on two mainstream novels which have not yet been published. One of these, set in Japan, was a finalist in the James Jones First Novel Fellowship competition.

Currently, Sara is living in Corvallis, Oregon. She recently found that she had a poem nominated for the Rhysling Award for science fiction poetry, which was when she first discovered that she had committed an act of science fiction. The story that follows, "Orange," is her first attempt at writing a science fiction short story, but Sara promises it will not be her last.

About the Illustrator

Ulia Semenenko was born on November 14, 1976 in the Kola Peninsula. In 1982, her family moved to the city of Lugansk.

At the age of twelve, Ulia enrolled in Sheevchenko Art School. In 1993 and through 1994, she attended college in the city of Lugansk where she studied art. Ulia has worked in many publishing companies and her work has been sold in the Ukraine and Russia.

The courier, a young man with a long ponytail, sat beside his mountain bike on the stoop of Arthur Snell's apartment building. He stood as soon as Arthur approached, and thrust an envelope at him. "Sign here."

Arthur saw his name on the delivery form and signed beside it. The courier quickly tore off the original, bounced his bike as he leaped on, and pedaled away. Envying the courier's energy, Arthur mounted the stoop and punched in his security code.

Today, at CompCare's staff meeting, he'd been assigned to do a special insurance analysis for Pratt, the most difficult and obnoxious salesman in the Company. Then he'd discovered his new secretary had mistakenly altered his hyperfile template, losing statistics on a two-hundred employee client in the process. The final blow, just before 5:00 p.m., was personnel telling him he had to repeat his routine blood draw for drug testing as the results from last month showed his sample missing.

"Can't this wait?" he'd asked.

"Well, no. Your group tests on the thirteenth, which is next Monday, and if you don't replace a former sample seven days before the current draw, your employment file has to go through automatic review. It's a real hassle. So it has to be right now."

He sighed. "You couldn't have given me notice?"

The clerk's voice turned harsh. "We're busy, too, you know. You're lucky I called in time for you to fix it."

He'd rushed down to the Company lab just as it closed, and had to offer to personally cover the medical technician's ten minutes of overtime in order to get her to unlock the door and draw a sample. Finally, Arthur reached home with a sore arm to have this packet shoved in his hand. He gathered his mail before climbing the stairs to his apartment door. Only after he got inside did he notice the courier had given him a court summons. The rest of his mail, bills and catalogues, slithered to the hardwood floor. As he tore off the perforated edges, he tried to convince himself it was jury duty, even though he knew jury taps came through e-mail. He peeled off the security liner and read the form.

As a result of a DNA test, he was among five suspects for the murder of Ivy Graham on August fourteenth, 2010. He was to appear in Criminal Court on September 7, 2010. If he did not appear, he would be considered a fugitive under Statute 56DA, which called for the police to capture him dead or alive.

The summons fluttered to the floor and Arthur felt faint as he bent to pick it up. This had to be a mistake. Arthur checked his name, address and social security number on the summons; all were correct. He had somehow clung to the notion that only criminals or marginal people would be rounded up in a DNA sweep. Not someone like himself, whose record didn't even show parking tickets. But now it had happened. To him.

His ribs clenched around his heart. He forced himself to breathe deeply, poured himself a glass of Cabernet and walked into his living room. He sat in his sofa, newly upholstered in raw linen, a gesture toward making his apartment inviting to a hypothetical woman he might ask out if he mustered the nerve. The sofa and the Persian rug centered on the wood floor were the only soft things in the room. Someone had suggested drapes for the windows, but he made do with the tan venetian blinds that had come with the place. The rest was a clutter of books, electronics, tools, mismatched end tables and a TV. This morning, his worst problem had been loneliness; now, he was a murder suspect.

How could he prove his innocence? Since the Citizens to Contain Court Costs ballot initiative drives, the mere act of hiring a lawyer weighed against you if you were charged with a second offense. On the other hand, this was murder. Just his luck to have had a DNA match with the worst crime in the book. The red wine stung his cheeks.

He needed a lawyer, and the only lawyer he could trust was the one who'd divorced him a year ago. He punched her number in his cellular phone and listened to it ring. If Current Husband answered, he'd hang up.

The "Hello?" was her unmistakable tense alto voice.

"M-M-Margot? It's Arthur."

Pause. "When did you pick up that stutter?"

"Just . . . ah . . . just now. I have bad news."

"Not Sneakers!"

"No, Sneakers is fine." At least Arthur assumed the cat was lounging on his bed as usual. He'd been granted cat custody when Current Husband turned out to be allergic. "It's me."

Margot sighed. "Well, that's good. I mean, that Sneakers is okay. Why the call?"

"Well, you see, it's a little something a courier delivered to me." Talking to Margot awakened his former habit of attempting cavalier banter. He never could pull it off. "That . . . uh . . . requires the pleasure of my presence in Criminal Court."

"Bummer. Is it bad?"

"Bad is an understatement."

"Tell me it's a witness call."

"I can't lie to you." He threw more wine at his cheeks. "I'm a suspect."

"You? For what? You don't even jaywalk."

"M-Margot, it's not funny. It's a DNA round-up."

"Shit. Okay, how bad is it? Armed robbery? Rape?"

Arthur swallowed, though the wine didn't want to go down. "Murder."

Silence. Then, "Would it help if I said I don't believe for a nanosecond you did it, that, despite your lack of a life, you're a sweet guy incapable of willfully harming his fellow man?"

"Or w-w-woman?"

"Don't push it."

"The victim's name is Ivy Graham. Someone killed her August fourteenth. I'm one of five suspects, and—"

"Five! There are four others?"

Startled, Arthur murmured, "That's what the form—"

"That can't be right. The whole point of DNA is that no two people have the same polymorphic strands." Margot snorted. "They must have messed up in the crime lab."

He knew Margot liked to defend forsenic accuracy, but she was ignoring his murder charge. "Margot, please. I need help. Would you . . ."

"Yeah, I'll defend you. When's your court date?"

"September 7th."

"Tomorrow, huh?" He listened to her computer beep. "Okay. I have a ten o'clock in Claims Court, but Criminal meets at two o'clock in the B Wing, so I'll have plenty of time to make it. I'll be over after dinner tonight to prepare your case. Around nine."

His ribs loosened their grip a tad. "Margot, I don't know how to thank you."

"Don't. I'm doing this for Sneakers. I'm charging you, too. Later, bye."

Arthur set down the phone. Dinner. He supposed he should try to eat some. He pulled a box out of the freezer, stabbed the cardboard with a fork and put it in the microwave. At the sound of the beep, Sneakers came into the kitchen, meowing. Arthur scooped kibble into a bowl and set it on the floor. Sneakers was a gray cat named for her white feet. "You'll get to see Mommy tonight." Sneakers chomped away, oblivious. If he were executed, Margot would make sure Sneakers found a good home. Sneakers would be all right. A few weeks and Sneakers wouldn't even miss him.

Arthur opened the slightly soggy cardboard. A chicken rice thing. He stood over the sink, chewing and swallowing each bite as if performing jaw-ups at the gym. He bent his head to drink water from the tap. He tried to remember what he had been doing August fourteenth. If the murder had occurred during the day, he'd have plenty of alibis. CompCare used an open floor partitioned into cubicles instead of offices with closed doors, obliging coworkers to notice each other. He raced to his wall calendar and flipped back a month. August fourteenth was a Saturday. Damn. He couldn't remember a weekend he *hadn't* spent alone. If the other four suspects had alibis, he'd be the one to get the lethal injection. Appeals court no longer existed. Taxpayers wanted justice swift and cheap.

He was going through his date book when the doorbell rang. He buzzed Margot in and waited on his doorstep above the flight of stairs. He saw the top of her head first, plain brown hair, thinning along the center part. She wore a red tank top with an ethnic embroidered vest over it, jeans and sandals. When she looked up, her face got to him the way it always did. It wasn't beauty but energy that made her attractive. The same brown eyes, double-bump nose and large jaw on another woman would be boring.

The first thing she said was, "You'll have to dress better when you appear in court. When you're guilty of wearing pants too big for you, you could be guilty of anything. And no ink marks on your shirt pocket, got it?"

"Hello, M-Margot. How are you?"

"And a jacket, an informal one. No necktie. Don't want to seem like you're trying too hard, and everyone knows insurance analysts dress like nerds. Nice haircut, by the way. You finally let it grow enough to show some curl."

"Thanks." He stood aside as she entered his apartment, catching a whiff of jasmine perfume as she brushed past him. "I, uh, can I get you anything?"

"Names of everyone you saw on August fourteenth." Margot placed her briefcase on his kitchen table and pulled out her laptop.

"I meant, like, something to drink?"

"No. Do you have any alibis?"

"Just one." Arthur pointed to Sneakers.

Margot knelt down to the cat. "Oh, Mommy's missed you, kitty-catty! Yes, you're a good, sweet lovey kitty, aren't you?" Nothing like a pet to reduce a no-nonsense lawyer into a babble of baby-talk. "Come sit with Mommy." She scooped the cat onto her lap. Sneakers jumped off at once. Margot's voice returned to normal. "Well, fine, break my heart, stupid cat." She turned her attention back to Arthur. "I downloaded the public record of the Ivy Graham murder. She was killed between three and five in the afternoon. Can you prove your location then?"

Arthur shook his head. "No."

"You don't remember what you did that day?"

"I'm afraid not. My calendar is blank."

"I'll check your August phone bill. If we get a time match, whomever you called is an alibi, even a mail-order company." Margot typed his name and social security number. His public record sprang onto the screen, surrounded by icons. She pressed the telephone icon, entered August 2010, glanced through his bill and sighed. "One call at 10:34 a.m. to 6782-3566. Should I look it up in the reverse directory?"

"That's the cinema-plex information number."

"That's progress." Her voice brightened. "You saw a movie? A matinee, I hope? With lots of people who said, "Hi, Arthur!" as you bought your ticket? Someone who sat beside you from three to five o'clock inclusive?"

"I honestly don't remember. I probably didn't go to a matinee, though. I hate to step out of a dark theatre into bright sunshine."

"I'll call the cinema tomorrow, on the longshot that your appearance was memorable to someone. Here's what I have from the prosecution. There were scratches and bruises indicating struggle, but she was killed either by poison—one that eludes an autopsy—or an air bubble injection. A needle fragment was found in her left arm. The DNA sample came from a blood stain on her jeans. They say the DNA had been degraded by bacteria. That's how they came up with five of you, but I still think someone botched the test."

"I'm going to court because a lab tech screwed up?"

"Look on the bright side: it gives you a twenty percent chance. For once, your lack of originality is going in your favor." Margot typed quickly and pressed the Enter key with a flourish. "Check out her picture. Know her?"

Arthur looked at the photograph on the screen. Ivy Graham could have washed up on the beach: faded seashell skin, eyes like murky water, sandy-gray hair that floated around her narrow face in waves. "I don't know her. But she doesn't look unfamiliar, either."

"Oh, great. You've slept with her, right?"

"No, I said I—"

"Joke, joke. Let's pull up her employment." Margot typed and waited for access. "*Are* you sleeping with anyone, by the way?"

Arthur petted Sneakers. "Yes."

"Oh." She was clearly surprised. "Well, good for you. What's she like?"

"Lazy. Quiet. Beautiful eyes."

Margot snorted. "Three ways to say boring."

"Pretty feet, too."

"Spare me." The screen filled with words.

"All four white paws."

Margot burst into laughter. "You had me going for a while. Here it is. Ivy's last job was assistant manager of Morning Glory Cafe—"

"I eat breakfast there."

Margot tsked her tongue. "How often?"

"Oh, I don't know. On Sundays. They don't hurry you out. You can read the paper and get coffee refills."

"But you don't recognize Ivy?"

"Not really."

Margot pointed a pencil at him. "Arthur, 'not really' doesn't cut it for murder one. Have you ever paid your tab with a credit card, even once?"

"Yeah."

"Then we can kiss the lying option goodbye." Margot rubbed the bridge of her nose. "Speaking of coffee, could you make me some?"

"Sure." Arthur filled a kettle with water, took a bag of beans from the freezer and shook them into his grinder. After he ground the beans, he asked, "What's my best defense for something like this?"

"Your best defense is what you haven't got: witnesses, alibis and a victim whose path you never crossed. Failing that, a time travel to the twentieth century could help you out."

"Wouldn't I be in jail, then?"

"Yes, but circumstantial evidence was easy to dismiss. I could argue the accuracy of forensics, put scientists and cops on the stand."

Arthur unfolded a paper filter. "When trials were long and lawyers were rich."

"Yeah." Margot sighed wistfully. "Lawyers used to make at least fifty grand a year, same as you. Twice my income. Even Jim makes more than I do, now."

Arthur dumped the grinds into a filter. He was used to her complaints about her salary, but the mention of Jim's name still bothered him. He preferred the term Current Husband, which made it seem possible he'd turn into Former Husband someday. "He found a job, I take it?"

"Swing shift at Bio-Gen."

"As what?"

Margot glared. "Specimen Injector, and don't you dare make a comment."

"Give him my congratulations."

"The last thing he'd want to hear. He gets testy if your name comes up." Margot got up and stretched, right hand on left elbow, pulling her arm straight behind her head.

"In that case, how does he feel about you defending me?" Arthur took the kettle off and poured water over the coffee. Steam moistened his eyelashes.

"I haven't told him, yet. He won't be home until after eleven."

"Why so late?"

"I *said*, he works swing."

"Oh."

"'Oh,' yourself. He'll deal with it. He'll have to."

Arthur felt he should be noble and offer to hire another lawyer. But he was up for murder, and he needed Margot. Current Husband was merely up for jealousy. Let him deal with it, as she had said. He filled a cup and handed it to Margot. "Things are going well for you two?"

Margot shrugged. "It's only been four months. I guess it's natural to have some conflict."

He and Margot hadn't conflicted. Her complaint had been that he was dull and she needed excitement, adventure, intensity. "He doesn't bore you, then."

"We're just . . . adjusting." Margot took a sip, slurping to cool it. "Hey, this might go in your favor. Before the Morning Glory Cafe, Ivy Graham worked for Shooter's, Grit Bar and Pussy In Boots. Serious sleaze, wouldn't you say?"

The scent of coffee alone was enough to make Arthur's stomach jiggle. "Didn't your husband used to work at Shooter's?" No need to remind her of the theft charge that had reduced Current Husband to dishwashing jobs.

"What's that supposed to mean?" Margot said sharply.

Arthur tried to think up a benign answer. "Maybe it's not so sleazy?"

"It's sleazy. After his trial, it was hard for Jim to get any job. The taint of being accused followed him for a few months. Ivy, on the other hand, shows a life-long pattern."

Arthur refrained from pointing out that Jim's previous career history was just as questionable. Why Margot had ever fallen for one of her clients was inexplicable to him. She knew better than to confuse sympathy with love, yet had married a man she had defended on his third charge of petty theft, who'd never held a job for more than a few months, and sulked in bars as early as eleven in the morning. Arthur knew; since he insured Margot and her husband, he knew Current Husband's social security number and had opened his file and browsed through his credit receipts. The only thing this down-and-outer had going for him was a quality Arthur dubbed 'Loser Charisma,' and that had to be powerful indeed to seduce a smart, competent woman like Margot.

Margot was talking. " . . . until we appear in court and see what they hit us with. Arthur? Have you been listening?"

"Yes. I mean, no. What could they hit me with?"

"Your personality profile, for one. You should never have said your favorite color was orange. That's the most unusual favorite, *except* among psychotics."

"It's a happy color. You know, sunsets, marigolds." Arthur glanced around his kitchen. Nothing orange.

"You should have lied and said blue. And your record is too clean. They'll peg you as a bottled-up type who exploded." Margot tipped her cup to finish her coffee. "They may even suggest you were depressed after the divorce and determined to victimize a woman, but my showing up as your lawyer should mitigate against that."

"Wouldn't they have fingerprints on the needle? I mean, syringe?"

"This record states the syringe is missing. With luck, they'll have found and dusted it before tomorrow afternoon."

"How about a motive?"

Margot shook her head. "Not necessary. A plausible scenario is good enough to convict a DNA match. Like, you're a loner, a regular at Morning Glory Cafe, you obsess on Ivy, and one Saturday go to her place to do her in."

Arthur began to wonder how many innocent people had been put to death in the name of plausibility. "That's scary."

She reached across the table and clutched his hand. "I know. But don't stay up all night dreaming up worst possible outcomes. I've gone to hearings many times to have new evidence narrow it down to one person and the false suspects go home without saying a word. Think about *that* possibility, all right?" She packed her computer away and knelt on her heels to stroke Sneakers. "Goodbye, my sweet, good kittycat. You take care of Daddy." She stood and opened her arms.

Arthur clasped her bony body. Then she was gone, a cold draft pushing back at him as the door fell shut behind her. He listened to her feet go down the stairs, and the apartment building door creak open and lock her out with a slam. He tossed his coffee down the sink and poured another glass of wine. He usually had only one glass, but he couldn't think of a better night to make an exception.

Ivy's face stuck with him. He tried to picture her bringing him pancakes, pouring him a cup of coffee, tried to visualize her in the sky-blue dress with the white collar and buttons, name tag on the twining leaf pin over her breast. Her face kept floating away from the Morning Glory Cafe uniform. Hers was a bar face, a night face, a street-lights-and puddles face. She had nothing to do with breakfast.

He checked his watch. Eleven. He should *try* to sleep. Maybe habit would take over. But in bed, lights out, Sneakers curled by his knees, he couldn't have been more awake. His pounding heart flogged him to get up and do something, anything. He threw off the covers and turned on his computer. He ran through the IDs of his online groups without finding a face like Ivy's. He entered his company's interface code and checked out his coworkers. Then he started through his clients, beginning at 1998. An hour later, he switched directions and moved back from 2010. He quickly found Ivy Graham. She had applied for health and life insurance on June fourteenth, 2010.

Arthur stared at the screen, willing a memory to emerge. As an analyst, he didn't work with clients the way agents did. He might meet clients briefly if the agent brought them by his desk, or he might phone them with questions, but mostly he checked backgrounds, ran figures through his charts, and came up with a monetary value for a person's life. Ivy Graham's face remained slightly familiar, nothing more. He vaguely recalled feeling sorry for her, but maybe he was projecting that on her now, knowing her fate. He called up her policy, and discovered she hadn't been issued one. He looked for his own code that showed the reason for denial: OR5F8DU3. This meant she was in the fifth level of occupational risk, had eight incidents of financial misconduct, and met third-degree criteria for drug use. Statistically, she was a very poor risk. It occurred to him that her unnatural death had proved his analysis to be true. If only he'd been wrong—now, her early demise might bring about his own. Saliva suddenly flooded his mouth, and he ran to the toilet, vomiting onto the lid.

Cleaned up and back in bed, Arthur stroked Sneakers and considered his life. Why hadn't he planted a window box of marigolds or watched sunsets, even one sunset, from beginning to end? Why had he wasted day after day in front of a mind-numbing computer, and so many nights in front of another mind-numbing screen, and on weekends, for a treat, sat in the dark with strangers facing a very large mind-numbing screen? Why had he ever let a marital night pass without making love to Margot? How many times had he pushed Sneakers away? He had lived for achievement and had achieved nothing. He was probably the most expendable man in the world. But now, without Margot, without friends, without success, without an interesting life, he desperately wanted a chance to live, to savor all the small pleasures he'd forgone. He didn't want his life stopped with a needle prick and a plunge. Arthur Snell stayed up all night.

• • •

He met Margot on the steps of the courthouse. The wind blew stray droplets of rain on his head, whooshed through poplar leaves, flipping their silvery undersides up. Margot's heels drum-rolled, slowed, stopped. She stood in a houndstooth-check skirt suit, hair clipped in a loose bun, suspicious look in her brown eyes. "You've changed."

"You told me to dress better," Arthur joked.

"It's the look in your eyes. Is it from sleep deprivation? You didn't sleep," she stated.

"I didn't want to. I was thinking about the meaning of life last night."

She hooked her arm through his and propelled him into the building. "Don't get philosophic on me. I struck out on the cinema-plex, but there's room for hope. I hear they have hair and fiber analysis today."

"Margot, you should know that I found out Ivy Graham applied for insurance last June. I was the one who denied her coverage."

Margot winced and covered her eyes with her hand, palm facing out. "Okay, we'll pray for the new evidence to rescue your ass. What kind of insurance?"

"Life and health." You couldn't get health without life anymore.

"Who was the bennie?"

Arthur opened his mouth and closed it. Of course. Why hadn't he looked for her beneficiary? Because he didn't have a criminal mind, that's why. "Is there time to check?"

"Not now there isn't," Margot grumbled. She raised her arms as the guard frisked her and sent her briefcase through X-ray. The guard took longer frisking Arthur and took his thumb prints before pinning a suspect pass on his lapel. Arthur wiped his thumbs on a detergent-soaked towel while the clerk ran his prints through the file. Margot used a microchip implant instead of prints. She pointed to her shoulder and the clerk scanned the chip to verify she was Margot Beacon. He buzzed them both into the courtroom.

Margot led Arthur to the front table. The four other suspects were already seated, three next to attorneys. Margot sat beside another lawyer and spoke to him briefly. Arthur looked up to the ceiling dome, which sheltered an electric chandelier. Around the dome's circumference, carved in walnut, was the phrase "With liberty and justice for all." They should change the last word, he thought, to "the lucky."

At exactly two o'clock, the judge entered and took the bench. He had a horseshoe of gray hair around his bald spot, bushy brows slanting up like an owl's, and long jowls. He carried thirty extra pounds, all on his stomach.

"Tom Winter," Margot whispered. "Conservative, old-school curmudgeon."

"Be seated." Tom Winter opened a file and put on tortoise-shell glasses. "We'll get the Ivy Graham case out of the way first. Due to new evidence and lab reports, we have ruled out all but one suspect."

Margot squeezed his hand hopefully.

"Joe Hill, Peter Seneca, Faye Martin and Benjamin Cook, you are excused. Arthur Snell, how do you wish to plead?"

"No! You're wrong! It's not me!" Arthur shouted.

Tom Winter took off his glasses and shook them at Arthur. "Your lawyer speaks, not you. Don't tempt me to slap you with contempt. Ms. Beacon?"

Margot cleared her throat. "Excuse me, Your Honor. My client and I are unaware of the nature of the lab reports. I request review of evidence before entering a plea."

Tom Winter chuckled. "Oh, no, you don't. No measuring the water before you dive in. Snell knows whether or not he did it. Are you going to make the taxpayers pay for a trial, or will you confess and proceed with sentence bargaining?"

Margot stated, "We plead not guilty."

"Fine." Tom Winter put his glasses back on. "Let the record show Arthur Snell pleaded not guilty and is represented by Margot Beacon. I order the police and prosecution to allow Ms. Beacon to review any and all evidence against Arthur Snell. Set trial for Tuesday, September fourteenth, at nine o'clock." He spoke in a monotone, getting it over with. "Implant a tracking device in Arthur Snell, who will be held in house arrest until then. Due to the brutal nature of the alleged crime, authorize police to shoot on sight should defendant attempt to leave his quarters. Require police escort to court on the fourteenth, to be paid for by defendant. Any questions."

"Your Honor, I have a general objection to—"

"Forget it, Ms. Beacon. I'm in no mood to pamper your client." Tom Winter banged his gavel. "Ivy Graham suspects are dismissed. We'll take a five-minute break and return with the Gerome Scott case."

One of the other suspects said, "I'm so glad they found out who did it. I can't believe I was summoned for this. What a nightmare."

Arthur toppled his chair and had to grab the edge of the table for support. He wished they had technology to expose his heart and mind, to prove his innocence.

"Take it easy." Margot's low voice soothed him. "It's not over until it's over. We'll get you implanted and find out what they have."

"The w-w-way he talked—"

"He's a bad-ass playing hardball. Too bad he scheduled your trial for a Tuesday. One in three, we'll get baldie on the bench again. This way." Margot led him down a dirty corridor, with urine-colored linoleum and chalk green walls. Fluorescent ceiling tubes hummed and crackled at them. She knocked on an unmarked door, which was opened by a woman with red hair sprayed up in a coxcomb, wearing round red glasses and a white smock.

"Hi, Jill. My client needs a tracking implant." Margot handed her a stamped form.

"Sure. Whoa!" Jill grabbed Margot's sleeve. "Isn't he your ex?"

"Yes. It's house arrest, so he won't need to pay for parole strength, okay?"

"Oh, my God! I can't believe you were married to a criminal."

Margot squinted a fake smile at her. "I wasn't. He's innocent."

"Yeah, right, sure. Why are you defending him?"

"Jill, just do your job." Margot let her hand linger on Arthur's shoulder. "Hang in there. I'll meet you here in ten minutes."

Jill motioned him onto a table. "On your stomach. Take your shirt off."

He propped his chin on the edge to keep his nose from touching the paper covering.

Jill jimmied a chip into a special syringe. "Actually, I shouldn't be surprised. It's the quiet types you can't trust."

"I didn't kill anyone," Arthur said. But he sounded defensive.

Jill lowered the long, thick needle under his nose. "It goes in the back of your neck. If an amateur tries to remove it, you could die."

"Did you have to show me?" he muttered.

"It'll hurt like hell, too." She plunged the needle in.

•••

Margot arranged for police escort back to Arthur's apartment. While the police made Arthur walk around to test the implant's sensitivity, Margot left to buy groceries for him. When she returned, Arthur was lying face down on his raw linen sofa.

"How are you holding up?"

Arthur laughed bitterly. "It's funny. So many weekends, I never left this room, and now all I want to do is go outside."

"You don't know what you've got till it's gone."

"Yeah. But it's one thing to say it and another to feel it. What's the new evidence?"

"I didn't have lunch, did you? You still eat cheese-and-onion sandwiches?"

"Uh-oh. You're delaying the blow."

"Yes. Get up and make me a sandwich. Whole wheat, Muenster and red onions, nuked." She pried him over. "Come on, I'm hungry."

Arthur played possum while she tugged at him, then quickly pulled her down onto his chest, an old gambit from their marriage. Face to face, he thought about kissing her. Her eyes almost signaled him to. Then he released her and she jumped away, nearly raced into the kitchen. He followed, wincing. If a microchip hurt this much, shrapnel must be agony.

Margot began to slice the cheese with his bread knife. Arthur took the knife out of her hand and replaced it with a paring knife. "What is it you want to delay telling me?"

Margot watched the knife, not him. "What is it *you're* not telling *me*?"

"Nothing." He shucked the papery skin off the onion and cut off the root end. This one had two sets of concentric rings, outlined in magenta. Why hadn't he noticed before that onions squeak faintly when cut? His eyes began to burn.

"No seemingly irrelevant personal details?" Margot's voice was as sharp as his knife.

"I don't know what you mean." He rubbed his eye on his sleeve.

"Where's your gray-and-white flannel shirt? The one I liked?"

"I don't know. I lost it, I guess." His voice remained soft and calm, although tears and snot flowed out of him. "What are you driving at?"

Margot flung her knife in the board. It caught on the tip and shuddered to a halt. "Ivy Graham was wearing your shirt the day she died. With a few Persian rug fibers and scads of Sneakers' hair in it."

"That can't be." Arthur rinsed his hands.

"Think hard."

Arthur thought. "How could they match my rug and my cat? They never sampled my apartment."

"Actually, they did. Not this one, the one we lived in before. Part of my background check for licensing, remember?" Margot pushed a rectangle of cheese slices toward him and he put the sandwich together and set the microwave. "But it's definitely your shirt. I recognized it, missing button and all. Sneakers' hair blended right in. How did Ivy get it?"

So even Margot didn't trust him anymore. He snatched a paper towel and blew his nose, hiding his real tears. "I don't know. I don't know Ivy Graham. I've never been to her place. I don't even know where she lives. Lived. And I certainly never gave her my shirt."

"I believe you. So you must have thrown it out. Could she have bought it at a thrift store?"

Relieved that Margot still had faith in him, Arthur wished he could remember what he'd done with it. "I wouldn't throw it out." Too many memories of Margot in that shirt, sleeves rolled up. He couldn't wear it and he couldn't trash it. "Didn't I give it to you? The day you took Sneakers away?"

Hearing her name and the microwave beep, Sneakers trotted into the kitchen, meowing.

Margot picked her up, pushing her nose into the cat's fur and said, "I never meant to hurt you."

"I know. You did it for yourself. I bored you. You needed adventure."

"I miss you so much."

Arthur looked up, startled, only to see Margot was talking to the cat. "I'm sorry . . . that . . . Jim . . . is allergic to cats." A major concession, speaking his name.

"He's not."

"Then w-w-why—"

"I got to feeling bad about you. I mean, I had Jim but you had no one. It didn't seem fair for me to get Sneakers, too. I made up Jim's allergy to spare your pride."

"What's pride?" Arthur took the plate to the table and sat.

"Pride is . . ." Margot sat across from him and laughed. "Funny how you never get my jokes and I never get yours."

"That's good, isn't it? To surprise each other?"

Margot swiped a string of cheese oozing from her sandwich and tucked it back between the bread slices. "Maybe. I hadn't thought about it."

Arthur watched her eat with her mouth open, absorbed in food and thought. "I never stopped loving you."

Margot put her hand over her eyes, palm out. "Don't say that. Please."

"Sorry." Her response hurt, after all these months. "We should discuss my defense."

Margot sighed. "Thing is, if I didn't know you, I'd think you were guilty. I wouldn't want to risk a polygraph. Even the brain-wave type detects stress more than it detects lies. All we have to prove your innocence is your character, and that won't work. Character never emerges in a courtroom. The situation is so unnatural that even if you could 'act natural,' as the oxymoron goes, you wouldn't be convincing."

"What if we can find out who really did it?"

"No one's going to confess when there's such a strong case against *you*."

"Based on my DNA?"

"Together with your shirt. Even if I can discredit the blood sample, the cat hair is a perfect match. Sorry to say, Sneakers nailed you."

"Could they have nailed me if you hadn't had our apartment sampled?"

Margot forced a laugh. "What? Trying to frame your lawyer?"

"A frame-up! Could someone have framed me?"

An onion slice fell onto the table. Margot picked it up and ate it. "What for?"

"How should I know? Whatever people frame people for."

"Last I knew, you didn't have any enemies. No friends, but no enemies. Acquired any this past year?"

"Enemies?"

"Or friends?"

"Not that I know of. I could hire a private detective to investigate CompCare clients."

"You can't research an infinite list of strangers in one week."

Arthur spoke softly, "Don't get angry with me."

Margot said nothing.

He looked at his untouched sandwich. "I think I'm having a reaction to this implant."

"How so?"

"I feel all hot and cold and buzzed. Like the flu. A bad flu."

"You're sweating." She reached across the table to touch his forehead. "Look, go to bed. You're probably in shock. Take the rest of today to absorb this." Margot packed up. "I have a few cop contacts. I'll check their scuttlebutt, talk to people at Morning Glory, that kind of stuff. Take care of yourself, okay? Don't panic, and whatever you do, don't leave your apartment."

"Might be better to take a bullet than a needle. At least I'd die in sunlight."

"And no wallowing in despair!" Margot tried to look stern. She wiped the corner of her eye, patted his shoulder and left him alone again.

•••

In bed, sore and shaking, Arthur distracted himself by pondering mundane details—starting with calling CompCare to request a leave of absence. Would they halt his computer access during his leave? He should download all his files first in case they did. Would they fire him? After he was released, would he get his job back or would he, like Jim, have to scrounge for a dishwasher job at Shooter's? He tried not to think of the other possible outcome, but he imagined the needle sliding into his elbow, the drugs flowing into his vein. What would he feel? "No!" He was surprised he'd spoken aloud.

He threw off the covers, turned on his computer and set to work. When the room began to dim, he stopped, poured himself a glass of wine and pulled open the blinds on his western window. He watched pale pink clouds in a blue sky turn into salmon clouds in an indigo sky and then into darkness over a glowing greenish band at the horizon. He ate his cheese-and-onion sandwich and went back to work.

At 4 a.m., shaky with fatigue, he ground coffee. If he only had a week to live, he wasn't going to waste time sleeping, especially when he didn't remember his dreams. Then he realized that even if he didn't remember them, he still had them, and that was a precious experience, too, to savor while he could. He joined Sneakers in bed and instantly went unconscious.

Friday morning, a sense of his dream lingered with him, a feeling of tension and euphoria. Something about jumping into a dangerous—boat? plane? car? He didn't know where he was going, but he knew he'd have been killed if he hadn't risked the jump.

He decided to fix waffles, a treat he rarely indulged in due to the labor involved. He paid attention to how the egg whites stiffened under the beaters. He studied the anatomy of walnut meat, two sides with two lobes each, joined at the top over a wafer-thin barrier inside the shell. Instead of stirring a tablespoon of frozen orange juice into a glass of water, he mixed the whole can in the Italian pitcher, hand-painted with a red rooster on the side. He would call a shopping service to get him real oranges to squeeze by hand. And marigolds, if they were still in bloom. He played a CD of Beethoven's Ninth Symphony while he ate. He opened his long-saved tin of pure Vermont maple syrup and poured until it puddled.

After breakfast, he called CompCare. He planned to call in sick—not entirely a lie—but when Dennis got on the line, he said, "I quit."

"Did you say you're sick?"

"No, I said I quit."

"What! Why?"

"To accept a better job." Arthur hung up, jubilant. His next call was to Margot. Current Husband answered the phone. Instead of hanging up, he said, "Margot, please."

"She's out."

"Would you tell her to call me as soon as she can? This is Arthur Snell."

"Oh, yeah. Margot told me you're on trial. Murder, isn't it?" Jim yawned.

Arthur wasn't sure if he meant the charge or a description of his situation. "Did she tell you anything about it?"

"Not much."

"I'm charged with killing a waitress, Ivy Graham."

"Tough luck, man."

"Does it bother you that Margot's my lawyer?"

"Uh, no." When Arthur said nothing, Jim faltered on. "She has to make a living."

An unexpected reaction. "I'm glad it doesn't bother you. For her sake."

"Yeah, well, I'll tell her you called. Bye."

Arthur hung up. Margot had said Jim got testy at the mention of his name—she wasn't giving Current Husband enough credit. He turned to his computer. CompCare had already locked him out of his work files. Good thing he'd copied everything last night. He remembered he hadn't checked the listing of Ivy Graham's designated beneficiary. On her application, the beneficiary line was blank. He checked her reference line ("Who referred you to CompCare?"), where she'd written "a coworker." Through Ivy Graham's social security number on her insurance application, he tapped into her life record and looked at her employment history again. Her job at Morning Glory Cafe began July 20. She had been employed at Shooter's when she'd applied for insurance. He drummed his fingers on his mouse pad. He accessed his telephone database and found the name of a private detective he'd worked with on insurance fraud. When Margot called at noon, he had made an appointment with Lou French.

Margot asked, "On a scale of one to ten, where are you?"

"I put myself around six."

"That good? What's wrong?"

"Isn't it good to be good?"

"Not when you're facing trial for murder. It's normal to be a blubbering wreck."

"A reason not to be normal. What's up?"

"That's my question. I'm returning your call."

Arthur hesitated, wondering if he should tell Margot he was hiring a private eye against her advice. He chose his other news. "I quit my job."

"Okay, I'm not falling for this one. What's the punch line?"

"No joke. I quit."

"Arthur, was that wise? Was that prudent? Why didn't you just ask for a leave? You have tons of vacation time stored up, don't you?"

"Not anymore. I got to thinking what you said about Jim. Even though he got off—I mean, was innocent—it was hard for him to find a job after his trial. I figured I should protect myself from getting fired by quitting."

"Your charge is on your life record, regardless."

"But my employment slate is clean."

"Splitting hairs, aren't you? Anyway, how will you pay your legal fees?"

"You're in my will."

"Don't talk like that! I schmoozed some cops this morning. One cop said your profile matched a 'perfect crime' type to him—your data indicates you could be a one-time killer, the loner kind who doesn't need to brag about it later."

"Just because my favorite color is orange?"

"I'm not done. So, to him, the victim wearing your shirt was too obvious. He felt you were too smart to do that."

"He thinks I was framed?"

"Unless you're smart enough to make yourself appear framed."

"Come on, Margot! You sound like the prosecution. This is good news, right?"

"It's only an opinion. You can't put speculation on the stand."

"It's done all the time. It's called expert testimony."

"When did you pass the bar, smart-ass?"

"I watch TV."

"Oh, well, *you're* the legal expert, then. Got any ideas how to find the real killer and make him confess within a week?"

Arthur deliberately slowed and softened his voice. "Why are you so testy?"

She sighed long and loud. "Sorry. I'm just so damn frustrated at not being able to get you out of this. Yet. But you're the last person I should dump on. I am sorry. Forgive me?"

"It's okay. I understand."

"Did you look up Ivy's beneficiary?"

"The line is blank."

A pause. "Figures. Anything else?"

"Zip."

"Nice try, anyway. I have to run to court. Later, bye."

Arthur took a hot bath. He brought the telephone and a stack of catalogs with him and ordered anything that struck his fancy. A silk suit, a build-it-yourself kit of connecting cat tunnels to amuse Sneakers, an umbrella holder painted with tiger lilies. He ordered cloth drapes the color of nectarines and a bright orange towel set, extra plush. He paid extra for next-day delivery. Out of the bath, he put on a charcoal cashmere pullover and natural linen pants he liked but hadn't worn because they required dry-cleaning. He wore the cashmere next to his skin so he could feel it, even though the V neck showed chest hair he normally covered up. Margot liked tan, hairless chests, not his curly mat.

The doorbell rang before his hair and feet dried. Arthur buzzed in the shopping service, and two teenage boys carried in groceries and potted marigolds. They had to make a second trip for all the marigolds. Arthur tipped them well. While Sneakers investigated the pungent flowers, Arthur sliced chocolate chip cookie dough onto a sheet and put it in the oven. Then he cut open an orange, watching a tiny spray erupt through the punctured membrane. The doorbell rang again, and he buzzed in Lou French.

Lou French's blue flannel shirt and heavy jeans were muscle covers passing as clothes. Her light brown hair had the ragged look of an amateur cut, and her hooded blue eyes seemed childlike without makeup. "Hi." She crunched Arthur's hand. "Does your doorman frisk everyone?"

"That's my guard. I have to pay him two hundred a day to shoot me if my implant beeps. I'm not allowed to leave my apartment." He shoved marigolds aside to clear a part of the kitchen table. "I'm sorry he frisked you. It must be his orders."

"I'll live. Cute cat," she said, as Sneakers jumped off the table. She sat and looked at Arthur. "You're different."

"What do you mean?"

"Sorry, I mean it as a compliment. At your office, I thought you were . . . oops, my foot's in my big mouth now, huh? I don't mean to imply that you used to be . . . I mean, shame on me for stereotyping you wrong, okay? I didn't have you pegged as a guy with a kitchen full of posies and . . . do I smell homemade cookies?"

Arthur was touched by her inarticulateness. "Cookies, yes, but not homemade. Would you like some orange juice?"

"From actual oranges?"

He smiled. "I take that as a yes."

"Sure, if you can talk and squeeze at the same time." Her face flushed deep rose as she fumbled with a pocket notebook. "That came out wrong, too."

Arthur pushed his sweater sleeves above his elbow and twisted orange halves on the corrugated cone as he filled her in on his case. Lou listened without interrupting and jotted notes until Arthur stopped to take the cookies out of the oven.

Then she summarized, "So you decided to hire me when you found out Ivy Graham worked at Shooter's the same time your ex-wife's current husband did?"

"Right." Arthur scraped a spatula under the cookies and piled them on a plate. "Ivy was referred by a coworker. Jim was a coworker. And the only person I know who dislikes me. Can you find out if he set me up?"

Lou chewed on her pen. "Why would he? He got the girl, right?"

"But Margot said their marriage has conflict, and that he resents the mention of my name. You don't know this guy. He's a sleaze-ball, goof-off barfly. He's been called up for theft three times. He's capable of anything."

Lou fixed her baby blues on him. "You're not fond of him, are you?"

Arthur clenched his teeth. "Does it matter?"

"Maybe not. Margot Beacon married Jim Hatch when?"

"May twenty-third." He set glasses of orange juice on the table beside the cookies.

"Okay. I assume Margot was insured by CompCare through you, right? So after she ties the knot, it stands to reason she'd try to get hubby on life and health through you as well, right? When?" Lou reached for a cookie, and jerked her fingers away. "Yeow! Hot."

"A week after they married."

"Fine. So now Jimbo's washing dishes at Shooter's and has to take time off for a medical exam to get insurance. Ivy Graham asks him where he's getting his. He tells her. And she trots over to CompCare to check it out. Sound innocent enough?"

Arthur grabbed a chair and straddled it backward, folding his arms over the back. "Except this morning, when I called for Margot, he pretended not to know her."

Lou French squinted. "Explain."

"He had no response when I mentioned the name of Ivy Graham. He just said, 'Tough luck.' Don't you think that's bizarre? To be completely nonchalant about the murder of someone you worked with?"

Lou nodded agreement. "It is. You might be onto something. I have to ask this: Why did you hire your ex as your lawyer?"

"She's a good lawyer. We're still good friends. I trust her."

"If you say so. You didn't try to get someone else first?"

Arthur didn't want her to know he was a loner. But she'd find out soon enough in her investigation. "I don't know many people. I don't . . . um . . . socialize much."

"A gorgeous guy like you? I don't buy it. What's the deal? Are you sleeping with your counsel?"

Arthur laughed. Little did she know he was Mr. Celibate of 2010. And what did she mean by that "gorgeous" crack? "I wish, but it's not that way."

"Aha! You wish, huh? Wish it enough to set up Jim Hatch?"

The room was hot. Arthur got up to check if he had turned off the oven. "I don't like him, I admit it. But setting him up wouldn't change anything for me. I mean, you can't make someone love you." The oven was off, but he was sweating. Implant sickness? "Margot doesn't love me." He wiped his forehead with a dish towel.

"So why torture yourself by having her handle your case?"

"It's not torture." Arthur grabbed ice from the freezer and pressed it on his forehead. "She's the only person in the world who knows me. She knows I'm not guilty."

"Are you all right?" Lou's hand touched his back.

Arthur leaned against the refrigerator. "I get waves of this. I think it's the implant."

"Some people are allergic to those. Want me to take it out?"

Arthur looked up, startled. "Isn't that dangerous?"

Lou French shrugged. "Not for me. I've done it several times."

"It's illegal. I don't want to get in more trouble."

"It's your call, but if you don't leave your digs, no one will know the implant's gone. They don't remove it if you're cleared, you know. You have to line up a private doctor, who has to check court records, and some cop usually talks the M.D. into leaving it in place. Makes it easier to arrest you again."

"How do you know that?"

She smiled, a small smile that twisted one lip higher than the other. "Experience."

"It's here." Arthur pointed to the back of his neck.

"I need antiseptic, gauze, tape, a real sharp knife and tweezers." Lou examined his kitchen knives and chose a slender poultry knife. Arthur foraged in his bathroom cupboard for the other supplies. His stomach felt queasy and he hovered over the toilet, wondering how to tell Lou he'd changed his mind. Yet, he wanted to get rid of the implant, and he trusted her to do it. As Lou said, no one would know the difference as long as he followed the rules of his house arrest. The very thought of removing the device gave him a tiny thrill of control. As long as he was stuck in this nightmare, he might as well take a chance. Arthur came out to find Lou sharpening the knife.

"Where do you want me?" he asked.

Lou glanced into his living room. "Hate to get blood on a white sofa. Got an old sheet or something?"

"I'll get it off the bed."

She crossed the living room into his bedroom. "Hell, why not do it here?"

"Is there enough light?" Arthur pulled the blinds wide open, hoping Lou wouldn't judge him by their ugliness. As the slats clattered up to the top, he added, "My new curtains come tomorrow."

"I never get around to putting up curtains."

He liked her for admitting it. "Neither did I, until today."

Lou stepped into the bathroom and washed her hands. She rolled her sleeves above her elbow. She had the sinewy forearms of a tennis player. She motioned to the bed.

Arthur pulled his sweater over his head, self-conscious of his hairy chest. When Jill inserted the implant in the court building, it had been impersonal, routine. In his own bedroom, it felt sexual to take off clothes in front of Lou French. Weird.

"Yeow!" Lou said. "Someone did a butcher job on you. Want a shot of tequila or something?"

"Just do it."

"About Ivy. Has anyone looked into the possibility of suicide?"

Arthur felt cold liquid on his sore skin. "Margot didn't say."

"Huh. Well, ask her. Count down from ten. Prepare for pain at blast-off."

"Ten, ni-HINE!" The knife seared through him. He grasped the edges of his bed with both hands and roared into his pillow.

"Don't move. Hang in there. I tricked you so you wouldn't tense up."

The pain prevented him from answering. Just as the pain slacked, intense stinging forced another pillow-roar out of him.

"Worst is over." Lou held the chip with tweezers in front of his face, a metal globe an eighth of an inch in diameter, smudged with blood.

He heard the scratch of torn tape, felt it attach to his skin. Lou's fingers pressed firmly on his wound, then, after a minute, gauze and tape took up the tension. "All done."

Arthur opened his eyes. He had to work to release his grip on the mattress. His fingertips were pale and cold. "Thank you. What should I do with the chip?"

"Don't throw it away before your trial. Afterward, you could destroy it, but I wouldn't recommend it. You never know what could trigger an alarm. I keep mine under the refrigerator in a cockroach trap."

Arthur rolled over. "You had an implant?"

"Years ago. A certain cop framed me for drug dealing."

"I'm listening."

"Thanks, but no thanks. I don't like to talk about my ex-husband. Feeling better?"

"Actually, I am." Arthur supposed it was too soon to be anything but psychological.

"I should check your white blood cell count for infection. I'll bring my medical kit tomorrow."

"Were you a doctor before you became a P.I.?"

Lou French laughed. Her laugh was raucous, but comforting. "A surgical intern."

"And after your trial you couldn't get a job?"

"You got it. Self-employment was my only option, and preparing my defense launched my current career."

"I'm glad you weren't convicted." He swung his legs over the edge of his bed.

"Every once in a while, justice prevails. Take it easy." She grabbed his chest as he wobbled to his feet. "Maybe we should stay in bed?"

When he looked down at her upturned face, she blushed.

"That came out wrong," she said. "You know what I mean."

"I'm fine," he said, but Lou French hovered as he headed back toward the kitchen. Lou asked a few more questions while they had cookies and orange juice. Then he transferred a retainer fee into her bank account and she left, promising to report any leads at once. Arthur worked at his computer until the room seemed dimmer. He poured a glass of wine and carried Sneakers to the window. The sun set yellow under dark gray cloud streaks. When the clouds sealed off the horizon, Arthur put lamb chops in the broiler. His hands were greasy when the phone rang, so he wiped them first, picking it up on the ninth ring. "Hello?"

Margot said, "You had me scared."

"Why?"

"I thought maybe you'd stepped outside to catch a bullet."

"You do have your way with words, counselor. Any news?"

"I went to Morning Glory Cafe. No one knew much about Ms. Graham."

"Probably because she hadn't worked there very long."

"How did you know?"

Arthur suddenly became aware of the danger of investigating his lawyer's husband. He could lose his lawyer right before his trial. "I remembered it from her insurance application, I think."

A pause. "You know, CompCare records might give me information it would take me weeks to find. Can you boot her file now?"

"CompCare deleted my access when I quit." He didn't tell her about his copy. He felt miserable, deceiving her.

She tsked her tongue. "Another reason not to have quit. I can't believe you were that impulsive."

He wanted to tell her he'd been even more daring, removing his implant, but then he'd have to tell her about hiring Lou French. He remembered Lou's question. "I had an idea. Could it have been suicide?"

"No go. She was left-handed and the needle went in her left arm."

"Oh." It occurred to him that Margot's path might cross Lou's. "Are you going to ask around at Shooter's next?"

Another pause. "Why would I do that?"

"You told me she used to work there. Part of her sleaze pattern, remember?"

"Right, right," Margot cut in quickly. "What I meant was that I'm going to try Pussy In Boots first. A better source for potential killers. But even another suspect doesn't get rid of your shirt and your blood."

His throat tightened. "Is there any hope for me?"

"There has to be," Margot said firmly. "You're innocent. I gotta go. Later, bye."

• • •

Arthur woke in the middle of the night. His body felt cool and strong. It must have been the implant that made him sick and feverish before. He opened his window and leaned out. Street lights cast dim circles on the empty sidewalk. He heard the thrum of the distant freeway, smelled a trace of pine in the night breeze. He longed to go outside. Of course, if he got caught, that would be the end, but how would he get caught now that he had the implant out? All he had to do was get past the guard in the building's entry.

The answer came to him at once. He pulled a sweater over his pajamas and thick socks over his bare feet. Then he went into his closet, unbolted the door behind his suits and stepped onto the fire escape. The metal slats cut into his soles, but he made no sound as he climbed the stairs to the third floor. He stood on his upstairs neighbor's platform railing and grabbed the edge of the eave. Then, he swung himself over onto the flat roof.

His apartment building was on a small rise, so he could look out at the plaid grid of city lights stretching to the east. To the north, the lights wound up a hill, thinning out in a rich neighborhood. A large dark patch marked the park to the south, and on the freeway by the ocean, an intermittent stream of white and red flowed opposite each other. The beauty overwhelmed him. He craned his neck and spotted a few stars between the rapidly moving clouds. He stepped back, and a pigeon shot up, flapping its wings close to his face. He took that as a good omen. He stayed until the gray of his pajama stripe hinted blue, signaling the approach of sunrise. Dangling over the eave, feeling for the balcony rail with his feet, he felt exhilarated by the risk he'd taken. When he let go of the eave, he lost his balance and fell onto his neighbor's fire platform. Quickly, he went down to his landing and back through his closet escape door. Sneakers sat on the sill of his open window, meowing forcefully. Arthur hugged the cat and closed the window. Then he went back to bed, alive and refreshed.

•••

The phone woke him and he let the answering machine take the call.

"Pick it up, Arthur; I know you're there." It was Margot. "Arthur!"

His foot tangled in the sheet and he hopped to the phone. "Hi, Mar—"

"How the hell am I supposed to represent you if you keep secrets from me?"

"What do you mean?"

"You hired a P.I., that's what."

"I-I-I w-w-w—"

"Yeah, stammer around. You paid Lou French five hundred dollars yesterday."

"How did—"

"Here I am, thanklessly searching your bank records to try to find you an alibi, and I come across this, which I do not appreciate."

"W-What harm can it do?"

Margot sighed, her you're-a-moron sigh. "If something pops out in your trial I don't know about, it practically convicts you. The judge thinks, if this guy lies to his attorney, he's guilty."

"I didn't lie to you. You seemed to be against the idea, so I thought I'd do it on my own. I'd let you know if anything panned out."

"Stupid, Arthur, stupid! If you had to hire a private eye, he should be working *with* me. What premise is he investigating?"

Margot hadn't yet discovered that Lou French was a she. Arthur said, "I don't know."

"You don't know? The dick does what you tell him to do. If he's trying to find a murderer out of the blue, he's ripping you off. I'm going to run a check on him, to protect you. Meanwhile, you call him and hold him off before he cleans you out, got it?"

"Okay, but try to understand my position—"

"It's all I can do to defend you without you making it harder for me. Later, bye."

When Arthur hung up, he realized he hadn't turned off his answering machine. The whole conversation had been taped. He popped the cassette out and put in a new one.

•••

When Lou French arrived, she reached under her chamois shirt and pulled out bubblewrap, from which she unwrapped a medical kit. "I had to smuggle this past the guard. Make a fist." Lou tapped the vein at his elbow. "What's this needle mark from?"

"Employee drug testing. CompCare lost my August sample and I had to redo it."

"When was this?"

"Monday. I barely made the deadline."

"What deadline?"

"I had to get the make-up draw at least a week before the September round. Since I'm scheduled for the thirteenth of each month, that boxed me into Monday, the sixth. Personnel told me two minutes before it would have been too late."

Lou French stared at him. "You're kidding."

"Really. Those are the rules. It doesn't matter, now that I've quit."

Lou put on plastic gloves, pushed in the needle and slowly pulled up a vial of blood. She gave Arthur a cotton ball to press in his arm. Then she stripped the gloves off and put them and the needle in a plastic bag. "While I'm drawing your blood, anyway, could Counselor Beacon get us a copy of the DNA readout?"

"Margot's not happy about you. I'll play you this morning's conversation."

Lou sat on his sofa and listened. She kept her shoulders still and her elbows at her side and looked straight ahead. Her jiggling foot attracted Sneakers.

When the tape finished, Arthur asked, "What should I tell her?"

Lou leaned over to pet the cat. "Whatever you want. Is she always that mean?"

Arthur was taken aback. "She's not mean. She's upset—quite understandably—that I didn't level with her. She doesn't want me to lose credibility."

Lou shrugged. "You know her, I don't. You want me to hold off on my inquiries?"

"No!"

"Okay." She walked to the door. "I'll be in touch."

"But what about Margot?"

"That's personal. I can't help you." Before she left, she added, "If we do nail her husband, you can't expect her to like it."

•••

Lou called Saturday morning. "Pay dirt," she said.

"Jim did it?"

"Here's what I found out: What you told me about CompCare drug screening? It smelled funny. The fact that your August blood sample was taken the day before Ivy Graham's murder. I thought drug tests had to be done by an outside party, to be impartial, and I was right. CompCare doesn't process its employee blood, but sends it to—keep your pants on—Bio-Gen."

"Where Jim works."

"Right. Not only has he been working there since the first of August, he's assigned to blood screening."

"Margot said he was a specimen injector."

"I don't think so. That takes some training. Blood tests are really simple. It makes sense Bio-Gen started him there."

"So he stole my sample and leaked it on Ivy's jeans!"

"I don't have proof of that, but he had the means. Also, the owner of Shooter's indicated Jim and Ivy had an ongoing affair. I want to feel Jim out on this face to face. I'd pretend to be a former friend of Ivy's, surprised at her death, wondering about her boyfriend. Any objections?"

"How would you keep Margot away?"

"That's your job. You must be due for a lawyer-client consultation."

Arthur sighed. "All right. But be careful. This guy has Loser Charisma. Don't let him charm you."

Lou burst into her raucous laugh. "Don't worry. I'm charm-proof."

Arthur arranged to meet Margot at one, and called Lou back with the schedule. Waiting for Margot, he realized he would have to tell her what Lou discovered. It was, after all, his defense. He decided to broach it as slowly as he could, pretending not to understand the meaning of the information. He would let her sharp mind draw the conclusion. Let her outrage fall on Current Husband, and her sympathy pour over Arthur.

Margot wore a black leotard with jeans and a jacket that looked like woven straw. Dark lines outlined her eye sockets, and pimples swelled at her hair line. "Hey," she said. "Things have changed."

Arthur looked proudly at the nectarine-colored curtains, tiger lily umbrella stand, potted marigolds and half-assembled cat tunnel system. "Do you like it?"

"Yeah." She wavered on the "yeah" as if there had to be a catch. "How come?"

"In case I don't live until next week."

Her neck tensed into a column of wires. "Don't talk like that."

"I would think you'd want me to be realistic about my chances. Face the future as honestly and bravely as I can."

She unshouldered her computer. "I guess it's my own feelings. Can you shut up about it for my sake?"

She cared about him. In time, could that grow back into love? "I'll try." Arthur led her into his living room. "Have you found anything new?"

"Only about this Lou French. *She* doesn't have a clean rep."

Arthur could tell Margot was gearing up for a grand announcement, so he quickly injected, "You mean the drug-dealing charge?"

Margot's open mouth snapped shut. She sat abruptly on his sofa. Her lipstick was a purplish shade Arthur found unsettling. "She told you about that?"

Arthur nodded, nudging her knee with his as he pushed in next to her. "She was cleared, you know."

"Of all the private eyes in the book, why *her*?"

"She's done contract work for CompCare."

"Not because of her tits?"

"Margot, you know me better than that."

Margot shrugged at the ceiling. "I thought I knew you, but you've changed. Not just your decor, you. Your expression. Your whole manner. What the hell happened, and why did it happen *now*?"

She seemed near tears. Arthur put his arm around her shoulders. They stiffened at once. "I haven't changed," he murmured. "I just stopped chaining myself to the future. I watch the sun set every day. It's amazing, all the shades of pink and the way the sky gets green on the bottom. It's like—"

Margot started to cry. "Have you gone crazy?"

"No, I've gone sane!" Arthur ached to share his insight with her. "Margot, listen. The other night, after midnight, I went up on the roof—"

Her eyes flared wide. "You could have been shot! Why weren't you shot?"

"I was lucky. But looking at the city—"

"Arthur Snell doesn't take any risks! Arthur Snell plays it safe! What's gotten into you?" Margot stood and started pacing his Persian rug. "I can't take this!"

Arthur watched her pace for a full minute. Then he asked, "What if I did it?"

She wheeled to a halt. "You didn't! You never do anything!"

"But what if I did?"

"If this is a joke, it is not, N-O-T, funny."

He chose words deliberately. "How would you feel about me, if you knew I killed her? Wait! Hear me out. Let's say I had a reason, that my motivation was love for you. How would you feel?"

Margot lifted a skeptical eyebrow. "What's your point?"

"I was only wondering . . . what your feelings are." He had choked up.

"You can't be telling me you killed a waitress just to find out if I care about you?" She shielded her eyes with her hand, palm out. "Arthur, I'm in love with Jim. You're—you're a good person, okay? But not for me."

Arthur couldn't speak without losing it. He bit his lip and nodded.

"I won't let you make me feel guilty." She nearly shouted at him. "I don't care if you're up for a murder: it doesn't change how I feel, all right? You have no right to lay this on me!"

Arthur barely got the words out: "I understand."

• • •

Arthur realized he had a choice to make. What was best for him or what was best for her. Why couldn't they be one and the same? Why did he have to love Margot who loved Jim? Why did it have to be *A Tale of Two Cities?* He looked at Sneakers, peeping out of the cat tunnel system he'd put together. "'Tis a far, far better thing . . .'" He wasn't noble. He hated Jim Hatch. He wanted him dead. But what about Margot? He supposed he'd hoped she would stop loving Jim the moment she knew the truth about him. That she would see, by his bright new curtains and bold new attitude, that he, Arthur Snell, was the man for her after all.

Wouldn't Margot's passion for justice prevail over her feelings for that creep who'd framed him?

Nope. Margot would forever hate him for exposing the truth about Jim. She would become his enemy and he would be entirely alone.

Suddenly, he clearly remembered giving Margot his gray-and-white flannel shirt. "The shirt and Sneakers go together," he'd said. He'd watched Margot descend the stairs, shirt slung over her shoulder. Sneakers, in her carrier, stared back at Arthur through the cage door, distraught, no doubt fearing a visit to the vet. And he had thought, there goes all the love; I'm alone, now.

• • •

Lou French reported her talk with Jim to be inconclusive. Jim claimed Ivy was no more than a friend, but she sensed he was covering up. He didn't hold back on snide comments about Arthur, which bothered her. If he framed Arthur, he should be playing it cool. But maybe it was a double bluff, acting natural so as not to appear to be playing it cool. She needed to do more research. She suggested Arthur try to find a dated photograph to prove the gift of the shirt.

Rain erased the sunset that night. Arthur turned pages of a photograph album, mourning his memories of Margot. The photos got sparse after she moved out. He had only two dozen post-Margot snapshots, half of them of Margot during Sneakers' visitation. He found one dated June 6 with her wearing the shirt. He put it inside an envelope so he wouldn't have to look at it.

• • •

Monday afternoon, Lou French came over without warning. She walked directly into his arms and hugged him. Arthur, surprised by this act, was more surprised by the feelings her stout body stirred in him. Her body fit against his. The pair of shoes that felt so good you couldn't bear to take them off, even to buy them. Odd that she felt so comfortable, while the woman he loved had the feel of spine and ribs and compromise.

Lou broke away and looked him straight in the eye. "Jim didn't do it."

Arthur swallowed hard. "Explain."

"He worked swing shift on August fourteenth. Not only does he have a time clock punching him in at 2:56 p.m., but his supervisor worked at his side from three to six, inclusive. Ironically, they were doing a rush order on the CompCare drug screening, which is why they came in on a Saturday. Ivy Graham was killed between three and five. Jim didn't kill her."

Dizziness forced Arthur to kneel on the floor. He stared at a dark red fleur-de-lys inside a navy blue diamond ornately edged in pale green. "You're sure?"

"Hundred percent."

He sat back on his knees. "My trial is tomorrow morning."

"I know."

"And I have nothing to present in my defense." His voice had all the juice drained out. He sounded robotic.

Lou took a deep breath and blew it out. "Except who the real killer is."

Sneakers came over to see what Arthur was doing on the floor. "But we don't know."

"Yes, we do." Lou's voice was resigned, but steady. "We have means and motive, a double motive at that.

Someone who inherits money and gets rid of the other woman. A triple motive, if she wants Sneakers again."

"You're wrong. You couldn't be more wrong." He tried to laugh. He couldn't.

Lou kept talking calmly. "She knows crime, knows how to get away with it. She knew they'd never have made a fiber and cat-hair match if it hadn't been for her background check. She had it all planned. I'm willing to bet that's the real reason she returned Sneakers to you. Her only guesswork was that you wouldn't have an alibi, but it was a chance worth taking, given your solitary habits, right? You have it on tape how she talks to you, Arthur—she has absolutely no respect for you."

"Stop. Stop now."

"She counted on you to carry the torch for her. She assumed you'd hire her as your lawyer, so with you under house arrest and her in charge, all she had to do was nothing to get you convicted. That's why she hit the roof when you hired me. She never dreamed you'd seek outside help."

He must be drowning for his lungs to rip apart like this. He had to snatch at the tiniest twig. "What about the blood? Only Jim could have got my blood sample."

"She knew your draw schedule was on the thirteenth. I have a witness who says she arrived to pick Jim up at work before eleven. The witness remembers because it was Friday the thirteenth. He saw her looking at a case of vials and had to tell her she wasn't allowed to do that, it was confidential."

Arthur mustered all his control to ask, "Would you please leave?"

"Okay." Lou patted his shoulder. "I'll leave the affidavits on your table. Oh, and carry your implant with you to court, just in case they check."

•••

Tuesday, September fourteenth, at nine o'clock, the court rose as Tom Winter took the bench. "Be seated."

Margot pushed a paper cup of coffee toward him.

Arthur didn't touch the coffee. Margot's anger about Ivy, her resentment of his income compared to hers, these he could understand. But to set him up for murder was to send him to his death. He couldn't believe she had that kind of malice in her heart. If he presented Lou French's evidence, it would lead to Margot's death. He wasn't sure he could survive that.

Arthur stretched his fingers to touch Margot's hand. "What did I do to deserve this?"

Margot smiled bravely, though her lips quivered. "Just bad luck, I guess. Try to hold a good thought."

Arthur tried. He went back to their wedding day. Their wedding night. Choosing Sneakers out of the litter of gray-and-white kittens. Those memories were all tainted with a sense of her contempt for his choices, and his habitual deferral. What had been purely good in his life? His night on the roof. Sunsets and real maple syrup. Lou French in his arms. By setting him up to die, Margot had accidentally brought him the best days of his life.

The State concluded the prosecution in an hour and a half. Snell met Ivy Graham when she applied for insurance. They became lovers; she wore his shirt. Cat hairs on the shirt matched those of his cat. As a life insurance analyst, he was familiar with methods of death. He knew an air bubble injection was the least detectable means of murder. His personality profile showed he fit the "perfect crime" type, the bottled-up loner with a psychotic leaning toward the color orange.

Illustrated by Ulia Semenenko

He had no alibis the afternoon of Ivy's murder. Most incriminating, the blood on her jeans at the time of her death matched his DNA. The People rested.

Tom Winter inspected his thumbnail. "Defense may proceed."

Arthur Snell raised his hand. "Your Honor, I would like to represent myself."

Margot yanked his hand down. "Objection!"

A few people laughed. Tom Winter looked over the rim of his glasses. "Objecting to the loss of your fee, eh, Ms. Beacon?"

"My client is incapable of serving his own best interest!"

Yes, Arthur thought, that's how she had always regarded him. Incapable. Expendable. Count on good old Arthur to lay down his life for her.

Tom Winter tapped his fingers on the bench. "Care to change your mind, Mr. Snell? It's your right to defend yourself, but you're better off with a lawyer."

"Not this lawyer, Your Honor." Arthur's voice shook, but he got the words out. "I intend to prove that Margot Beacon herself killed Ivy Graham and framed me for the murder."

"He's insane!" Margot screeched. "He can't do this! Stop him!"

Tom Winter hammered his gavel over the uproar. "Quiet! Order! Clerk, note Ms. Beacon's reaction in the record. Mr. Snell, proceed."

As Arthur stood up, he caught a glimpse of Lou French in the audience. She gave him a thumbs up signal. He began his defense.

BLACK ON BLACK

Written by
Kyle David Jelle

Illustrated by
Jack Hines

About the Author

Kyle David Jelle began writing in the sixth grade, where he turned out mini-epics about dragons fighting F-16s over Mount Rainier, but, like many writers, he was slow to recognize his true calling. He considered several "normal" occupations, including teaching and the military, and dropped out of college three times (though, calling himself a "hopeless information junkie," he suspects he's probably doomed to get a degree eventually!), before deciding to pursue writing seriously. He currently drives a truck for a local newspaper, where he finds he has plenty of time to consort with his muse on the road.

He says that he usually writes in a slow and meticulous fashion, however this story was an exception—it came out in only a couple of days and was delivered to the post office three minutes before closing on the last day of the quarter.

We don't normally recommend that you try to write a first-place story overnight, but it seems to have worked for Kyle. The fine tale that follows will compete for the Grand Prize.

About the Illustrator

Jack Hines is twenty-nine years old and lives in Arizona with his fiancée and three cats. He has enjoyed drawing since childhood, and has studied art at a number of universities and art colleges.

He has worked in advertising, production art, and silk-screen printing. He's also done a bit of graphic design on computers, and spends a good amount of time on the Internet. He is currently creating illustrations for a role-playing game called "Genesis Down."

Jack enjoys travel, art, reading, computers, nature and music and history.

didn't panic when the alarm went off. Overreacted a little, perhaps—and that's no shame; I never claimed to be fearless or heroic—but I *didn't* panic.

I had been nestled in my sleep restraint, pressed gently to the side of the lifepod, sleeping soundly as I always did in free-fall, and then the sirens started wailing and the lights started flashing and I tore open the restraint and scrambled out through the privacy curtain—

And they were just floating there in the aft compartment, almost indistinguishable in their black Space Corps duty uniforms and matching crewcuts, watching me. Ensign Nguyen's broad grin gave the prank away, and I knew he was behind it. Ensign Gutierrez smiled, but turned away, a trace of guilt in her eyes, which I noted and filed away for future use. Lieutenant Junior Grade Schoeler just floated stiffly next to the hatch that led to the airlock juncture and watched. No guilt. No mirth. No expression at all. She held my eyes for several seconds before she spoke.

"The next time you hear a hull-breach alarm, Mr. Kancheli, you would probably be better off climbing into the lifepod instead of out of it," Schoeler said.

Then she turned and disappeared into the cockpit. That's when I realized I was wearing nothing but my briefs and, urged on by Nguyen's half-stifled guffaws, pulled myself back into the pod and shut the privacy curtain.

•••

My wake-up beeper went off three hours later and I glanced at the clock: 0300 hours. I had twenty minutes to vacate the pod before the next sleep shift. I unzipped the sleep restraint, pulled on a pair of athletic shorts, grabbed my stowage bag and slid the curtain open. Only Lieutenant Kemp, our commander, fresh from the night watch, was waiting for me this time, floating in front of the autogalley with a sealed hot beverage container and a steaming tray of the sticky protein-pudding by-product that the life-support biosystem put out. She gave me a brusque glance, the whites of her eyes bright against her jet-black skin, and turned back to her food.

"Good morning," I said, trying to be civil. They had shown me nothing but open hostility so far, but returning it wouldn't help me win them over, and the prospect of three and a half more weeks of stony silence and mean-spirited practical jokes was intolerable.

"Did you sleep well, Mr. Kancheli?" Kemp asked.

"Oh yes," I replied. "Tell me, does warning your crew in advance about emergency drills really improve their efficiency?"

"They've been through it plenty of times," Kemp said, "they know what to do. Lieutenant Schoeler just thought we should do something to help you get acclimated." Kemp took a drink from her beverage container. "She said you showed some confusion about what to do in the event of a hull breach."

"I'm sorry," I replied, concealing my surprise that Schoeler had been responsible for the alarm. "Perhaps if you gave me access to a list of rules and procedures I could be better prepared next time."

"That information is classified," Kemp replied, turning away from me. She stuck her tray to the wall by one of the monitors, and tucked her toes through the footloops near the floor.

"I know," I replied. I could see I wasn't getting anywhere. "If you'll excuse me . . ."

Kemp turned on the monitor and brought up a status report. Never even looked back. I pulled myself into the lavatory, used the commode, showered, air-dried and dressed in the black fatigues they had issued me before I boarded SP 92.

Only three weeks, four days and twelve hours to go.

• • •

SP 92 was a DS-132C Nightwing, a stealth patrol craft designed for maximum efficiency with minimal crew. The Space Corps had commissioned the design in response to congressional pressure to "do something" about the growing threat of piracy in the asteroid belt. Nearly eleven million people, of every race, religion and nationality, inhabited the belt on a permanent basis, more than three million of them holding US citizenship, and by that virtue establishing US territorial claims in the region according to regulations provided by the space treaty of 2111. This large and widely distributed population had quickly been targeted by persons and organizations bent on hijacking, robbery, kidnaping, and, when expedient, murder—not to mention various "opportunistic" crimes, like sexual assault and beatings, inflicted on victims in the course of other activities.

The Europeans and Chinese had responded to the problem by restricting the areas their citizens were allowed to settle, and organizing regional shipping and transit in military-escorted convoys. Milder legislation to that effect had been passed by the US Congress, but the limitations did not sit well with many of the more expansion-minded senators and representatives or their constituents, hence the push for a program to turn pirate tactics *against* the pirates.

Funded from the black budget, usually reserved for covert operations against foreign governments and corporations, the Right Of Passage Enforcement division had gone into operation with total secrecy, functioning only in international space, with few restrictions on their activities. The government consistently refused to provide figures on how many "kills" they'd made, but reported pirate activity in the belt dropped 2.3 percent in their first year of operation, 3.1 percent the next year, and 3.3 percent the year after that.

Oddly enough, as one Space Corps liaison put it, this did not have the intended effect of reassuring the belt population. Rumors of unidentified spacecraft and mysterious disappearances had fostered unprecedented levels of fear and paranoia among not only pirates, but average citizens as well—not to mention generating hysteria among UFO enthusiasts and at least one religious group which attributed the events in question to demonic activity.

Into this morass stumbled Mahmoud K. Al-Khouri, a respected net journalist who had correlated the available data and verified ROPE division's existence with the help of a still-undisclosed source, which many commentators have speculated may have been a deliberate leak from the Senate Intelligence subcommittee designed to force ROPE division out of hiding. It is known that several major corporations with substantial belt investments suffered serious stock declines even as the piracy figures dropped, an effect many analysts have attributed to the unease provoked by ROPE division's covert activities. At least one US representative—from Arizona, a state well known for its ties to belt commerce—was turned out of office by constituents angry over the government's perceived failure to address the problem.

Hence the new policy of openness. Official confirmation of ROPE division's existence was released and, to allay fears and improve public relations, the government invited American journalists from all over the solar system to submit applications for a "ride along" experiment.

Which is where I got involved. The liaison officer told me that Al-Khouri himself had been disqualified by his cyber-implants—the unpredictable electromagnetic emissions associated with bioelectronics made them difficult to mask—but rumor had it that he had actually been rejected because the administration felt they could not guarantee his safety in the hands of the ROPE division field officers he had just exposed. Needless to say, I did not expect a warm welcome.

I did not get one.

•••

By the time I got out of the lavatory, Lieutenant Kemp had disappeared, probably into my recently vacated lifepod to sleep. Assuming the schedule—one of the few shipboard documents I did have access to—hadn't been changed, Nguyen would be sleeping in the other pod, Schoeler would be exercising in the physical conditioning unit, adjacent to the medi-scanner on the other side of the aft compartment from the lavatory, and Gutierrez would be standing the morning watch.

Gutierrez was the only member of the crew who had shown me even a touch of courtesy. If I was going to establish any real communication with anyone on the ship, she was the one to start with. I pulled myself forward, through the airlock juncture—a small cubical with four spacesuit lockers and hatches that led to two separate cylindrical airlocks, each of which had external hatches on both the upper and lower hulls—to the cockpit, a cramped, windowless compartment toward the spacecraft's nose with stations for the command pilot and copilot up front and two turret gunners behind them.

Gutierrez was strapped into the command pilot station. She turned to face me as I approached, her eyes invisible behind the opaque visor of her helmet. She was still easily recognized by her full lips and dark tan skin.

"What do you want?"

"I'm an observer. I want to observe."

"Well, don't touch anything. And don't get in my way."

"Yes, sir." I pulled myself into the copilot's seat and strapped in.

Hooked to the command console in front of me was another helmet. It bobbled up and down in the breeze from the ventilation system. I held it up without unclipping it.

"May I?"

"Yes. It knows who you are. The auto-lockouts will keep you from seeing anything you shouldn't. Put it on."

I unhooked the helmet and slipped it on.

"I'm not seeing anything at all."

"I know," Gutierrez replied. I heard her fingers run across the console in front of me, and a detailed virtual environment appeared. Only Gutierrez, the flight operations panels, and the hot beverage container attached to the communications panel appeared in full detail. SP 92's shape was etched in multi-hued vector graphics, each subsystem denoted by a different color. In the distance, all around, the stars shone hard and bright. Only one asteroid was within visual range, a dark, carbonaceous rock designated by the number 29756 C superimposed over its virtual image. The sensation of floating in empty space was unnerving.

"What do you think?" Gutierrez asked.

"Impressive. Can you talk about what's being locked out?"

"Sure. I'm seeing full schematics of the weapons systems, propulsion, navigation and maneuvering systems." All I could see was the general saucer-shaped outline of the ship and its internal bulkhead arrangement. The lumps that jutted up and down from the rear of the saucer, on either side of the main fuselage, theoretically contained four ion drive units. The hollow-looking spaces on either side of the cockpit held the forward weapons bays. The only critical items I could see were the dorsal and belly weapons turrets, located in the center of the saucer, between the airlock outer doors.

"Doesn't that create a lot of clutter?"

"You learn to ignore it unless it's flashing, which indicates a failure. If you're trying to focus on something outside the ship, the graphics tend to blur out of sight anyway."

"Can I assume this system handles targeting as well?"

"You can assume anything you want, but I can't confirm or deny it."

"Sorry."

"Don't worry about it," Gutierrez laughed. "We expect you to be nosy."

"Yeah, well, I could've gotten all the information you guys have given me so far in a thirty-minute tour. I'm starting to question the need for three weeks of this."

"Oh, it'll get a lot more interesting," she said. "By the way, did you sleep well?"

•••

The second time an alarm jolted me awake, I took my time responding. No one else was pushing into my pod, so it couldn't have been too much of an emergency. I slipped into my fatigues and slid open the curtain.

No one was watching me this time. They had all gathered in the cockpit.

"Where is it?" Lt. Kemp demanded from the command pilot's seat.

"Bearing oh-three-two-mark-seven, elevation thirty-two degrees, range twenty-two thousand kilometers and closing," answered Nguyen, from the copilot's station. "Transponder negative. Visual ID running. No response yet."

"What's going on?" I whispered to Gutierrez, in the starboard gunnery station.

"Potential target acquired. ID unknown. Told you it would get more interesting."

"We have ID on the target," Nguyen said. "European heavy cruiser *Thatcher*."

"Emissions stabilized at forty-three percent," Gutierrez said. "No forward or lateral seepage." I noticed that many systems had been shut down—communications, waste management, food synthesizers, even internal lighting. Only critical flight operations, navigation and defensive systems remained active.

"Sir," Schoeler said, from the port gunnery station. "Projected eclipse situation in thirty-two minutes. Roll-through parameters acceptable."

"Do it," Kemp said.

"Reduce emissions to twenty-two percent," Schoeler ordered.

"Yes, sir," Gutierrez replied. "We can maintain safe internal temperature for forty-three minutes."

"Target range eighteen thousand kilometers," Nguyen volunteered.

"Initiate roll-through program," Kemp ordered.

"Yes, sir," Schoeler replied. "Target locked. Program running."

They all fell silent. Gutierrez exhaled.

"What happens now?" I whispered.

"Now, we wait," Gutierrez answered. "You wouldn't happen to have a deck of cards, would you?"

"I assume we're hiding?"

"Right," Gutierrez replied. "By cutting forward emissions, we've gone dark up and down the spectrum. They can't see us."

"What about active radar or laser tracking systems?"

"Our adaptive armor can absorb them. No signal bounces back. We're black on black."

"So what's an eclipse situation?"

"That's what keeps it interesting. Absolute black is a great color for hiding in space. Not so great for hiding in front of a bright background object, in this case, an asteroid. But if we can retune our armor, we should be able to blend in with the asteroid when we pass between it and the cruiser. The trick is that the armor can't adapt fast enough, which means the only way we can do it is if we prepare a spot on the surface in advance, then roll that spot to face them at precisely the right time."

"I see," I said. I could feel damp spots forming under my arms. "Is it getting warmer in here?"

"Yes," Gutierrez said, "ordinarily we discharge waste heat through the armor. We had to cut emissions to zero for all surfaces facing our target, but by cutting power consumption, we could keep internal temperatures stable. But the roll-through requires us to cut emissions on all—"

"Ensign," Schoeler interrupted. "You are talking too much."

"Yes, sir," Gutierrez replied.

"Target range fourteen thousand kilometers," Nguyen said.

"Temperature thirty-six degrees," Gutierrez offered.

But for the periodic updates from Nguyen and Gutierrez, we waited in silence. With all the monitors shut down, I couldn't even see the approaching spacecraft, but I could get a general idea of its location by watching which direction my companions faced; the way they turned their heads in unison made me wonder if I was missing a very slow tennis match.

The temperature had reached forty-one degrees, sweat was pooling on my skin, and Nguyen had just given the target range as ten thousand kilometers, when the ship silently began to turn. I thought I had simply become disoriented from the heat, but then Schoeler announced, "Roll-through maneuver initiated," and I realized what was happening. The Nightwing used an inertial attitude control system; rings around the spacecraft's outer edge spun, forcing the spacecraft to spin the opposite direction without using external thrusters that might reveal its position. I reached for a handhold to steady myself.

"What happens if this doesn't work?" I asked.

"Don't worry," Schoeler said. "They're armed with rapid-fire rail guns, neutral particle beams, and one-point-three gigawatt lasers. We won't even know what hit us."

"They're a government ship, not pirates," I said. "Wouldn't it make more sense to just identify ourselves?"

"We can't compromise our mission," Kemp said. "And if you can't stop distracting us, you should go back to your pod."

"Range nine thousand kilometers," Nguyen said.

"Temperature forty-three degrees," Gutierrez added.

We waited.

Schoeler chewed on her thumbnail.

Nguyen laced his fingers together as though he were planning to crack his knuckles, or perhaps pray, though he appeared to be doing neither.

Gutierrez fidgeted with her helmet.

Kemp sat motionless.

"Roll-through maneuver complete," Schoeler said.

I started breathing again, and experienced another episode of mild disorientation as the ship's rotation slowed and stopped.

"Approaching point of closest proximity," Nguyen said. "Eight thousand kilometers."

"Temperature forty-two degrees," Gutierrez said, then, glancing at me and smiling, "Looks like we're going to make it."

•••

I was sitting out the day watch with Gutierrez and Nguyen, who rounded out his morning shift by running systems diagnostics, when Schoeler woke up. I was wearing a helmet at the time, and when she emerged from the unscanned privacy of the pod, she appeared to materialize out of nothing. Her shorts and sport bra indicated an imminent physical conditioning session.

I took off the helmet, unfastened my seat restraint, and kicked toward the rear compartment. Nguyen watched me leave, glanced at Schoeler, and rolled his eyes.

"Good luck," he mumbled.

"Thanks. I'll need it," I answered. Nguyen hadn't turned out to be so bad after all, once he saw Gutierrez warming up to me. A little obnoxious, perhaps, but he treated everyone that way. Said it was a defense mechanism he developed after living with a crew of women for six months. I could already sympathize.

By the time I got back to the aft compartment, Schoeler had cracked the cover on the physical conditioning simulator, a full-body exoskeleton tied to a virtual environment in which the pull and resistance of gravity could be simulated.

"Excuse me, Lieutenant?" I asked.

"What?" Schoeler said.

"I was wondering if we could talk for a moment."

"I'm scheduled for conditioning," Schoeler said. "If it's important, you can plug in with the CI jack." She climbed into the exoskeleton, fastened its connections, and shut the lid.

I found a cerebral interface headset, slipped it on, and plugged it into the jack on the physical conditioning unit's operations panel. The blue field of a blank simulation appeared around me, the main menu suspended in mid-air before me laying bare all of the ship's functions, even the virtual flight systems. I slaved my interface unit into Schoeler's simulation, and the blue background vanished.

I found myself standing on a bridge over a small river. Roads ran into the distance in either direction, one disappearing into a shadowy forest, the other into a small town of brick buildings and courtyards. A small, not terribly ornate church stood in the town square. Just upstream loomed a dark, foliage-encrusted stone fortress.

Schoeler stood by the rails on the bridge, stretching. I almost didn't recognize her with long, blonde hair, lightly tanned skin and a white sweatshirt. "It's an old scan," she remarked, noticing my stare. "I had it made before I joined the service."

"Where are we?" I asked.

"My hometown. Neustadt am Rübenberge."

"It's beautiful. Germany, I presume?"

"Used to be, as my dad always said."

"He didn't support the Union."

"Not after what they did when England tried to secede. That's why we came to America." Schoeler finished her stretching, and tied her hair back in a ponytail. "Are you coming?"

"Sure." Just what I always wanted. I was already spending four hours a day in the physical conditioning unit to control the muscle atrophy, cardiovascular weakening and bone decalcification that came with life in free-fall, and I wasn't terribly fond of it. Even worse,

Illustrated by Jack Hines

since I was only connected by a CI headset, which cut off voluntary neural impulses to the rest of my body, this wouldn't do anything for me.

Schoeler started jogging toward town, then abruptly cut left onto a path that led us under the wall of the fortress. "I'm sure you didn't decide to bother me because you wanted to know about my childhood, Mr. Kancheli, so what do you want?"

"Well, good background is important, especially since I don't have access to much multimedia information. People are what bring good stories to life." I could tell by her expression that she didn't buy it. "But you're right, that's not why I'm bothering you. I know you don't like me very much, but I want to assure you I didn't come to this assignment with any intention of doing a hatchet job on you or ROPE division. I was hoping we could patch things up and get along a little better for the next two weeks."

The trail curved around the crumbling bastion into a fen area.

"It's not you personally," Schoeler said. "It's what you stand for."

"And what's that?"

"Surprise is a tremendous advantage out here," Schoeler said, "the pirates didn't even know we were hunting them. Oh, maybe they suspected something was prowling around out here, but they didn't know what. The devil you don't know is always more frightening than the one you know. Since Al-Khouri's article came out, we've gone from being the devil they don't know, to just another Space Corps division. I think it will be extremely detrimental to our mission."

"I see," I said. "And just what, exactly, is your mission?"

"Our orders are to use stealth tactics to acquire and pursue vessels suspected of intent to commit acts of piracy against American citizens and other free people in the unregulated portions of the asteroid belt. If possible, we track them and provide information to Space Corps intelligence to be passed on for law enforcement purposes. If necessary, we intercede when we catch them in the act."

"And why do you think you've been ordered to do this?"

"To suppress piracy and maintain order in the belt."

"And what's so important about that?" I asked. Schoeler slowed to a walk.

"What are you trying to get at?"

"Blowing up pirates is all well and fine, but isn't the whole point of this operation to restore public confidence? What's the point of controlling piracy if rumors of unidentified killer ships and shadowy government agencies scare away all the colonists and investors?"

Schoeler started running again. Around the corner of the fortress we found a flight of stone steps. She started up them. I followed. On top was a park-like garden. We ran down between two parallel rows of oak trees to the edge overlooking the river.

"I'm sorry. It still doesn't make this any easier. We've been trained for silence and secrecy. Our assignment to ROPE division was based on psych exams and performance during training. We were selected specifically because we were well suited for this kind of work, and now it's all going to hell."

"Do you really think going public will make it that much more dangerous?"

"Yes. I do," Schoeler said. "And not just because the pirates know about us. We're the only Space Corps division currently engaged in active combat duty. Since Al-Khouri's article hit the net, the administration has been swamped with people who want in. Now, instead of persons chosen for ability, we're going to end up with hotshots who want to make names for themselves. I think that's going to be a lot more dangerous."

"Do you think they'll lower the standards like that?"

"They'll have to. I doubt they'll change the height and weight restrictions, but everything else is fair game. Sooner or later, some senator's daughter will want in, and they won't be able to keep her out. Even if that never happens, I've never met a psych test that can't be fooled by a well-motivated individual."

"Can I quote you on that? I've never met a democratic government that couldn't be manipulated by bad press."

That was the only time I ever saw her laugh. I found it hard to believe this smiling long-haired girl—she couldn't have been more than eighteen when the scan was made—was the same stone-faced woman who'd been making my life unpleasant for the last two weeks.

"By all means . . ." Schoeler said. "I usually like to run some martial arts programs after I've warmed up. Care to join me?" She smiled at the expression on my face. I did *not* come in here to be assaulted and battered.

"Maybe some other time," I answered. "CI gives me headaches after a while."

I exited the simulation to find myself duct-taped by my collar to the wall.

"What the hell?" I mumbled.

"You were floating all over the cabin," Nguyen responded. "What did you expect?"

•••

"Well, you see, my great-great-grandfather immigrates to the US after the big war in the late twentieth century," Nguyen said. We were sitting out his watch in the cockpit, helmets on, watching the stars while he regaled me with the history of his family, beginning with the French conquest of Indochina. "So he hates the way the Americans treat him, that was back when racism was still a real problem, you know. Skinheads, the Klan, all that. He gets totally sick of it and moves to Canada. You can imagine how he felt after the breakup, especially when BC and Alberta voted for statehood. Nobody was expecting ... Oh my, what have we here?"

"What?" I asked.

"Electromagnetic emissions off the starboard bow." He hit the alarm.

I looked off the starboard bow. The computer-generated image in my visor indicated a faint, high-frequency radio source.

"What is it?" Schoeler asked behind me. I decided that this might be a good time to get out of the way, so I removed the helmet, unlatched my restraint and floated up over the seat. She slid in under me and put on the helmet.

"We have a radio source, looks like an unshielded electronic component, bearing oh-seven-eight-mark-three, elevation two-hundred-ninety degrees, range fifteen hundred kilometers."

By now, Gutierrez was sliding into the port gunnery position. She gave me a brief smile, but turned all business as she slipped her helmet on.

"Transponder negative," he continued. "And no visual contact. Whatever it is, it's trying to hide."

"Lock on and hold position," ordered Kemp. I hadn't even noticed her behind me. She slipped into the unoccupied gunnery position and put on the helmet.

"I've got a silhouette," Gutierrez said. "Running ID scan."

"Range fourteen hundred kilometers," Nguyen announced.

"Gotcha," Gutierrez said. "It's a Merganser."

The SLC-1035 Mergansers were fairly common mid-sized rock hoppers. Their cargo capacity, range and adaptability had made them popular among the smaller belt mining operations. Unfortunately, the same features had also made them popular among smugglers and pirates.

"Approaching point of closest proximity," Nguyen announced. "Thirteen hundred kilometers."

"Intercept plotted," Schoeler said, looking to Kemp for further instructions.

Kemp said nothing.

"Sir, should we engage the target?" Nguyen asked. Gutierrez turned to her as well.

"Negative," Kemp said. "Maintain silent running. Let it go."

"Yes, sir," Schoeler replied.

Surrounded by the uncomfortable silence, Kemp watched the proceedings for a few minutes longer, then removed her helmet and crawled out of her seat.

"Keep me informed of further developments," Kemp said, and disappeared into the aft compartment.

"Well, there's something you don't see everyday," Nguyen mumbled.

"You couldn't ask for a more perfect target profile," Gutierrez said, pulling off her helmet. "Sometimes we go for months without detecting anything like that."

"You know," Nguyen said, "she's been acting strange ever since we got our orders."

"You just noticed?" Schoeler asked. "I wouldn't read too much into it." She turned to me. "She's been in the program since its inception. She was even in the pilot program. She's probably having a harder time with these changes than I am. And we *were* given explicit orders to bring you back alive. Taking you into active combat probably wouldn't be the best way to assure your safety."

"Oh, come on," Nguyen said. "We could follow that thing to Jupiter without half as much risk as we had facing down that cruiser."

"Do you remember what she said when we received our orders for this mission?" Schoeler asked.

Nguyen took a deep breath. "Yeah."

They all fell silent.

"Okay," I said. "I'll bite. What did she say?"

Schoeler gave me a wry smile. "'We do not obey our orders because they are smart or because they are right. We obey them because they are given.'"

• • •

The next eight days passed uneventfully.

In conversations with Nguyen, I learned the rest of his family history, how proud his parents had been when their little Toby was accepted to Officer's Candidate School and how he had been forced to tell them he was running a supply ship out of Ceres, so they had no idea what he was really doing.

Gutierrez told me all about growing up in California before the quake, how her father had lost his job when she was seventeen, forcing her to scramble for college tuition, how the Space Corps' ROTC program had helped her with scholarships and she had found, for the first time, some place where she really felt she belonged. She showed me a delightful simulation of Malibu beach that she used for physical conditioning.

Kemp never did engage me in any real conversation. Every time I asked her a question, I felt as if I were interrogating a foreign agent. I haven't seen such thinly disguised suspicion since the last administration got turned out of the White House. I did manage to get a few details about the pilot program, when she was an ensign on one of the eight modified SC-2112 Wavepounders that had been used to test the operating theory behind ROPE division. Wavepounders, originally sub-orbital, ballistic troop carriers with stealth design components, had proven surprisingly adaptable to deepspace operations. Pirates had been known to use them as well.

But only Schoeler gave me anything dramatic.

"Last week," I said during her watch one afternoon, "you quoted something Kemp said about obeying orders. Do you really believe that philosophy?"

"Absolutely. That's my job."

"So you would never, under any circumstances, disobey a direct order?"

Schoeler paused, twisted her mouth to one side.

"If the order in question was in direct violation of a superseding order, or if it seriously conflicted with my loyalties, I might have to consider disobeying a direct order."

"Describe a conflict with your loyalties."

"If I were ordered to, say, fire on an unidentified ship, I might have no choice but to refuse. We can't go around killing innocent civilians, or we become part of the problem. Frankly, I'd rather risk being killed than serve in a

Space Corps that doesn't respect life. That's what makes this job so stressful. They can shoot us on sight. We can't shoot them until we know, beyond any doubt, reasonable or otherwise, that they're hostile. Which usually means letting them shoot first. And sometimes one shot is all it takes."

We also tracked five legitimate ships—two mining company ore-haulers, a medical supply ship, one passenger transport, and a Sundodger lightsail yacht. All were following properly logged flight plans. All had properly functioning ID transponders. All were easily evaded. The more I learned about ROPE division operations, the more amazing it seemed that Al-Khouri had been able to dig up anything more than a bunch of odd disappearances.

•••

The first day of my last scheduled week on SP 92 began quietly. My beeper went off. I climbed out of the pod. I spent four hours in physical conditioning, hiking the Olympic Rainforest, showered, dressed, and sat part of the morning watch with Nguyen.

I was eating lunch with Schoeler—and getting sick to death of that protein-pudding; each of the two hundred available flavors was uniformly bland, but we had to eat it so we'd be prepared for hibernation if we were forced to abandon ship in the pods—when Gutierrez sounded the alarm. We all scrambled to the cockpit.

"You're not going to believe this," Gutierrez said. "I think we've got another one."

"Location," Schoeler demanded.

"Bearing two-nine-one-mark-five, elevation twelve degrees, range five hundred kilometers. This one's quiet. They made a course correction and I caught their exhaust."

Nguyen had already climbed into the port gunnery position by the time Kemp climbed up behind me. She did not take the starboard gunnery position, but merely grabbed a handhold and held her place behind Gutierrez.

"I've got target ID," Gutierrez said. "Looks like a DG-3."

"Emissions stabilized at forty-two percent," Nguyen offered.

"Intercept plotted," Schoeler declared. "The sun's in our favor." Everyone's attention was instantly riveted to Kemp.

She glanced at each of them, then at me for what seemed a long time.

"This is what we're here for," Kemp said. "Let's do it. Ensign, may I take your station?"

"Yes, sir." Gutierrez climbed out of the command pilot station and took the starboard gunnery control. Kemp slid into the command station and donned her helmet.

"Optimal burn position in four minutes, thirty-two seconds," Schoeler said. We would be using solar glare to hide our main thruster exhaust.

"Mr. Kancheli," Kemp said. "If they spot us, we'll probably be seeing action. You might want to wait in one of the pods."

"Thank you," I said, "but I didn't come here to hide during the action. I'll take my chances."

She pursed her lips. "I'll allow it for now, but I am responsible for your safety, and if I order you into that pod, you *will* go, immediately, no questions asked. Is that clear?"

"Yes, sir," I lied.

Shortly after I left the political beat in DC and moved to the belt, I had seen part of a video in which a federal agent, who had been caught infiltrating one of the distribution organizations the pirates used to convert their stolen goods to hard currency, had been tortured to death over the course of seventeen hours. In a conversation last week, Gutierrez, Schoeler and Nguyen had all mentioned seeing it. We knew what it would mean to be taken alive.

That was why none of us had complained about being stationed on a ship with only two two-person lifepods. If we were forced to abandon ship under fire, the lifepods' limited evasive capabilities would be no match for even a moderately well-equipped opponent.

But if Kemp suspected I planned to disobey a direct order, she didn't let on. "Find something solid and hold on," she said. I tightened my grip on the handhold and waited.

"Ignition in thirty seconds," Schoeler said.

Gutierrez and Nguyen began arming their weapons systems.

"Twenty seconds."

"Weapons status active," Gutierrez said.

"Ten seconds," Schoeler announced. Then, after a short pause: "Ignition."

The acceleration—couldn't have been more than .75 G's—had the smooth and quiet qualities characteristic of most ion drive systems. When it pulled me back toward the aft compartment, I managed to balance on the edge of the port airlock hatch and held tight to the handhold.

"Main engine cut-off in ten seconds," Schoeler announced. Shortly thereafter, the G-forces vanished.

"Course and speed now match the target vessel. No indications that we have been spotted. All systems nominal."

We followed the DG-3 for thirteen hours before they made another course correction, probably to shake off any possible tails, though the random direction of the maneuver indicated that they hadn't discovered us yet. We drew as close as two hundred kilometers over the two hours it took to line up with sun again and make our correction to match them.

We paced them for another twenty-six hours—returning to a roughly standard duty schedule, except that there were never less than two people on watch at any given time—before Nguyen detected the transponder signal.

"The *Tamerlane*," he said. "Registered as an independent surveyor out of Ceres, complement of three, plus two dependents. Range four thousand kilometers."

"They spotted it," Gutierrez added. "They're changing course."

"Course plotted," Schoeler said. "Recommend a three-hour delay. That will put seven-hundred-fifty kilometers between us to mask our exhaust. A twenty-minute burn will put us in intercept range before they reach the survey ship."

"Good," Kemp responded. "Do it."

It took a total of eleven hours to complete the burn and draw within one hundred kilometers of the DG-3. Schoeler let me use her helmet to get my first really good look at a pirate ship. Like most DG-3s, it had a sphere-shaped command module attached to a laterally-extendible superstructure designed to carry standard cargo containers and a separable chemical-rocket booster. Unlike most DG-3s, this one was plated with nonreflecting, possibly adaptive, armor and bristling with augmented weapons emplacements. Schoeler pointed out twin 30-megawatt laser cannons mounted on the superstructure, and what looked like a rail gun underneath. Formidable firepower for such a small craft. There seemed little doubt as to their intentions, but we did nothing but pace them.

We anticipated their next course correction by watching how they adjusted their angle, and made our adjustment simultaneously, so we could hide behind their exhaust. They fell in behind the surveyor. We fell in behind them. This continued for another three hours, the pirates showing no evidence that they had spotted us, the *Tamerlane* showing no evidence that they had spotted either of us.

Then we received a transmission on the standard ship-to-ship band. It came from the *Tamerlane*; a swarthy, bearded, middle-aged man in grease-stained blue and yellow coveralls, an expression of wide-eyed terror in his eyes. "Please," he said. "We don't have much, we'll cooperate fully. We're opening our cargo bay. Please, God, don't shoot. . . ."

"The bad guys are using a tight beam," Schoeler said. "We can't pick them up."

"Damn," Kemp said. Without first-hand evidence to confirm the pirate's hostility, she could do nothing. "Can we send a signal to that ship without the pirates intercepting it?"

"No, sir," Schoeler said. "Not at this angle."

"Sir," Nguyen said. "Our target is closing on the surveyor. Estimate three minutes to hazard boundary."

"Mr. Kancheli," Kemp said.

"Yes?"

"In three minutes, that DG-3 will be too close to the *Tamerlane* for us to fire on it without putting the civilian ship at risk. If we fail to act before then, we will be able to do nothing but watch. It will almost certainly mean the deaths of the *Tamerlane*'s crew and any passengers or family members. Therefore, we are going to attack and disable the DG-3, deliberately, based on the circumstantial evidence we've already seen. I trust you will present this objectively in your story."

"Count on it."

"Thank you. It's time for you to go to the pod. Now, please."

I withdrew from the cockpit, into the rear compartment, but no farther. "Two minutes," I heard Nguyen say, as I unlatched the physical training unit, climbed in, and shut the door. The exoskeleton and smart-surfaces felt strange through my clothing, and failed to completely synch with my scan. At the main menu, I accessed the flight control virtual environment.

I found myself in the center of the cockpit, and I could see and hear everything that happened, in or out of the spacecraft.

"Inertial attitude control system off line," Schoeler said. "RCS thrusters active."

"All weapons hot," Gutierrez added.

"God help us all," Kemp said. "Target and fire on my command only. Main engine ignition in ten seconds."

When it fired, the vibration from the RCS thrusters—we didn't need to be invisible anymore—thrummed through the ship, and the engines shoved us forward.

On my right, Gutierrez aimed her hand-controller at the DG-3, and the dorsal turret above me tracked her movements. On my left, Nguyen did the same for the belly turret. Schoeler brought both forward weapons systems to bear on the target. And Kemp drove us down on it.

"All weapons fire," Kemp ordered.

A digital inferno broke loose below. Graphic simulations showed where SP 92's turret lasers, invisible in the vacuum, streaked across to the target vessel. White-hot lines were drawn on the armor of its engine module where the laser beams connected. Then Schoeler cut loose with the particle beams, targeting the command module. A fiery but brief explosion erupted when one of the beams struck an oxygen tank. Then the lasers burned through to the main fuel tanks, and a thin mist boiled out into space away from the ship.

The DG-3's lasers tracked toward us, but both turrets stopped before they could reach us. Sparks amidships suggested a severed power conduit.

They never got off a shot.

"Hold your fire," Kemp ordered.

Schoeler, Gutierrez and Nguyen complied, but kept their weapons hot and fixed on the target. The DG-3 *appeared* to be crippled, but it may have just been doing a very good job of playing dead.

Kemp slowed us down as we passed over the DG-3 to inspect the damage.

"What a piece of junk," Nguyen said.

The DG-3's armor looked like thin sheet metal, painted black. Makeshift repairs were evident and sloppy. The superstructure had clearly been welded together from two separate components that didn't quite match, as if the halves had been scavenged from two different ships.

Not very intimidating.

Not much fight in them either, considering the belt pirate reputation for ruthless, unrestrained violence. We did, of course, have the advantage of surprise, but if they were leveling threats and demands at the

Tamerlane, their weapons systems should have been armed and ready . . . How could they fail to return fire at all?

Unless they never intended to fire.

I turned to the others. Could they see me in their visors? Could they hear me? Were they putting this together?

"It's a decoy!" I shouted.

No response. They all stayed focused on the wreck.

All but Kemp.

I followed her gaze to the survey ship, to the open cargo bay we were approaching.

"Oh, my God . . ." I said.

Couldn't she see it coming?

She still had time to brake or change course.

Kemp glanced at Schoeler.

The bay drew nearer.

Kemp closed her eyes.

Something flashed.

The Nightwing was jolted hard to port. The starboard external cameras went dark, but the schematics stayed active, subsystems blinking from bow to stern.

I left the virtual environment and shoved the cover open.

"My control system's down!" I heard Gutierrez shout. "Dorsal turret's off line."

"Belly turret intact," Nguyen said. "Request permission to return fire."

"Negative," Kemp said. "Hold your fire until we can clarify—"

Schoeler was already on the communications system. "*Tamerlane*, this is SP 92. We are a Space Corps vehicle. We are not hostile. Repeat, we are not hostile. Please respond!"

As I crawled through the cockpit hatch, another shock pounded the ship.

"*Tamerlane,*" Schoeler repeated, "we are not hostile! Please—"

"They know," Kemp said. "We've lost starboard engines, weapons and control systems. We're dead in the water. Take the crew, get in the pods, and go."

"Sir, we can't leave you!" Gutierrez shouted.

"She's right," Schoeler said to Kemp.

"Do it! That's an order!"

Schoeler looked to Gutierrez, then Nguyen, then back to Kemp. "Yes, sir." She yanked off her helmet, unstrapped, and crawled back to Gutierrez.

"Denise, we've got to go," Schoeler said, reaching for Gutierrez's helmet.

"No, sir," Gutierrez replied, shaking off Schoeler's attempt to remove the helmet. Schoeler withdrew her hands.

"This is a direct order," Schoeler said.

"Request permission to stay and fight," Gutierrez said.

"Denied," Schoeler answered. "Get to the pod."

"You know what they'll do if we're caught!" Gutierrez said, her voice breaking. Schoeler pulled off Gutierrez's helmet. Gutierrez was in tears, and shaking like a frightened child. Schoeler unbuckled Gutierrez's seat restraint and pulled her out of the gunnery station.

Then she pushed Gutierrez toward me. "Take her with you. I don't want her alone in the pod," Schoeler said. "I'll get Nguyen."

Nguyen had already removed his helmet and safety restraint, and was climbing out of his gunnery station. "I'm ready," he said, with no apparent qualms about saving his own skin.

Gutierrez used the distraction to twist away from me. I tried to restrain her. She drove an elbow into my chest. The absence of gravity blunted her impact, the blow pushing her back with equal force, but it was enough to force me to let go of her.

"Denise!" Schoeler said, grabbing Gutierrez's wrists, "We don't have time for this!"

I pushed in next to Schoeler. "Ensign," I said. "I'm a civilian. I'm not trained for this. I *need* your help to get out of this alive."

Gutierrez stopped struggling, but held Schoeler's gaze for a moment before relaxing. Schoeler released her. "Go to the pod," Schoeler said. Gutierrez hesitated, then started toward the aft compartment. Nguyen and I followed her. Schoeler brought up the rear.

Gutierrez drifted toward the upper lifepod, hesitated again at the hatch, glanced back at Schoeler, then me, and climbed in. Nguyen had already disappeared into the lower pod. Schoeler moved in after him.

Then she hit the lower lifepod's hatch cycle button. It snapped shut, sealing Nguyen in alone.

"What are you doing?" I demanded.

"I'm not going," Schoeler said.

"They're going to kill you," I said.

"I can't leave her."

For a moment, I forgot that no one else had seen Kemp steer us into their line of fire, and my jaw dropped open in astonishment.

"She set us up!" I shouted. "She *knew* this was going to happen. This whole incident was staged!"

"I know," Schoeler replied.

Another shock rocked the spacecraft, but I just floated there, mouth gaping.

"I've worked with her for two years," Schoeler said. "I saw how she was acting. I couldn't understand why she let our first target go until—"

Another impact hit. The monitor panel by the food dispenser shorted out with a shower of sparks, and the fire suppression system enveloped it in foam. The shriek of twisting metal echoed through the compartment, structural integrity had to be failing....

Schoeler punched the intercom panel. "Nguyen, go now!"

"Yes, sir," he replied. The spacecraft lurched as the lifepod was ejected. Schoeler turned back to me.

"This is my *life*," she said. "What am I supposed to do?"

I didn't know what to say.

"Get in the pod," she ordered.

No point in arguing anymore. I climbed through the hatch.

"Just one more thing," Schoeler said.

I turned back to her.

"Don't discuss this with anyone until they release you. They may be listening. Even in the pod." She paused, glanced toward the cockpit. "And don't forget what you promised her."

"What?" I asked.

"An objective story."

She sealed the hatch.

I punched the jettison button and fell onto the hatch as the lifepod rocketed away from the Nightwing's tail. On the monitor, I brought up an external view of the receding spacecraft.

Heavy structural damage. Gaping holes in the weapons bays and engine pods, characteristic of kinetic kill weapons. Exposed wires sparked. A fuel tank leaked a glistening trail of mercury droplets.

Then the image twisted sharply and vanished from the screen as the lifepod initiated its antitracking program.

I stared at the empty screen.

"They're going to kill us," Gutierrez said. She was shivering. I pulled her closer, and she buried her face in my shoulder. "They're going to kill us."

"Shhh," I whispered. "It's going to be okay. It's going to be okay."

THE ART OF LOVE

Written by
Ron Lindahn

About the Author

Ron spent eleven years as a photographer and film maker for a Fortune 500 company. In 1978 he moved from California to North Georgia to teach meditation and work at a spiritual retreat facility. Ron met Val and they were married and began working together in 1983. The couple's book cover illustrations have graced many top science fiction and fantasy authors' works, both in the U.S. and abroad. In addition to book covers, they have produced movie posters and video packages, posters promoting the North Georgia Mountains, T-shirt designs, images of TSR's Dungeons and Dragons series, and for a time they produced a monthly feature for Heavy Metal Magazine.

Ron and Val are frequently featured as artist guests at science fiction conventions and they are both judges for the international L. Ron Hubbard Illustrators of The Future competition. They are often invited as guest lecturers for civic groups and school art classes.

Ron and Val are now collaborating on their own book projects. **The Secret Lives of Cats** *gives a whimsical view of* *cats, with each painting based on a visual pun, like "Skating on Thin Mice."* How to Choose Your Dragon *is a delightful children's book which features an enchanting selection of pet dragons and their individual traits.* Olde Misses Milliwhistle's Book of Beneficial Beasties *offers a humorous alternative look at some classic mythological creatures and the couple is currently working on* Twizzle Takes a Ride. *In his spare time Ron makes furniture from dogwood, laurel, rhododendron and barn wood and plays bass guitar.*

Good art, the stuff that stands up over time, is always a labor of love. Writing, illustrating, sculpting, designing a beautiful house or making a quilt are all forms of art, the end result of the creative process. And the creative process has only two basic elements, labor and love.

"Bah! Romantic claptrap. You have to be born to it. It takes talent, knowing the right people and having lots of luck," I hear you saying.

It is just such self-limiting notions that keep most people from achieving their true potential. The first step in any creative endeavor is to believe that it might actually be possible to succeed. To be willing to try. And the willingness to try is borne up on the wings of desire. And what is desire if not the first step toward falling in love?

We see a painting that takes our breath away or read an enchanting story and think, "Oh, if I could only do something half as good, I would be delighted. What a thrill it must be to create." All creative activity begins in this way. It is like seeing that beautiful red-haired girl across the lunchroom and thinking, "Oh, if only I had the courage to go and talk with her." Then in the face of possible rejection, if we take the chance, we may find acceptance and possibly fall in love. In the same way, if we are willing to take the chance, to attempt to create in spite of the possibility of failure, we may end up falling in love with our work.

What is it like being in love? We are obsessed. We think of the person we are in love with all of the time. We can't wait to be together with them. We rise early and retire late, just to spend more time together. In their presence we lose track of time. We may even forget to eat. We are willing to do almost anything to make the other person happy. We go the extra mile, dress nice, bring gifts and pay close attention to their every word. In short we work at developing the relationship by paying attention.

The coin of our payment is our energy. Energy always follows attention. The more attention/energy we contribute to our relationship, the richer and more fulfilling it becomes. We can think of any relationship simply as an exchange of energy. A kind of dance.

We have the same experience in the creative process. With the impetus of our burning desire we become engrossed in the relationship with our work. Frank Kelly-Freas tells aspiring illustrators that if they can do anything else to make a living, they should. He says that one becomes an artist because they simply can't do anything else, they have to make art, they are called, compelled. In other words, we must be totally head over heels in love with our art for it to be fulfilling. We must find our joy in the dance.

As to the question of talent, I believe that talent is actually the ability to become obsessed, to fall in love. Very few great masters have ever been born with the skills required to practice their art. Most took many years to develop their technique, to acquire the sensitivity to their medium, to learn to observe and then reproduce their unique vision. And what sustains them through the long solitary hours of practice, trial and error, learning all of the things that don't quite work in order to discover the few that do? It is the love of being involved with the creative process.

One must become immersed in one's work in order to develop the skills to produce good art. In her wonderful book *Writing Down the Bones*, Natalie Goldberg says, "If you wish to be a writer, write every day, spend every spare minute putting your thoughts down on paper. If you want to be an artist, draw or paint every day."

Technique doesn't come naturally; it comes from time and practice. A great concert pianist once told me that when preparing to perform, he plays his selection the first hundred times to get the piece fully in his mind. Then, the second hundred times to get the piece into his fingers, so that when he sits to perform, he no longer has to even think about the music. Instead of making the music happen he feels himself to be part of a process where the music flows and there is no feeling of separation between himself and the piano and the audience.

Some engage in art with thoughts of reward. They think that painting a nice picture, or writing a story, will bring them financial gain or earn them the respect of others. In fact this is often the motive for starting a creative endeavor, but along the way one must fall in love or they are doomed to failure or mediocrity.

The masters report that it is the very process of creating that is the reward. Being in the flow, dancing with our love. Once this kind of relationship is established with one's art it no longer matters whether anyone even sees it, the doing of it is enough. A good example of this was when it was discovered that the great American artist Andrew Wyeth had buried what many consider to be some of his best work, the Helga paintings, in his backyard for many years.

Once we establish this relationship and fall in love with our work, we find that our experience is profoundly altered. We discover a wealth of resources that were previously unknown to us. One of the most common questions asked to those working in the arts is, "Where do you get your ideas?" Most artists respond to this question with a smile because they know that they don't have a method for getting ideas. Ideas simply come to them because they are open to ideas. Einstein reported that none of his ideas were the result of using the rational mind to figure things out, the thoughts just came to him.

Where do ideas come from? They automatically emerge in a quiet mind. Pay attention next time you work a crossword puzzle. You look at the available spaces and you look at the clue. Then you try to figure out an appropriate word to fit both. Finally, when you stop thinking about it for a moment, the word just pops into your mind. Where do those words come from? Silence.

When we are truly in love with another, we are content just to be with them. We don't have to talk, or be doing anything in particular. When we are together and quiet we feel, experience, a sense of connection. It is this feeling of connection with our work which keeps us open to inspiration.

Walter Russell, another great American artist, sculptor and architect, talked about the importance of spending time in the silence in order to fully participate in the creative process. He had been working for many years as a successful illustrator when he was asked to sculpt the bust of Thomas Edison. He felt a tinge of reluctance to attempt such an important commission in a new medium. After all, going from flat, two-dimensional representation with paint and brush to working in three dimensions with stone and chisel would be quite a challenge under any circumstance. But to have the world-famous Thomas Edison as a model for his first project was nearly unthinkable.

Fortunately Russell was in love. He understood the creative process and trusted both his ability to tap its resources and its ability to provide him with the inspiration and sensitivity to accomplish his task. He reported that on the train ride down the East Coast to Florida, where he would meet with Mr. Edison, he did not engage in any of the activities that most people would have. Instead of depleting his energy by worrying about how he would be able to perform his assignment, or talking, or distracting himself with a book, he simply sat quietly and emptied himself of all thoughts. In this way he arrived in Florida psychologically empty, open to inspiration and creativity. Not only was his sculpture extraordinary in having captured the essence of Edison, but it propelled him into an entirely new career as a world-renowned sculptor.

The ancient Greeks personified their source of inspiration in the nine Muses. They said it was the Muses who brought the creative ideas for an individual to express. The word *muse* means to contemplate or to meditate. Creative thinking is a process of emptying. Letting go of preconceived notions and ideas about the way things are, in order to be visited by our muse and inspired (to breathe in).

As to the question of how to make a living from one's art, there is no good answer. There is no cook-book approach to a creative life. As you can tell, it is my contention that one's art is one's life. It has been my experience that the same source of creative inspiration which arises from the love of one's work also provides the means for its continuance. If people can set aside ideas about how they think things are supposed to work and simply trust the creative process, then, almost magically, they are led to make the right connections, meet the right people, or find the appropriate outlet for their work.

In order for this process to work you must learn to trust your love, the creative process, without reservation. If you are inspired to attend a conference or convention, to submit to a contest, or to sit on the side of a road with your paintings displayed in the back of a pickup truck, you must follow through. You never know when just the right person may happen by, or when you might be referred to the friend of a friend, or when someone may ask you to sculpt a very special bust.

It is possible for anyone to produce works of art if they are willing to work long hard hours, all alone, with no promise of reward, simply for the love of participating in the creative process.

Those who have succeeded by following this path in life will tell you that it has not always been easy, there are many challenges along the way. They will also tell you that they wouldn't trade this life for any other. After all, they are in love.

A PRAYER FOR THE INSECT GODS

Written by
Morgan Burke

Illustrated by
Karen Pollitt

About the Author

Morgan Burke has in his background an artistic mother and a scientific grandfather, and thus has spent much of his life with divided interests. He received a degree in astrophysics at the University of British Columbia, where he spent his spare time writing, fencing, and riding his motorcycle.

In an effort to combine some of his interests—computers, fencing and writing—he edits an online reference for fencers. He's also recently spent a good amount of time riding his motorcycle in Eastern Europe and Asia Minor, and has worked in astronomy and particle physics.

For the past several months he has been devoting himself to writing full time, to good effect, I think. "A Prayer for the Insect Gods" is pretty much a perfect story, and won first place in the first quarter of competition this year. Thus it will compete for the Grand Prize of $4000. I suspect that we will be seeing a good deal more of Mr. Burke's work in the future, and I for one will be following his career with interest.

Morgan Burke is twenty-eight years old, single, and currently lives in Vancouver, B.C.

About the Illustrator

Karen Pollitt has been an avid reader of fantasy, mythology and history for most of her life. She has studied art since childhood, and finds that she has been influenced by the paintings of Hieronymus Bosch, by the engravings of Francisco Goya, and by such fantasy masters as Virgil Finlay, Frank Frazetta and the Hildebrandts.

Karen graduated from California State University in 1989 with a bachelor's degree in fine arts.

Her first published magazine illustration recently appeared in the Winter 1995 issue of Deathrealm magazine. She plans to work toward developing a full-time career in the fields of speculative fiction. Currently, she maintains a studio in Crestline, California, where she lives with her husband Marc.

The bug attacked while they were cruising down the alleys behind the auto wreckers in the warehouse district. It was a big one, maybe thirty kilos, and it was fast. It came charging out of the dumpster where it was foraging and went straight for the rear tires.

Perez floored it, and they felt as much as heard the impact when the bug pounced, too late, and hit the rear fender. But it must have got its claws around the corner of the wheel well or something, because Perez didn't see it in the rearview mirror as he sped off. There was a bad grinding sound coming from the rear of the car.

"Shit," he said. "We're dragging it."

Jones reached behind the seat and pulled the electric cattle prod out of the equipment bag. She quickly checked to make sure the capacitors were charged, and then nodded to Perez.

"Whenever you're ready," she said.

Perez slammed the brakes on hard, and spun the truck sideways to disorient the bug. Jones was out the door before the pickup had even stopped moving, and Perez heard the snaps of the discharging cattle prod as he climbed out, his taser gun drawn. Jones was good, though, and she had the thing immobilized before it could get to the gas tank or engine bay. Together they dragged it out into the light, being careful to avoid its twitching mandibles and #8-bit proboscis.

"Jesus, that's a mother," said Perez, counting eight articulated legs.

"It's beautiful," agreed Jones, wrapping bungees around the legs to hold them out of the way while she peeked under the armor plates for the proper nerve lines to cut. "Looks like it matches the bounty spec. Get my bag, will you?"

Perez grabbed her canvas backpack from the cab, and handed it to her. As she began searching through it, the bug gave a mighty twitch and flipped over onto its feet. Jones jumped back as its mandibles slashed wildly at its bindings. It went hopping and skipping down the alley, dragging the bungees and trying its damnedest to make a getaway. Perez scooped up the cattle prod and chased it down.

He dragged it back to her by the legs, cattle prod over his shoulders, looking for all the world like a caveman returning from the hunt. "Did it hurt you?"

"Nah," she said as she flipped on her logic analyzer and attached the ground clip to the bug's exoskeleton. Within the minute she had found the primary nerve corridor, and cut it with wire clippers. The bug's legs went slack.

Jones started unbolting dermal plates and removing legs. "God, this is great, look at this," she said, pointing to a dense collection of circuit boards tucked in behind the bug's fuel tank.

Perez shrugged. "Bug guts," he said.

"Separate neural nets for each leg. That's pretty innovative, don't you think? I've never seen that before. Looks like they were adapted from voice-recognition systems stolen out of cars. This is really great. It's probably a new species. What do you think?"

Perez spat on the base of a telephone pole, unable to share her enthusiasm. "Bug-us Jones-us," he said in his best imitation of Latin. "Can't wait to find its nest and kill its whole fucking family." He grinned at Jones' expression of disgust.

"It's people like you, Perez, that wiped out three-quarters of the species on this planet," she said.

"Hey, it's my job, I'm an exterminator. Boss says kill the bugs, I kill the fuckin' bugs. It's your job too, don't forget."

"My job is to control bug migration and development so as to minimize interference with human activities."

Perez rolled his eyes. "Is that so, Dr. Death?" He teased her with that moniker whenever she refused to admit her talent for killing. Fact was, none of the crew knew the chinks in bug armor like Jones.

"Shut up and help me lift this baby into the truck." They hoisted the partially dismembered bug into the truck bed, and tossed a few of its detached components after it.

"You know what the trouble with you academics is," began Perez.

"I don't want to hear about it."

"You think that any kind of extinction is bad, and that all kinds of conservation are good. Extinction is good, see? You think the extinction of the dinosaurs was bad? If it weren't for that, we wouldn't be here. Without extinction there can be no progress. That's how life works."

The corner of Jones' mouth twisted. "That's a killer, you telling me how life works. Spare me your rationalizations, Perez. Unless your idea of progress is ending up the only thing left alive on the planet, choking in your own shit, don't second-guess nature and exterminate anything that's mildly inconvenient, okay?"

Perez raised his eyebrows and spat again. "Cool," he agreed. "Are we going to find that nest or not?"

Jones looked around. "Yeah, I guess." They both climbed back in the truck. Perez turned it around, and they began cruising back toward the dumpster that the bug had pounced from.

"Careful," said Jones. "The spec said these new ones attack in packs."

"Right on!" snorted Perez. "That I'd like to see. Who was the poor bastard who reported that?"

"City garbage crew. Five bugs attacked their truck and chased them off. By the time they got help, the truck was mostly stripped."

"That's hilarious! Did they track 'em down?"

"Nope. Never found them. They made off with a lot of high-power hydraulics and fuel."

Perez revved the engine as they got close to the dumpster, trying to coax any other bugs out. None came, so he parked the truck and they both got out, packs over their shoulders. Perez holstered his taser gun, and slung a goo gun with a two-liter magazine over his shoulder. Jones looked inside the garbage bin, and seeing nothing, climbed in.

"Goddam scientist," grunted Perez. "What the hell do you think you're doing?" Jones didn't answer, so he looked inside to see her rooting through soggy cardboard boxes and packing foam. She squealed with delight suddenly, as a little four-legged bug scrambled out of the light when she moved a box aside. Diving after it, she fought with garbage for a few seconds before emerging triumphantly with the little bug in her hands.

"Isn't it cute?" she grinned, a strip of packing tape stuck to her hair. "Ow! Stop that!" The bug was pinching her fingers, trying to free itself. It was constructed mostly from old tape deck motors and plastic mounting brackets. "Tetrapod. Looks like a derivative of the Frisco Garbage Gremlin. Hold it for a sec. I want to take some pictures."

Perez juggled the bug while Jones fished out her cam and took ten seconds worth of footage. Then he tossed it back into the trash bin, where it quickly climbed inside a paper bag. "I don't know why you like those goddam things so much," he said, wiping his hands on his pant legs.

Jones climbed out. "Some people like cats. Some like fish. I like bugs. Besides, I'll never finish my dissertation if I don't collect field data. Artificial life, Perez! Don't you think it's kind of magical?"

"They're a bunch of greasy parasites and thieves. They shoulda jailed that Jap who set them loose when his grant was cut." Perez looked around as if trying to spot something worth shooting.

"Konaka was a genius," retorted Jones, inspecting the bug footprints in the dust and decomposed newspapers at the foot of the garbage bin. "Where do you think our space program would be right now, if it weren't for his research into Von Neumann machines?"

"Yeah, yeah, tell that to the folks in Tokyo. I saw on TV the other day that a whole family was killed by a hunter pack that broke into their house. They ate the TV and stereo, and stole a kilowatt-hour of power." Perez was strolling idly down the alley, following a meandering set of wheel tracks.

Jones didn't answer. She had seen that story, too, and it had disturbed her in the way she imagined it would be like to discover that your fourth-grade teacher was a child molester. She had often entertained the notion that the bugs would eventually evolve toward intelligence, mutating through successive generations by replicating themselves with improper replacement parts. It would be a wonderful world, she imagined, coexisting with these benevolent machines. We would be like gods to them, but we would be kind gods. They could work for us, but they would be free.

The Tokyo slayings had raised the possibility of violent strife, even wars between humans and bugs. The police had hunted down and destroyed the murderous machines within hours. A mass extermination program had been launched. If bugs ever did evolve intelligence, it wasn't going to be in Tokyo. Watching the news clips over and over, Jones had come to the belated realization that there were no free servants, and certainly no kind gods.

Perez whistled from down the alleyway. "Yoo hoo, Jonesie," he cooed in his worst falsetto. "Bug highway!" He was pointing at a peeled-back section of chain-link fence that led into an auto-wrecking yard. The weeds and litter at the base of the fence were all trampled from the traffic that passed through the hole. The wrecking yard beyond the fence was prime territory for a bug nest. The only trouble was that the main gate, farther up the alley, seemed to be chained and locked shut.

Perez was pulling the broken chain-link back as Jones came up. They could easily squeeze through, but they would have to leave the truck in the alley. And of course there was the matter of getting permission from the yard owner to go hunting on his premises.

Perez slipped through the fence and started to follow bug tracks beyond a doorless Korean hatchback. "Where you going?" asked Jones. "We gotta call in first."

"Yeah, yeah," mumbled Perez. "This is reconnaissance. I'm not killing anything."

"You're still trespassing."

"Fucking tight-ass. Do you want to get the bugs, or do you want to fuck with red tape all day?"

"I don't want to lose my commission because you dicked with the procedure," said Jones. It had happened before, and Perez hesitated, considering this powerful piece of logic.

Suddenly the blare of horns and sirens filled the alley behind Jones. She jumped out to see the beacons and headlights of the company truck flashing wildly, as its security system tripped. The truck was rocking like it was full of manic children, and the alarm was shouting, "Stand back from the truck! Stand back from the truck! Occupants will be stunned in fifteen seconds!" Jones caught glimpses of mechanical legs and other appendages flicking in and out of the engine bay and wheel wells.

Perez was quickly beside her. "How many?"

Jones shrugged. The security system boomed, "Stand back! Occupants will be stunned in ten seconds!" She and Perez stood passively, waiting for the system to send its thirty-thousand volt spike through the chassis and bodywork. That was usually sufficient to fry any bugs that were trying to disassemble the vehicle. Worked well on people, too.

"Five seconds!" bellowed the security system. "Four. Three. Two." And then the truck shut up. The lights shut off, safety beacons stopped flashing, and the security system went silent. But the vehicle continued to pitch and rock.

"Christ," groaned Jones. "They cut all the power."

"Lucky bastards. Let's go!" said Perez. They were responsible for half of all damage to their truck, levied against future commissions. Fortunately the company trucks were all fortified against bugs, but that didn't mean they were invincible. It just meant the bugs took a little longer to finish their business.

Jones ran after Perez. "I left the cattle prod in the truck!"

Perez tossed her his taser gun. She juggled it to avoid the electrodes, not sure whether he had left the safety on. A check of the magazine revealed three remaining shots.

"You got cab and cargo bed," commanded Perez. "I got engine and gas tank!" He ran right up to a wheel well that had a bunch of legs protruding from it, and whacked off a couple rounds of the goo gun.

Jones looked through the open driver's side window and noticed a big octopod disassembling the dash. It had already completely removed the truck radio, and was working on the air conditioning system. Jones leveled the taser gun and pulled the trigger from a range of half a meter. The round popped audibly when it discharged, snapping the bug's legs straight and launching it straight into the windshield. The safety glass shattered into a million fragments, and the bug tumbled upside down onto the seat, legs twitching spasmodically. Jones threw open the door, and dragged the bug onto the pavement. It was still fighting, but couldn't muster any coordination of its limbs. The shock of the taser shot must have cleared its memory or blown its feedback sensors.

She left the bug squirming on the ground and hopped up on the rear bumper. There were two bugs in the cargo bed, having a field day with the toolboxes and testing equipment. The carcass of the bug from the dumpster was also a subject of intense interest. Jones aimed and fired at the closest bug, catching it right on the carapace, just behind its monocular eye. The bug twitched, and then sprinted for safety, running right into a steel tool chest. It about-faced, and charged right into the tailgate. She had only managed to fry its visual circuits, and had to use her last taser shot to put it down.

The second bug didn't ignore this turn of events. It turned on her and raised its forelimbs, like a crab preparing to fight. It was similar to the bug from the dumpster, close to thirty kilos, and Jones wasn't willing to take it on without any more ammunition. She hopped off the bumper and backed down the alley. The bug scampered to the edge of the cargo bed to watch her retreat. Jones took a few more steps back, keeping her eye on the bug. With an unknown species like this, you couldn't be too sure of its pattern recognition algorithms. Bugs occasionally mistook humans for machines and tried to disassemble them.

The bug kept its attention on her, though. It hopped down from the truck and scuttled in her direction to get a better look at her. Jones froze and started to sing softly. This was usually enough to convince bugs that the subject of their attention was not of mechanical interest, and sure enough the bug stopped, reevaluating.

Jones could hear Perez cursing and kicking something around the other side of the truck, then the liquid whunk of the discharging goo gun. The bug in front of her remained fixed and staring at her from a few meters away. It was evidently having some difficulty deciding if she was worth the effort of disassembling. Either it was incredibly stupid and lacked the usual selection criteria for spotting machines, or else it was unusually intelligent, and the usual criteria were insufficient. Whichever, it wanted more data.

"Piss off!" said Jones, stamping her foot.

The bug perked up, and advanced a few steps. Jones swore softly. Evidently, she hadn't done the right thing.

She relaxed and began to retreat again. The bug accelerated and resumed its pursuit.

"Perez!" screamed Jones. "I've got a tail!" She dodged the bug and ran back toward the truck, the bug trotting close behind. Perez whacked it as they passed by, and the bug tripped up, trapped in the goo gun's congealed ammunition. With the barrel of the gun, he flipped the bug over on its back and then methodically broke each of its legs with the heel of his engineer's boots.

Jones walked back toward him. "Take it easy, it isn't going anywhere."

"Piss me off," said Perez. "Peckers cut the brake lines, the ignition system, everything! They're getting so fast, we're not going to be able to stop them, soon."

"How many did you get?" asked Jones, looking under the engine.

"Jesus, at least five, I don't know," spat Perez. He shook his goo gun. "Just about drained it. Can't be more than a couple shots left."

"Don't worry about it. Your five plus my three, that more than covers the damage to the truck."

Perez sighed, nodding. "Yeah, I guess you're right. We're still gonna need a tow. I'll call in."

"Don't bother. The radio's trashed."

Perez rolled his eyes. "Coffee break, then." He tossed the goo gun into the cab, and pulled out his lunchbox.

Jones breathed deep, surveying the carnage. Eight bugs. That was rare for a single incident; bugs generally had little in the way of cooperative or social instincts. Nevertheless, coordinated attacks were becoming more common, as the Tokyo incident had shown. The most remarkable example of pack coordination was a recent riot in Mexico City. It involved an estimated one thousand bugs who laid waste to an industrial park during a three-day rampage that caused almost two hundred million dollars in damage. Academic circles were abuzz with all sorts of scientific speculation about cooperation and communication in this and other, similar, bug incidents. The subject was of intense interest to Jones. Her thesis was entitled "Communication via RF Interference in Von Neumann Insectoids."

She popped the hood, and looked around the engine compartment. Congealed goo covered everything, with the occasional trapped bug twitching stubbornly in its sticky grasp. "Jeez, Perez, you look like you were trying to ice a cake or something."

"I was cooking, that's for sure," said Perez, stuffing a muffin into his face. "Speaking of which, we can't go back for the nest until I get more ammo."

"It's a good thing you used the goo gun," decided Jones, still watching the writhing bugs.

Perez raised his eyebrows. "Let me guess: because it's nonfatal? Jones, you crack me up." Jones just shook her head; it was pointless even debating the topic with him.

They both looked up as another company truck turned into the alley, its safety beacons flashing. Head office would have been signaled when the security system tripped, and it was company policy to dispatch extra agents to lend assistance.

Perez swore under his breath. "Is that who I think it is?"

Jones nodded, "Malkovich and whatsisface."

"Bunch of cowboys." They both looked away down the alley, feigning disinterest.

"I shoulda known it was Bonnie and Clyde!" called Malkovich from the truck as he pulled up. His partner,

Chan, giggled maniacally from the passenger seat. They jumped out, bristling with weaponry, and swaggered over with the relaxed gait of the self-important.

Malkovich let out a whoop of laughter when he looked at the engine. "Perez, you been jerking off again?"

Chan cackled, slapping his thigh. "That's it, Malkie! I bet Jones was giving one of her lessons in Bug Love!" The two of them exchanged ritual punches in the arm.

"Yeah," said Malkovich. "You two are redefining the meaning of buggery." Chan snorted with laughter, despite the fact that it had to be the oldest joke around.

"Shut up, you morons," growled Perez, closing his lunchbox and throwing it back inside the truck. "I need to borrow a magazine of goo."

"And two clips of taser shot," added Jones.

Malkovich pursed his lips and rocked back on his heels. Chan nodded enthusiastically, looking back and forth between Perez and Jones. "What's up?" said Chan.

"Nothing's up," said Perez. "One bug got away, and we gotta hunt it down."

"Yeah right, one bug," said Malkovich softly. "Two liters of goo and a dozen tasers for one bug. That's some serious bug, eh? Must be one mother-fucker bad-ass bug, huh, Chan?"

"Worst bug I ever heard of," admitted Chan.

Malkovich nodded. "Well, if the bug is that bad, me and Chan will have to help you get it."

"We don't need your help," said Jones.

"I'll bet you don't," hissed Malkovich.

"You found a nest," said Chan. "Where is it?"

Perez snorted and looked away. Jones shook her head, "Do you think we'd tell you?"

"We're coming with you," said Malkovich.

Perez's face contorted as he wound up to eject some expletive. Jones put out her hand to stop him. "You can't," she said.

"Bullshit," said Malkovich. "You guys can't keep a commission like that to yourselves."

"Doesn't matter," replied Jones. "I was just telling Perez here that these bugs are all of tremendous biological interest. I was going to declare them all lab specimens, but didn't get around to filling out the forms, yet. Perez and I need to find that nest pronto, so you guys are going to have to tag and bag them all for us. Section 3-17, Scientific Priority."

Perez grinned.

"Don't shit us, Jones," growled Malkovich. "These bugs aren't no lab specimens."

"Check out those big octopods," said Jones. "New species."

"So what?" complained Chan. "They look pretty dead. No 3-17 priorities on dead bugs, sorry."

"That's right," said Malkovich.

"The ones in the engine bay, too," said Jones.

Malkovich glanced at the bugs still wriggling in the engine bay. "You can't be serious. That's just a Jumping Mucksucker and a few Portland Gutter Scooters. Stupidest bugs on the face of the earth."

"That's what you think," said Jones. "For your information, those Scooters were exhibiting signs of an evolved locomotion algorithm that is really amazing. And that Mucksucker, I coulda sworn it was talking Morse."

"My ass," said Malkovich. "You pull this, Jones, you'll get no favors from me."

Jones shrugged. "My loss, I guess." She grabbed the cattle prod and nodded to Perez. "Got your ammo?"

Perez smiled, and put his hand out to the other two. Chan reluctantly unhooked a bottle of goo from his belt and handed it over. "And two taser clips," said Perez, wiggling his fingers. "Thanks," he said when Chan coughed up these as well. "And don't wait up for us."

He and Jones turned and trotted down the alley, trying to suppress laughter. "Not bad, Jonesie, you're not bad," smirked Perez. "3-17, that's a good one."

"Fifteen minutes!" called Malkovich from the trucks. "Then we're coming after you!"

Jones waved at them, just before disappearing through the chain-link fence. They didn't need permission now that their truck had been disabled. It was justifiable under one or another of the protection of property clauses in the bug laws.

They ran between rows of rusted cars, following the bug trails like frantic bloodhounds. If Malkovich said he was following in fifteen, he could be expected in ten. They would have to be fast to avoid splitting the commission from the nest.

"Check there," said Perez, pointing down a dead-end row of minivans. Jones searched it to no avail, as Perez did the same down another row. Jones came back, dragging the cattle prod across rows of sun-bleached doors and fenders. The noise flushed a six-legged bug out of the weeds, and it tore down the road, making its best getaway from what it assumed were predator bugs.

"Perez!" called Jones, sprinting after it. She stopped at a Thunderbird sans doors, as Perez ran up behind her.

Perez looked under the car. "What is it?"

"I don't know, looked like a Banzai Express, about five kilos." She swung the cattle prod under the car, as

Perez kicked the frame noisily. The skittish bug broke out, making another dash for safety. Perez charged after it, banging like crazy on any cars the bug tried to hide in, to keep it moving. Jones stumbled along behind him, watching at each stop to see which way the bug was going to run. Suddenly the bug charged across an open gravel space, and straight down an open storm drain.

Jones and Perez ran up and listened. The scrabbling of the bug's metallic legs as it scampered through the sewer echoed out of the dark hole, audible over their panting. The storm drain grate lay beside the open hole, where it had been pushed aside some time ago.

"Bingo," said Perez. "Who goes in first?" He looked at Jones cheerfully, but she didn't seem keen. "I guess it's me." He removed his pack and pulled out a head lamp, which he strapped over his forehead. "God, I love this part!" He winked and lowered himself into the sewer.

Jones followed, pulling both packs in behind her. The sewer was cramped, and they were forced to crawl. Their pant legs and gloves were quickly soaked by the trickle of water running along beneath them.

Quickly enveloped by darkness, Jones considered stopping to pull her own flashlight out of her pack, but the sewer pipe was too small to turn around and look through the pack or pull it up from behind. She lurched forward and bumped her face on Perez's wet thigh. Her heart jumped.

"What's the matter? Why are you stopped?" she whispered.

"Take it easy," grunted Perez. "I'm just adjusting my head lamp."

"Are you going the right way?" Jones asked.

"Yup," said Perez, too sure of himself. He always took on these underground jobs a little too keenly. Made him think he was some kind of medieval spelunker.

Jones wrinkled her nose at the mosaic of pungent odors, and looked at Perez's butt, filling the sewer pipe just in front of her. "How do you know?"

"Follow the water flow. It'll take you to the main sewer lines. That's where the nest will be."

Jones looked down to see that they were in fact following the trickling water. She shut up and crawled along behind Perez, dragging the packs behind her. She hoped they wouldn't come to a dead end and have to back up all the way to the storm drain. She briefly fantasized crawling backwards and having the packs get jammed in the sewer behind them so that both directions got blocked, and they'd have to lie there for days or until swarms of psychotic bugs found them and disassembled them, feet first. She closed her eyes and continued her dogged crawl.

"Ah ha," said Perez. "Here we are." He crawled out into a black space and stood up. They had reached one of the main city sewers, and it was more than big enough to let them stand up fully. Jones rubbed her neck and breathed deep.

"Now which way?"

Perez looked each way, inspected the water they were standing in, and shrugged. "Keep following the water, I guess." They set off, footsteps splashing in the shallows.

Perez stopped, pumping his goo gun and aiming it down the sewer.

"What is it?" asked Jones, drawing the taser gun. She looked around him, and saw the shape of a bug glinting in Perez's head lamp beam. It wasn't moving. "It's dead," she said, moving around him to inspect it. It was stripped of electronics and motors, leaving only a bare metal frame to rust in the city's runoff. Maybe it had run out of fuel and was scavenged. Maybe it was caught by predators. She took a few more steps and spotted a detached leg a few meters farther along, and a plastic armor plate a short distance past that. These were probably dropped by the scavengers/predators as they hauled the booty off to their nest. She waved Perez forward. They were on the right track.

Emboldened, they picked up their pace, trotting down the sewer, now certain that they were close. Perez was eager, rushing forward, panning his head lamp back and forth across the tunnel. Smaller pipes joined the main line at periodic intervals, along with the occasional access shaft, which Perez slowed only briefly to scan, goo gun raised. The splashing of their feet and the echoes of their breathing filled their ears, and too late, they realized they were surrounded by bugs.

"Shit!" bellowed Perez, firing two rounds of goo in random directions. Jones covered her head, and fired at the first moving thing she saw: her own shadow in the light of Perez's whirling head lamp beam. The taser skipped off the wall, discharging against the moist masonry with a blue flash that illuminated bugs everywhere. On the walls, floor, ceiling. Several ran toward them, and slipped by on the walls, scooting back up the sewer from where Jones and Perez had just come. Perez whirled to chase them, goo gun at his shoulder, and ran off with a battle cry.

"Perez! Don't leave me!" shouted Jones, too late. He was gone, and she was left in darkness. She fumbled in her pack for her flashlight, trying to ignore the clicking, clacking noises around her in the gloom, and the echoes of Perez's splashes and cursing filtering down the sewer. She spotted the red glow of a light-emitting diode, and fired at it. There was an electrical crack, a scrambling noise, and the light went out. Two small incandescent light beams appeared, and swept toward her. She fired at one, and the light popped and went out. The other light blinked out before she could get a bead on it.

She took a careful step backward in the dark, and felt her leg brush against something. She screamed, trounced it with the heel of her boot, and whacked it with the cattle prod several times to be sure. They were everywhere.

"Perez! Get back here, you prick!"

Perez's voice came back down the sewer. "You okay?"

"I'm surrounded, I got no light!"

"I got several cornered up here," he called back.

"Jesus, Perez, that's the oldest trick in the book. They lured you away from the nest! Get the hell back here!" She kicked at the water around her feet, and swung the cattle prod around her to fend off imagined attackers. The area seemed to be clear for the moment, so she dug deep into her pack, pulling out pliers, analyzers, bungees, and finally her flashlight. She flipped it on, and pointed it around her, accusingly.

A few adult bugs scampered back when the flashlight beam swept past them, not sure about the predator in their midst. Two twitching bug corpses lay in the water, the victims of her shots in the dark. Junk lay everywhere—struts, brackets, bolts, wheels, all scattered about like bones in a wolf den. Rickety scaffolding had been erected along the walls, to keep the nest above the water that regularly coursed along the floor. Shelves and cubbyholes in the scaffolding contained partial motors and incomplete bugs, missing legs, electronics, or armor. These were the bug young, in mid-assembly, just waiting for the adults to find the appropriate components to complete them and give them their independence. An electric conduit, spaced with light bulbs for maintenance workers, was strung along the ceiling, and the bugs had tapped into this power source at numerous points to feed their hungry families.

Jones looked at one nearby adult, perched on a shelf in front of an incomplete bug with no legs. It was big, like the bug from the dumpster. She pointed her cattle prod at the adult, and took a step forward. The bug raised its forelegs in defense, but took a few steps backward. It was afraid, but it was also willing to die to protect its young. Jones hesitated.

She lifted her taser gun and pointed it at another bug that was dancing nervously on the ground behind her. The bug skittered back underneath a shelf. Intrigued, Jones aimed the gun at another bug, and it, too, tried to hide. These bugs had some amazing pattern recognition algorithms, to recognize a danger in her mere gestures. They knew she was here to kill, they knew she was capable of it, and they even knew how she was going to go about it.

"Jonesie, what are you doing?" came Perez's voice from behind her.

She looked over her shoulder, to see the light of his head lamp a short distance up the sewer.

"I don't know," she said. "I've got a very strange feeling about this. They seem to understand why we're here."

"They're machines, Jones. Don't empathize. Just do your job."

Jones shook her head. "No, no, they're intelligent. Look." She re-aimed her gun at another bug, and it tried to duck behind a box. "Lots of bugs hide from predators, but these ones aren't afraid unless I take aim at them. How do they know that's when they're in immediate danger? They're a new species. They've never been exposed to exterminators. They haven't had a chance to develop an evolutionary response to us." She shook her head and looked back at Perez. "They must be figuring it out for themselves."

Perez walked up beside her, his goo gun at his shoulder, and swept the barrel around the nest. Everywhere he aimed, the bugs scrambled and hid. After a few seconds, the bugs began to peek out and creep forward again.

"Huh," grunted Perez skeptically. "I don't know." But he didn't fire.

A short distance down the sewer, a bug crept slowly out from a shelf, and climbed down a truss to the ground. In its forelimbs it carried a small electric motor, from a blender or power drill or something. This item would undoubtedly have formed the core of some bug's locomotion system.

Perez swung the barrel of the goo gun toward the bug, and it dropped the motor and hid under the nearest shelf.

Jones hit him in the arm. "Stop it! Put the gun down." Perez looked at her like she had just popped a brain artery, but he lowered the barrel anyway. After about ten heartbeats, the bug inched its way out, and examined the two exterminators with its monocular eye. Then it slowly went over to the dropped motor, picked it up, and resumed a cautious advance toward them.

Perez shifted his weight. Jones kept her hand on his arm to quell his urge to shoot. The bug slowly moved forward, every movement of its eight legs slow and deliberate, so as not to provoke alarm. Other bugs watched the whole episode from their positions on the shelves, their eyes panning back and forth with barely audible whirrs.

The bug stopped about two meters from Jones. It placed the motor down on top of a metal sheet that protruded from the water covering the floor. Then it scampered back a few steps and hesitated.

"What the fuck?" said Perez.

"Holy shit," whispered Jones. She put her hand to her cheek. She was dizzy. She squeezed her eyes shut and then opened them again. The motor sat in front of her like a small, glistening fruit, with two wires hanging off of it. The bug stood a short distance away, looking at her with that inscrutable eye.

Was she misinterpreting this? Was she somehow blowing this all out of proportion? Or had this bug just tried to bribe her?

"It's an offering," she said.

"Huh?" said Perez.

"It's making a sacrifice in the hope that we'll take it and leave the nest alone."

The implications were phenomenal. Social interaction and communication between bugs was a radical enough concept. But communication between bugs and humans—outright trade that was initiated by a bug!—this was completely unheard of.

"Ha!" said Perez. "It's not enough! We got 'em by the balls. Can you tell 'em that?"

"My God, Perez, you're missing the point. They're trying to talk to us." She looked into the monocular eye of the bug, obviously recycled from a video phone, and saw fear, love for its offspring, and a powerful enough

Illustrated by Karen Pollitt

sense of community that it would potentially sacrifice its life in an effort to make peace with the invaders.

She felt a powerful urge to pick up the motor, and walk away. To accept the bug's offer with grace and without hesitation. It was the only way she knew of saying, "I hear you. We are not that different, you and I. We can come to an understanding."

And then it exploded. Great chunks of its carapace shot into the air, four of its legs were completely severed, and the eye lens shattered. A searing roar whistled down the sewer, the unmistakable howl of a shotgun blast in a tunnel. Jones gagged with horror.

She whirled on Perez, but he was on his knees, with his hand covering his head. Perez never used firearms—she wouldn't work with him if he did. Suddenly two brilliant halogen spotlights fired up just behind them, blinding her completely.

"Get down, Jones," came the voice of Malkovich. "We're gonna clean this place up."

"No, stop, you can't!" Jones had her arms up, but the spotlights were incredibly bright, and she didn't know where to look. "Please, this is very special! Section 3-17, absolute Scientific Priority!"

"Bullshit," said Chan. "That scam only works once."

Somebody was muscling past her, but she couldn't see who it was. She grabbed at the air. "Stop! Please don't do this!"

"Fuck, let go of me!" said Perez. "I'm not doing anything!"

"Make them stop!" screamed Jones.

A thunderous roar ripped through the sewer once again. She could hear creaking and splintering as scaffolding toppled. The air was full of the sharp scent of gunpowder. Big red spots danced in her vision, everywhere she looked.

"Taser grenades, take cover!" shouted Malkovich. Buf-buf-buf went his grenade launcher, and Jones stumbled toward the wall to get out of the water. The grenades popped and zinged as they sprayed highly charged capacitors into the scaffold wreckage, discharging on bugs, shelving and sewer water alike.

"Look at 'em all!" called Chan. Another shotgun blast tore through the air. "Run, motherfuckers!"

"Sorry, Jones," came the voice of Perez. "Can't let 'em have all the commission." She vaguely saw him get up and charge into the heat of the extermination.

She couldn't breathe. Her chest heaved, and no breath would come. Everything was wildly off-balance. She put her fists to her temples, and sank against the wall, fighting to center herself.

She was six years old, horrified that her uncle was slaughtering a hutchful of rabbits for their meat and fur. She was fourteen, slack-jawed as the family car crawled past the scene of an accident as the police waved them on, their flashlights reflected in blood. She was nineteen, standing in a crowd in an alleyway as two drunken skinheads kicked another man senseless, screaming incoherent strings of profanity.

She was twenty-six, curled up in a sewer tunnel, choking on gunsmoke and a profound sense of betrayal.

Her ears rang from the furious orgy just a few paces away. With each blast and roar, the commissions ticked over. That's what they do, she thought. I can't stop it, it's just what I do. Jones shook her head and blinked the fogginess from her eyes.

She pushed herself to her feet and followed Perez into the madness of halogen beams and smoke. She had done this many times before. It was just like any other job. She was good at it.

She scrambled over the toppled scaffolding, stabbing through it with the cattle prod whenever she spotted the occasional bug scrabbling for cover. The pickings were pretty easy, since the bugs were big, and many were trapped by the fallen shelves. Four, five, six. She spotted one juvenile trying to make an escape with only three legs. She booted it, snapping one leg, and when it refused to stop, dragging its belly on the ground, she whacked it with the taser gun. About three meters away, Malkovich was clubbing something with the butt of his grenade launcher. Jones stepped over the twisted corpse of an adult that had been hit by a shotgun blast, and glanced at the object of Malkovich's fury. He was trying to bend a panel of metal shelving enough to get underneath, where Jones spotted the glint of several eyelenses and the nervous flicker of legs. Using the barrel of the grenade launcher as a crowbar, Malkovich pried an opening, thrust the weapon inside and fired. A terrific banging and screeching erupted as the bugs thrashed themselves to death under the weapon's intimate hail of lightning.

Jones staggered forward through the nest, trying to get to the other end, where the bugs would be fleeing. Great pink splotches of goo, like the droppings of a giant bird, covered the wall on her left. Perez was up ahead, shooting gobs of goo down the sewer. She noticed a bug upside down in the wreckage. No marks on it, so she hit it with her cattle prod to be sure. It gave a mighty kick as the prod discharged, and then twitched spasmodically. Clever. It was playing dead.

The shelving wreckage ended as she came up to Perez. "Is that it?"

"Yep. I don't think any got away," he said. A half-dozen bugs were visible farther down the sewer, their limbs gummed together by the goo gun.

The sounds of Malkovich, cursing behind them as he banged on something, echoed down the sewer. Chan joined them. "How many escaped?" he asked. Perez shook his head.

Chan nodded. "Good nest, guys. Maybe twenty-five adults, fifteen juvies. Close to a ton of live product." He grinned. "We all made a lot of money in the last five minutes."

He turned and headed back up the sewer. "Give it a rest, Malkie, you're rich!" he shouted. Malkovich's laugh rolled down the tunnel.

Jones looked at the floor, watching the murky water run over the toes of her boots. Then she looked at Perez, who was watching her silently.

"I think I'll buy me a new TV," said Jones.

Perez patted her on the back. "Of course you will, Jonesie," he said quietly. "Of course you will."

THE WINDS

Written by
Heidi Stallman

Illustrated by
Nathan Hale

About the Author

Heidi Stallman grew up in Columbia, Missouri, and received her bachelor's degree in biology from the University of Missouri and recently got her master's in animal ecology from Iowa State University.

Since graduating, she's worked as an instructor of ornithology and conservation biology, and as a research associate in avian ecology. She soon plans to look into research and scientific exchange programs in other countries.

Heidi has always considered herself a writer, but has written mostly in technical and scientific fields. She won an award for a poem as a child, and her first publication was a poem, but she only recently began writing short fiction. With the support and criticism of some fine instructors at Iowa State, her parents and the writers in her university writing club, Heidi produced this story, and earned her first fiction sale.

About the Illustrator

Nathan Hale was born and raised in Orem, Utah. His father, who had recently graduated from Brigham Young University with a bachelor's degree in art, recognized Nathan's early talent: Nathan could draw recognizable objects at the age of one, and Nathan began to constantly study books on art history before he could read.

The local arts community also recognized his early interest, and invited him to figure-drawing seminars and to be in the National Fantasy Art Show in Park City at the age of 16, where he was commissioned to do a drawing for Orson Scott Card.

When he doesn't have a pencil or brush in hand, Nathan has a book of SF or fantasy. After completing a year of study at Cornish School of the Arts in Seattle, Washington, Nathan is taking a two-year hiatus to serve as a missionary for the Church of Jesus Christ of Latter-Day Saints.

I sit on the front porch swing sipping my latest tea experiment and watching the first rays of the morning sun spread slow and beautiful across the sky. That's what Harlan always loved best about Iowa, the sky.

"Everywhere you look," he'd say, "you can see more blue than anywhere else in the country. It almost engulfs you." And I'd have to agree with him on that. But it's the greens I prefer. There are more shades of green in an Iowa cornfield in July than you ever imagined possible, and then the winds pick up, rustling through the leaves, and bring you even more.

Iowa winds... In the summer they bring such sweet relief, but in the winter they roll across the plains, building up speed until they crash right through you like thunder. The one time I left Iowa, it was the winds I missed the most.

My tea starts to taste bitter as I near the end of my cup, so I drain what's left over the edge of the porch. I still must be adding too much clover, or maybe it's the rose hip and lemon grass, but it is getting better. I never imagined I'd become such a weed-tea connoisseur, but then I never imagined being left here alone, either.

I take one last look at the rosy sky, then sweep the remains of my soybean and zucchini breakfast into the food bag for later. I'm about to go back inside, when suddenly the roar of the harvesters' engines rips through the empty countryside like a shot, and my chest goes hollow.

October 23, right on time. I grab my gun from under the swing, collect my food bag, and retreat quickly to the back shed. My land isn't planted because I haven't abandoned it yet or sold out to Uncle Sam, but the neighbors' land needs harvesting, and I'm not taking any chances. I set a chair near the boarded window where I can shell beans or tie cords of dried grass while watching through the slats, just wide enough for my eye and the shotgun. I won't let them take me.

The harvesters arrive in a cloud of dust, then branch off into the neighbors' fields where they spend the morning crawling among the corn and the beans before converging on the transport semi like ants on a hill.

I shell beans into an old gunny sack I salvaged from the Johnson's place and wonder how much fuel a monstrosity like that semi burns in a day. If I could have just a little fuel to plant my fields or power up the old generator in the barn, things would be so different here, but no. Uncle Sam's controlled the gas supply for so long, I have trouble remembering the last time we filled the truck, just Harlan telling me we had to save that last tank for emergencies, how he yelled something awful when I used it up making special trips to see him in the hospital. Now Harlan's gone, and the truck sits rusting under the old oak next to the barn with less than half a liter in the tank, but I might still be able to make it to Ames in an emergency, if I tried.

By late afternoon all the harvesters but one have moved on down the way, ignoring me and my farm. I start to relax, thinking maybe they won't try to talk me out of my home this year, when I see a man drop from

Illustrated by Nathan Hale

the lone combine and start heading toward me. I brush the soybeans from my lap and quickly level my gun through the slats. They haven't used force with me, yet, but I heard old Ms. Taylor was taken from her farm on account she was too feeble to care for herself anymore, and I wouldn't put anything past them. Uncle Sam is full of tricks when it comes to taking private property, so it's best to let them know I've still got claims on this land from a fortified position. They may have driven out all the neighbors, but I'm not so easy to budge.

The man is almost to the house. He hesitates a moment, then walks up the front porch steps and knocks on the door.

"Mrs. Williams, are you there?" calls a voice so familiar, my heart flutters. Could it be, after so many years? I strain to get a better look, but he's disappeared into the house, calling my name, and I'm left switching hold on my gun.

A moment later he's back on the porch and walking around the side of the house, a large man with an awkward gait and a shock of blond hair over his sun-browned face. Billy!

"Mrs. Williams? I know you're here. It's me, Bill Porter. Where are you?" Then he's striding toward the shed, more careworn since the last time I saw him, a young man striding so confidently next to Jeremy, duffle bags slung casually over their shoulders as they left home to enlist.

"That's far enough, Billy," I call, standing up to get a better hold on the gun, the anger rising in me like a wave, drowning out any joy I might have felt at seeing him again. They've got some nerve sending a boy I practically raised.

He grins and picks ups his pace. "Thank God, I've found you. Jeremy's been worried to death. He sent . . ."

"I said hold it right there," and I wave the gun so he'll see it. I can't afford to waste ammo on a warning shot or even to shoot him if he gets too close. Not that I would, of course. I couldn't hurt Billy any more than my own son. But I'm not leaving this farm, and that's that.

Billy comes to a halt about ten feet from the shed. "Mrs. Williams, is something wrong?" he asks, not even stopping to consider the absurdity of the question. He might as well ask, what's right?

"Where's Jeremy? Is he coming home?"

Billy shakes his head. "Naw, he got sent to Oklahoma, 'cuz they knew you were still in Iowa. I got to come this season, 'cuz the whole family is in Dallas with me now."

I let out my breath slowly, feeling the rush of disappointment and anger at myself. I know Jeremy has one more year on the harvesting crews, and the army rarely sends boys to their home states, too much desertion. I shouldn't waste energy on false hopes.

"So, how is everyone, Billy?" I ask quietly.

He's still eyeing the gun, but a slow smile spreads across his face as he starts talking about Carry's new job, the apartment they share with Jeremy on the base, his mother's volunteer work at the refugee camps. I listen carefully, wishing I had tea and cookies or even bread to offer, but all I have are beans, so I guess hospitality's out. It's just as well. I don't want him relaxing too much, anyway.

"I think Jeremy's taking things the hardest though," Billy is saying. "He worries about you, and he misses Iowa. He said he was gonna defect and hike over here this fall, but I told him it was too dangerous and he probably wouldn't make it before the snows come. I don't think he'll try it now, unless I fail."

I smile at Billy, knowing instinctively what he's planning even as he looks at me so innocently. How I wish we could sit together and really talk, but Billy wouldn't think twice about hog-tying me and hauling me on his back all the way to Dallas if need be. I don't trust him as far as I can throw him.

"Why are you here, Billy?"

"The army sent me, though I would have stopped by anyway. Jeremy wants me to bring you back to Texas. The army just wants you off your land."

"You know I'm not going to Texas."

"I know, but neither am I. I was thinking I'd hide out for a while until the army has moved on, then spend the winter in Ames. Come spring I'm going north to build me a cabin and live off the land."

"Now Billy, what do you want to do that for? You know they might shoot you if you're caught AWOL." Leave it to Billy to come up with some crazy plan.

He shakes his head. "You don't know what it's like down south, Mrs. Williams, with all the crowding, and most people ain't got work or shelter or food or nothing. We thought it'd get better when things stabilized up north, but it hasn't happened yet. People just keep coming, and we don't know what to do with them."

"But Billy, you're in the army, Carry's got a job, and you live in a city that still has full power. You're doing okay."

He scuffs his shoe against the ground and looks at his feet. "Well, maybe, but I guess that's not really it." Finally, he looks up. "It's just I belong up here where I can see the sky, and growing things, and not so many people around me all the time. You know, they got that wind generator up in Mason City still powering half the city, and there's big areas of abandoned farms and woods around Clear Lake with so many deer you've never seen anything like it. I'm gonna set up a trading post, just like the pioneers. I could make something of myself there. I know it."

Well, I just nod my head as I listen to him, because there's nothing I can say against it, really. I might do the same if I were a young man, but why can't he just wait out another year in the army and then come back home?

"You been by your folks' place?" I ask.

"Yeah. I've been there."

"Well, why don't you try claiming it again? Squatter's rights, huh? Then, you could make your trading post here with Jeremy when he comes home."

A slow smile spreads from the corner of Billy's mouth. "I'd like that, Mrs. Williams. I really would. But this will be the first place they look for me after I desert, and even if I did finish my tour, all that stuff about temporary seizure was just bull, anyway. They've got this whole county zoned Ag-One, now."

"Ag-One? What do you mean, Billy, Ag-One?"

Billy looks away before he speaks. "It means no one's coming back. They're gonna come through here and level all the buildings and roads until it's just corn and beans and nothing else. I've seen it in Missouri. Not a barn or fence in sight, and so quiet, like a great corn desert."

I just look at Billy, too stunned to speak. My house, my land, my community, totally gone. How could they do such a thing? "Rural areas are expendable." That's what they said. But people aren't, and neither are dreams. I always thought we'd rebuild.

"Mrs. Williams, I'm sorry I had to tell you that, but you need to know what's going on in the world. Things are getting worse, not better. It's time for you to leave."

"You're not going to Texas and you're not going home, so what do you want from me?" I finally ask.

"Come to Ames with me. It'll be safe."

I smile at Billy thinking how the last time I hiked the ten miles into Ames, they were trying to restore power to the old town section, how everyone was working hard together. Most northern cities shut down when the coal stopped coming, but Ames took advantage of their experimental wind generators and solar conductors. A few people stayed, built a nice little community. If I was going to move, it would be there, but what would I do without my farm and the memories that live here?

"I'm not leaving my home, Billy."

"But Mrs. Williams, you can't live out here another year."

"I've lived out here just fine up till now."

"But what are you going to eat? How will you stay warm?"

I hold up a cord of grass and some beans.

"You can't heat that house on just grass. It's too big."

"I've got some wood, too."

"I saw your wood supply. It's not enough. Neither are your beans, nor your wormy apples. Come to Ames with me, please."

Well, he's almost begging me now, but I don't care if he stands there until he's blue in the face. I'm not leaving. This is my home. The same one I was born in, the same one I'll die in, and I'll be damned if I let them tear it down because of some new plan Uncle Sam's come up with, now. I release the safety on my gun. It's time Billy left, before he gets any ideas.

"Billy, it's been good seeing you, but I'm not going anywhere, you hear? Now move on back to Ames or Texas or wherever you're going, okay? I don't want to shoot you."

"Jeremy made me promise not to leave without you."

"I'll tell Jeremy you made a grand effort. Now leave me alone, please." I wave the gun at him to let him know I'm serious. I sure hope he thinks I'm crazy enough to shoot. He takes a step forward.

"You got till the count of three and I'm shooting, okay? One . . . two . . ."

He keeps coming until he's only a few feet away and it's point-blank range.

"Three . . ." I say and lower my eye to the sight.

Billy hesitates. "Okay, okay," he finally says. "I'm going," and he starts walking backward.

Well, I guess he must really think I'm a lunatic, or maybe he just remembers the time he and Jeremy were fighting over who got to lick the bowl, and I gave them until the count of three before I started whacking them with the wooden spoon, chocolate-frosting covered and all. But he's leaving.

He keeps backing up until he gets to the porch, then he smiles. "You can't get rid of me so easily, you know. I'll get us all set up in Ames, then I'll come back for you, okay? It'll just be a couple weeks."

I don't say anything, and he finally waves goodbye and shuffles off down the gravel road. I watch him disappear, then release my grip on the gun and relatch the safety, surprised at how fast my heart is beating, the sweat on my brow. That was close, old gal. He could have called your bluff, and then what would you have done? I have a hard enough time shooting deer, let alone a person, but I'm not giving up my home. They say I'm a crazy old woman, that I'll never survive out here another year, and perhaps they're right. But I don't feel crazy. I just don't want to live without this farm. Anyway, dead or alive, as long as my body is in this house, they can't take it from Jeremy. At least I have that.

I set down the gun and try returning to my beans, but my hands start to stiffen in the cool fall air and I keep mixing the piles. Finally, I brush the beans from my lap, sit quietly listening to the night fall around me. A flock of geese is on the wing, and their lonely calls echo across the open sky. A lone cicada buzzes from behind the shed, the barn door clanks on rusty hinges, and all evening, as I replay the memories in my mind, I hear laughter and the sound of children's voices on the wind.

• • •

It has been over a month now and Billy hasn't returned. Maybe he's decided not to stay in Ames, or maybe the army caught him AWOL and is forcing him to return to Texas. Either way, I'm somewhat relieved. It's tiresome carrying this gun around all the time.

A blanket of snow dusted the ground last night, turning the world white and bringing the first taste of winter winds. It's too early for the freeze to last, only November 22 if my count is right, but I've decided to try for a deer this morning. I don't have strength for the deeper snows of December, and as long as it freezes at night, the meat shouldn't spoil.

I sit in the Schroeder's wildlife blind all morning, tying cords of grass until my hands grow numb, then rest my head against the butt of the gun. What happened to all the deer? In the last few years, as people moved out, the animals moved back in and deer have been plentiful. In the summer, they glide into the fields at dusk to graze, then bound away easily when the dog packs come. I don't know what those mutts ever catch, but it's sure not the deer. All their natural smarts were bred out of them long ago, and only a few have adapted to the wild. I even got soft last summer and fed the Schroeder's old coon dog, Kelsey, for a while, although he stopped coming around lately. I miss him, but it's just as well. I've nothing to spare, and he'd only scare the deer.

I close my eyes and have almost dozed off when I hear a crash below me. A young doe, probably last spring's fawn, is grazing about fifteen meters away. My heart skips a beat and my hands shake as I pick up my gun and take aim at her chest. She bends her slender neck toward a tuft of grass, so small and delicate, I think maybe I should wait for a bigger deer. But who knows how many chances I'll get later on? I take a deep breath and pull the trigger just as she lifts her tail and bounds across the field. I hold the breath tight in my chest until her pace slackens and she starts to stumble.

Climbing down from the blind, I follow the bright red stains through the snow, Jeremy's flexible flyer in tow. It's not too deep, but I move slowly, testing each step for buried ice before trusting my whole weight. A broken arm could cut my chances of survival in half this winter, and a broken leg would finish me for sure; I can't be too careful.

I keep trudging after her, but soon she's out of sight and I start to panic. What if I only hit a leg or shoulder and she keeps running for miles? Or what if it gets dark early? I can't track her very far and still make it home safely, but I can't let her go, either. I pick up my pace, walking faster and faster until I'm almost jogging, my mind now set only on retrieving her. Sure I've got to be careful, but I've got to live, too. I need this meat. Nothing else matters.

The wind cuts into my cheeks and my feet are blocks of ice. I forgot how cold it gets, how desolate the winter landscape becomes. The sky has turned gray and heavy, and it seems to be weighing down on me, pressing out my energy like cider in a sieve. I know I can't go on much farther, when I catch a glimpse of the deer up ahead, turning a corner around the Frantzen's barn. Relief floods through me as I give a final spurt of effort and find her backed up against a rusted old shed.

She has dropped to her side, but she starts thrashing wildly when she sees me. The snow is streaked red with blood, and she's not making any progress getting up, but what if she can still get away? I need her if I'm going to make it through this winter, if I'm ever going to see Jeremy again. I raise my gun, about to use the last shot, when I see a pile of boards stacked near the shed.

Almost in slow motion, I drop the gun and move forward, my body acting apart from my mind as I grab a large board and turn to the struggling deer, just inches away from me in the snow. The wind howls in my ears and my breath comes in ragged gasps as I close in on her, her efforts to stand almost frantic as I lift the board above my head, bring it down across the back of her skull. I raise the board over and over, filled with new strength, the deer struggling wildly under my blows. She's not getting away.

Finally, my shoulders give out, my arms shaking so hard, I can't hold the board any longer. I take a step back and drop the board into the darkened snow, my body trembling and my legs so weak, I can't stand. I drop to my knees, staring at the still form of the deer, my hope for another year, and I start to weep.

• • •

The sun came out dazzling this morning, bright prisms of light shattering off the snow's surface, ice melting away in rivers from the dirt road. I'm trying to haul wood from the Johnson's old barn, which fell in the storms last summer, but Jeremy's wagon keeps getting stuck in the slush and mud, making it slow work. It's pretty unusual to get a complete thaw this late in December, but believe me, I'm not complaining. I need to stock up on wood before the real snows begin, and it's so beautiful and still out here, I can't get enough fresh air into my lungs.

It's late afternoon and I'm on my third load when a blue jay's alarm call pierces the stillness, and I see a lone figure walking toward me down the road. My breath catches deep in my throat, and my chest tightens. I scan the sides of the road, but I can't make it back to the house in time. There's nowhere to hide. Finally, I grab my shotgun off the top of the woodpile and bring it to my shoulder. The figure approaches steadily, then stops just outside my range.

"I didn't think you were coming back," I say.

Billy smiles. "A promise is a promise, Mrs. Williams. I'm just sorry it took so long. I didn't get a chance to get away until we hit Missouri, then I slipped off and hiked back up. I've been in Ames this last week, waiting for the storms to break."

"I'm glad you're okay, Billy. I was worried." I smile, surprised to find I really was. I guess I've been looking forward to his return as much as I've been dreading it, and suddenly I feel somewhat foolish, like a schoolgirl in the presence of her first crush.

He shifts his weight from foot to foot, and eyes my gun. "I talked to the Headleys in Ames. You remember them, don't you?"

I can't say that I do, so I shake my head.

"Well, they remember you from the PTA. They said we could stay with them for the winter, and come spring, they'll help you set up a new place."

"I've got a place, Billy."

"Come on, Mrs. Williams. Have you been to town lately? It's real nice."

"I'm not leaving. You know that."

"Listen to me. They've got most of the downtown and about twenty blocks of residential area north of it on full power. They've got a communal grocery and garden system going, and they've even opened the library as a community center. It's a bit crowded, but it's warm and you could live there, make a home for yourself and maybe Jeremy."

"I've got a home, Billy, and when Jeremy comes back, it'll be waiting here for him."

"But you can't survive by yourself out here. Why can't you see that?"

"I've survived well enough up till now."

"They said the only reason you made it last winter was the early thaw and because you had canned food stored. What will you do this year, if you're not so lucky?"

I shift the weight of the gun against my shoulder and just stare at Billy. I know he thinks he's trying to help, but I can't leave this farm. Maybe I'm being a fool, but this is my home, and I'm too old to change now. Besides, just one more winter and Jeremy will be coming home for sure.

"Billy, I'm sorry you hiked all this way, but I told you I won't leave, and that's final. Now if you don't mind, I need to get another load of wood before nightfall."

Billy looks at the wagon and the deep ruts it has left in the road. "May I help?" he asks.

I'm not sure I should let him—no telling what he has planned—but my muscles are sore after working all morning, and suddenly I don't want him to leave. I step back another ten feet and gesture at the wagon. "Thanks, I'd appreciate it."

Billy takes the handle and slowly pulls the wagon toward the house. We walk in silence, and I find myself relaxing in the warmth of the sun and his company. This could be dangerous, I know, but I try not to think about it, just enjoy his presence for a while.

When we get to the house, he stacks the wood on my front porch, then steps back and looks at me.

"Could I get you a drink of water before you leave?" I ask.

He shakes his head no. "Why won't you come to Ames with me?"

I don't answer. I wish I could tell him so he'd understand, but I'm not sure how, and anyway, I'm through explaining myself.

"God, you're stubborn. What do I have to do to make you see what a fool you are?"

"Goodbye, Billy."

He takes a big breath, like he's just made a decision. "I'm not leaving here without you." He takes a step toward me.

I step back quickly. Damn, why is he pressing me? I don't want to threaten him, but it's past time he left. I raise the shotgun, then lower my eye to the sight and aim two feet off his shoulder. "You do what you have to, and so will I."

Billy stares at me and the gun. He smiles. "I know you're just bluffing, Mrs. Williams. You won't shoot me. You couldn't hurt a fly." He takes another step.

"Billy, I'll shoot," but he keeps walking toward me. I don't know what to do. I don't want to hurt him, but I can't let him take me away. My hands start shaking wildly. My heart is beating so hard I think it might jump from my chest to the ground. I'm almost as surprised as Billy when the gun goes off.

Billy crumples to the ground, then lays staring at me with wide eyes, his hand against his shoulder. Oh, my God, I've killed Billy! But then he's moaning and rolling around and trying to rise back to his feet. I take a step toward him, then hesitate. What if he can still overpower me? I run into the house and return with an old sheet and a flask half full of whiskey.

"God damn," Billy is yelling. "God dammit to hell!"

"Are you okay, Billy? Do you need bandages?" I quickly tear the sheet into strips, my hands trembling wildly. I can't believe I hit him. I was aiming two feet away. If he dies, I'll never forgive myself.

Billy just stares at me. "You shot me! I can't believe you really shot me."

"Here," I say, throwing the strips of sheet and the flask at him. "It's all I have."

Billy hesitates, then starts removing his coat and shirt. There's so much blood on his arm, I think I might be sick, but he wipes it away easily and I feel waves of relief. Billy is okay. He's going to be all right. I take a deep breath, then reach down to pick up my gun. I just hope he doesn't realize it's empty.

Billy is shaking his head as he cleans his arm. "Well, I guess you're as crazy as they say. Or maybe I'm the crazy one for walking all this way to help you, just so I can get shot. I could have stuck around the army for that."

"I appreciate you coming out here, Billy, I really do, but I never asked for help. All I want is to be left alone."

"Well, I guess." He ties the last strip of sheet around his shoulder.

"I'm sorry I hit you. I didn't mean to shoot."

"Which is why you're still aiming at me, I suppose?"

"I'm not leaving."

"Well, don't worry. I'm not trying that again." He gingerly pulls on his shirt and coat, then stands looking at me, holding his shoulder.

"So this is it. You really want me to just leave you to die out here?"

"I don't plan on dying," I say, though I guess I might. It's better than leaving, though. It has to be.

"Yeah, well, I don't think the choice is yours." He stares at me a moment, then looks at his feet.

"Damn, Mrs. Williams, what do I tell Jeremy? His mom's even crazier than everyone thought? He won't understand this."

"Tell Jeremy that the farm will be waiting for him this summer when he comes home, and that I'll be waiting here with it."

"Why can't you just do both of you a favor and tell him yourself. We can be in Ames by nightfall. The Headleys have a phone."

"I'm not leaving."

"And you're an old fool."

I smile slowly this time. "You may be right."

He kicks at the ground, then looks out over the farm. "This sucks, you know. This really sucks."

And I'd have to agree with him, but I don't know what to say, so I'm quiet. Billy stares at me a moment, then turns down the road toward Ames. His step is slow but steady, and it's a long time before I lose sight of him fading into the empty countryside like a dream.

When he's gone, I walk to the wagon and pick up the flask of whiskey. I do wish I could make Billy understand why I stay, but the truth is, sometimes I don't even understand it myself. Sometimes I can't believe how my life has gone, and I think if I pinch myself hard enough, I'll wake up with my family around me and neighbors down the road. I guess I just never believed it would last. Crises belong to California and New York, not the Midwest, where life is slow and change comes gradual on the wind. Things just kept getting worse, and then one morning everyone was gone. Jeremy asked me once right after the power was turned off, "Why don't you leave, Mom? The house is dead." But it's not electricity that gave this farm life, it was the people who lived here, and the memories of love.

They say I'm just holding on to ghosts, now, and maybe they're right. But if I can hold on just a little longer, I'll save this farm for Jeremy, and maybe, someday, he'll fill it with life again. I lean over for the handle of the wagon, then taking a long draught of whiskey, head off to the Johnson's for another load.

•••

Time passes slowly in the dead of winter with only the wind and the ghosts of old memories for company. Harlan used to say the best thing about being a farmer was that you could take January off and go to Florida if you wanted. Of course, we liked it here and never went anywhere, but the thought was always comforting during the long gray days. Now, I sit for hours on the sofa thinking I could go to Texas if I really wanted, but I'd rather stay here, wrapped in the warmth of old memories and my mother's afghan. Of course, some days it's easier to believe than others.

Today, I sit in my usual spot on the sofa, rummaging through old magazines I salvaged from the Johnson's barn before it fell last summer. Today is a special day, January 29, Harlan's and my thirty-fourth anniversary. Harlan used to bring me a rose and a poem each year, and once he even arranged for Jeremy to stay overnight at the Porter's, and Harlan fixed us a candlelight dinner. Such a romantic, that Harlan. God, how I miss him. But I'm glad he never saw the farm like this. It would have broken his heart right in two.

I flip through the magazine's pages, occasionally skimming an article I've read twenty times before, until I find a picture of a rosebud from an ad in *Woman's Day*. I cut around it carefully, putting down the scissors more than once; my hands get so stiff in this cold. Then I mount it to a scrap of cardboard off the burn pile and bundle up to go outside. If Harlan can't bring me a rose this year, I'll take one to him.

The air is biting and the wind whips through my coat like it's nothing as I push through the snowdrifts to the north side of the house. When I reach the snow bank that is Harlan's rose garden in the summer, I stick my rose into the snow, then stand back to recite Robert Burns' poem.

"Oh my luve is like a red, red rose that's newly sprung in June. Oh my luve is like a melodie that's sweetly played in tune."

And I wish I could do it right and sing it, like Harlan used to, but my teeth are chattering so hard and the cold air stabs through my lungs like a knife. Anyway, I don't think Harlan will mind. He used to grin at me whenever I'd try to sing, and he'd say, "Why, Miss Betty, I believe there's a hole in your bucket. You've lost the tune," and then we'd both laugh at how awful I sounded. Harlan was always ready with a joke.

I finish the poem, then stand next to Harlan's rose, looking out over the white expanse of farm, listening to the wind whistling through the barn, thinking about my days with Harlan. In the winter, with the snow to cover up the emptiness, the farm looks almost the same as it did ten years ago, before my world began to crumble. For a moment I think I might see Harlan as he goes about the evening chores, laughing with Jeremy at some joke, whistling through the barn. It seems so real, I can almost see the light seeping from under the barn door, smell the freshly shoveled manure on the air, hear the squeal of hogs waiting to be fed.

I sink lower into my coat, burying my hands deeper into my pockets, shaking and shivering something awful. I don't want to go in, don't want to leave this vision of comfort, but my feet have lost all feeling and my nose is so cold it burns. I can't afford to get frostbite, and I know it's not real, no matter how much I want to believe.

Finally, I turn back toward the house and start retracing my footprints. I'm almost to the front porch before I see the basket and some bundles wrapped in newspaper stacked against the door. I look around cautiously, then hurry up the steps. There's a note stuck to the basket's lid.

"Thought these might come in handy. Have you changed your mind, yet? Bill."

I look up quickly and scan the farm. "Billy? Are you there?" But the wind takes my words and tosses them carelessly through the air, the only movement in the yard the swirl of snow and the bending of the old oak.

I reach down and open the basket's lid. It's full of candles and matches, dried fruit and jerky, a box of shot, a couple of books, and a battery for my old transistor. He even remembered my mail: a letter from Uncle Sam—full of tricks to talk me off my farm, I'll wager—lots of other junk I can't believe they're still sending, and a postcard from Jeremy! I drop the other mail back into the basket, my hands shaking and tears blurring my vision as I scan his familiar writing. "I'll see you soon, Mom," he says and then I really start to cry. Jeremy's coming home soon.

Still clutching the card, I reach down and unwrap one of the bundles. It's a large deer steak. I tear open another and another, but they're all the same. It must be at least a side of deer, and just when my own deer was running out.

"Billy?" I call again loudly. "Billy, where are you?"

I look around frantically, but I still don't see him. God, where is he? He couldn't have left that long ago. He has to be around here somewhere.

"Billy, come out if you can hear me. . . . Please?" But he doesn't show himself. I take a step off the porch, then stop. What am I thinking? I can't go out looking for him, not in this cold. So I start to talk, instead, hoping maybe he can hear me, wherever he's hiding.

"Thanks for the supplies, Billy. I can sure use them. Today is my anniversary. Did Jeremy tell? I'm still not going to Ames but I've missed you. God, I felt terrible about last time. I wish we could do that day all over again, but I still wouldn't leave. You know that, don't you?"

I yell as loudly as I can, the wind catching my words and tossing them into the bleak winter landscape. I start telling him about my days here, the sweater I'm knitting for Jeremy, the shed I started to chop down, the things I hope to accomplish this month. I just keep talking until the numbness in my feet and hands starts to burn, the biting cold against my cheek becoming a lash of fire. Billy, where are you? But the farmyard is empty, the countryside desolate.

"Come back soon, Billy, okay? You're always welcome." And I wave at the far windbreak of trees, where I think he must be hiding, then turn to pick up the basket.

•••

I leave all the meat except for one steak in the front foyer where it will stay frozen and be safe from wild animals, then spread my green linen tablecloth over the old computer system in the dining room and start setting it with my best china. Tonight, I'm celebrating my anniversary in style. No handful of soybeans for me.

I set the candles in my best silver candlesticks from Aunt Irene, display Jeremy's postcard between them, and find an AM station out of Little Rock that is playing old-fashioned jazz. The steak is only partially burnt over the wood stove, and there's dried apples and peaches for dessert, which I reconstituted with water and what was left of the whiskey. Best of all, Harlan's memory floats around me, whispering old conversations and love songs I'd thought long forgotten.

It's much later that evening when I hear fumbling on the porch and a loud scratching at the front door.

"Billy, is that you?"

I scramble for my gun and the extra shells, cursing myself for not loading it right away. What was I thinking? I've grown careless this winter, lulled by the quietness of the countryside and the false security that comes with solitude. The scratching grows louder, then the door slams open and I hear footsteps in the foyer.

"Who's there?" I call, but the only answer is a tearing noise and the raging of the wind as it bangs the door back and forth against the porch rail.

I light the end of a long cord of grass from the stove's fire and walk slowly toward the noise, torch held high, my heart thumping so loud, I can barely think.

"I've got a gun, you hear me? I'll shoot!"

I hesitate at the edge of the living room, taking deep breaths to calm myself. Then, taking one last breath, I turn the corner into the foyer, my gun raised to kill.

A black-and-tan dog is tearing at one of the frozen deer steaks, growling low in his throat. His fur is matted against his side and I can count every rib along his spine. It's the skinniest, most pathetic creature I've ever seen.

I let out my breath in a rush and lower the gun.

"Kelsey! Kelsey, boy, is that you?" The dog's tail wags a little, but he doesn't look up. I take a slow step toward the open door, and Kelsey growls louder. He looks up and snarls, teeth bared in warning.

"Easy, old boy, I'm not after your steak. I just need to close this door, okay?" I take another slow step toward the door, then drop the latch as the wind throws the door shut.

Kelsey watches me carefully, then drops his muzzle back to the steak. He's finished gulping down the first one and is tearing into a second one before I realize, he won't stop there. He's so close to starving, he'll eat himself sick before he stops. I raise the gun again and aim right between his eyes, willing myself to shoot. That steak is my life, but I can't pull the trigger. He's probably even had a rougher time at it than I have. I can't just kill him.

I change my grip on the gun until I'm brandishing it like a club, then walk slowly forward. "Get back, now. Go on!" I yell, waving the gun.

He growls loudly, but his back is quivering and he's about to bolt. This dog sure knows fear, and once he's moving, I back him easily into the corner, steak in tow. Quickly, I gather the remaining steaks and shove them into the shelf in the hall closet, keeping a weary eye on Kelsey as I work. When I finish, I back slowly from the foyer and return to my bed by the stove.

I huddle into my blankets and coat, shivering uncontrollably, suddenly so cold, I think I'll never be warm again. The wind scrapes branches of the old cedar tree against my window, grating at my nerves like sandpaper, fingernails against a board.

So close. What if it had been more than a half-starved dog? Someone to steal my food or take me away, and I wasn't ready for them? I'm losing my edge, my wits.

And what fool thing am I doing now, not turning that dog out immediately or even shooting it for food? I can't keep him. That's for sure. I can barely feed myself, let alone a dog. But he looked so desperate, so alone. I couldn't just kill him. I'll have to turn him out first thing tomorrow morning, that's all, and I close my eyes to sleep.

It's much later when I wake to Kelsey's comforting warmth pressed against me, his breath on my hands. I smile slowly, then stroke his ears and nose as I curl my body tightly around him, happy for his presence in the cold night, even if it's just for a while.

•••

Another storm came through last night, dumping a foot of snow on the ground and trapping me inside, inert and useless. I have to get out of here. I have to go outside where I can find wood, find food, but I'm trapped in this house, my refuge turned into a cage.

Kelsey and I have been on half rations for weeks now, but the bottom of the food bag is near and the steaks are all gone. We ran out of wood last week and grass cords two days ago, so there's not much left to burn. Yesterday, it was the sofa, and today, the book cases with all their books consumed in fire. I know the piano should be next, but I keep holding off, just in case it clears up outside. I remember how Jeremy's legs used to dangle from the bench as he practiced, how he hated his lessons and me for making him take them. But in high school, we couldn't drag him away, and oh, could he make that piano sing. It should be waiting here when Jeremy comes home. I know he's coming home.

I emerge slowly from under the covers and throw another piece of my bedpost on the glowing coals. It doesn't catch right away, but then flame's slow fingers embrace it, and the stove breathes warmth upon my hands. I rub them slowly together, so stiff from the cold, from so much inactivity, like a migraine has settled into each one of them. I stare at the fire a moment, then walk toward the living-room window, the only window in the house not kept filled with corn husks between the storms.

The ground is coated white and the sky is so gray, it's almost like night. The wind tosses snow carelessly into the air, building drifts against the house, more walls to keep me in. At least the drifts will insulate the house a little, but not enough. How could it be enough? The weather mocks me, my hope. I never thought winter could last so long.

I pace the house, stretching my frozen legs and trying to decide what else to burn, anxious to get outside, needing to be outside. If the storms would just break, I could make it. I know I could. The snow will thaw to reveal frozen carcasses and broken branches, and the spring rains will bring green shoots and worms pushing up to the soil's surface. There's food out there, and fuel, if I could just leave this house and find it. Damn these storms.

I finally turn toward my bed, I should be lying down, not pacing uselessly, and I glimpse the computer terminal where I've taped pictures of Jeremy, his postcard, a note to Billy, the army's letter. I will myself to keep walking, but I stop, stare back and forth between them, the postcard and the letter. I was saving them for Jeremy, to show him what dirty liars they were, how they'd stoop so low to trick an old woman from her home, but a bolt of fear stabs through me, and I rip the letter from the terminal, cast it furiously into the stove's dwindling fire. He's not dead, not shot going AWOL, not gone, the dirty liars. Jeremy is coming home, I know it. And I'll be waiting here for him.

•••

The winds howl through these old walls like laughter, chilling me to the bone and leaving me shivering under all these blankets. I can't get warm, can't remember ever being warm, even with Kelsey's body huddled close against me.

The storm has been raging for almost a week now, with no end in sight. I don't ever remember a storm this bad in March, but then there's no accounting for Iowa weather. So much for global warming. We ran out of food two days ago, and there's nothing left to burn. Just the blankets off our backs and a few odds and ends: the piano keys, Jeremy's baby pictures, and Harlan's carvings. I can't imagine any of them in flames, but I guess they'll be next. After that, I don't know what I'll do.

Kelsey whines in his sleep, pressing his body even closer to mine, looking for warmth that's not here. I stroke his back slowly, feeling each rib under folds of loose skin, the coarseness of his fur. He's so weak now, so feeble, and I thought I was saving him. I thought we had a chance.

I pull the blankets tighter around my face and huddle deeper into my cocoon, thinking Billy was right after all. I don't feel crazy, but I guess I've been a fool all along, believing an old woman like me could find a way to survive out here alone. I knew this could happen, that things might not go my way, but I never thought how it'd be. I never thought how the truth would slip in so quietly until it expanded to fill every part of me like a cancer, crowding out any room left for hope.

I told Billy I would die here, and I will. But God, I'm not ready yet. Jeremy will be home soon, I know he will, and I've got a garden to plant, a shed to mend. And what will happen to Kelsey when I'm gone? There's so much life left in me, so much I want to do. I'm not ready for this. Not yet.

I huddle even deeper into the blankets, thinking about the truck parked out back under the old oak tree. Were the chains still on it, the bags of sand in the back? Maybe I could still make it to Ames, if I could get the truck to start? Or maybe I should start to walk? But no.

This was my choice. I have to stay here for Jeremy, for all the people who have been lost in these times.

I close my eyes and let my head grow fuzzy with whispered prayers and voices on the wind. My body's trembling so hard, I can't control it, but eventually it stops and I feel lighter, warmer somehow. I'm drifting off into emptiness when suddenly, I feel strong arms lift me and heat pouring down the back of my throat.

"Billy, is that you?" I try to open my eyes, see his face in a halo of light.

Just relax now. I'll take care of you a voice is saying, and I feel his warmth seeping through me, my mind growing heavier. I struggle to stay awake, I have so much to tell him.

"Billy, promise me you'll stay until Jeremy gets here. You have to stay," I whisper, and he smiles at me and nods.

I smile back, then let my eyes close slowly, stroking Kelsey's ears and listening to the winds howl against the night.

Harlan told me once, if you listen to the winds just right, you'll hear their stories. On a warm spring day they're the songs of birds wooing a mate and the promise of flowers to come. Summer winds whisper of children playing and cool running streams, and in the fall, they're a chorus of thanksgiving for the harvest, a dance of leaves to celebrate the year's end. But it's the winter winds that really speak to you. On a cold winter's night, the winds move endlessly through you, becoming the voices of everyone you have ever known or loved, calling you home.

I am haunted by winds.

THE GARDEN

Written by
Cati Coe

Illustrated by
Eric Williams

About the Author

As a child, Cati lived in Chile, Ghana and India. Her school in India encouraged students to rewrite stories, so she began writing at an early age. But she says she never wanted to be a storyteller; instead, she wanted to change the world.

In the years since, Cati (whose name is pronounced Cah-tee) has gone on to study the writings of such fine craftsmen and storytellers as Terry Bisson, Octavia Butler and Suzy McKee Charnas.

Cati currently works as an assistant editor for the SF magazine Terra Incognita. *She's also working on her PhD in folklore and folklife at the University of Pennsylvania.*

The following tale is a quiet one, and brilliant in many ways. I hope to see much more of her work in the future.

About the Illustrator

Eric Williams was born in Belleville, Illinois, in 1968. He won a $10,000 art scholarship as a senior in high school. His entry was published in 1988, in both Scholastic Scope and Voice Magazine.

He attended the Savannah College of Art and Design, where he specialized in computer illustration, graphic design and oils.

Eric has displayed his work at the Howard County, Maryland Art Guide, at the Gateway East Art Guild of Southern Illinois and he won the Grand Award for a work displayed at the Bond County, Illinois Fair in 1991.

I push through the gate, an' the sun bounce off the concrete, hurtin my eyes. There be nothin but concrete all round. But the grass, it try to grow through the cracks. I kick at the pebbles an' glass. I the only one here.

I come to the old playground an' jump up to swing on the rusty chain. It use to be that it had a seat.

I member when Darryl use to push me on the swing.

"Harder! Harder!" I scream.

An' up I went into the blue sky. An' back to earth. An' up again. An' Darryl, he yell, "Jump, Keisha! Jump!"

But that be before Darryl got the implant in his arm. An' now the red light glow through his shirt to let everyone know the drug be workin right. I let go of the chain an' head for home.

•••

When I open the door, I see Mama an' Jeanie from upstairs sittin on the sofa. I shut the door after me, an' stay right where I am. Mama ain't seen me yet.

"Shit," Mama say. "I spectin this ever since the day he born. Well, at first, I spected he'd go to prison or get shot. But when he got drugged, I knowed he wouldn't get mixed up in all that. But he would never amount to nothin anyway if he was drugged, so why should I be upset? Ain't no reason for me to be upset now."

"Honey," say Jeanie. "Have somethin more to drink." An' she hol' up the bottle to Mama. Mama drinks, but she keep lookin right in front of her, not at the woman an' not at me. She been cryin all this time.

"You know what happen to my first one?" say mama. "Little bitty baby boy. I was fifteen, livin with my daddy, his girlfriend, all their children, takin care of my kid an' my daddy's kids. You know what happen? My baby die! I go to the doctor. You know, at one of those clinics. You have to sit, sit, sit round all day. Then the doctor yell at me for not takin good care of my child, cuz you know what this sweet little thing have? He have rabies!"

"I bet he bitten by rats," say Jeanie.

"Uh-huh!" say Mama. "But that doctor blame me. As if it be my fault there rats in the place."

"Uh-huh," say Jeanie.

"So I don't know why I bother with all these other children."

"It's the men," say Jeanie.

"Yeah," say Mama, "but now they all drugged. I pass 'em on the street, an' they wouldn't mind if I beat their asses. They ain't even men no more. Oh, man, what am I gonna do?" She start cryin again, an' the woman jus' hol' her. I wish I wasn't here. Maybe I be movin or somethin, cuz Mama see me an' lift up her head.

"Well!" she say. "Would ya look at this, Jeanie! Can't have no privacy, can we? No privacy in here, huh?" She walk over to me, put her hands on my shoulders, turn me sideways, an' push me over to my cot. "You sit down right there, hear? An' you stay there, an' you mind your own business!" Then she an' Jeanie walk to her room an' she slam the door.

I jus' sit there on my cot. There ain't nothin else to do, an' I don't know what's goin on.

There a knock on the door, an' Aunt Jolene come in with Tommy, Crystal an' Willie. Jolene all dressed up. "Keisha, you wanna watch 'em this afternoon? I gotta go to a class."

"Okay. When you be back?"

"Round six. Maybe later."

Mama an' Jeanie come outta her room. The bottle empty now. "Well," she say. "Don't Jolene look fine."

"Yeah," say Jolene. "I'm takin a class down at the Center."

"That so?"

"Yeah, honey, I'm gonna make it out of here so fast."

"This my sister," say Mama to Jeanie. "If she amount to more than shit, it gonna be a big surprise."

"Jus' you wait an' see," say Jolene. "Actions speak louder than words. Soon, I'm gonna have a nice job downtown, we gonna move to the suburbs, have a nice big house—"

"There ain't no way they lettin you out there, cuz number one, you from this place; number two, you ain't a man; an' number three, you as black as me. You jus' gonna sit here with the rest of us."

"Jus' you wait an' see," say Jolene. "I'm gonna make it, no matter what you or anyone else say. An' you, who won't do nothin to help yourself, you gonna be the one stayin right here."

"Let me tell you somethin," say Mama, raisin her voice. "The only reason you get to take your class is cuz of my Keisha. You gonna rise to the top by takin advantage, jus' like everybody else. That's how you gonna make it. Now don't that make you feel proud!"

"I'm gonna pay her for her time," say Jolene.

"Uh-huh. Let's get outta here," say Mama to Jeanie. "The smell of that perfume—uh-uh." They walk out the door.

"Huh! I feel sorry for you, Keisha, havin to live with her," say Jolene. She brush off her skirt even though there ain't nothin on it. "Hey, Keisha, you doin such good work, I'm gonna pay you a dollar each time. You hear?"

"Yeah."

"Don't tell your mama. You know what she would do with it."

My money. My very own money!

"You really gonna make it out of here?" I ask.

"Baby, you gotta believe it. God's on my side. He's fightin for me. You gotta believe in somethin, or you can't live. Bye, Keisha. Take care of my babies." She go out the door.

My own money.

"Hey y'all," I tell 'em kids. "Now sit down. We gonna watch TV."

And that's what we do.

When the baby wake up, I feed her an' change her diaper. Mama come home, an' she go to the kitchen to cook dinner.

"I ain't feedin Jolene's kids!" she say.

"Don't worry," I whisper to 'em. "You mama gonna come back any time now."

Then I yell, "Mama, where Darryl? How come he ain't home yet?"

She don't answer, so I go to the kitchen an' say, "Where Darryl at, Mama?"

"I don't know. He ain't home yet?" She don't look at me.

"No."

"He went to get his drugs checked at the Center."

"Somethin wrong with it?"

"I don't know. They jus' check it now an' then."

"He gonna be okay?"

"Stop botherin me, Keisha."

• • •

I wake up in the mornin real early. Jus' gettin light outside. But I can see that Darryl ain't on the sofa. Mama's there, watchin TV. "Where's Darryl?" I say, sittin up. "He ain't come back from the Center?"

"Nope," she say, still lookin at the TV. She prob'ly feelin the letdown.

I start gettin dressed. "Where you goin?" she ask.

"To school, Mama," I say.

"You stay here. It too early for school."

"Mama, I hungry."

"So go then. Jus' leave me alone."

I finish dressin, an' I open the door.

"Come over here, baby. I'll braid your hair."

"Mama, I real hungry. How bout tonight?"

She don't say nothin.

"Bye, Mama."

Then I'm runnin down the stairs, all the way down. Then I'm outside headin toward the Center. I get all outta breath. I don't know where the clinic is, so I walk round the Center, lookin at the big cement walls an' the big tall iron gates. I go past the doors to the school, the police station, an' the stores, an' then on the other side, I come to a door which say "Free Clinic." I go through the big door an' the metal detectors, an' inside it's a big room with lots of people sittin there. I think some of 'em might have TB, so I try not to look at 'em. Some of 'em be kids, too.

A white lady in a white uniform sit behind the desk at the end of the room, an' I walk over to her. She stop writin an' put down her pen. "Come over here, little girl."

I go over. "What's wrong with you?" she say. "Where's your mommy or daddy?"

"I'm lookin for Darryl Whitacker."

"Oh," she say. "So you're not sick or anything."

"No'm."

"Who's this Darryl Whitacker?"

"My brother."

"Why are you looking for him here?"

"He was supposed to come here yesterday, cuz they needed to check his drugs. But he ain't come home."

"You'll have to check with the school, honey. Drugs are the school's business."

"But is he here?"

"Check with the school."

Outside, on the street, I see Lydia. "Lydia!" I call. She turn round, an' I can see she ain't drugged for fightin yesterday. I run to her.

"I jus' spend the whole night in there," she say, "poked an' pricked an' everythin. They ask me all kind of questions. They wanna know—"

"Were you scared they might drug you?"

"Keisha, I's a girl!"

"There be drugged girls."

"You know it's only boys who be violent. So only they need to get drugged."

"You jus' lucky."

"Keisha, wake up an' see the light! Most every boy be drugged. But only one, two girls."

"Uh-huh, what I tell you? Some girls get it!"

"But Keisha, I's light." She hol' out her arm. "If any girl gonna be gettin drugged, you the one that gotta watch it."

Then we go inside the school. Lydia head straight for the cafeteria an' I go to the office. There a lot of people here. I push an' I make it through the people to the front. When I get the attention of the secretary, I say, "I'm lookin for Darryl Whitacker."

"Is he a student here?" ask the secretary, tapping her pen on the desk.

"Yeah."

"Well?"

"He missin."

"Well, that will show up on the school's records."

"The clinic told me to ask you—"

"Is he on medication?"

"Yup."

"Well?"

"He went there yesterday to get it checked. They told me to ask you bout it."

"Who told you to ask me?"

"The lady at the clinic."

"I don't know about such things. But I don't see what the school has to do with checking medication. We only recommend it. Please don't waste my time." She already turnin to the old lady standin nex' to me.

I get out from all the people, an' I go back to the clinic, to the lady behind the desk.

"Hello," she say.

"The school don't know neither. Can't you check?"

"This is about the missing person?"

"Yeah."

"What's the name?"

"Darryl Whitacker."

"When was he supposed to come here?"

"Yesterday afternoon. After school."

"I can't check for everyone who came in here all afternoon. Do you know how many people we get a day? But I'll look up for the time he was supposed to be here. When was his appointment?"

"Uh . . . three?"

"Okay." She go through a few papers. "No," she say, "there was no Darryl Whitacker at three o'clock. Sorry."

"How bout—"

"Hey, 'scuse me," say a man walkin up with a clipboard.

"What this say?" He hol' the clipboard out to the lady.

"Previous illnesses," say the lady.

"An' this?"

"Asthma. Will that be all?"

"Yeah." The man walk away.

"Please, can't you check nothin else?" I say.

"That's all I can do," say the lady. "I have a lot of work to do."

I don't know what to do, so I walk away. "These people," I hear the lady say. "Can't even say 'Thank you.'"

I run back to the school. I's too late for breakfast, an' I ain't learned nothin. Did Darryl come here? Maybe I said the wrong time? How'm I supposed to know what time he come? An' I gonna be hungry all mornin.

The Garden

• • •

When I come home from school, I see Darryl ain't in his place on the sofa. He still missin. Mama come out of the kitchen swingin a bottle an' sayin, "Shit, shit, shit."

"Hi, Mama. Darryl still not home?"

She throw the bottle at me, but miss. It smash against the wall an' the drink run down onto the floor. There glass everywhere.

She got me by the ears 'fore I know it, an' she draggin me to my cot. "I don't wanna hear another word bout Darryl from you," she say, shakin me. "You hear me? He gone. He gone, Keisha. He gone he gone gone. . . ." She lets go of me, an' starts cryin, sittin on my cot, curled up with her head touchin her knees. I sit up an' touch her arm, but she push me away.

"Mama, Mama, Mama," I say. "It be all right."

"No more lies," she say.

"Mama, it gonna get better. Come on, Mama."

"No," she say. "I try to do my best by you an' Darryl, but it ain't enough. It ain't enough. Lost my boys."

"But you got me," I say. "Come on, Mama." I move off the cot, an' I move her so she be lyin down. The cot too small for her. Then I jus' stroke her head, an' keep sayin, "Mama, Mama, Mama." Then, she fall asleep. Prob'ly from the alcohol.

Then I go to her room an' check on the baby. She doin fine, jus' sleepin. I put a bottle in her crib. An' I tell her, "Be a good girl, baby, cuz Mama's sleepin."

Then I go, shuttin the door behind me slow, an' I head for Grandma's house. She live further than the Center, so I pass it. I cross the street when I see a gang of teenagers hangin on the corner, in a circle, lookin over they shoulders an' blowin smoke at one another.

All the drugged guys, too, they sittin on the street, jus' come back from prison. Their red lights be shinin strong. No one's gonna feed 'em, so they sit there. They don't do a thing but snooze. Guess they gonna starve to death. Them I jus' step over. They so harmless you can take money from 'em. They more dangerous to themselves than to me.

Grandma live in a house between other houses, an' she got a backyard where she put her washin. Ain't got no grass or trees. She live on the first floor.

When I ring the bell, it take some time for Grandma to come to the door, but I's use to that. When she open it, she glad to see me. "Why, hello, Keisha. Come right on in."

So I go into her livin room, which is where she sleep, an' I sit down in my favorite chair. "Would you like some juice?" she ask.

"Yes, please." I go get it, while Grandma sits down.

"So what gives me the pleasure of your visit?"

"I wanted to see you."

"How's the family?"

"Everybody's okay. But Darryl . . . he missin. He was supposed to go to the Center to get his drug checked, but they tol' me he didn't go there, an' he ain't been home since yesterday mornin. Nobody know where he at."

"How's your mama?"

"She unhappy."

"Feeling guilty I bet. She probably sold him to a gang for some crack."

"Mama's real unhappy," I say. "Cryin all day."

"Yup, I bet," she say. "Comin down off a high, I'm sure. I know her like the back of my hand, an' if she's unhappy, I say that's good! She should be unhappy . . .

with the way she's livin her life, with what she's doin to you all. I'm glad to hear it!"

"You're not gonna help her?"

"Honey, you gotta understand. The only help she wants is money for her crack. Or is it something new now? What's it called? K? An' that's right, I'm not gonna help her. Uh-uh. Not me, her mother. I ain't gonna kill my own daughter. If she kill herself, I'm not gonna have a thing to do with it. An' you should be ashamed of yourself for beggin for her."

I don't say nothin.

"His medication workin before he left, right? No blinkin red light?"

"No'm. It was steady."

"That's good. Then the police won't get him."

"What you mean?"

"The police—they got a good excuse to shoot you down if your red light be blinkin."

"Cuz the drug not workin? An' then you be violent?"

"That's right. They figure you not in control of yourself. They love *that*. Those Negroes can't control themselves, so let's feed 'em drugs to keep 'em down. No, no, no, to 'protect' 'em from themselves. To protect 'em from they violent natures. We calls it *legalized* crack, an' they mean to keep our menfolk down."

She sigh. "In my mind, that boy your brother died when he was put on that drug. He started missin then. Ain't no big tragedy now. But I guess you don't feel that way."

"No'm." I sip my juice.

She smile. "You got you own mind. You want to stay for supper?"

"Yes'm!"

We finish dinner bout five. "You better be off," say Grandma. "Fore it gets too dangerous. Maybe I'll walk you to the end of the block. I command some respect in this neighborhood." She smile.

I get her cane, an' I help her get down the steps. We go real slow down the block. At the end of the block, she say, "Good luck, Keisha. Come again sometime." She kiss me on the cheek an' I start walkin home. There more teenagers out now, grouped together in the lots. They look at me as I go by, but I don't look at 'em. Some of 'em be throwin bottles at the wall. Then there's some beatin up someone who's already lyin on the ground, an' I go past fast. It gettin darker an' darker. I go past all the prison men. Most of 'em be sleepin. Two women are talkin to one. "Hey, you! You got any money?"

He jus' smile. Then he say, "No."

"Search him!" That's when I walk by. Course, he ain't got no money. Million people a day tell him to give it to 'em, an' he jus' does, cuz he ain't got no resistance no more. That's Darryl all over. Only Darryl ain't so skinny. His hair ain't fallin out. Not yet.

Then I get home. I round the corner of my buildin, an' I trip over somethin. It the leg of that K user that always be sittin round the buildin. I so scared, cuz that leg take me by surprise. I run through the door, an' all the way up the stairs, hopin there ain't nothin else in my way.

An' then I stand outside my door, jus' hearin my heart an' tryin to breathe.

When I open the door, there ain't no lights on. "Mama?" I call. But no one answer. I reach for the light, but I stumble over somethin. I get the light, an' I see that everythin's all messed up. The sofa's upsidedown. Pillows, they all over the place, all ripped an' torn. The TV jus' gone. The rug is over on one side of the room, in a heap, an' my cot is on its side. My clothes is all over the room, an' the cardboard box been stepped on. They still pieces of glass on the floor, an' the alcohol be smellin up the room. I open up the window. Mama must of gone real crazy.

I go to her room an' turn on the light. The baby be in her crib, sleepin, but Mama's bed all a mess. Her mattress been thrown to the floor an' torn up, an' all her drawers open too, an' her clothes all over the place too.

I go to the kitchen, an' all the food in the fridge an' the cupboards be gone, but there still be paper plates, forks, an' spoons. There wasn't much food anyhow.

Where did Mama go? Why she done mess up the place? Maybe I should go ask her friens upstairs?

I go out the door, an' jus' then Jolene come up the stairs with Crystal, Tommy an' Willie. "You can look after 'em, can't you, Keisha? I can't trust your mama no more. She sent 'em down this afternoon all by themselves."

"How come you here at a different time?"

"Oh, well, since you take such good care of 'em, I figure I would take two classes—typin an' business management. It'll mean more money for you. You see, Keisha, we're all together in this."

"When you be back?"

"Maybe nine, maybe a little later."

I take the kids inside, but they holdin on to me.

"Keisha, Keisha, Keisha," sing Willie. He must be glad to see me.

"Tell her," say Crystal to Tommy.

"You know what happen today?" ask Tommy.

"Bam, bam," say Willie.

"What happen?" I ask.

"You wasn't here," say Crystal.

"I was with Grandma," I say.

"We here with your mama," say Tommy.

"Three people come in!" say Crystal.

"Bam, bam," yell Willie.

"With guns!" yell Crystal.

"They shoot Mama?" I ask.

"No," say Tommy.

"They take the TV!" say Crystal.

"Bam, bam," say Willie.

"Stop that, Willie," I say. "That it?"

"Yes," say Crystal. "The end."

"No," say Tommy. "There's more."

"You lie," say Crystal to Tommy.

"You mama—" say Tommy.

"Bam, bam, bam!" yell Willie.

"Shut up!" Tommy yell at Willie. "Let me tell the story."

Willie start cryin. "Look at what you did," I say to Tommy. I pick up Willie, an' give him a clip from my hair to play with. "Keep talkin," I say to Tommy.

"Well," say Tommy, "you mama ask, 'You know where Darryl is?' An' they say, 'Come with us.'" He look proud of himself.

"Mama go?"

"Yeah."

"An' we go down the stairs," say Crystal. "An' now we here with you!" She start runnin round the room.

"She go with 'em people? The ones with guns?"

"Yeah," say Tommy.

"And she ask 'em if they know where Darryl at, an' they say they know?"

"Yeah."

"Clio here!" yell Crystal from Mama's room.

"Shush," I tell her, rushin into Mama's room. But Clio already awake an' cryin. I pick her up. "Gimme her bottle, Crystal." I take the bottle from her. I give it to Clio who suck an' suck, she so hungry. I walk back to the livin room, an' Willie's bendin over to touch the broken glass. "Willie, no! Crystal, get Willie! Tommy, hol' Clio." Crystal grab on to Willie by his pants, an' Willie screamin an' tryin to hit her. "Stay there," I say while I push the sofa back up. Then I pick up Willie an' put him on the sofa. "Stay there," I tell him. "Don't go near the glass." Then I get the broom an' the dustpan from the kitchen, an' I hear Crystal an' Tommy yellin, "Keisha!" I come back in the room, an' Clio is screamin an' there's milk all over. I pick up Clio.

"Crystal an' Tommy, sit down!" I put Clio, who still be screamin, between 'em on the sofa. "Jus' put the bottle in her mouth," I tell 'em. "Willie, stay where you at! I ain't picked up the glass yet."

"TV?"

"No TV. Look!" I point to the empty space on the floor. Then I sweep up the glass, an' wipe up Mama's drink with a sponge, keepin one eye on 'em. Then I go to the kitchen to dump it out, an' when I come back, Crystal hittin Willie.

"Stop it!" I say. "Okay, I gonna hol' the baby. We gonna play cards." While we play, Willie fall asleep, an' so do the baby. I didn't change her diaper, but I don't wanna wake her up now.

Jolene come by. "Wow," she say. "You all sure made a mess. You better pick it up, Keisha, or you gonna be in real trouble with your mama. Here's a dollar. Goodnight!"

First, I put the baby in her crib. Then I put Mama's clothes away in her drawers. Then I stack my clothes against the wall since the box is broken. Then I put the pillows on the sofa even though they torn an' ripped.

Mama still ain't home. I lie down on my cot.

But I leave the light on, jus' in case she an' Darryl come home.

• • •

I wake up. The baby cryin. The light still on, an' it still dark outside. I go into Mama's room an' pick up the baby. Mama still ain't home. I get Clio's bottle from the fridge. She only got a little bit of formula left, an' then I'm gonna have to give her water. Maybe Mama was killed by 'em people. Maybe they be usin Darryl as a runner. Tomorrow, I gonna go on the streets an' start lookin for him, cuz if he be runnin for 'em, then he be on the streets. Or maybe Mama's findin him right now.

While the baby's drinkin from her bottle, I change her diaper, an' sure enough, she dirty. I clean that up, an' by the time I's done, she asleep, but when I pick her up, she cry, so I rock her a little, an' she close her eyes again. But when I put her down in her crib, she cry real loud, so I pick her up again, an' she close her eyes again. So I wait till she real, real asleep, an' then I put her down, but she roll from side to side an' she wake up again, an' cry some more. So I pick her up again an' try again, but she cry when I put her down. I so tired now that I jus' let her cry, an' I go back to my cot an' I lie down.

But I can't fall asleep till she shut up, which is a long time. Maybe she worryin bout mama an' Darryl jus' like me.

The Garden

• • •

When I wake up in the mornin, Mama ain't there. Darryl ain't neither, an' I spose I didn't spect it no other way. It's up to me now. I so tired, but there things I gotta do. First I dress. There ain't no more formula for Clio, so I give her some water, which she don't like. Then I dress her an' change her diaper. She don't cause much fuss. I pack her bottles an' diapers an' clothes into my knapsack till it be burstin. Then I's ready. I put the knapsack on, pick up Clio, an' I walk down the stairs. I got my two dollars in my pocket cuz I need to buy some food.

I sure am hungry.

When I get to the bottom of the stairs an' open the door, ain't nobody outside. Only the K man leanin there against the wall.

"Hey, mister K man," I say. I walk toward him, but not too close.

"What you want?"

"You seen my mama?"

"You got any money? I be quittin tomorrow, but you know. . . ." He stare at me.

"What you mean?"

"You how old? Nine, ten, eleven?"

I nod.

"It gonna cost you fifty cents a question. What you wanna know?"

"You seen my mama since yesterday afternoon?"

"Nope. That be fifty cents."

"You seen my brother Darryl in the last three days?"

"Yup. That be a dollar."

"Where?"

"He walkin away one mornin with some guys, right here. Dollar fifty."

"You know 'em?"

"Yup. Two dollars." I give him my two dollars.

"That be all I got," I say. "Can't you tell me who they is?"

"Okay, okay—since you so little. But don't break my rules again. They be my connections, you know, my suppliers. My friends."

"Can you show 'em to me?"

"For a dollar."

"When do you see 'em?"

"Uh, uh, uh. Don't you push it. I already give you a free ride. Fifty cents a question."

"I need to get more money."

"Uh-huh. That's a good idea. That some pretty baby you got there."

"Don't you touch her!" I yell, an' I start runnin, but I don't run far cuz the knapsack jogglin on my back an' the baby jogglin on my chest, an' I afraid to drop her. But he ain't followin me.

He seen Darryl! Maybe it was the day he disappear. Or maybe he seen Darryl before he disappear, an' it got somethin to do with why he disappear. If Darryl be part of a gang, then I know sooner or later he gonna die. Or maybe he in prison an' we don't know it. Or maybe his arm start flashin red, an' the police shoot him.

I still don't know nothin!

When I get to Grandma's house, I's afraid she not up, so I ring the doorbell loud an' hard. She come quick.

"Why, Keisha. What a surprise!"

I go straight to the livin room an' I put the baby down on the bed, an' then I start emptyin my knapsack. "Put those things in the kitchen," she say, an' I take 'em there.

When I come back to the livin room, she ask, "What happened?"

"You gotta take care of the baby today. Mama didn't come home last night, an' I gotta go to school."

"So this is Clio."

"You ain't seen her before?"

"Nope. I haven't seen your mother in three years, either. I don't care to. But Clio, why, she's so pretty!"

"I gotta go to school."

"Listen, if your mama doesn't come home tonight, you come here an' sleep."

"Okay," I say.

I go an' shut the door behind me. I walk to school, an' there's more people out. I see Lydia, an' we walk through the big gates an' upstairs to the cafeteria for breakfast. I keep yawnin an' yawnin.

"Cockroaches or maggots today, Keisha?" ask Lydia. I smile at her. She make this joke every day.

When we're sittin with our 'cockroaches,' she say, "You know what's gonna happen tonight?"

"What's that?"

"Big things."

"Like what?"

"The Panthers plannin to break into the Center an' take all the medicine from the clinic, an' then they gonna set fire to the buildin so there won't be no more school."

"Yeah?"

"My brother Robert tol' me so. He's a Panther. Real high up." She whisper, "He's the only boy, so they like him a lot."

"Oh," I say. "That so? You think he know somethin bout Darryl?"

"What's wrong with him?"

"He missin."

"He drugged, right?"

"Yup."

"Oh." She take another bite of 'cockroaches,' like she finished with the conversation.

"Why you ask?" I say.

"I heard my brother an' his friends talkin bout that, but when I walk up, they went all hush-hush. Like they can keep somethin secret from me! Well, I gonna ask him, but maybe he'll ask me to do somethin for him. You know, in payment. You help me do it, right? Whatever it be?"

"Yeah," I say.

• • •

When I get home from school, I open up the door an' there's Mama. She kneelin on the floor, with her back to me, an' she got somethin in front of her.

"Hey, Mama. Where you been?"

When she hear me, she take what's in front of her an' go into her room.

"You find Darryl?" I ask.

She don't say nothin from behind the door.

I jus' sit down on my cot. I don't know what else to do.

She come out in a few minutes, an' she carryin a big garbage bag. It ain't big enough for Darryl, maybe big enough to hol' Tommy. "What's that, Mama?"

"None of your business," she say. She open the front door.

"You leavin us, Mama? You leavin us like my daddy done?"

She stop an' look at me. "No," she say. "I'm tryin to do what's best. I got a big night tonight. But when the time comes, I'm gonna treat you right."

"What bout Darryl? You find out bout Darryl?"

"Not yet," she say.

"You gonna die tonight, Mama?"

"No," she say. "I'm finally doin somethin right in my life, an' I ain't gonna die now." An' then she gone.

I think bout what I'm gonna do this afternoon, how I better get movin quick fore it get too late. Someone knock on the door, an' it's Jolene, ready to drop my cousins off. They gonna slow me down. "Thanks, Keisha."

"All right," I say when Jolene gone. "Crystal, come here! I got somethin important to say. We gonna do somethin different today—"

Someone knock on the door again. I open the door, an' it Ms. Fuentes. She got a policeman beside her. "Hello, Keisha, how are you today?"

"Hi."

"Is your mother here?"

"No."

"She been here lately?"

"Last five minutes."

"Who are all these kids?"

"Tommy, Crystal an' Willie."

"They can't be your mama's."

"No, they Jolene's. She my aunt."

"They're staying here?"

"No, they stay with Jolene."

"Why are they here?"

"I'm watchin 'em."

"I see. Can I look around the apartment?"

"Yeah." She always do.

She go to the kitchen, an' she open up the fridge an' the cabinets. "How come there's no food here?"

"I think Mama's gone shoppin right now."

She move on to Mama's bedroom. "Where's Clio?"

"With my grandmother."

"Why is that?"

"My grandmother wanted to see her."

"How long is she going to be there?"

"It jus' for a visit."

"She's never gone for a visit before."

"This time she do."

"Don't lie to me, Keisha."

"I ain't lyin to you! It the truth."

"Where's Darryl?"

I don't know what to say. "I don't know where he at," I say.

"You know he's been absent from school the last three days?"

"No."

"Have you seen him in the last three days?"

"No."

"And your mother didn't try to contact social services?"

"I don't know."

"Was he on medication last time you saw him?"

"Yeah."

"Red light flashing?"

"No'm."

"You got your period yet?"

"No'm."

"Maybe soon, though," she say. "You tell me when, an' I'll get you all fixed up. Okay, tell your mother I stopped by. I'll try to come by again, but I got a lot of places to cover. Will you give your mother this note, just in case I don't see her?"

I nod. Anythin to get her outta here. She scribble on her pad, an' give me a piece of paper.

"Goodbye. Keep well, Keisha." She go out the door with the policeman.

"What's it say?" ask Tommy.

"Gi' to me, gi' to me," say Willie.

"Ssh, y'all. I'm gonna read it." The note say: TERMINATION OF WELFARE SOON UNLESS: 1) DARRYL BACK AT SCHOOL, 2) CLIO AT HOME, 3) YOU AT HOME WHEN KIDS ARE HOME. POSSIBLE REMOVAL OF CHILDREN TO INSTITUTIONS.—MS. FUENTES.

"What it say?" ask Crystal.

"We gotta find Darryl," I say. "Today we gonna search this neighborhood from top to bottom to find him. So Crystal an' Tommy, I want you to hol' hands. 'Member, if you hear shots, you lie down." I pick up Willie. "Hol' hands, I said."

We walk down the stairs an' across the lot. We walk down the blocks, walkin close together, first walkin in areas I know, then gettin to ones I don't. The teenagers already out, so I know we don't got much more time. Tommy an' I checkin out each corner an' lookin at every group, lookin for Darryl in new clothes, as a seller, a user . . . anythin. We look down the alleys, but they jus' full of trash.

"We gonna look through there?" ask Tommy.

"If he in there, he dead," I say.

"An' the empty houses?" Tommy ask. He pointin to broken windows in an apartment buildin.

"Tommy," I say, "we ain't gonna go through every buildin. Some people use those places."

"Who?" ask Crystal.

"You 'member when all 'em men got sent back from prison? People like that, who don't got no place to go. An' people who can't live without crack or K or somethin else. We can't go through there."

"But what if Darryl be in there?" ask Tommy.

"Then there ain't no hope for him."

After some time we get to the wall.

"Wow," say Crystal.

"High," say Willie.

It real high. Not so high as an apartment buildin, but maybe three stories high. Straight, no footholds. I didn't know it was so high. No place to climb neither. None of the buildins touch it.

"You see those wires way up top? My daddy say you touch 'em an' you die. An' those, they guard towers, so nobody can get over," say Tommy.

"Yeah," say Crystal. "They tore down Grandma's place to make it. She live right here." She stamp her foot on the street.

"Okay," I say. "Now we jus' go back an' forth, from one wall to the other."

We get to the other wall later, an' we go down the streets. Then Willie start cryin. "I hungry," say Crystal.

I done saved some bread from lunch, an' I split it up three ways.

"Juice," say Willie.

"No juice," I say. "This all I got."

"I wanna go home," say Crystal.

"Home," say Willie.

We never gonna find Darryl like this. "Jus' a few more minutes," I say. "Come on. Willie, I gonna carry you. Crystal, you too big. Use your own feet." I move along real fast, cuz I don't got much time, but I don't wanna get too far away from Tommy an' Crystal neither. Tommy stop lookin anyhow. He tryin to hol' Crystal's hand, an' she tryin to catch up with me.

"Hol' my hand," say Tommy. When he get close, she raise her hand to hit him.

"Look, y'all, we need to find Darryl."

But it ain't no use. I can't carry Willie for long, but when he walk, he so slow. We walk down a block, an' I too busy watchin Crystal an' Tommy to look for Darryl. "All right," I say, "let's go home."

"Thirsty," say Willie.

"When we get home," I tell him.

We walkin down a street when I hear someone callin, "Hey."

"Come on!" I say. "Walk faster."

But the man catch up. "Hey," he say. He a big man, with gray hair.

"What you want?" I say.

"You better go home," he say. "It ain't safe to be out here, four kids like you."

"Unsafe to be home, too," I say.

"Oh," he say. "It's like that, huh? Well, I could take you over to social services."

"No," I say. "Leave us alone."

"Look," say Crystal. She pointin to a picture painted on the wall. The picture got kids of all colors playin together, an' it say "I have a Dream." In front, there be a rusted-out old car an' an empty lot. A few people pickin beer cans out of the weeds.

"You like that? We did that," say the man.

"You did that?" ask Tommy.

"Yup. Last year. This year we clearin out that lot over there. We gonna make it into a park, with swings an' stuff. Then y'all can play in it."

"Come on," I say. "Let's go home."

He a big man, but he squat down an' ask Willie, "You wanna go home?"

"Yeah. I hungry," say Willie.

"How bout you?" he ask Crystal.

"Yeah," she say.

"You like bein at home?" he ask Tommy.

"Okay," say Tommy.

"Okay," say the man.

"Come on," I say. "Let's go. You don't need to check up on us, mister."

But the man walk beside us all the way home, an' he talk bout his empty lot. An' Tommy an' Crystal an' Willie talk to him. But I don't pay him no mind. I didn't find Darryl today, an' I don't know where he at.

The man walk us to the door of our buildin, an' we climb the steps. I gotta push Willie an' Crystal up. Tommy ask, "How come you didn't ask the man bout Darryl?"

"He wouldn't know nothin," I say.

"How you know that?"

"He ain't that kind of person. He different. He wouldn't know nothin bout it, bout Darryl."

One more flight up, Tommy say, "I like him."

"Maybe that explain why he don't know nothin. He too nice," I say. Willie cryin, so I pick him up.

"Me too!" say Crystal.

"No, I can only hol' jus' one," I tell her.

We get to the ninth floor, an' I open the door. We all head for the couch, an' Willie an' Crystal fall asleep right away. Tommy an' I don't say nothin to one another. We play cards. Then Jolene come.

•••

I wake up in the middle of the night to gunfire. It must be what Lydia talked about. I go over to the window, an' the sky is all lit up. Must be a fire somewhere. There a lot of smoke. Maybe no school tomorrow.

Mama still not in. Lots of bodies tomorrow. I hope Mama ain't one of 'em.

My eyes go all blurry. All I see is the light, the purple sky lit up. Can't see no buildins. Only light. An' then I can't see that. It all darkness, an' I start screamin, an' I can hear my screamin, an' I can hear the gunfire, but I can't hear nothin else, an' it seem like it go on forever. But then I's fightin to open my eyes, an' then I see light, an' then I see the ceiling, an' I breathin hard, an' I lyin on my back. An' I stay there til I can breathe okay an' see the window an' the wall an' I can turn my head from one side to the other. Then I crawl to my cot, an' I lie down. My head hurt.

•••

I wake up in the mornin, an' Mama still ain't home. My head still hurt, but I go to the window an' look for the Center. That cement buildin still there, an' I glad, cuz I awful hungry. No dinner last night. Maybe I gonna eat cockroaches *an'* maggots today. I don't meet nobody on my way to school, an' the Center looks fine. No dead bodies, no new gun holes, no windows broke. It look the same as always.

When I walk into the cafeteria I see Lydia, an' I sit next to her with my food.

"Hey," I say.

"Do I have news for you!" she say.

"Bout Darryl?"

"No, no. Robert, he won't tell me a thing bout that. All hush-hush about it. A big secret." Maybe she didn't ask. "I'm talkin bout all that gunfire. You hear it last night?"

"Yeah."

"Well, it gonna be on the news. You know why?"

"Why?"

She lean over the table an' whisper, "It happen outside."

"Outside?"

"Yeah. You see, there's this big ole truck that carry all the hospital stuff, an' medicines an' drugs, but it was gonna go to, you know, 'em rich people outside. Not to us. So, the Panthers take it, an' then they rob a supermarket since they outside, you know—fresh food! Anyway, they sellin it today on 41st Street, in case you want some."

"But how they get outside?"

"They got a secret route. Ever since that last wall was planned, they been makin their plans, an' they got an out. They been usin it all this time, but only for little things, you know. K, crack, heroin. But this make 'em famous. Watch for it tonight! It gonna be on TV."

"I ain't got no TV."

"You wanna come over an' watch on mine?"

The Garden

"No," I say. "I gotta find Darryl."

"Forget Darryl. I's your friend, ain't I? I bet Robert won't tell me cuz your brother dead!"

"Liar! You didn't ask him!"

"Who you callin a liar?" she say, standin up, an' she put her shoulders back an' start lookin all tough. I know she ready to fight. She pickin up the cereal bowl full of milk, an' she ready to hit me with it or throw it if I say somethin. I ready to fight her too, only people's watchin an' I don't wanna be drugged for bein violent, an' she tougher than me anyhow. So I jus' walk away, an' I glad she don't follow me.

I ain't got nobody now.

• • •

After Jolene come by with Tommy, Crystal an' Willie, I take 'em to look for Darryl. We go down the stairs an' out the door. Along the wall by the door it the K man.

"Hey," I say, a few feet from him. But he lyin down, eyes starin, in some dream world. "Shoot," I say. I got my dollar, I work out what question I wanna ask him, an' here he is all shooted up. "Okay," I say. "Let's go."

When I turn round, there's a group of people standin round one guy, an' paper bags an' money changin hands, people comin away serious. Some people round shootin up. This guy's gotta be our K man's connection, right?

"Y'all wait right here," I tell Tommy an' Crystal an' Willie. I go an' stand on the side of the group, but in front of him, so he can see me.

When everyone satisfied, he turn to me. "I don't sell to minors," he say, laughin.

"No," I say. "That ain't it." I so nervous. This man prob'ly killed so many people in his life, who's me? If I say the wrong thing . . . I gotta be careful.

"Wait, wait, let me guess. You want to be a runner? Yeah, lemme hear the sob story. You supportin your mama's an' daddy's habit, an' you buyin milk for the kids. 'Jus' gi' me a job, daddy!' Uh-huh, I hear 'em all."

"No," I say. "I wanna know bout Darryl Whitacker."

"Darryl Whitacker. Ain't that news? What's he to you?"

"He my brother."

"Oh, you want him to support the family. Got it. He drugged?"

"Not crack or K—jus' in the arm. He wouldn't hurt nobody."

"Oh," he say. "Uh-huh. He got a government-supported drug habit." He laugh. "Well, you come to the right place, cuz I know everythin, I mean *everythin*, that happen in this place. Yup, I do recall now. An', sista, I got bad news for you. He dead. Yup, definitely dead by now."

I shakin now. "Gang fight?"

"No. Somethin worse."

"Can I see him?"

"Gotta join the organization for that. Work your way up till you can get into our secret headquarters, our chambers."

"He squeal on you? That it?"

"Yeah, why don't you work as my runner? Work your way up. You live round here, right? You eleven or twelve? Why not work for me? You be all taken care of. We be like family to you. You be makin big money, *big* money. An' I see you got guts."

I don't know what to say. I don't wanna dis him by sayin no.

"Still too young, huh? You think bout it."

"Uh, huh, sir," I say. We walk away fast, but not so fast that it look like that's what we doin.

When we round the corner, we start doin the other part of the neighborhood, up one street an' down the other, from wall to wall, but I'm not lookin too hard. I'm wonderin if this walkin is useless. Or maybe that dealer, he lie to me. I don't know why they would kill Darryl. He don't do nothin, jus' lie round. An' if you tell him to do somethin, he jus' do it, jus' it might take him a long time. He never gets mad. Maybe he was doin somethin for 'em, an' he make 'em angry an' they shoot him. Or maybe they get mad cuz he so slow. Why didn't the dealer tell me why or how? Maybe he don't know nothin. Maybe Darryl be runnin on the street, an' the K dealer think he dead cuz he so stupid an' all runners die sooner or later, specially if they don't pay attention. Maybe the dealer don't know nothin.

Tommy an' Crystal been lookin, but they pointin at people, an' that dangerous. "Don't," I say, pushin Tommy's arm down. "Don't point." He look at me in surprise. "But you keep lookin. You too, Crystal."

All the alleys, they filled with trash. When the walls was finished, they stopped pickin up the trash, an' people jus' throw it out the window. In the summertime, it smell. But I don't see Darryl.

Finally we get to the third wall, an' we walk all the way down it. We got most of the neighborhood done. "Hey, y'all want somethin to eat?" We all stop, an' I give 'em the bread an' pass the bottle of water round. I got a dollar in my pocket if I need it. Tommy an' Crystal an' Willie, they tryin to read the graffiti.

We turn down a street to get to the fourth wall. It's not a busy street, an' lots of the houses is all boarded. If mama loses her welfare, maybe we gonna end up here. We pass a K house, with the people lying round outside, an' a man leanin against a tree. They don't pay us no mind. No Darryl.

I see lots of people up ahead, round a big truck. Then I 'member what Lydia say. So we walk up to the truck, an' there's rows an' rows of medicines, an' there's food too, shiny tomatoes an' pineapples an' potatoes. There's green stuff too, like cabbage an' other funny lookin vegetables. Lots of people round too, an' people inside the truck be busy sellin it all. They wearin pink caps, so they Panthers.

"What you want?" I ask Tommy an' Crystal an' Willie.

"That," say Willie, pointin at an orange, all big an' shiny.

"Okay," I say. "How many oranges for a dollar?" I ask the woman sellin.

"Two."

"Ok. I'll take two." An' I hand over the dollar.

We go to the side of the road, an' I peel the oranges for 'em an' divide 'em in half. The juice run down Willie's face. "Good," say Crystal.

Then I hear gunshots. "Get down," I yell. An' I push 'em over, an' I try to cover 'em with my arms as I gettin down. I can't see what's happenin, cuz the shots, they comin the other way. Willie got hurt comin down, an' he cryin an' tryin to sit up so he can look at his knee. "Get down!" I shout at him, an' I take his arm an' pull him down, an' now he really cryin. Jus' like Clio do. Then the gunshots is comin from the roofs of the houses round us, too, so I jus' lie there with my cheek against the pavement, waiting to die. People lyin down all round us, an' they scared too—I can tell. One woman prayin in my ear, "Allah, be merciful." Then I hear the truck movin, an' I turn my head the other way to see it. It movin down the street real fast.

An' then I see my mama, in a green jacket, in the back of the open truck, firin at the roofs. "Mama," I yell. But the truck turn the corner at super high speed an' is outta sight.

The gunfire stop, but we all lie there till it's clear that's it. We all pick ourselves up. "That the Hoodlums?" ask someone.

"Yeah, I saw the green jackets," someone answer. Willie, Crystal an' Tommy ain't hit, but other people are screamin an' cursin. Some of 'em got hit, an' some of 'em are screamin cuz someone else they know got hit. We was lucky, cuz we walked away from the truck to eat our oranges. Them who was still buyin is the most wounded, on all sides of the truck. All the Panthers from the truck are dead too, but some of their friends are now movin off the roofs an' onto the street. "Get lost," they say, wavin their guns. They start to pick off the jewelry an' the fancy clothes from the bodies.

"Come on," I say. We go round the corner. Crystal an' Tommy don't say a word, an' Willie's cryin an' holdin on to me.

"Keisha," he moan. An' then Crystal's holdin me too, an' then Tommy, an' we all cryin' there together.

"Shit," say someone. I look up an' it a girl a little older than me standin near us against the wall.

"What's up?" I say.

"Nothin much." She spit in the dirt. "I jus' needed some medicine. Now the Hoodlums gonna sell it for three times the price, I guarantee it. You know what my father gonna say?"

"You sick?"

"No, my father be—for maybe four, five years. My sister say it heartbreak; the doctors say it somethin else. But the clinic, you know, they give him only a little medicine. So he want me to buy more. It help a little. You know, with the pain."

Her arm is bleedin. "You get hit?"

"Naw. That jus' my implant. I don't know—maybe it got put in wrong. I got it cuz my father get that little bit of medicine, you know, from the government. How bout you?"

"I too young. But one day they gonna make me get it cuz my mama on welfare."

"Well, I guess it's a good thing. I can't do what my mother done."

"You got a lotta brothers an' sisters?"

"Yeah."

She point at Willie. "How old he?"

"Three."

"His mama have an implant?"

"Yeah," I say.

"I don't see many little kids," she say.

"His mama only got on welfare a couple years ago." Her arm still bleedin. "It okay?"

"It hurt like hell," she say.

"You live over here?"

"Yeah."

"Oh. I live on the other side."

"Oh. Well. My father don't like me bein out too long."

"Yeah," I say. An' she go off, holdin her arm.

"Well," I say to 'em. "Let's go home too." It not a good idea to keep lookin. It too hot, too much trouble out here. All the streets empty, 'cept for the trash. I guess everyone knows to be inside. 'Cept us. We start walkin. We so far from our buildin.

We pass by Grandma's, an' I got a good idea. I knock on the door, an' she open it. "Come on in," she say. "How nice to see you all." She put Willie in a chair, an' Tommy an' Crystal on her bed. She pick Clio up from the bed, an' put her in her lap. "Get 'em some juice, Keisha," she say. I get 'em some juice from the fridge.

"You want some, Grandma?"

"No thank you, Keisha," she say.

When I come back with a tray, Willie already asleep. Tommy an' Crystal sit up when they see me with the juice. I sit down on the floor, near Willie.

"Keisha," say Grandma. "Why on earth were you outside with my grandchildren?"

"We was lookin for Darryl."

"Keisha, you better listen to me carefully. You endangered these children for Darryl? There are three of 'em. They can't take care of themselves. Yet you take 'em outside to find one big drugged-up boy?"

I don't say nothin.

"Well?"

"Tommy's eight," I say.

"And Crystal's six an' Willie's three. You got somethin more to say for yourself?"

I don't say nothin.

"Go get me the switch," she say.

I go get the switch from behind the kitchen door. I don't look up from the floor, an' my face be all hot an' burnin. I know Tommy an' Crystal is watchin.

"Stand right here," she say. I turn an' face away from her. She gets me once, twice, three times cross the legs, an' then I run an' sit in the bathroom, cryin an' tryin not to cry. Then when I done, I come out.

"Put the switch away," she say.

"Yes'm."

When I come back, she say, "I hope that will be a lesson to you. If you're put in charge of my grandchildren, no matter how old they are, you keep 'em safe. That's the most important thing. An' if you can't do that, then you don't deserve to take care of 'em. Do I need to tell Jolene about this, or shall I assume that you will mend your ways?"

"I mend my ways, Grandma."

"Okay. I want you to go straight home with 'em, as fast as you can. These little children shouldn't be out on the streets." I pick up Willie, an' he don't wake up.

"An' Keisha," say Grandma. "How come you didn't stay with me last night?"

"I was hopin for Mama to come home."

"I'm findin you to be a very disobedient child, Keisha. Be careful that you don't grow up like your mama. I want you here tonight. You take those kids home, give 'em to Jolene, an' come right back. You hear?"

"Yes'm," I say.

"Good. Bye-bye, Tommy an' Crystal. Come again sometime."

"Tommy, Crystal, hol' hands," I say.

I ain't on the lookout for danger, cuz it so difficult to carry Willie. He so big, he keep slippin outta my hands, an' he wake up an' start cryin, so I put him on the sidewalk, but he keep cryin an' reachin for me, so I pick him up an' carry him.

"Hungry," he say.

"Your mama be home soon," I say.

"I hungry too," say Crystal.

We walk some more an' then Tommy say, "When I grow up, I'm gonna get drugged, right? Jus' like Darryl."

"We gonna find Darryl," I say.

"Why did Darryl get drugged?" Tommy ask me.

"The school give all the boys a test to see if they gonna be violent," I say. I surprised to find myself cryin. "They only test girls if they fight. An' Darryl have dark skin." Jus' like Tommy.

It still quiet out. I mean, some people, they's out, but not many. But we safe. We don't cause nobody no harm, we jus' mind our own business, an' we'll be okay. Unless we get caught in a cross-fire. So I don't understand bout Darryl. I'm gonna have to spend some time lookin in that other area. Gotta go tomorrow afternoon. Four days since he gone. He better show up soon, before he get himself killed.

We get to our buildin. Ain't nobody round. I can't get Willie up the stairs. I can't push nobody else up neither, cuz he in my arms. Crystal start cryin, an' she jus' stop on a landin, an' she sit down.

"You better get offa your butt, Crystal," I say in the dark.

"Aaaaaah," she whine. "I tired."

"You won't get no food if you stay there."

I stand there a few more minutes, an' then she start goin up the steps again. They all tired. I hope Jolene come soon cuz I gotta go back to Grandma's.

• • •

Jolene ain't here yet. It eleven at night. There ain't no food. The kids cryin an' cryin no matter what I does, an' they can't fall asleep. "Mama. Mama," Willie's cryin. They all lyin on the sofa, an' I on my cot, but I sure can't get to sleep with this noise.

"Shut up!" I yell at 'em. "Go to sleep!"

Even Tommy's moanin.

I walk over to the sofa. "Y'all makin too much noise," I say. I see their faces in the light from the streets an' the searchlights. They all lookin at me. "Shut your eyes," I say.

"I hungry," say Crystal.

"Me too," I say.

"Bathroom," say Willie.

"So go," I say.

He get up, but before he get to the bathroom, he start to pee, an' the pee's runnin down his legs an' onto the floor. "Keisha!" he say.

"Big boy like you . . ." I say. "Take 'em off. Yeah. Your underwear. You gonna sleep with jus' your shirt tonight."

He take 'em off, an' I take him to the bathroom an' wipe him off. "Go back to bed," I say. He don't move. "Go back to bed!" I yell. "Now!" He go to the sofa an' he lie down.

I wash off his underwear an' then I wipe up the pee on the floor.

Then I go lie down again. "Keisha," say Willie. "My underpants?"

"They wet," I say. "You can't wear 'em. Tomorrow."

"Cold," he say.

I get up. I pick him up an' take him to Mama's room. I put him down on the bed, an' then I shut the door an' lock it. I so angry, an' then I'm glad. When he realize what's happenin, he rush for the door, an' he bang on it an' scream an' scream. I go lie down. Tommy an' Crystal sittin up, lookin at me, but I don't say nothin. I's tired of 'em all. Willie stop screamin after a while, an' then everything's quiet.

•••

In the middle of the night, I hear the front door shut.
"Who there?" I say.
"Keisha?"
"Mama!" I say. I sit up. I so happy. She come over an' touch my face.
"How's it goin, Keisha?"
"You alive."
"Yeah, I's alive."
"Mama?" say Tommy all sleepy.
"Who else in here?" ask Mama.
"Tommy, Crystal, Willie. Jolene never come."
"I'm gonna get her," say Mama. "She jus' livin it up at your expense." Mama leave.

•••

I wake up when they come back.
"Where Willie?" ask Jolene.
I get up an' go to the door of Mama's room, an' unlock it so no one know. I pick up Willie, an' come back out. Tommy an' Crystal standin, their eyes closed, their clothes all a mess, an' Jolene's holdin 'em by the hands.
"Hey, Keisha, carry Willie down for me, will ya?" she say. I nod. I go get Willie's wet underpants an' we walk down the stairs. When we get to Jolene's apartment, there a lot of people in there, but I so sleepy I don't pay 'em no mind. There a lot of smoke in the room. I jus' follow Jolene to the other room.

"Put him on that cot," she say. So I do that, an' I's careful so he don't wake up. Jolene's puttin Tommy an' Crystal down, but their eyes, they shut before they even lie down.

"They ain't had no supper," I say. "An' Willie wet his pants." I give her the wet clothes.

"Thank you, Keisha," she say. "Here's your dollar."

I take it an' walk out, past all those people. Then I go up the stairs an' to my apartment. Mama's in her room, with the light on.

"'Night, Mama," I say, gettin on my cot, an' pullin up the blanket.

"'Night, Keisha," she say.

• • •

In the mornin, Mama's already up, an' she dressed. She got her green jacket on. "Hey, Mama," I say, an' I go to the bathroom to brush my teeth an' wash my face. Then I dress in some clean clothes, an' then I go to the kitchen to talk to Mama, cuz I 'member bout Darryl.

"You didn't find Darryl, did you?"

"He got kidnapped," she say, "by another gang."

"Why? What'd he do to 'em?"

"I don't know."

"I mean, he always respectful. Jus' slow."

"Yup," she say. "But that ain't gonna happen again. It ain't gonna happen to you, cuz I got protection now. I got friens."

I almost tell her that I seen her an' her friends in action, but then I 'member what Grandma done to me, an' Mama might do worse. She ain't drunk now, though.

"What about the other gangs, Mama? They gonna try to kill you."

"Like I say, I's protected. Look." She go to her room, an' take out three guns. One's tiny. "That one fit in my jacket. I can whip it out. No one else know. They never do." The other two, they big. She don't talk about 'em. They for killin lots of people at a time, I know. "So you be safe," she say.

"Goin shoppin today," she say. "Anythin you want?"

"We rich, Mama?"

"We gonna be, I promise. I gonna take you outta here. We go live someplace nice, with trees an' grass, maybe even a stream in back. Big, big TV."

"Mama, you crazy," I say, giggling.

"You'll see," she say. "Now get goin. Don't be late for school. Last breakfast you'll eat there, I promise."

"You gonna be here tonight?" I ask.

"I don't know, honey. I gonna try."

It strange the way Mama so happy, I think as I go downstairs. Never seen her this way before. Like she a different person. Like somethin happen to her. The guns change her, an' the new clothes, an' the money. Problem is, she happy, but I jus' know she gonna die. I's happy she's happy, but I's sad cuz I know I won't see her long. Can't fool myself no more.

Then I hear someone callin my name. I look round an' it Lydia, runnin up to me.

"Keisha!" she say. "I figured out what happen to your brother."

"You ask Robert?"

"I *did* ask him yesterday, like I said. An' like I said, he wouldn't tell me. Keisha, you know what I think Darryl did?"

"What?"

"You know that secret passage to the outside?"

"You tol' me bout it."

"I think he take it, an' he now outside."

"Why you think that?"

"Because it make sense!" she say. "I mean, we stuck in prison here, you know, with the walls—an' Darryl, he jus' decide to escape to freedom." She see that I don't believe her, cuz she say, "Keisha, you know what it like out there? People walk round with jewelry an' nice clothes, an' there's forests an' trees an' lakes an' grass. An' there be *things* out there—the food good an' tasty, an' it ain't rotten, an' the streets paved, with no holes an' no trash. I mean, they got everythin out there! So I think Darryl decide he tired of this kind of life an' he jus' leave. He watch a lot of TV, right? Well, that's what it's like out there. An' he prob'ly out there right now, livin it up. That's where I think he go."

"You think he went out the secret passage?"

"Yeah. See, he captured by the Panthers. That's why Robert won't tell me nothin. But he break off his chains an' run an' run an' run through the secret passage into freedom!"

"Lydia, he drugged!"

"I think they take it off," she whisper. "I think they find a way."

"Why you think that?"

"That's why they won't talk about it. See? I think they kidnappin drugged people so they can test how to take it off."

"So he outside now, you think?"

"Yeah! You ain't found him nowhere else, have you?"

"No. I been watchin the streets every afternoon. Where you think he be?"

"Well, where would you go if you went outside?"

"I gonna go," I say. "I gonna find him."

"An' bring him back?"

"I dunno. I jus' wanna see him again."

"Don't go," say Lydia. "He prob'ly gonna send you a postcard from . . . from Italy! How you gonna get out, anyway?"

"I don't know. I ain't got me no pass."

"You want me to see if Robert got one? You know, they won't let no men through, so it ain't no use to him."

"Yeah," I say.

"You really gonna go?" she say.

"Yeah," I say.

"We friends now?" she ask.

•••

When I come out the school gate, Mama standin there on the sidewalk in her green jacket. "Mama," I say. "Whatcha doin here?"

"I gonna take care of you now," she say.

"Hey," say an old woman walkin to us. "Ms. Adrienne, you got any asthma medicine?"

"Yeah," say my Mama.

"Aspirin?"

"Yeah. Lots of that."

The old woman smile. "Can't get none of it at that clinic," she say. "They run out first day of the month."

"Yeah," say Mama. "That's why we do what we do. We better than the government. Oh, her name Francine. She at the corner of Duke an' 30th."

"Thank you," say the woman.

It take us an hour to get home, cuz so many people stop Mama, callin her Ms. Adrienne or Sister Adrienne, an' sayin "Thank you" an' talking bout how wonderful it is to get medicine or food. It nice to be walkin with a famous person, but it also make me sick.

"Mama, why they ain't thankin the Panthers?"

"Well," she say, "the Panthers steal it from the Zulus. They the ones that took the truck first."

"Mama," I say, "why you keep takin from one another?"

"That jus' the way it is, honey."

"Somebody gonna steal the food from you?"

"Don't you worry. It well protected," she say. "It ain't public knowledge, neither."

But she lyin to herself. She gonna be lyin on the street soon, gettin her clothes picked off.

"We gonna be livin high soon," say Mama. "Gonna buy me a car."

"Where?"

"From outside," say Mama. "I got myself a pass. Gonna go get me a nice bright-red, shiny car. Then I gonna buy some people to guard it."

"You goin tonight?"

"Nah, some other time. Tonight's business."

•••

When Mama leaves, I look for the pass. It right in the top drawer of her dresser. Then I go to the kitchen. I know I'm gonna be hungry later, but I don't wanna take any of the food Mama brought. I don't wanna have nothin to do with her death when it happen. We went out to eat, too, at the McDonald's at the Center, an' I had to eat that, cuz Mama so happy an' proud. She never take me out before. She so pleased. I don't want to see her die, not when she so happy. When she crazy, I can take it better. Not now. Uh-uh.

I don't know what to take outside. I don't know what it be like out there. I ain't never seen it, 'cept for the high buildings that I can see past the wall, with their shiny glass windows sparklin in the sun. That's what I know. I don't know what the people is like.

I look at the pass. It say Latreece Hylton on it, an' it got her picture. Looks nice. 'Cept she's 35, an' I don't look 35. The other problem is she can only go out at 5 a.m. Monday to Friday, an' she gotta return by 8 p.m. at night. It now 8 p.m. I gotta hope that they don't check good.

There be only one entrance through the wall, a big tall gate, an' it got two towers either side. I gotta walk a long way to get there. It only open once in a while, an' it not time yet. There benches there, though, an' I sit down. I look at the pass again. It say Latreece work at Mr. an' Mrs. Fields, an' it say their phone number. I wonder what she do for 'em, an' how far she gotta go to get there.

Two women old as Grandma walk up an' sit down on the next bench. They both carry huge bags. One wearin a dress, an' the other wearin jeans.

"Back to work again, Shirley."

"Ain't it a shame, Jermaine."

"It don't even keep my head above water."

"Don't I know it."

"Work all night, cleanin up someone's garbage, come home to clean up my own."

"Uh-huh."

They silent for a little time.

"Hey, Jermaine," say Shirley. "You think they tryin to kill us? The women got the implants—no more babies. Not enough police to protect us when those kids start fightin, but lots of police outside. Not enough medicine. Bad food. They don't pick up the garbage, so there's disease. Liquor stores. They give the men drugs so they helpless.

"But they give us school. They give us welfare, classes at the Center, social workers. I jus' can't figure out what they tryin to do. I wish they'd make up their minds one way or the other."

"Yup," say Jermaine. "Ain't it the truth."

"You know what I think? I think they tryin to fool themselves. They spendin a lot of money jus' to fool themselves that they good. But they don't fool me!"

"You said it," say Jermaine.

They silent again.

"'Scuse me," I say. "They check the passes good?"

"Oh," say Shirley. "You been listenin in all this time, ain't you? Invisible at night, invisible by day too! Ain't that the way it is!" They laugh an' laugh, but I don't see what so funny.

"Huh, huh, huh," say Jermaine. "What'd you ask, honey?"

"They check the passes good?"

"You wanna go outside?" ask Shirley.

"Yeah."

"No kids allowed out there. Not unless you got a job. Which kids don't. How come you got a pass there, anyhow?"

"From my mama."

"Your mama's pass?"

"Yup."

Illustrated by Eric Williams

"No, honey, they won't let you through. How come you goin out there, anyhow?"

I don't say nothin.

"I bet she's tryin to visit her brother or father in prison," say Jermaine to Shirley. "One of those that ain't affected by the drug."

"That what you tryin to do?" ask Shirley.

I nod.

"Ain't it a shame. Well, honey, he don't need you. What you gonna do for him in prison? You be concerned bout yourself; that's the best thing you can do for anybody. Your daddy's gotta work himself out."

"There ain't no way to get out?"

"Not for you, honey."

I hear somethin grindin, an' Shirley an' Jermaine stand up. "Keep well," say Jermaine.

"Take care of yourself," say Shirley.

"Yeah," I say.

I watch 'em go toward the gate. Two men with rifles come out an' check their passes. Then they open the gate, an' let 'em out. I try an' look through the gate, but I don't get a good look at the outside. I don't see what it like.

Bye-bye, Darryl. I hope you fly far.

ONLY HALF THE EQUATION

Written by
Ed Gorman

About the Author

Ed Gorman has been called "The poet of dark suspense" by The Bloomsbury Review *and "One of today's most original crime writers" by* The San Diego Union. *Gorman has a screenplay in the new* Screamplays *collection from Del Rey and his science fiction novel,* Zone Soldiers, *recently appeared from DAW under his Daniel Ransom pen name.*

A few years ago, I taught a writing class at a large midwestern university. There were eighteen students, and not a dud in the bunch. They'd come to learn.

The few first days in this week-long class, we talked about writing, everything from how one starts a story to how one finishes. I like to teach by example. I gave them pages and pages of xeroxed openings and closings, everybody from Charles Dickens to Joe Haldeman to Stephen King.

The third day I asked them about reading. They'd already told me how they set aside time for writing every day. But when I asked them about reading—well, most of them said that they read when they could but between jobs, families and social lives, they could barely make time for writing, let alone reading. One student said that he "just didn't have time for the pleasure of reading." I told them that I felt reading wasn't a pleasure but a necessity.

A digression, if you will: I was recently working on a piece on Elmore Leonard for *Mystery Scene*, the magazine that I own part of. "Dutch," as he prefers to be called, made a point in the course of our first conversation that I'll quote for the rest of my life: "To develop your own writing voice, you've got to read and write for at least ten years. You learn by imitating." Notice he said read *and* write. Equal halves of the writing equation.

Another excellent crime writer, Lawrence Block, has gone so far as to suggest that the beginning writer should write out the plot lines of the books he reads. No need for great detail; just a page or so. You do this enough, you begin to see how novels work, their ebb and flow, their twists and turns. Their craft.

I took Block's advice. Before I sold my first mystery novel *Rough Cut*, I read and outlined perhaps twenty mystery novels. I did the same thing a few years later when I decided to write two science fiction novels, sf being my first love as a teenager, and a field I was eager to return to.

Outlining these books showed me how chapters are constructed, how foreshadowing works, and how (in the words of the great playwright Henrik Ibsen) "when you introduce a gun in the first act, it must go off in the third."

I know that there are professional writers who don't read any fiction at all. They're afraid that they'll be overly influenced by the style of others. I don't criticize this, I simply don't understand it. While I don't believe that there are any rigid rules about writing—for most quotation rules "you cite," I can show you a dozen brilliant exceptions—I really don't understand how you can write without reading.

I get all kinds of ideas, and learn all kinds of craft points, from reading other writers. Hemingway once said that great writers don't borrow—they steal. And he wasn't kidding by much. While he wasn't advocating plagiarism, he was certainly advocating learning from others. I'm presently reading a great new novel by a bestselling author. The book is very much his own. Yet just last night, when I read fifty-some pages before falling asleep, I recognized, in various places, the influence of Theodore Sturgeon, John D. MacDonald, Stephen King and Joe Haldeman. Was this writer ripping them off? Not at all. But he'd learned things from them, and learned them well, and wisely used what he'd learned in his own novel.

I remember Robert Silverberg saying somewhere that he used to keep a Keith Laumer novel close by while he was writing. Laumer was very good at the basics, Silverberg said, and so whenever he got stuck, he'd open up his Laumer and read a few pages or so. Laumer would help get him back on track. John D. MacDonald did his own version of that. When *he* got stuck, he'd open up somebody else's book and started typing *their* words. He couldn't resist changing a word or two—or phase or two—here and there and very quickly he'd be in the mood to write his own story again. In much the same spirit, F. Scott Fitzgerald once told his daughter that she would write only as well as she read, meaning, of course, you need good literary influences to produce good work.

So, just as you set aside writing time, set aside reading time. I'd try to read at least one novel and a few short stories a week. And don't be afraid to imitate. That's how you'll learn. Read writers you admire. They'll be the best teachers you'll ever have.

WINGS

Written by
Alan Smale

Illustrated by
Arthur Roberg

About the Author

Alan Smale is from Bowie, Maryland, by way of an English childhood and an Oxford education. He's a mild-mannered NASA astrophysicist by day, but sings bass by night with an up-and-coming a cappella group, "The Chromatics." He also performs in community theater and at Renaissance festivals, which leaves only the early morning hours for writing.

Alan has recently sold stories to A Wizard's Dozen, A Nightmare's Dozen, Marion Zimmer Bradley's Fantasy Magazine *and* Terminal Fright, *among others. He is also currently marketing one novel while writing his next.*

About the Illustrator

Arthur Roberg was born and raised in Salt Lake City, Utah, where he developed an interest in many arts—fine art, sculpture, costume-making, animation and photography.

He's particularly interested in the human form, in portraying not only motion, but also emotion and story.

He says that his art is a passion—as other artists have called it, a "blessed curse"—which he would not surrender for anything in the world.

He has had a few formal classes in art. Primarily he has studied in the Academy of Hard Knocks and his art serves as his diploma.

Beth found the first pair of wings as she tidied up the living room for Jack's visit. Fine as gauze, veined with white, they rested on the gray carpet beneath the ficus plant in her bay window.

She picked them up and arranged them on her palm, like two halves of a tiny stretched-out heart. The gentle curve of the outer wingtips contrasted with the torn, ragged lines of their innermost edges.

Cockroaches, grasshoppers, moths—no insect she knew matched the thumb-sized wings she held.

Until now her house had stayed insect-free. In the springtime mice had stormed her basement, burrowing into the bag of grass seed in the box room and leaving little mouse turds behind them, until General Jack brought in his arsenal of infernal machines and drew a line in the sawdust—springloaded wire blades, little plastic tunnels to nowhere with one-way doors, violet poison bottles. The mouse menace was quickly routed.

The wings worried her. It might be time to bring in the big guns again.

Beth pulled herself together. It was four-thirty. Jack would expect her and the house to be spotless and dinner to be on the table at six. She had no time to fuss over bugs. The tiny wings crackled as she closed her hand and took her dustcloth to the window ledges.

Illustrated by Arthur Roberg

Jack was punctual and hearty. "How's my little girl?" His arms wrapped her, and her feet briefly left the carpet. Clean wool and Old Spice mingled in her nostrils as he kissed her cheek.

"I'm fine, very well," she gasped, and reached around him to push the front door closed. Thickening around the middle, with crow's feet around her eyes and more chin that she felt she really needed, Beth would have died if the neighbors heard her answering to diminutives.

"Good, great, so am I." As he released her, his gaze roamed over the twin glass coffee tables and black picture frames, looking for dust. The house seemed to pass muster, for his next words were, "Except that I'm hungry enough to eat a horse."

"I'm afraid there was a run on horse. I stuck my neck out and went for ostrich," said Beth, and led the way to a chicken dinner.

With Jack in it, her house seemed smaller, more shabby. He held up his fork to the light and cleaned it with his napkin. He said, "Patrick fell off the roof today."

The breath thickened in her throat. Jack spent his workdays out of doors, putting insulation, roof tiles and plastic siding on new townhouses. She'd been to see him at work exactly once, and at the sight of him strolling around on the sloping roof three stories up, she'd suffered an attack of vertigo so profound that she had been sick to her stomach. Just thinking about Jack daring gravity was enough to banish hunger. She embraced his career as part of her weight-loss program even as she blanked out the recurring image of him tumbling through space.

"What happened?"

Jack shrugged. "I don't know. He was fixing chimney fittings, I think. I was on a ladder with a nailgun by the middle floor. I heard a bump-bump noise, and then he passed me going down, with the skylight in his hands. They'll probably take the skylight out of his pay."

How should she react? Should she show her distress, or match his toughness with wisecracks about brains dashed on paving stones? She risked his disappointment either way. And why would he tell her this, anyway, knowing how she worried for him?

"Did he die?"

"He was still alive when the ambulance came. Guess we'll find out for sure tomorrow. This is good chicken."

At least Jack pulled out his fear and confronted it in the cold light of day. So many of Beth's fears could not be named; sly, darting creatures that pricked her without revealing their true natures.

Perhaps he was saying, *Patrick was hurt, not me. I wouldn't be that careless.*

She ruffled his hair. "That'll never happen to you, right?"

"Right. I've got the luck of the Irish."

"Didn't help Patrick much, did it?"

He snorted. "Patrick is Korean. His real name is Pa Moo Phun, or something like that."

Gravity was selective, then.

"I found wings today," she said, needing to change the subject. "I may have bugs in the house."

So Jack quizzed her about the wings—what shape? What size?—but she found that the details eluded her. They, too, had slid from easy view.

After dinner he carried the plates into the kitchen for her. They sat on the sofa to watch the news, and when it was over his hand moved on her thigh. Beth still felt full from dinner and guilty from eating so much of it when the Korean builder and his skylight were shattered and ruined, but she smiled and took him upstairs.

She'd made the bed and tidied her vanity, but her open closet door revealed a basket half-full of dirty laundry. She felt him wince, and slid the door shut before turning to unbuckle his belt. He was a bear of a man and quick; he pushed her blouse off her shoulders and the top of his head bobbed as he kissed her breasts.

His need made him clumsy, and Beth unzipped her skirt before he could rip it. She sat back on the bed and kissed his tight stomach muscles, smelling the clean musk of him, hoping for time to get in the mood, but tonight Jack would accept no delay.

His urgency overwhelmed her. Beth tried to close her legs a little, to keep him back, but his strength allowed her no quarter and she gasped and turned her head aside to breathe, and strained against him, and thought of his largeness and her full stomach and finally of Daniel Day-Lewis, until she came almost in self-defense and felt his hardness break inside her.

Jack rolled away. "Was it good?"

"Yes," she said, because it was the only answer that would do, and because no man before Jack had ever waited for her to finish, and that *was* good of him.

"Mmmm," said Jack. "Yeah, dessert was good today, little girl," and smiled and ruffled her hair, and went to the bathroom, and she heard the shower start up.

With the gentle hiss of falling water in her ears, Beth pulled the sheets around her neck and closed her eyes.

• • •

After ten minutes the water stopped, and Jack came in to sit on the side of the bed, wrapped in white towels, with his hair sticking up. As usual, he looked a little perturbed to find her still lying there.

"I wanted to talk tonight," he said. "About us."

He's going to leave me, she thought. I'm overweight and I don't wash often enough for him and he's had enough of me.

He patted her butt under the sheets. "Don't look so worried. It's not so bad. I've been thinking that maybe we should move in together. Make all this more official. Like regular folks."

She felt joy and fear, hot and cold. "I don't know. . . . Could you stand to see me every day?"

"Well, we'd have to get a few things straight, discuss one or two things. But I'd be good to you, Beth, you know I would. I'd do anything for you."

"I know you would."

"So what do you think?"

The walls and carpets and furniture watched her. The house was silent, awaiting her answer. A disquiet draped itself about her shoulders.

"You said you'd never live in a townhouse, because you now how crappily they're made."

He laughed. "For you, I think I'd put up with it."

"Let me think about it. Can I think about it, Jack? For a few days? It's a big step, and you know I've never lived with anyone before."

"Well, neither have I," said Jack. "But that's fine."

He looked so hurt that she rushed in with, "Will you stay tonight? You've never stayed a whole night. Maybe we should practice?" She smiled at him, trying to be winsome, to make up for the other stuff she'd said.

Jack fingered the sheets absently. It was nearly a week since she'd changed them. "Got to be up early tomorrow. I shouldn't really. I'll be tired as it is."

Her gut clenched as she saw him falling through space, arms outstretched. "Of course. I mustn't be selfish. You must get your sleep."

He dressed in the clean clothes he had brought, and folded the dirty ones neatly to be washed.

"Well, think about it. I'll see you tomorrow."

Then he left. The house grew and became empty, and yet not empty.

Beth tried to picture Jack's face, calm in sleep, lying on the pillow next to hers, but the image would not come.

She slept.

•••

Tiny wings littered the utility room floor.

Beth dropped Jack's clothes and the bedsheets outside, and knelt to look. Twenty, perhaps thirty pairs of wings lay strewn between the door and the washer. She collected a handful.

Some felt soft as tissue paper, others dry and brittle, with soap bubble colors dancing across their surface in the light of the unshaded sixty-watt bulb. They came in a range of sizes from pinkie-fingernail to over two inches long. Although they were scattered, she could easily have paired up the wings according to their sizes and colors.

The dryer door stood open, and fluff from the lint trap hung down, gobs of spittle from the mouth of a drunk. She saw marks where the bugs had torn into it.

This was getting serious.

She wasn't alone. Something was already living with her. Creepy-crawlies were shedding their wings, maybe growing through their life cycle. Building a nest?

The pressure of eyes on the back of her head made her look up. *Something* whizzed past her head in a blur. She caught a flash of red and heard, quite distinctly, the thrumming of wings.

And a high-pitched, bell-like laugh.

• • •

Beth decided not to tell Jack about the fairies.

On Wednesdays she worked from noon till eight at the Sears in the mall, so Jack usually got his dinner at Subway and came around at nine, to give her time to shower and change.

She walked into her house at eight-fifteen, and there he stood in the kitchen, up to his arms in froth, washing dishes that were already clean. All the cupboards lay open, revealing cans neatly arranged and saucepans ranked in order of size. A pile of fluff waited on a newspaper so Jack could show her the magnitude of her failure. The washing machine clanked away in the utility room.

"How did you get in?"

He had the grace to look slyly apprehensive at her tone. "I borrowed your spare key last night. Everybody keeps their spares in the cutlery drawer or the spice cupboard. I'll give it back if you want, but I was rather hoping you'd let me keep it." Out came the smile. "I've been putting things in order. I wanted to show you how serious I was about helping out around the house, if I move in. I thought you'd be pleased."

Fairy wings stuck out of the fluff pile. She picked them out, one by one, and arranged them on the newsprint.

"I saw those. You were right about the bugs. I'll inspect the whole place at the weekend, and I'll buy some Raid tomorrow. How are the mice doing?"

"The mice are fine. You can't stay, Jack."

"What?"

The house was so small tonight she felt almost claustrophobic. Nothing was her own anymore. "You can't clean the house. And I'd like the key back, please. What I'm trying to say is that I like my house the way it is." At the expression on his face, she hurried to say, "It's not because of you. Don't be angry. It's just because of me."

Jack blew out a breath and sat down at the kitchen table, watching her fidget with the fairy wings. She knew she was a puzzle to him, and he was eager to solve her.

He began to talk quietly. "Let's put our cards on the table, okay? I know I've got my flaws. I'm a bit pushy, a bit keen, I know that. People have said that I notice dirt and mess more than average, so don't think I haven't heard about it." She opened her mouth, but he held up a hand. "There's more, I'm sure. But I really care about you, Beth, really I do, and I want to make this work. I'm willing to put in the effort. Make compromises. You see?"

"You're a good man, Jack. I know it, but . . ."

"But?"

"You make me feel . . . *dirty*. How can you bear it?"

He thought about that a little longer than necessary, in her opinion, but when it came, his answer was worth waiting for. He stood and put his arms around her. "Because it's you that's the normal one and me who's strange, I guess."

It was the most beautiful thing he'd ever said to her.

He grinned at the tear in the corner of her eye. "Isn't every day a guy volunteers to keep your house clean for you. Most women'd jump at the offer. So, how about it?"

"You said you'd give me a few days, Jack. I don't know if—"

Her feet left the floor and before she knew it he cradled her in his arms like a baby, and began walking upstairs. She feared for his spine. "I really like you, Beth. We've known each other five or six months now. It isn't like we're rushing into anything."

They arrived in the bedroom, and still she couldn't think of anything to say. He still held her in his arms. She felt trapped, pinned like a butterfly before his loving stare. She briefly considered honesty, but shrank from it. There was only one way to buy time.

"Make love to me, Jack."

He put her on the bed and grinned as he slid off his jeans. Sex was something he knew he was good at. With sex, she might be persuaded.

"Thought you'd never ask. I feel hungry like the wolf tonight." He pushed her skirt up over her hips and pulled at her panties. With a faint ticking sound, the stitching gave away.

He often chose the wolf position when he wanted to assert himself. It was uncomfortable for her, but she owed it to him because of her indecision. She crawled up the bed on her forearms and knees, vulnerable and alone with her ass in the air. She couldn't see his face, that was the first bad thing about being bitch to his wolf, and the second thing was the penetration; as he slid between her legs to hilt himself against her buttocks, he buried himself deeper inside her than in any other position.

Tonight he got especially rough, wedding his body to hers by main force. Thrust after thrust made her breasts quiver and her forearms slide up the bed until she was pressed against the wall, being stabbed to her core as he grunted behind her, unseen.

Beth knew that he was holding back as he always did, trying to be a good lover in his way, and that he would not finish until she came.

And in this discomfort, an orgasm seemed unthinkable. There was no way. She would have to fake, and faking made her feel worse than dirty. Tears began to leak from her eyes.

Suddenly she felt less alone. With a dazed certainty she knew they were being watched; the house itself watched them, eyes on her body and his, and she responded to that involvement, as if her figure were perfect and she were beautiful and twenty. Fifty, a thousand tiny, flawless winged men and women were enjoying her with their eyes, and a thrill skittered along her aching back to her womb and beyond. The feeling took root, beating on her inner softness until it bloomed into red flowers of heat and she pounded the wall and cried, and Jack spurted inside her and became soft and plopped out, and she collapsed onto the pillows.

"Thank you," she said to the fairies. "Thank you."

"You're welcome. Whoo-ee!" said Jack, and howled cheerfully on his way to the shower.

•••

Beth hugged her knees to her chest, seeing only the white wall. Her fairies were not chained to the earth by gravity, but floated in the air like dust motes. They were hers, and to them she was glorious.

The torrent of shower water stopped. Soon, Jack would return.

She stood and walked gingerly into the guest bathroom. Before she could bathe, she had to clean fairy wings away from around the plug hole. The hanging end of the toilet paper had been shredded by tiny hands.

She sat in the tub and turned on the water, full and hot.

•••

Beth was clean. The sheets were crisp. Jack stayed.

He fell asleep easily on his own side of the bed, and did not snore. His face looked calm in the dim brown light from the windows, resting there in her bed, and she realized that this was what she loved about him; his easiness and his calm.

The house creaked and relaxed into night. Homey noises.

She thought of her previous boyfriend, who had developed a fascination for her shoe closet and who had ultimately become impotent unless she wore boots in bed, and the boyfriend before that, who had arrived each night complete with a long list of compulsory TV viewing, during which he forbade her to talk. Compared to those two and the other losers she'd picked recently, Jack wasn't so bad. He didn't like dirt, but he never got mean about it. He was demanding in his way, but he was a man, after all.

But something about the thought of sharing her life with him drove away sleep. She slid from under the covers and pulled on a robe.

On the stairs, something buzzed her in the dark. She swung and missed.

She descended farther, and something small crunched beneath her bare foot.

At the limit of her hearing, she became aware of a faint crackling sound, like a gift being unwrapped at the end of a long tunnel. The living room clock ticked once. Time slowed around her. Moving became difficult as the air turned to molasses at her feet.

The blackness of her living room seethed with subliminal movement.

An insect lighted on the skin of her upper arm. The hairs rose, but by the time her other hand arrived to swat at it, the creature was long gone.

The clock ticked again.

The air buzzed.

Like a picture coming into focus, or a veil falling, she saw.

Faint lights in the dark. Little people studded against black velvet.

She saw two kinds. There were stocky forms three inches high, clad in skins of leather, with wings that folded down their backs. These had teeth that bulged out from their lower jaws to wrap the upper lip in dirty ivory, and red caps that they wore like badges of honor.

And there were pale, thin, green creatures, a little shorter, garbed in fresh leaves, with wings held high and wide, and translucent hair that barely covered their scalps. Their faces were pointed but not unpleasant, and she recognized the shape of their wings.

Her living room had become a slaughterhouse.

Four redcaps hauled on a flat length of ribbon stolen from Beth's sewing chest, dragging it across the floor toward their master. On the ribbon lay half a dozen green fairies, their wings pinned, their legs and arms bound tightly with black cotton.

Just ahead of them went a small phalanx of the savage soldiers, marching in pairs, with each pair of reds holding a green up between them, its gauzy wings stretched almost to tearing point. The prisoners' hands were bound behind their backs or held over their heads. Their feet were hobbled with little glass beads.

And at the head of the receiving line King Redcap, with a razor blade, cut through the tendons of a green fairy's wing. When the blade caught in the wound, he placed his boot against the fairy's stomach to tear the wing free from his body. Blood poured from the ragged holes in the green fairy's sides, and the leathery soldiers doused their caps in the blood and placed them, still dripping red, back on their heads.

The green fairy had swooned, mouth open, chin resting on his chest. They tore the second wing off him, and when they released him he tumbled to the floor in a heap.

Wherever she looked was butchery; green fairies pinned and immobile, flat against the tablecloth and carpet, lined up against the molding, lying in piles beside the sofa. Even the fairies who looked dead still glowed by their own faint internal luminescence. One had tiny wings like little stubs, just beginning to grow back. Beth could see that the scars from the last time had barely healed.

The soldiers hustled another green fairy forward to meet their king, and his blade flashed.

Then King Redcap noticed her. He threw the razor blade contemptuously to the floor, placed his hands on his hips, and stuck his jaw out. Wings unfurling, he jumped into the air, a hummingbird with bloody hands and a sneer.

The clock ticked. Beth's questing hand reached the light switch at last, and she flicked it on. The explosion of light dazzled her. The air buzzed with motion. A small body hit her in the face and spun away.

When she opened her screwed-up eyes, she saw . . . her living room, empty and normal. Sprinkled with a fine dusting of fairy wings.

• • •

Jack woke as she sat on the end of the bed. The reek of tannin from the cup of over-brewed tea in her hands spread to fill the dark corners and secret places in the room.

"You're dressed." Jack rubbed sleep from his eyes. "Christ Almighty, Beth, it's two in the morning. What's the matter?"

The tea burned, but could not cut through the smell of blood that clogged her throat. "You have to go."

"I thought we agreed—"

"*You* agreed, Jack. You never asked *me* at all. You know you didn't."

With the sheets tangled around his legs, and his hair pointing every way at once, she thought he looked like nothing so much as an adorable little boy.

That didn't help, not at all. She turned away, and a void opened between them. He must have felt it too, because the hand reaching out to touch her shoulder stopped in the air and retreated.

"You want me to leave? Right now?"

"Yes, please."

"I'll be tired at work tomorrow. Today."

He wouldn't fall. She knew that now. Strong, bloody protectors watched over him.

"Live with it," she said.

"I see." He rubbed his eyes again. "'Live with it.' Well, thanks a lot." He swung his legs off the bed.

"I'm sorry, Jack." It just came out.

He dressed, still shaking his head, while she watched his strong body being covered and hidden away under progressive layers of clothing. Doors closed in her life.

"I'm really sorry."

His shoes were lined up neatly by the dresser. He went to fetch them. "Forget it," he said. "It could have been good, Beth. I'd have made it work. You know I would. But let's just forget it."

Tears began to dribble down her cheeks. Damn, damn, damn.

He touched her. "You're trembling."

"Please, Jack. Just let me tremble, and go."

Fully awake now, his mind whirred and clicked behind his eyes. "I'll go. But first you have to tell me exactly why I have to go."

"You're taking me over, Jack. I have to stop you, or there'll be nothing of *me* left."

"That's bullshit. I respect you, Beth. You know I do. I'd do anything for you!"

He was raising his voice. He'd never raised his voice to her.

"Then do what I want you to do, and go. You hurt me in bed tonight, Jack. You always do. You enjoy it."

Beth couldn't believe she'd actually said that. But what else could she say? Your fairies are ripping the wings off my fairies, and if they keep it up, I won't have any left?

Jack's jaw dropped. "But you like it that way!"

He didn't know. He really didn't. Somehow that made it worse.

"Beth. It's very late. Can't we just—"

"Go home, Jack. Please."

He gave it up.

Beth was a rock as he kissed her on the forehead and walked to the door. He said, "When you change your mind, call me."

Then he went. She heard her spare key clank back into the cutlery drawer, and the soft click of the front door latch.

Jack was gone.

She listened carefully, but there was nothing else to hear.

●●●

The redcaps were leaving, she knew. Through the roof and up the flue and under the doors and out of the pipes. In the secret places of the house, the green fairies licked their wounds and waited for their wings to bud again.

She saw only one. As she sat at the kitchen table, dazed with tiredness, a single redcap flitted up the stairs from the basement and swooped low across the carpet, to disappear under the front door.

However much tea she drank, the heat never reached her fingers and toes.

"Are you here? I'm glad you're here," she said. Her fairies did not answer, of course, but Beth knew they heard her.

A floorboard cracked. A bird began to sing. The sun rose, casting its rays of pitiless orange past her and into the living room.

Beth waited until its warmth melted the ice on her skin.

Then she fetched the dustpan, and the vacuum, and went to clean the house.

THE GODS PERSPIRE

Written by
Ken Rand

Illustrated by
Viktoria Dunayeva

About the Author

In 1992, Ken Rand ended two-plus decades as a reporter in Utah and Wyoming. That's when he accepted an invitation to move from Wyoming—where he was a grumpy, overworked newspaper editor—to West Jordan, Utah, to remarry his ex-wife, ending a nineteen-year divorce.

That day he began writing science fiction as a career. He now writes much of the time, paying for stamp glue and pumpkin seed addictions with a part-time job shelving books at a library. He's written almost a hundred SF short stories, two hundred humor columns, two SF novels and a lot of nonfiction. Much of his work can be seen in the small press, and he's recently made sales to larger markets.

He's also a member of the Pilgrimage writers group, which now boasts seven of its ten members as Writers of The Future winners.

Ken has worked as a reporter, photographer, talk-show host and producer, editor, PR flack, furniture mover, temporary secretary and an announcer for sports events, daredevil shows, air shows, mudbogs and stock car races.

He grew up in the little town of Port Chicago, California, which no longer exists; the Navy bought it because it was in the way of their ammo depot. Twenty-nine years after his home town vanished, he's still angry at the Navy.

A hippie before he lost his hair, he lived in San Francisco in the 1960s, where he attended the first Be-In.

His writing (and living) philosophy can be summed in two words: Lighten up.

About the Illustrator

Viktoria Dunayeva was born in Kiev, Ukraine, in 1970. She attended the Republican School of Art for three years and graduated from the Ukrainian Academy of Art in 1996. Viktoria has been working as a drawing teacher at the Youth Center of Art since 1991.

A granite-jawed muscleman out of an old Russian propaganda poster stood across the counter from Jack. "Mister The Pipe," he said, "I have come to place a wager."

Who was this guy? Nobody never came to Jack "The Pipe" Lombardo unless they was regular guys. This guy sure as hell wasn't regular.

Course, enough came to Jack's Pipe Shoppe to just buy butts and papers and stuff that the IRS never paid him too much mind. It was the *other* customers, the ones who seemed to try to look over both shoulders at once when they slipped into the shop off the street real sudden, like they was playing hide-and-seek from cops or their bosses or wives, that The Pipe was dead set on doing right by. They was his meal ticket. They was the ones who called him "The Pipe." Most he knew personal, some was one-timers. They brought in regular white envelopes with all the necessary stuff in it—which horse, which team, whatever—and sometimes money if they was owing, slipped it across the counter at him, yakking about the weather, politics, women—but never sports, not even Superbowl or the World Series—and they got an envelope when they bought their newspaper or whatever, gave Jack a knowing smile and left. Some looked grim. Others, with fatter envelopes, left whistling.

It was an okay life. Course, the regular payoff to Big Augie was a pain in the butt, cause Augie would tack on what he called "special fees" whenever he knew Jack had had a pretty big day. So Jack never got to sock away much of a nest egg to move to Wyoming like he'd wanted for the past—geez, ten years now? But Augie and his boys never gave Jack no trouble so long as he paid and the shop got along okay, so it was an okay life. It would do 'til Jack could go where the picture was taken, the one by his cash register, the one of the Teton Mountains reflected in a lake. Then, life would *really* be okay.

A couple of kids leafing through his comics looked over at the giant customer and muffled giggles.

"Hey, you kids," Jack yelled. "You bend the merchandise, you buy it, you got me?"

The kids tossed the comics on the floor, gave Jack the finger and left, laughing.

Jack looked back up at the guy in front of the counter. *Up.* Six-ten, maybe seven foot. The giant's barrel chest, shoulders—maybe four foot wide—and thigh-thick arms strained his suit fabric, a cheap off-the-rack Sears job. He had long yellow hair that looked like straw made up in two pigtails that hung over the front of each shoulder down to his lapels. Clean-shaven. The guy looked like some Norwegian skier just off the boat. He smelled a bit fishy.

Jack wisely refrained from laughing out loud. After all, the guy *was* big, and he didn't look nervous at all.

Maybe this is Augie's new runner. Naw. Spencer was doing okay. And Augie would have brought a new runner by, personal, to introduce, if he'd replaced Spencer. And Augie's runner wouldn't be laying no bets with The Pipe. Maybe Sabatini sends me his enforcer, still wants to bust into Augie's territory. The putz. Never learns.

Jack reached a casual hand under the counter. He touched the cold metal of the shotgun and released the safety. It was already aimed at the guy's gut.

"You got me wrong, buddy." Jack forced a smile. "I don't do no book."

"I am not here to purchase a book, Mister The Pipe," the big guy said. "I am here to place a wager."

The guy's voice was flat, his eyes steely, no expression. *Don't never play poker with this one.*

"Who you working for, bud? Sabatini send you? You ain't one of Big Augie's boys."

"I work for no one. I am not Bud. I know no Sabatini, nor one of Big Augie's boys. I am from Valhalla. I am Thor."

Suddenly, it hit Jack. Somebody was playing a joke on The Pipe. There was a theater right across the street, a ragtag outfit where any number of his cronies could buy themselves use of an actor for a couple of twenties. And the gym down the street where the pro wrestlers worked out. Some was more hard up for cash than others. This guy looked like a wrestler—a new guy, cause The Pipe knew them all, it was his business to know—and new in town, judging by the ridiculous new duds.

But no, Jack decided, looking at the hair. A wig. Too yellow, too long. Too fruity.

"Thor, huh? God of thunder and all that crap, huh?"

"Of thunder, it is so. But not of crap."

Jack laughed and reached up to grab one of the pigtails. He intended to whip it off the actor and toss it and him into the street. If he was an actor, he was likely a fag despite his size, and he'd squeal and run. Fun joke, though.

But the wig didn't come off. Instead, the big guy was pulled forward a few inches when Jack tugged on the hair, a surprised look on his face, the first change of expression Jack had seen on the guy. Then the guy straightened, Jack let go of the hair, and the guy's gunmetal eyes turned hard, like Jack had seen in boxers when they went berserk.

Jack took a step back, the shotgun forgotten. He could run pretty good, out the back door, into the alley—

"Mortals do not touch gods," the guy—Thor—said. "It is forbidden. The punishment—"

"Look, uh, Mister Thor. Pal. Buddy. It was a mistake. Honest. I saw this, uh, bug on your shoulder and I was trying to get it off. Wouldn't want it to bite you or anything like that, would I? Give The Pipe a bad reputation, if I let things like that happen to my customers. Augie'd be pissed. I don't know squat about this god business. I ain't read the rule books. It ain't like Thor is a Catholic god, you know? Jesus, maybe I ought to go to church more often—"

"Cease talking."

"Right, you bet. *Bet*. That's what you came here for, isn't—"

Thor slid an envelope across the counter.

"Great," Jack said extending a hand, "let's shake on—"

But Thor had already turned and walked out the door, ducking under the lintel.

Jack let out a sigh and was amazed he hadn't wet his pants. He sat on a stool behind the cash register and glanced at the picture of the mountains. *Someday. Someday.*

Then he opened the envelope, his hands shaking. Some nag named Thunder Hooves. To win, in the third, this afternoon. A twenty-to-one glue factory. Ten K. In cash.

"Jesus H."

He hung up the Out To Lunch sign on the door, locked up, and called Spencer, Augie's runner.

While Spencer was coming over, Jack called Augie, told him Spencer would be by with a package.

"How much?"

"Ten K."

"No friggin way."

"Friggin way."

Spencer was at the shop in a flash. A fresh black kid with no gang contacts. Didn't shoot, snort or smoke. Stayed away from the babes. Raising money for college. Smart kid.

He took the envelope, smiled and waved at Jack and left on his bike.

Jack watched him pedal across traffic, down the street, around the corner. Just another city bike courier, lost in the crowd. With ten grand.

Jesus H.

Big bets scared Jack cause they always drew Augie's attention, and even though he needed a big score to retire out West, he didn't need no attention from Augie. Last time he'd taken a big bet was back at Superbowl XXV. Some guy with a diamond on his pinky and a thousand-dollar hooker on each arm. Bet five grand. Said if he won, he'd be back. Jack smelled a fix, turned him to Augie direct.

Now, here was this, this— Naw. It had to be a gag. *Had* to be. Jack shrugged: Augie's business. He done right.

Jack put on his coat cause it'd started to get cloudy out, locked up the shop and walked across the street to the theater. The Egyptian, they called it. Old, rundown. Used to be a movie house. "Opening Soon: The Gods Aspire," the marquee said. Avant-garde, artsy-fartsy fairy stuff.

The front door was open. Inside, some guy was on a ladder on the stage, tinkering with the lights.

"'The Gods Perspire,' huh?" Jack said, loud.

The ladder-guy looked down, squinted into the dim house.

"'The Gods *As*pire,' yes." The guy started down the ladder. "Our new show. Opens the twentieth."

"The twentieth? But there's a title fight that night. Mountain Rivera and—"

But it was clear to Jack that the tall, skinny hippie-looking guy walking toward him down the narrow aisle didn't know from sports, didn't know nobody would come see his show when there was a heavyweight title on the line the same night.

"How may I help you?" The theater guy extended a slender hand. Jack could tell a lot about a guy by his handshake. It was a talent. The guy shook Jack's hand with delicate grace.

"Don't tell me," Jack said. "You were a dancer. A pretty good one, too, right?"

"Yes. My knees gave out. How did you—"

"A talent. Comes in handy in my business. I got the shop across the street—"

"Ah, yes, the tobacco store."

"Yeah, that's me. Anyway, I just had a customer stopped by, bought a paper, left his, uh, coat. Didn't get his name, but he looked like maybe he was an actor. I wondered if—"

"What'd he look like?"

Jack described the man. The theater guy shook his head.

"But I figured maybe with this new show you got—"

The theater guy laughed. "It's a work of experimental theater. The gods, you see, rise up and contend with each other for control of—"

"Yeah, this guy, I remember now, said his name was Thor."

"God of thunder."

"So he's here?"

"No. Actually, we don't use live actors in this show. Just lights, audio, props, screens, visual effects. That sort of thing. Experimental. The flies are computerized. Would you like to see?"

Jack waved the guy off and left. *Computerized flies? What the hell was he talking about?*

He glanced across the street at his shop before turning down the sidewalk toward the gym. Two punks were spray-painting gang stuff on the wall under his front window.

Damn city's going to hell. Where're the cops when you need them?

The gym was hot, the odor of honest sweat hung in the air. Dim, like the theater, only noisier. Guys grunting and panting. The rhythmic thump of fists on bags, running feet, jump ropes slapping floors, metal weights clanging.

Jack described the big guy to the manager, an old cronie.

"Not one of our people," the manager said.

"Lemme just have a looksee."

The manager shrugged. "Have at."

No dice. All the gym guys looked like they belonged. The big guy—okay, *Thor*—would've looked as out of place as—

Jack frowned in thought as he walked back to his shop, hands buried in his coat pockets, head down thinking hard. It had become cold, overcast.

—About as out of place as a Norse god in downtown—

Jack almost bumped into the man standing in front of his door. The guy was *big*.

"Let me guess," Jack said, "you must be Zeus, right?"

The big guy nodded. His massive, curly beard arched around a rosy-cheeked smile which threatened to burst into a booming laugh. Not as tall as Thor, but rounder. Dressed just as cheaply, though. Smelled garlickly.

"I wish to place a bet with Mister The Pipe," Zeus said.

"Look, buddy, would you keep your voice down? We're standing on the for-gods-sake *street*."

"This is the shop of Mister The Pipe, is it not?"

"Yeah, this is—"

"Are you acquainted with Mister The—"

"I *am* Mister The goddam—"

"Cease talking."

The bearded man extended a thick envelope toward Jack, who took it in numb, shaking hands. Zeus turned to walk away.

"Now just a minute," Jack yelled. People on the street turned to look, and looked quickly away, hurrying past. Zeus stopped and turned back to peer through beady eyes at Jack, a puzzled expression on his face.

"Zeus, you say?"

Zeus nodded.

"Yeah? Look, buddy, I know a little about Greek mythology. I'm a high-school graduate and I took me some college courses. And I figure no god is going to go around in the middle of the city in the middle of the day placing his own bets. I mean, you got Mercury, for chrissake. Isn't he your messenger or something? How come you don't get him to do your running for you? How come—"

Zeus laughed a gut-jiggling bellow, shook his shaggy head, turned and walked away.

Jack gritted his teeth. He opened his shop, locked it behind him and went into the back room to open the envelope.

A bet on a marathoner in a track meet in Oregon. Guy with a Greek name Jack couldn't pronounce. *Mercury, I'll bet. That's why Zeus was busting his britches laughing.*

Jack had forgotten about the meet. Not much action there.

But now—

Twenty grand. Cashier's check. On the Greek runner. Fifty to one.

"Jesus H."

He called Big Augie immediately and Augie sent one of his boys over. Not that he didn't trust Spencer, but this was *big*.

"Next time one of these friggin god fellows come by," Augie said, "you call me. Hear? Nobody bets like this. Unless they got the friggin fix on."

If Jack was lucky, there wouldn't be no gods coming back.

The nag won, and the Greek in Oregon. Both set records.

When Thor came by the shop to collect the next day, Jack immediately threw out a couple of straight customers, closed shop and phoned Augie.

"The one named Thor. He's here."

"I'm already on my way." Augie hung up. It was then that Jack noticed two of Augie's boys hanging out, real casual-like, across the street by the theater, shoulders hunched against the rain that had just started. Watching. Just in case.

Augie arrived in two minutes flat, another record.

"You have my money," Thor said as Augie walked into the back room of Jack's shop, flanked by two of his best boys. It wasn't a question.

"Sure, I got your money, wiseguy."

"I am not Wiseguy. I am Thor. God of thunder."

"Yeah, right. And I'm the friggin Duke of Windsor."

"Give me the money, The Friggin Duke of Windsor."

"I saw your nag run today. I don't know how you did it, but either the fix was on or my name is John friggin Wayne."

"I know of no fix on. I thought you were The Friggin Duke of—"

"Enough of this. My associate, Gino," Augie nodded to one of his boys, "will now proceed to teach you better than to friggin mess with Augie Costello. Gino?"

Gino took a step toward Thor—

—and turned into a fish.

"Jesus H." Jack smelled urine, but it wasn't his. He'd already gone to the bathroom, just in case.

Augie's jaw dropped as he looked at the fish flopping around on the floor and his other guy, Orville, made a noise in his throat like it was being cut.

"What the friggin hell have you done?" Augie squeaked.

"Your Associate Gino has just been taught better than to friggin mess with Thor, god of thunder."

"Turn him back, mister," Orville whimpered, eyes brimming with tears. "Please turn my buddy back."

"I got the money, Mister Thor, sir," Big Augie said, reaching into his coat pocket. "Will a cashier's check do, sir? Or would you prefer cash?"

Augie extended a cashier's check toward Thor. Thor took the check, looked at it, nodded, and Gino changed back from a fish into one of Big Augie's boys.

Nobody spoke as Thor turned to leave the back room and go out the front way.

But as he did so, the little bell over the front door chimed, announcing another customer. *But I locked the door.* Jack shot past Thor into the front room, followed by Thor, Augie and his two boys.

There stood Zeus.

"Mister The Pipe, I've come for my—"

Then Zeus saw Thor.

Outside, lightning flashed and thunderous peals shook the building as the two gods glared at each other.

"I don't think they like each other, boss," Orville said.

"What the friggin—"

But Augie's comment was drowned in cacophonous noise. Without their lips moving, Jack heard the gods yelling at each other in what sounded like several languages, none of them English. They stood six feet apart, facing each other, brows knit in anger. They didn't move, stiff as bird-shit-covered statues in the park, yet Jack's head ached from their guttural screams and barks.

He, Augie and the boys covered their ears. To no avail.

"Hey, gods, why don't you take it outside, for cris—"

A sudden silence left Jack's ears ringing. The two gods turned to him as if seeing him for the first time.

"Oh, shit," Jack said.

"Mister The Pipe," Thor said. "The Greek and I have reached an agreement to settle our differences. First, John Friggin Wayne will pay Zeus what is owed to him."

Augie took out a checkbook and began writing frantically. He handed the check to Zeus.

"It won't bounce, I swear," Augie said as Zeus eyed the check with a frown. Zeus nodded, put the check in his pocket and folded his beefy hands over his stomach.

Zeus nodded to Thor. "Continue."

"We now want you, Mister The Pipe, to hold our bets until we settle our differences."

"Yeah, sure," Jack shrugged, "but Augie here's got a nice big safe and a lot of muscle—"

"We trust you, Mister The Pipe," Thor said.

"That's why we placed our bets with you in the first place," Zeus said. "It may appear a coincidence that we both came to you, but in fact we both have shopped around."

"Independent of each other, of course," Thor said.

"We both require honesty in our gambling," Zeus said. "You are a crook, but you are an honest crook. The only such one we could find at present. Hence our both coming to you was not a coincidence."

"A coincidence that we were both on the Earthly plane to recreate at the same time—" Thor said.

"But in choosing you—"

"Thanks, I guess," Jack said. "I didn't realize you gods like to gamble."

"Some do," Thor said. Zeus nodded agreement.

"You've done this a lot?"

"Yes," Thor said, "but we seldom cross paths."

"Seldom? You mean—"

"The last time," Zeus said, "was World War Two."

"You guys had something to do with—"

"We argued," Thor said.

"Petty, I realize now," Zeus shrugged. "But—"

"World War Two," Thor said. He nodded at the downpour outside.

"But, really, guys, *gods*, when it comes to big money—"

"We do not wager cash," Zeus said. "This time."

"We cannot risk future chance meetings between us," Thor said. "Too hard on the furniture."

"You will write down our wager, Mister The Pipe," Zeus said. "And *you*—" he caught Augie and his boys with steely eyes, "will witness."

"Yeah, sure, Mister Zeus," Augie said. The boys nodded vigorously.

"Okay," Jack said.

Zeus dictated, with frequent interjections from Thor. Jack wrote the wager being made between the Norse and the Greek in cramped, stuttering lines.

The two would wrestle on the twentieth, on stage at the Egyptian during the opening of "The Gods Aspire"—they'd "rewrite" the script, so to speak, using their godly powers—and the winner would take all.

All.

The stakes were the universe and everything in it. The loser was to retreat—to Valhalla, if Thor lost—to Olympus, if Zeus lost—and never enter the affairs of the world again, forever. The universe, and everything in it, would then become the domain of the winner. Forever.

The agreement went on and on page after page, until Jack's hand cramped and his writing became illegible. When Jack complained, Zeus waved a finger and Jack's hand became uncramped, his handwriting became as legible as type and he stopped sweating.

Rules of the match. Illegal holds defined. Boundaries of the ring. Number of rounds. Time per round. Point system. Zeus agreed to shave off his beard and hair. Thor would clip his golden locks. They'd wrestle nude. All the details.

Jack, of course, would referee.

"Can we watch?" Orville asked.

Augie interrupted. "Is it okay with you gods, sirs, if we take some side bets? You don't mind? Sirs?"

Both gods shrugged.

Augie and his boys left quickly, before anything else weird happened. As they hustled through the downpour to Augie's waiting car, Jack heard Augie say: "Get the friggin word out. I'm giving the Norse a five-to-one edge over the Greek. That Thor, he's friggin *big*."

"Good day, Mister the Pipe," Zeus said, a slight nod.

"Until the twentieth," Thor added.

Both turned to leave.

"Just a sec, gods," Jack said.

They stopped and turned to him.

"Hows about a handshake," Jack said. "For luck."

"Mortals do not touch gods," Thor said.

"It is forbidden," Zeus added.

"Yeah, I know. But this is a special occasion, don't you think? I mean, it's for all the marbles, right? So hows about a break with tradition, just this once? For luck. Do it for The Pipe. You guys said you trust me, right? Right?"

The two gods looked at each other, shrugged and extended a hand to Jack.

Jack shook Thor's first. "Cause I met him first," Jack explained to Zeus. "And he's before you in the alphabet, too."

Illustrated by Viktoria Dunayeva

He then shook Zeus' hand.

"See you gods on the twentieth," Jack waved as they left.

The sun was coming out.

When they'd walked down the street and turned their separate ways, Jack went back behind the counter and picked up the phone. He dialed.

"Lemme talk to Sabatini," he said.

A moment passed, then Sabatini came on the line. "The Pipe is turning or what?"

"Just placing a little side bet, Sabatini," Jack said, glancing at the picture of the mountains. *Soon. Pretty soon.*

"The Pipe gambles? Has the world come to an end or what?"

"Just listen—" and Jack told Sabatini about the match at the Egyptian on the twentieth. He laid down his shop, all his savings and his insurance money on Zeus to win. He knew a few loan sharks. Maybe he'd add to the bet later.

"You know this Zeus fellow or what?" Sabatini asked.

"Let's just say I got a grip on some pretty good information," Jack said, kneading his aching hand, the one he'd used to shake hands with Thor. And then with Zeus.

THE BIGGEST LITTLE JOB IN FICTION

Written by
Janet Berliner

About the Author

In over twenty-five years as a writer, editor and publishing consultant, Janet Berliner has worked with Peter S. Beagle, Larry Bond, Ray Bradbury, David Copperfield, Michael Crichton, Dean Koontz, Eric Lustbader, Joyce Carol Oates and F. Paul Wilson, to name a few. She has counseled prime ministers, public figures and media personalities on all aspects of the ever-changing publishing world.

Among her eight books seeing publication since 1995 are the two volumes of a tribute to magic and illusion she created and edited with David Copperfield, Peter S. Beagle's Immortal Unicorn, *and The* Madagascar Manifesto *series (*Child of the Light, Child of the Journey *and* Children of the Dusk*) examining a little-known aspect of the Nazi plans to exterminate the Jews.*

She has short stories forthcoming in such diverse volumes as Marilyn: Shades of Blonde, Peter S. Beagle's Immortal Unicorn Volume II *and* Alternate Generals. *In 1998,* The Michael Crichton Companion, *which she edited, will come* out. It includes a one-on-one interview, conducted by Janet Berliner, with the author of such colossal bestsellers as Jurassic Park *and* Airframe.

Currently, Janet divides her time between Las Vegas where she lives and works, and Grenada, West Indies, where her heart is.

In my not always entirely humble opinion, there is no more challenging task in the writing of fiction than the crafting of a memorable short story. That's because the rules of good writing have to be obeyed in a framework which allows little margin for error.

As a traditionalist, in form if not subject matter, I believe in the imperative of knowing the rules before breaking them. Until we have learned to dot all i's and cross all t's, we have not earned the right to veer from convention.

The rules seem simple enough: Have a working skeleton that includes a beginning, a middle and an end. Give the reader a sense of time and place as early as possible in the story. Show what your protagonist looks like. Make sure that the story contains conflict and that the protagonist changes in some way. Provide layering and foreshadowing, build the story from its skeleton, and make every word count.

I'll repeat the last phrase: *Make every word count.*

Take this article for example. I was asked to contribute one-thousand words about writing short fiction. Seems simple enough, given the fact that I've been publishing short stories for decades, but it's not simple at all for me. I could write a full-length book on the subject and have material left over.

How then, do I approach the process of distilling a book into about three printed pages?

The answer is with great difficulty and with a great deal of forethought.

The same applies to a short story.

You have a concept, an idea, a character or set of characters who are demanding your attention. Now you want them to command the attention of readers. If you are going to achieve that end within the constraints of what is, in the writing lexicon, a few bold strokes, you are going to have to appeal swiftly and equally to the reader's intellect and viscera and—here's the rub—you are going to have to bring all of your skills to bear in using the right words to draw your reader into your story in such a manner that he brings to the story his own related experiences.

The boundaries of the short story allow none of the luxuries of novel writing. Subplots are out; digression is out. If you're going to Paris, you'd better not go via Versailles. There simply isn't the time. You have to travel the straight road from point A to point B.

That straight road is the skeleton of your story. The passing scenery is your layer of flesh. Still, you think, how much more interesting it would be to travel the side roads too.

So what do you do? You provide spaces for the reader to fill. Signposts that say, "Versailles this-a-way." The reader who has been to Versailles enhances the story with that experience; the reader who hasn't, enhances it with the desire to go there someday. The signpost adds thousands of words, not one of which is actually on the page, and there is no avoiding the side trip.

This is the true skill of the short story writer, the one for which we should all be reaching.

One of the writers who most ably achieves this unwritten texture, if you will, is Edward Bryant. He has certainly been *my* teacher. Read any one of his short stories, think about it, then go back and examine how much of what you thought was on the page is actually there and how much has been drawn in by careful omission, in breathing spaces deliberately placed in such a manner that you were forced to create texture out of your own experience. That is Bryant's art, his particular skill. Learn from it. Read constantly and learn from everything you read. Read advertising if you want to fully understand about making each word count. Ask yourself about the overt message and about the subliminal message.

Go back to the last draft of your most recent short story and apply the same test. If each sentence and every thought, isn't there for a reason, it's time to apply some tough editorial surgery.

Since I am now approaching the end of my allowable word count, let me add some practical advice about paring your story down to its bones. I started my writing life as a journalist, which gives me an edge. If anything, fearing my editor's wrath, I have always written too tightly. I start a short story with my crux sentence, a novel with a few paragraphs. Then I begin the process of opening up what I hope is a rosebud into a fully blooming flower. For those of you without that training, I offer the following advice. It's what I do and it has never failed me.

I look upon the editing process as a party where I go to meet old friends and make new ones. The words and phrases that make my authorial heart pound are the party guests. They all look and sound beautiful just the way they are and I cannot conceive of keeping any of them out. Yet among the most attractive of the party-goers are those who don't belong. Perhaps one day they will be allowed to join the party, but not here, not now.

Sadly, I bounce them, but not before I note their names and addresses.

Telling them that they will have to wait for "another time, another place," I take them—those words, phrases, paragraphs—and put them in my writing address book, a file of 3 x 5 cards that I keep ready and waiting for that other place, that other time . . . that other story.

I've cut and pasted, I've written and rewritten. I have a deadline and an editor waiting. Is it soup yet?

Not quite, at least not for me. I have to let the soup simmer in the pot for just a while longer, and then I have to have a taster, a reader, a critic—a bouncer with a practiced eye.

How I choose that person and how I do or don't implement the advice I get will have to wait for another article. I've run out of space. No words. Not ever words. But I am constrained by rules, by the boundaries of this article which is not a book. I will respect those boundaries, even when it is not easy, as I hope you will respect yours.

The more you do, the more you'll succeed. And when you do, break all the rules. That's why they're there.

Be reading you!

TRODER

Written by
David L. Felts

Illustrated by
Eric Williams

About the Author

David L. Felts is thirty-two and resides in Tucson, Arizona. His work in the Air Force has taken him to a variety of locations, including Texas, Mississippi, Florida, Alabama and Tokyo, Japan. David currently works as an information management officer.

David credits his success to the support of his wife and his persistence to the example of his three-year-old daughter, who taught him to never quit no matter how many times he heard the word "no."

He's taken writing classes through the University of Maryland and is in a writing workshop with Simon Hawke.

David has been writing science fiction and fantasy and submitting to various markets for five years. "Troder" was his first try with our Contest and is his first professional sale.

The desperate energy of the crowd buzzed in Panda's head, enticing and frantic, so thick she could almost taste it.

She took a deep breath, smelled sweat and incense and tobacco smoke. Pink neon glowed, strobes pulsed white, holobeam projectors flashed thick streams of brilliant color in patterns complex as any spider's web. Panda's gaze wandered across the battered bar, the scattered circular chrome and plastic tables. The huge dance floor was packed, an amorphous multicolored mass throbbing to the thrashing sounds of a band named Data Stream. The Virtual Razor was the place to be on Saturday night. She heard her sister sigh, turned as Lucie finished snorting powder off a palm-sized plastic mirror.

"Feels good," Lucie said, shivering. She licked the residue, dropped the mirror on the smudged table. "My head's swelling." She stood, twirled in place, head back and arms out, a wind-up ballerina from some antique music box. "Love that music. Data Stream's my band. Mmmmmm." She stopped spinning, pointed. "Who's the zipper?"

Panda looked to see a man in slick black leather weaving through the pulsating crowd. Zippers crawled across his suit in gleaming quicksilver patterns. The man's bald head flared sharp and bright under the strobes.

"Don't know," Panda said, staring. Nice face, all planes and angles, attractive and cruel, unlike the uniform and perfectly sculpted features that flashed *bioteched*. His body though—lean and loose and muscular under the skintight zipper—bioteched for sure. Panda felt a surge of warmth between her legs.

The zipper passed close, in the edge of the crowd, a sable shark cruising through a sea of neon minnows. Panda saw marks on his scalp, dozens of tiny circles a shade darker than the rest of his skin.

"He's a troder," Panda said, pointing. "Look, Lucie. At his head. See those marks?" The zipper saw her pointing, looked right at her. Eyes blacker than spun carbon crystal. Panda shivered with anticipation.

Lucie laughed. "So? Means he's got money, likes to spend. He's a taste, just my flavor. Bioteched bod and slick zipper suit. Wonder what else he teched?" She laughed again and wet her lips, twitching to the music like a puppet. "Never troded before," she said. She touched her fingertips to her face, her eyes shiny, the pupils black pits. "Am I glowing?"

She laughed again and twirled. Glistening sky blue skin, a shade matched by her skimpy panties and slippers, the only clothes she wore. She'd taken skintint before they'd left for the clubs. Lucie always picked blue, to complement the bright red hair tumbling loose to her shoulders. Panda didn't skintint, it made her itch.

"Tingle, Panda, tingle, Panda," Lucie sang, spinning. "Tingle, Panda. It feels good! Got any more?"

"Not for you," Panda said. She wasn't about to give Lucie hers. Government dispensers doled one hit a day. Tingle, Bliss, Placid—it didn't matter which one—you got one hit and one hit only. No saving them either. The drugs degraded in twenty-four hours, becoming just so much colored powder, iridescent dust tasting like ash.

Lucie simply giggled, stopped spinning and began swaying, smooth and loose on drug-oiled joints. She chanted in a singsong voice, "Got any more, got any more, got any more?"

"You're droning." Panda tried to grab Lucie's arm, but her sister whirled onto the dance floor, slipping through the frenzied, twisting bodies effortlessly. "Dance, Panda," she sang, laughing, dancing. "Dance, little sister!"

Panda emptied her packet of Tingle on the mirror, hunching over to snort it up. Her reflection stared back through the powder; short dye-black hair in a spiky Asian cut, wide-set green eyes, high cheekbones and an angular jaw. People told her she was attractive. She thought her eyes were too far apart.

She leaned close and inhaled, sucked the prismatic powder through her nose, licked at the residue like Lucie had done. It tasted like peppermint, made her tongue numb. Heat surged in her head, swelled, spread through her body in rippling waves. Sound flowed across her skin in a silky caress. Panda stood, ran her hands over her body, cupped her breasts through her skintight green bodsuit. Green to match her eyes. She looked for Lucie.

Her sister was in the arms of the zipper, her hands fluttering like moths over the black membrane of his suit, fingertips tracing the zippered patterns. The man touched her breasts, squeezed her ass. Panda felt a rush of anger and jealousy. Her sister was always doing this shit, getting in the way. Why should she always get what she wanted?

Then the Tingle took over and Panda shrugged. Screw it. Lucie could have him. There were plenty of others. Panda melted into the crowd, surrendering herself to the music and the drug. She thought about Hardwired. He was nice. Why hadn't he ever tried anything with her? She wondered, not for the first time, if he was gay. Or maybe asexual. A lot of net jockeys were, getting their thrills on the wire instead of in the flesh.

The Tingle rush continued to swell, and she forgot about Lucie and Hardwired and the zipper, and even herself for a time.

The supple young jacker she went home with had blood-red cybernetic eyes and teeth so white against his night-black skintint they almost blinded her when he smiled.

•••

The jacker was already linked and online when Panda woke, fiberoptic cables twisting from his eyes like glistening snakes. His black skintint had faded to a natural light brown, the smooth, rich color of coffee and cream. He cocked his head as if listening while she dressed, but didn't say anything. Panda let herself out.

She was somewhere north of Ashbury. A ten-minute walk got her home, a tiny two-bedroom government apartment she shared with Lucie, furnished with white plastic government-issue furniture gone gray. She heated some water, stirred in caff crystals since she couldn't afford real coffee, and sat at the table in the kitchen, sipping, wondering where Lucie was. It was almost eleven.

A loud knock at the door startled her. Hot caff slopped onto her hand, stinging. She cursed. It couldn't be Lucie. Lucie wouldn't have to knock.

Panda rinsed her hand in the sink. Another knock. "Just a second!" She went to the door, peered through the peek hole. Two men, motionless as statues, wearing long coats the color of dried blood. Both had short brown hair and honest open faces. Neutral brown skin, plastic good looks. Anyface USA, that's what Hardwired would have said. They looked exactly alike. Sniffers.

"What?" Panda asked without opening the door.

"Patricia Marlan?"

Panda hated her real name. "Yeah?"

"Could you open the door?"

"PDCs," Panda said.

Both men pulled Personal Identification Cards from their pockets and held them up to the peek hole. Across the top the cards read *Investigator, Level 2, San Francisco*. One read *Reed Bailey*, the other *Jensen Murket*. A holo of each man's face was underneath. Panda looked at them and shrugged. She wouldn't know if they were fake anyway. She opened the door, the molybond cable lock stopping it at a three-inch slice of face. The sniffers put their PDCs away.

Panda peered through the gap, wary. "Yeah?"

The sniffer on the right, Murket. "Know Lucie Marlan?" Voice deep and smooth, soothing as a hit of Placid, professional as any media caster's. Panda found herself liking him. Then she was mad. Sniffers were bioteched to make you like them. It was part of what they were.

She glared. "My sister."

The sniffers traded a quick glance. Panda felt a pang of alarm. Was Lucie in trouble?

"Need to come with us," Bailey said in a voice identical to Murket's.

"Why?"

"Need to answer some questions," Murket said.

"And determine disposition for the body," Bailey added without emotion.

Panda stared at him a brief moment, numb, replaying what they'd said in her mind. She slammed the door, slumped against it, wrapping her arms around herself, squeezing tight. Lucie wasn't in trouble then. She was dead. Panda shook her head. No. They were wrong. Lucie couldn't be dead. They must have made a mistake reading the identity chip. Panda fingered the small lump on the inside of her wrist, an implanted IC. Yes, a mistake. Lucie couldn't be dead. Not Lucie. Not her sister.

From the other side of the door. "Miz Marlan?"

"I'm getting my coat!" Fucking sniffers. Showing up, telling her Lucie was dead. What did they know?

In the kitchen, Panda splashed water on her face, ran wet fingers through her hair. The oversized gray coat she got from the closet hung to her knees, over the green bodsuit she'd worn the night before. When she opened the door, Bailey and Murket were waiting, looking bored. She wanted to smash in their perfect trustworthy bioteched faces. Instead, she jammed her hands into her pockets.

"Let's go," she said.

She followed them downstairs to a faded brown four-door car, a battered Nissan electric. Panda rode in the back. Inside smelled of sweat and old vomit. The light brown seat was splotched with dark stains, like a street painter's recycled canvas. She stared blankly out the tinted windows at cracked sidewalks and dim alleys choked with piles of shredded paper and plastic. People lounging against buildings or talking in small huddled groups. People fighting for a place in the long lines at the government drug dispensers. She stopped seeing.

She thought about last night, about Lucie. The only family she had.

The car whirred to a halt in front of the station. Low, worn steps led up to wide glass double doors.

"I want to see her," Panda said when she got out. "Need to make sure it's her."

"We scanned her IC," one of the sniffers said, frowning. She thought it was Bailey, but wasn't sure; she'd lost track of which one was which. "Matched it to her PDC. We know who she is."

Panda clamped down on her anger. It wouldn't do any good to lose her temper. "I want to see her," she repeated stubbornly. "You could've made a mistake."

"No mistake, Miz Marlan. IC scan, PDC match, and DNA." He shook his head. "No mistake."

Panda poked a stiff finger at him, her voice low and threatening. "You fucker. It's my sister. I need to see. I need to!" A corpie walking by, sleek and shiny in her ash-gray spunsilk suit, stopped to stare. Panda glared and the corpie hurried on her way, clutching her briefcase protectively.

Murket and Bailey exchanged glances. One shrugged. "Take you to the cryostore," he said. "Where we keep the terms. You can see her."

Terms. Panda shuddered. It's a mistake. It had to be. Lucie was probably at home now, taking a shower. Panda followed the sniffers up the stairs and into the station. More sniffers in the dingy off-white halls, men duplicates of Murket and Bailey, women no more than female versions of the same. They all looked alike. One big family. Sniffers gave up a lot to be what they were. Panda wondered if they ever got it back.

She followed Murket and Bailey down a flight of stairs, along a dim hall lined with doors. They stopped in front of one bearing a rectangular red sign stamped with white letters: *Cryostore 3*. They opened it, gestured for her to enter. Chilly room, bright ivory walls and yellowed tile floor, the smell of chemicals not quite masking a rank, sour scent that reminded Panda of the inside of a meat-grower's shop. Rows of halogen bulbs on the ceiling washed everything in raw white light, making her squint. On one wall, three rows of square silver doors, the top row just above chest level. Another sniffer here, in a long white coat.

One of the sniffers beside Panda pulled a minicomp from his pocket and read the number off the screen. "We're here to see 78772," he said.

The man nodded, went to a terminal on a desk set against the wall, typed something. A muffled pop as one of the silver doors opened. A puff of white vapor curling up. Panda felt abruptly dizzy, queasy from the smell. She took a few faltering steps, afraid she would fall. One of the sniffers grabbed her arm.

Panda shook loose. "Don't touch me."

A metal shelf slid out. Something lumpy under a gray plastic shroud. The sniffer in white drew the shroud back. Panda's heart thudded as a bald head appeared, the scalp mottled with faint spots. It *was* a mistake.

She staggered closer, not wanting to look, unable not to. Smooth white skin faintly tinged with blue. Familiar features. Her knees sagged. Lucie. Her sister's face was calm, unlined, eyes closed. No trace of the red hair she'd been so proud of.

"Your sister?" one of the sniffers asked, impatient.

Panda glared at him. Despite the engineered looks, the smooth voice, Panda hated him. She hated them all. The sniffer returned her look blandly, waiting. She had to swallow several times before she could speak. Damned if she'd let these clone-cult freaks see her cry.

"That's her," she finally said.

"She a troder?" the sniffer in white asked.

Panda shook her head. "No."

"Got the marks." He pointed at Lucie's scalp. "Trode marks."

"She's no troder," Panda repeated through clenched teeth. One of the other sniffers touched her arm. Panda jerked away. "What happened?" she asked.

"Found her this way," he said.

"Off Mission," the other sniffer added. "Near Fourth in an alley, under a pile of shred." He shrugged. "Some street verm phoned it in."

The room began to tilt, the walls wavered. Panda stumbled, reached out and caught the edge of the plastic shroud, pulling it partway off. She gasped. Lucie was naked, her body a mass of cuts and burns and tiny red-rimmed punctures. Panda sank to the floor, crouching, stomach churning, the plastic sheet cold and slippery in her grip. The room spun. The harsh halogen glare stung her eyes. Lucie. Poor Lucie. She blinked back tears. She wouldn't cry. Not in front of *them*.

Someone helped her up. The sniffer in white pulled the sheet from her fingers, covered Lucie again. Murket and Bailey led her upstairs to a small room, the dim light and dark blue walls soothing after the razor-edged brilliance of the halogens. They got her a cup of lukewarm caff tasting two days old and started asking questions.

Panda answered, told them about clubbing the night before, about ending up at the Virtual Razor because Data Stream was playing there and they were Lucie's favorite band. She told them about the zipper with the marks on his head. About the man she'd gone home with, the one with cybernetic eyes. They whispered notes into a minicomp while she spoke. They seemed disinterested.

When they were done, they took her out to a desk, one of dozens in the middle of a loud, crowded lobby. A sniffer sat at the desk, a woman, a thin cable jacking her head to a terminal.

"We'll have someone take you home," one of the sniffers said. Panda had never managed to figure out which was Murket and which was Bailey.

"That's it?" Panda asked. "That's it? What about the guy I told you about? The one with the marks? He's the one—"

"We have your statement," the sniffer interrupted.

"But what are you going to do?" Panda asked, already knowing they weren't going to do anything.

The sniffer looked bored. "Miz Marlan, a lot of people die in San Francisco every day—"

"But they're not my sister!"

"—and we do our best to find out who killed them."

"I know who killed her, the fucking zipper! It had to be him!"

The sniffer was silent.

Panda's rage pulsed white hot inside her skull. "You're not going to do shit, are you? Are you, Murket? Or Bailey? Or whoever the fuck you are!"

He ignored her and turned to the woman behind the desk. "Please see Miz Marlan gets home." Before Panda could say more, he and his partner strode off.

"What about her body!" Panda shouted after them. They kept walking. "You fuckers! She was my sister!" They disappeared around a corner. "She was my sister." It came out as a sob.

"Cremation?" a female voice interrupted. The sniffer behind the desk. "You could fert her," she continued in a businesslike voice. "Pays . . ." she glanced at her terminal ". . . seventeen yuan, currently."

Seventeen yuan? Was that all Lucie was worth? Panda had spent more than that in one night on drinks at a club. The thought of her sister fertilizing vegetables on some government farm brought a sour taste to her mouth. "Cremation," she finally said. The lump in her throat felt as large as a fist.

"State storage? Or disposal?"

"Disposal," Panda said. "No storage." Lucie wouldn't have wanted her remains packed in some cheap plastic urn and stuck on a shelf in some city storage facility. Panda's eyes stung. She wiped at them angrily with the back of her hand.

"Ten yuan for the cream," the sniffer said. "Five the disposal fee." She slid a thumber forward. Panda pressed her thumb against the print pad and entered her PDC code. The terminal verified the print and code and processed the contract.

"Copy'll be netted in a day or two," the sniffer said. "Money'll be autoducted from your account."

The car they drove her home in stank even worse than the first.

•••

Panda fiddled with her napkin. The tiny café was empty except for her and Hardwired and a bopping waitress with music plugs jammed in her ears and set so loud Panda could hear the song. "I Got Chrome Bones" by Data Stream. Lucie used to wear music plugs.

"Data Stream was her favorite band," Panda said absently.

Hardwired nodded, running a hand through his short brown hair. The cybernetic jack in his right eye socket glittered copper and gold. He was a wire jock, a peeler, stripping info and credit off the globe's vast electronic nervous system, for himself or the highest bidder. Illegal as hell. He wasn't affiliated though, not with one of the information syndicates that made fishing the data streams their business. He was a loner.

"Sniffers won't do anything," Panda said bitterly.

"Sniffers never do anything," Hardwired replied. "They don't give a shit about people like us. You have to be somebody for the sniffers to care."

Panda nodded.

"So what're you going to do?" Hardwired turned his head slightly. Panda noticed his real eye; beautiful clear blue flecked with gold, bright and piercing. She wondered why she'd never really noticed it before. "Do anything to help?" he asked. "I owe you."

Panda sighed, wishing he'd stop saying that. It had been a year since she'd stumbled over him lying battered and bloody in an alley as she staggered home from the clubs. She'd phoned a medic and five minutes later they'd shown up and pumped him full of healies. She'd helped him back to his apartment, stayed the night to make sure he was all right. The tiny nanocules did their job; by morning, he was fully recovered. Weren't even any scars. He never let her forget.

"Don't know what you can do to help." She sipped her coffee, real coffee, compliments of Hardwired, savoring the taste, the smell. "That zipper did her. I'm sure. He was a troder. I saw the marks on his head, just like the ones on Lucie."

Hardwired picked up his spoon, tapped it against the edge of his cup, a one-two beat. "Tried troding. Did it a few times. Liked it. It's scary though." He set the spoon down and looked away. "Binds you, you know? You feel whatever the other person does. Physical sensations I mean. Pleasure, pain, whatever. Ended up too scary for me. Too intimate. Like I was losing myself."

Panda squeezed her cup till her knuckles ached. "That fucking zipper did her. It had to be him." She shook her head, puzzled. "Don't know why, but he did."

Hardwired managed to get the waitress's attention by waving his arms frantically. He pointed at his cup and she nodded. "So," he said. "If the sniffers won't help . . . ?"

"I'll help myself."

The door to the café opened and a young woman with long red hair walked in. Panda's heart lurched. For a moment, the briefest instant, she'd thought it was Lucie. The woman staggered, eyes glazed, telltale mark of a virtual reality contact band like a vivid red tattoo across her forehead. She glanced vacantly around, then turned and left. Probably didn't even know where she was, or if it was even real.

"I'll find the guy myself," Panda said, tearing her thoughts away from the girl. She allowed the waitress to refill her cup after Hardwired's. They drank their coffee in silence, Panda glancing from time to time at Hardwired.

"It should have been me," Panda finally said.

Hardwired looked at her. "What?"

Panda met his gaze. "It should have been me. I saw him. The zipper. I wanted him. I was pissed because Lucie got him. It should have been me." Her eyes burned. She didn't want to cry, but couldn't help it. It should have been her on that slab at the station. Not Lucie.

"It doesn't work that way." Hardwired reached out and held her hand, squeezing softly. It's not your fault." He handed her a napkin.

She wiped her eyes, angry. "Fucking zipper. I'll find him. I'll get him. For Lucie."

"I'll help you," Hardwired said. "We'll get him."

Panda nodded, thoughts and memories whirling in her head.

• • •

"I want a Tooth," Panda said, walking into the biotech shape shop.

The shaper looked up. Tall and muscular, perfect vidstar face and glistening emerald eyes. "What kind?" His voice was a deep masculine rumble.

"Protection. A Sleeper."

He eyed her doubtfully. "Got the yuan? Be at least four hundred."

Panda flashed her PDC. Everything Lucie'd had was hers, not that it was much. Hardwired had asked to borrow her card yesterday when they left the café. When he'd given it back that morning, he'd said there were five thousand yuan in her account. Panda had been stunned. Hardwired had winked and said to let him know if she needed more. "It's hard," he'd said, "and risky. But I can get you more if you need it." She'd given him a hug and a kiss and been rewarded by seeing him blush. For some reason that had made her feel special.

The shaper ran her PDC. "Got enough," he said, looking at her with new respect. He gave the card back. "Go in back, on the table." He hit something under the counter. A buzzer sounded and a door opened, leading into the guts of the shop.

Panda went through into a medium-sized room that smelled of disinfectant. Shiny steel cabinets on three walls, big cryostore in the corner. A raised examination table covered with brown vinyl and a mirrored floodlight on a movable arm occupied the center of the room. Panda was sitting on the table when the shaper came in.

"Lie down." Panda did. The shaper turned on the light, moved it to illuminate her mouth. "Open." He examined her teeth with a critical eye. "Which one?"

"Which one's best?" Panda squinted against the light.

"Molar holds more gas. Front one's cheaper. Four hundred for a front, five-twenty for a molar."

"Molar." Panda closed her eyes. The light glowed pink through her lids.

She heard the shaper moving around, then felt his presence again at her side. "Open. Hold still. I'll do a bottom right. That okay?" Panda nodded. He poked something into her mouth. She heard a hiss, felt the slight sting of a pnuemojector. An antiseptic taste in her mouth. "Sit up. Hold your mouth open. Lean over so you don't swallow it by accident." He gave her a metal tray. "Spit it on this."

Panda did as she was told. A burning sensation on the right side of her jaw and suddenly something in her mouth. She spit it out. A tooth with the root dissolved. She probed the empty socket with her tongue, tasted a hint of blood.

The shaper took the tray with the tooth and went to the cryostore, returning with a small box. "Lay back again. Open." The light warm on her face, a bit of pain as something was pressed into the socket, the hiss and sting of another pnuemojection.

"All done," he said. "Takes a couple hours for the roots to grow and seat. Chew on the other side from now on. Bite something too hard and it'll break." The light went out.

Panda sat up, blinking, blue and violet after-images floating across her vision. She explored the new tooth with the tongue. It was loose. "How do I use it?"

"Bite down hard and twist your jaw. Try it now. Bite down, but not too hard."

Panda did.

"Now sort of twist your jaw a little. No, the other way. Feel that point?"

Panda nodded.

"Bite that point, the tooth breaks. So. Take a breath, bite, blow. Blow hard. Breathe in and it might knock you out."

"How long's it last?"

The shaper shrugged. "Ten, fifteen minutes for a good face full. Five or less, or not at all, if not."

"Thanks," Panda said. The new tooth felt big and too evenly square. She gave the shaper her PDC. He went and ran the transaction, returned with a thumber. Panda pressed her thumb to it and entered her code. He gave her card back along with a receipt.

He looked her up and down. "Doing anything later?" He smiled. Plump lips, straight white teeth, smile lines like surgical incisions framing his mouth. Three days ago, before Lucie had died, Panda might have been tempted. Now she wanted to laugh. He looked like a freak, fake as some holodummy in a store window. She thought of Hardwired. She doubted if a kiss would make the shaper blush.

"Give you a twenty percent discount," he said.

Panda headed for the door. "Thanks anyway." She hurried out before he could reply.

•••

Net-Work was bopping. A smaller club than VR, but just as crowded. Zippers, jackers, skintints, beefcakes, and everything in between, all whirling and twisting to the shrill, shredding strains of a band named Red Laser Cuts.

Panda sat on a tall stool at a small table in a back corner, facing the entrance, scanning the crowd. Clubbers zoned on the dance floor, or snorted government drugs at the tables. Panda felt sorry for them. Strange to think that two weeks ago she would have been out there with them. Desperate for fun, everything warm and fuzzy through a haze of drug-induced happiness. She hadn't taken anything since Lucie had died. Sometimes she missed the way the drugs made everything fun and new. But it wasn't real.

Panda watched the crowd. How many tonight would be dead soon? Would anyone care? How many would die tonight?

She sighed. She was about ready to give up. Ten days and no sign of the zipper. Would she ever find him? If he'd bioteched, he could be right next to her and she wouldn't recognize him. Hardwired was at the table with her. He was saying something.

"What?" she asked, yelling to be heard over the music.

"I said, do you see him?"

Panda shook her head. Hardwired had been a great help. Besides the money he'd somehow gotten an IC tracer, same as sniffers used. If she saw the zipper, she'd leave with him. Hardwired would use the tracer to follow in case there was trouble before she used her Tooth.

"Getting a drink," Hardwired said. He raised his brows in question and Panda shook her head. He headed for the bar, threaded his way through the multihued bodies. Panda lost sight of him.

She let her gaze rove. A man near the door caught her eye. She hadn't seen him come in. Tall, good-looking, lean and muscular. Iridescent green skintint matched by briefs and slippers. And bald. His face stirred something in her memory. It could just be that she'd seen him before and didn't remember. She wished she'd looked harder at the zipper that night—the Tingle she'd taken made her memory of him indistinct.

He danced next to a beefcake, a bioteched freak so huge with bulging slabs of muscle he didn't even appear human.

Panda stood, worked her way over, danced around the beefcake, looking. A surge of adrenaline set her heart thumping. Trode marks. Hard to see under the skintint, but there. That didn't lock it though. There were a half-dozen or so other people with trode marks. But something about him nagged at her. The shape of his head, his mouth. It was him, she finally decided. Face a little different, a little rounder, not so chiseled, not so cruel. But it was him.

The zipper from VR.

Panda danced her way closer. The man was alone, eyes closed, swaying to the song. Panda touched his shoulder, his eyes snapped open. Pitch black, a gaze she felt like a physical touch. Scary. Then he smiled, straight white teeth gleaming, licked his lips, eyes examining her body through her skintight bodsuit. Panda smiled in return, tried not to act nervous. He wrapped an arm about her waist, pulled her into his dance. Panda matched his rhythm, rubbed her body against him.

They left the dance floor two songs later, when Red Laser Cuts took a break. He led the way to an isolated corner. Panda looked for Hardwired, didn't see him. Two orange women with drug-glazed eyes had claimed their table.

The man gave his name as Tommy Luster when she asked. She told him hers.

"Good group," she said, making talk.

Tommy shrugged. "They're okay." He pulled her closer, ran a hand along her spine, made her shiver.

"I like Data Stream, too." She nuzzled his neck, holding her breath, waiting.

Tommy shrugged again. Bioteched muscles bunched beneath her hands. "Better than Red Laser Cuts," he admitted.

"I saw them at the Virtual Razor." Panda tried to sound calm. "Maybe two weeks ago? They played there."

Tommy pulled back, his eyes guarded. She thought the corners of his mouth twitched in a slight smile. "I saw them. I like the VR. Good club."

"Yeah," Panda said. She licked her lips. "Maybe I saw you?"

Shrug. "Maybe."

"Yeah, I think so." Panda felt hot, sure her face was flushed. But the light was dim. Could he tell? "You were there? Wearing a black zipper?"

She thought Tommy's body tightened, just for a second, but so quickly she might have imagined it.

"Got a zipper. Lots of guys have zippers."

Red Laser Cuts started again, staccato syntho winds clashing with irregular rhythm drums. The singer jacked his formwave and the club filled with a wailing, warbling sound. The formwave read his brain waves, turned them into tones. Music of the mind. Panda had the brief image of a hundred kids pounding on a syntho keyboard, each playing a different song.

Tommy leaned close again. Breath tickled her ear. He seemed urgent. He ran a hand through her hair. "Nice. I like black and short. Like bald more though." He wet his plump lips with the tip of his tongue. "Nothing sexier than a bald woman."

Panda was so anxious she felt nauseous. She struggled to keep her breathing even. "I see your marks. Troder?"

Tommy touched his head absently. His eyes were hard. Something peeked out. Anticipation? "Sometimes. You?"

Panda nodded, acted interested, ran her hands up and down his chest, massaging the muscles, rubbing his nipples. "Tried it a few times," she lied. "Liked it. Can't afford my own."

Tommy grabbed her hand and squeezed. Not hard enough to hurt, but hard just the same. "Got one. At my place. Let's go."

Panda leaned into him, looked over his shoulder while licking the side of his neck, searching for Hardwired. "One more song," she whispered in Tommy's ear, trying to stall. "One more dance."

Tommy shook his head, pressed her hand to his crotch. "Come on," he said. "Now." He thrust urgently against her hand, rubbed his chest against her breasts.

"One more dance." Where was Hardwired?

Tommy shook his head and began walking, pulling her behind him. Panda allowed herself to be led from the club. She didn't want to lose him. She looked back, hoped to catch a glimpse of Hardwired. Nothing.

•••

In the cab, Tommy reached over and ran a hand along her thigh. Panda shivered and he must have taken that for excitement. He pressed closer, hands moving to her breasts, rubbing the nipples through the thin fabric of her bodsuit. Panda didn't have to fake her rapid breathing, though she added a few moans for good measure. Tommy grew more insistent and Panda started to respond, the sense of danger adding to her excitement. She reached down, rubbed his erection through his tight briefs.

She thought about using her Tooth, but decided to wait. She was positive he was the zipper from VR, but she still didn't know for sure if he'd killed Lucie. She had to be certain. And if he was, she wanted it to be private. She didn't want to be interrupted.

They groped each other until the cab whirred to a halt before an elegant high-rise, a shiny black grid of steel and glass. Somewhere on Beach Street, Panda saw, down near the wharf. Expensive. No viruses wandering blankly about, no piles of shred clogging the sidewalks, no trippers sprawled on the concrete. It seemed foreign, like another city altogether from the one Panda knew.

Tommy led Panda into the building, typing the entry code to open the doors. They took an elevator to the twenty-seventh floor. Down the hall, footsteps muffled by expensive slate-colored synthetic pile, to a door inset with a shiny brass plaque reading 2720. Tommy entered his code on the lock and the door opened with a click, soft fluorescent lights in the apartment coming on automatically.

Panda's breath caught in her throat. Tommy must really have money. She ran her hand along the cool, smooth back of a chair, wondering if it was real wood. She smelled real leather. Authentic paintings on the wall, not cheap 3-D holoposters. Tommy moved behind her, wrapped his arms around her waist.

"Nice place," she said, and meant it.

Tommy pressed his lips to her neck. "It's okay." He took her hand, pulled her down a hall into a bedroom. Panda looked out the huge one-way window that made up the wall behind the bed while Tommy peeled her bodsuit off. The city seemed so different from this far up. Twinkling lights on black cloth, shot through with shifting dots of white and red; vehicles tracing the grid of streets like particles of data transiting a vast electric lattice.

Tommy turned her, pushed her back on the bed. He was naked, having removed his briefs and slippers without her noticing. She reached down, gave a quick squeeze. He'd obviously bioteched more than his muscles. Panda stifled a giggle. She felt giddy, filled with a strange, twisting mixture of dread and anticipation and excitement.

He indicated a night stand next to the bed where a squat gray metal box crouched, red digital readouts leering, bundles of thin gray wires sprouting from its side. "Trode box," he said.

The hot surge of adrenaline in her chest, an electric shock that set her heart pounding, raised goose bumps on her skin. Her mouth went dry.

He touched her hair. "Need to lose this. Got some biotech stuff that'll drop it."

"A kiss first," Panda murmured, trying to control her trembling limbs. She pulled Tommy's mouth toward hers, took a breath, twisted her jaw, and bit down. The Tooth burst with a bright crack.

Panda blew as hard as she could, right in Tommy's face.

Tommy must have heard the Tooth break, or been warned by her sharp intake of breath. He jerked away at the last moment, twisted aside, managed to avoid most of the gas. He rolled off the bed and sat on the floor, breathing deeply, shaking his head, stunned.

Shit! Panda scrabbled off the bed. She'd fucked that up. Tommy was still conscious. She had to get away. Forget the clothes. She darted for the door.

He lunged, caught her ankle, tripped her. She slammed into the floor with enough force to knock her breath away. She gasped, tried to squirm away, kicking at Tommy with her other foot.

He was groggy, but still strong. He kept his grip, pulled her toward him. Panda kicked at his face. Her heel crunched into his nose. Bright blood gushed out, dripped on the cream-colored carpet.

"You bitch," Tommy said, gasping. He pulled her closer, got on top of her, pinned her to the floor. His hands fasten on her throat. She flailed at him, raked her nails at his face. Purple spots swelled to float before her eyes. A gray mist rose in her brain, leeched away her strength. Semiconscious, she felt him stretch her arms above her head, drag her back onto the bed. Something soft and warm wrapped around her wrists, fastening them in place. A heavy weight settled across her hips.

She sucked air convulsively. Her neck ached and her lungs burned, her pulse throbbed in her head. The gray mist receded; her vision returned, swimming into focus. Tommy sitting above her, straddling her waist, panting, glaring down at her. Blood dripped from his nose onto her stomach, bright red against her pale skin.

When he saw her open eyes he slapped her sharply in the face. Pain chased the last of the fog from her brain, edged everything with razor-sharp clarity. She twisted her hips, tried to buck him off. As she squirmed, she noticed whatever held her wrists in place growing tighter.

"Thought you were smart, didn't you?" he asked, gingerly touching his nose. "You bitch! Think you broke my nose."

"Good!"

He slapped her again, making her ears ring. "Who's smart now?" He climbed off, tried to grab her feet. She kicked at him until he punched her in the stomach. Her legs drew up in pain. She tried not to vomit. Tommy grabbed one foot at a time, fastened each ankle to the footboard of the bed. Warm and soft, like whatever wrapped her wrists.

When her feet were secured, he looked at her. His eyes were small and cold and black. He wiped blood from his chin with the back of one hand. "Squid cuffs. Know what they are?"

Panda knew. Sniffers used them for uncontrollables. The more you pulled, the tighter they got. She'd heard stories of them squeezing limbs right off.

"Yeah," he said, gloating. "I was at VR. I remember you. You were with that red-haired bitch. What was her name? Lucie? We had a good time. She hurt bad. But it felt good. Tasty." He made smacking sounds with his lips.

"You bastard," Panda said, wheezing, stomach still knotted from his punch. "You killed my sister!" Her voice was hoarse. Talking hurt. She pulled against the squids. They tightened. She stopped, lying still, chest heaving.

His eyebrows rose. "Really?" He sniffed. "Too bad," he said, not sounding like he thought it was too bad at all. He walked away, went into the bathroom. Panda heard running water. She glanced wildly about, testing the squids again. They tightened. She felt the blood pulsing at her wrists, her ankles.

His face was free of blood when he returned from the bathroom, though his nose was red and swollen. He carried a spray bottle and a brush. He pointed the bottle at her, spraying, covering her whole head with a cold, medicinal-smelling foam. Panda tried to twist out of the way, but couldn't. Her efforts only made the squids tighten. She blinked as the stuff ran into her eyes. It stung, making them tear.

After finishing with the bottle, he began to use the brush. Panda saw strands of red hair tangled in the bristles. The sight made her crazy. She lifted her head, bit at his hand, thrashing on the bed, not noticing the squids or anything else.

He avoided her teeth easily, laughing. Panda finally stilled, panting, her hands and feet beginning to tingle from the loss of circulation. He dropped the brush, left the room again, returned with a hand vac he used to suck up the hair piled around her neck and shoulders. He dried her head with a towel. When he was done, he ran a hand over his naked scalp, then hers, giggling. Panda shrank away from his touch.

"We could pass for brother and sister," he said, winking.

He went to the trode box, got a large bundle of wires with small, circular electrodes on their ends, then sat on the edge of the bed. He tried to fasten the trodes to Panda's scalp, attempting to press each self-adhesive metal tab against her skin.

Panda threw her head from side to side, trying not to pull on the squids, yelling as loud as her sore throat would allow. Tommy managed to get a few trodes attached, but she was moving too much. Finally, he dropped the trodes and grabbed her jaw, fingers and thumb pinching. Panda winced in pain.

Tommy's face was close, his breath smelled of cinnamon. "You're going to hurt," he said in a low voice.

Illustrated by Eric Williams

"You're going to hurt bad." He squeezed her jaw tighter and Panda clenched her teeth to keep from moaning. "Your choice when it starts. Understand?"

"Fuck you."

He released her jaw and picked up the wires again. Panda threw her head from side to side.

"Goddammit!" He threw down the wires, grabbed her neck with both hands and squeezed. Panda's chest heaved. She couldn't get any air. Again the gray mist filled her vision, this time turning black.

•••

Panda jerked awake, sputtering. Water ran into her eyes. Her head felt stuffed with shred, her neck throbbed. Someone stood above her. Tommy, an empty glass in his hand. She wondered how long she'd been out.

"Ah, back again," Wires ran from his head to the trode box.

Panda swallowed past the pain. Her throat felt raw and swollen. "Bastard." Her voice was a croak.

A flicker of irritation in his eyes. "Give it a rest." He set the glass on the night stand. "Said you troded before. Know about inverters?" Panda remained silent. She'd never heard of an inverter.

He continued, obviously enjoying himself. "A trode box interprets brain waves and neurological pulses and relays them," he explained. "It lets you share physical sensations with another person." He paused to wet his lips. "An inverter reverses it. That means you feel the opposite of what the other person feels. See? So when you feel pain, I feel pleasure." He grinned hugely. "Get it?"

Panda felt the stirrings of real terror coiling beneath her anger. She squirmed, trying not to pull on the squids. She couldn't feel her hands or feet.

"I set the box for one-way read and feed. So when you hurt, I'll feel good." He stroked her cheek gently. She jerked away. "Tell you something." He giggled. "A secret." He leaned over to whisper in her ear, his breath tickling her cheek.

"It's a lot easier to cause pain," he said, "than pleasure."

He walked to a closet, wires trailing like thin gray vines, opened the doors, wheeled out a tray, pointed to it with evident relish. "Scalpel, sonic saw, laser pulse drill," he looked at her and winked, "needles, a good, old-fashioned knife . . ." He picked up a small square silver object, flicked it. A tiny flame appeared. "An antique lighter—that's especially fun." He set the lighter back on the tray. "Shall I continue?" Tommy wheeled the tray over beside the bed.

He bent and turned on the box. A few seconds later he smiled, moaning softly. "Yes. Hurts already, doesn't it?" He picked up a large needle from his tray. "Sometimes I have to turn it down," he told her. "Otherwise I pass out from the pleasure."

He held the needle up, right in Panda's face. She was afraid he was going to bury it in her eye. The point glittered sharp and brilliant. Tommy moved the needle slowly away, until she couldn't see where he held it. A prick in her side, near her stomach, then sharp pain as he jabbed the needle into her flesh. She jerked, but that made it worse, and made the squids tighten. Her hands and feet began to burn. She squeezed her eyes shut and clenched her jaw. She wouldn't let him know how much it hurt.

But he knew. The trode box told him. He sighed. "Ohh. We're going to have fun." He withdrew the needle, jabbed her again in a different spot. Panda quivered, but still made no sound. Tommy moaned.

He used the needle again and again, varying the time between jabs. Panda clenched her jaw, tried not to jerk so the squids wouldn't tighten. Finally the jabs stopped. Panda slitted her lids. He stood by the bed, green skin glistening with a light sheen of sweat, masturbating. When he saw her watching, he stopped. His eyes were bright.

"Now, now," he said, wagging a finger at her. "Mustn't rush. Plenty of time." He reached out and cupped her breast, pinching the nipple. Panda hissed through her teeth. He frowned. "Feel free to make all the noise you want, Panda dear. No one can hear. Screaming adds to the atmosphere." Panda squeezed her lips together tighter.

He released her nipple and set the bloody needle down, fingers drifting lightly over the instruments on his tray. "What next," he mused aloud. He turned and winked at her.

Motion in the doorway drew her gaze. A man materialized, a ghost stepping from shadow. Hardwired! Slow-motion vid in her head as he rushed into the room. Blue eye wide, cybernetic link in the other socket glittering copper and gold, lips drawn back in a grimace of desperation edged with fear. Something small clutched in an outstretched hand, crackling white-blue.

Tommy whirled at the last moment and Hardwired crashed into his side, instead of his back. Tommy staggered, caught hold of Hardwired's wrist, kept the flickering device away. They struggled. Tommy used his greater strength to slam Hardwired against the wall.

"Get him!" Panda shouted. "Come on, Hardwired!"

Tommy had his other hand around Hardwired's throat, pinning the slighter man against the wall. Panda pulled against the squids, struggling. They tightened. "Come on!"

Tommy glanced at her, grinning. Hardwired's face was bright red, his real eye bulged.

Panda's hands and feet throbbed and burned from lack of blood. She pulled harder. The squids tightened, the pain swelled, radiating down her arms. Tommy moaned, shivering, his grip loosening for an instant. Hardwired almost broke free. Suddenly she knew what to do.

She steeled herself, stuck her tongue between her teeth, squeezed her eyes shut.

And bit.

White-hot agony flared, a nova of pain cutting through her senses like a hot razor. Panda moaned, bore down, grinding her teeth into her tongue, slicing the flesh. Blood filling her mouth, a metallic, coppery taste, almost making her gag. Warm blood running down her chin. Ah, it hurt! Tears leaked from the corners of her eyes. Her whole existence was the pain.

"Panda!" Someone grabbed her shoulders. "Panda!"

Hardwired? Slowly she relaxed her jaws. Her tongue pulsed, flared with pain in time to her heartbeat, made her whole head hurt. She opened her eyes. Hardwired. A red swelling over his real eye, a faint trickle of blood from his lower lip. Red marks on his neck from Tommy's fingers.

"You with me?"

She nodded. "Yes," she croaked around her swelling tongue, drooling blood.

Hardwired used Tommy's scalpel to cut the squids holding her wrists and ankles. She sat up, flung her arms around him, hugged him as tightly as she could with her numb hands. She wanted to kiss him, but her mouth hurt too much.

"I owe you," she said, smiling, her words clumsy because of her injured tongue.

Hardwired grinned. "I'll get you a towel," he said, heading for the bathroom. Panda sat on the edge of the bed, shaking, flexing her fingers. She was alive.

She saw Tommy, lying on his back on the floor, muscles quivering. A thin line of spittle leaked from his mouth, his nose was bleeding again. His eyes met hers. He was helpless. She poked him with her numb foot.

"Stung him with a tangler," Hardwired said, returning from the bathroom. He patted a small bulge in his pocket. "Screws up the nervous system. Be hours before he can move on his own."

He handed her a wet towel. Panda saw his hands shaking. Hers too. She wiped the blood from her face, her chest, daubed gently at her tongue as best she could. It felt as big as her arm.

"He was kicking my ass," Hardwired said, glancing at Tommy. "Those bioteched muscles of his. Then he went rigid and started moaning. Like he was coming or something." He gave a short, nervous laugh, touching the swelling over his eye. "That's when I got him with the tangler."

"Thought tanglers were illegal," Panda said. She was giddy with reaction, still buzzing with adrenaline.

Hardwired grinned. "A lot of stuff's illegal." He began pulling the trodes off her scalp, jerking each one sharply to break the bond. "I saw you leave Net-Work," he said. "Used the tracer, followed you in a cab. Took me a while to decode the locks."

He finished pulling off the trodes, went to the box next to the bed. "This unit's got an inverter," he said looking at her. "That's serious shit."

Panda laughed, trying not to smile. Her tongue hurt ferociously. She spit blood into the towel. "Tell me about it."

Hardwired bent over Tommy, began attaching the trodes he'd pulled off Panda to Tommy's head, amidst the wires already bristling there.

"What're you doing?" Panda had found her bodsuit and was struggling into it, wincing. Tiny punctures in her stomach and thighs seeped blood. There were vivid red circles from the squids around her wrists and ankles; her feet and hands prickled with the needles of returning circulation.

Hardwired kept attaching the wires. "Hook him up. Switch off the inverter, set the box to amplify, two-way read and feed. He won't be able to stop it."

Panda limped to the door and leaned on the wall, watching. "Stop what?" The adrenaline was fading, leaving her shaky and weak.

Hardwired finished attaching the trodes, went to the box, fiddled with some buttons, adjusting the digital readouts. Finally he grunted in satisfaction. "I turn the inverter off, see? So it doesn't reverse sensation. Amplify makes it stronger. Then I set it for two-way read and feed to make a loop."

"But there's only one person."

"That's right." Hardwired looked at her. His blue eye sparkled with anger. "Cause a little pain, like this." He took a needle off the tray, bent and poked Tommy in the arm, drawing a bright spot of blood, crimson on pale green, then threw the needle down. He grabbed Panda's arm and led her from the room, supporting her as she limped on her tingling feet.

"Started a loop," he said. "Box reads the pain, amps it, feeds it back stronger, reads it, feeds it back stronger . . ." he looked at her. "Feedback loop. See?"

Panda understood. "Sending him his own pain, but stronger each time."

Hardwired nodded, licked his lips.

"Kill him?"

Hardwired nodded again. "Burn him out."

Panda pulled free of Hardwired's helping hands to stand alone, swaying. Tommy had killed Lucie. Would've killed her. Bastard deserved to die. All the better if it hurt. He deserved it. She turned to leave. She *tried* to leave. She couldn't.

She hobbled back to the bedroom, stood for a moment in the door. Tommy lay where they'd left him, body convulsing, eyes rolled up and showing white, heels and palms thrumming on the carpet, tendons like cables under his skin. His mouth was stretched wide in a silent scream. She'd dreamed of finding Lucie's killer, of making him pay. She looked for the elation, but it wasn't there. She wasn't sure what she felt, but she didn't like it, whatever it was. Why didn't she feel good? Shouldn't she feel good?

Panda limped over to Tommy. "I hope it hurts," she said, kicking him. She looked at the door, tried to walk toward it. Then she knelt, jerking angrily at the wires on Tommy's head with her numb and clumsy hands, over and over, until they were all disconnected. Tommy lay limp, eyes glazed and unfocused, breathing harshly, his muscles quivering and twitching.

Panda looked up, saw Hardwired in the doorway.

"I can't kill him," she said, shaking her head. "I thought I could, but I can't. I'm not like him. And even if I could, they'd find me. He matters. The sniffers wouldn't brush off his death like they did Lucie's."

Hardwired didn't answer, but she read the understanding in his face.

"We'll call the sniffers once we get out of here," she said, mouth dripping blood. "At least he'll get in trouble for having the box." She stood stiffly, glanced down at Tommy. He was watching her, recognition in his eyes, and something else. *I knew you couldn't do it*, they seemed to say. *I knew you were weak.*

"Fuck you," she said. She kicked him. *That* did feel good. She did it again, then limped to Hardwired, wrapped an arm around him, and leaned heavily on him as they left.

FOR THE STRENGTH OF THE HILLS

Written by
Lee Allred

Illustrated by
Steve Turner

About the Author

Lee Allred has had the usual assortment of writerly jobs—radar maintenance technician, cartographer, commercial artist, butcher's assistant, soldier, missionary, construction foreman, ranch hand, newspaper sports photographer and so on. Currently, he works as a desktop publisher for an international electronics firm.

He has lived and worked extensively in the Orient—Thailand, Korea, Hong Kong, Guam and Japan—as a missionary, electronics technician and as an English teacher. At one point, he was staying in the Royal Plaza Hotel in Korat, Thailand, in 1993 when the hotel collapsed, killing and injuring hundreds of people. Lee served as an interpreter for U.S. officials on the spot and assisted in the rescuing of victims and salvaging property.

Lee has nearly completed his undergraduate work and has presented several papers at regional literary conferences on topics ranging from Rudyard Kipling to John Gardner and Mormon SF writers. For the last two years, Lee has also been a co-chairman for Life, The Universe & Everything, one of the nation's largest academic symposiums on SF.

Lee has produced a number of fine stories (he's been a finalist in this contest before). Many of his stories incorporate his love of history, an interest in moral dilemmas coupled with powerful conflicts. His tales are often accompanied by a sly sense of humor.

In this story, Lee writes an alternate history based on an incident that most people are not at all aware of—the "Mormon War" of 1857. In the actual incident, U.S. government forces were dispatched to Utah to "quell" a nonexistent rebellion. The Mormons, who had survived an extermination order in Illinois a few years earlier, felt compelled to use a number of innovative defensive tactics—such as burning off the prairies, salting wells, stealing food shipments and using psychological warfare—to dishearten and defeat the U.S. Army without ever firing a shot.

In the fascinating tale that follows, Lee posits another possible ending to the scenario. . . .

About the Illustrator

Steve Turner was born on December 4, 1968, in Reigate, Surrey. A keen draftsman from an early age, he was encouraged to study graphic design when he left school. However, Steve became disillusioned with this and took other employment as it seemed unlikely he could succeed as an illustrator.

Between the years 1994 and 1996, Steve traveled through Russia, China, America, Canada, Australia and New Zealand, where he painted a number of murals in Backpacker accommodation.

Steve is still not employed as an artist, but having developed his own interest and style, he now intends to produce an illustrated book based on some ideas for a fantasy story he conceived some years ago.

The resupply column reached the blackened remains of Fort Bridger, flags flying, brass bands playing. Even the brackish dust billowing majestically across the prairie behind them joined the celebration. Fifteen hundred US Army Regulars marched west across the vast Utah Territory toward Fort Bridger. A line of ox-drawn wagons, two thousand strong, followed behind. The line curved eastward over the sage-dotted horizon, the first supplies to reach Fort Bridger since the snows of autumn.

From the dugout revetment on the banks of the tiny Black Forks Creek, just outside the fort proper, the starving men of "B" Battery watched the column approach.

"Cap'n?" The soft, timid voice belonged to young Private Danby, of course—young enough, his face was still as smooth as the brass cannon barrel he stood polishing. The twelve-pounder Napoleons gleamed in stark contrast with the rest of the muddy, derelict fort.

Captain Peck turned and looked down from atop the mud-plastered log wall of the revetment. Peck's once proud blue Army uniform had faded. Patched and patched again, his ragged tunic hung loose over his starved frame. Three disastrous marches down Echo Canyon and three hellish Bridger winters had chiseled a cragginess to Peck's face until it seemed carved out of the same rocks that lined the Echo.

"Supposing they're here to spell us off, Cap'n? Take us home, I mean. Or at least Ft. Levenworth, maybe?"

Peck remained silent. He looked back toward the approaching wagons.

"They *are* here to spell us off, I mean, aren't they, Cap'n?" Danby persisted.

Rufus Ferguson, the battery's grizzled sergeant-major, pushed back his threadworn cap with a dirty-looking thumb, tattooed by years of burning gunpowder. He squinted at the billowing dust clouds. "Too many wagons, boy." He spat on the ground and rubbed it around with a worn boot. "Too many wagons. Too much food in 'em. Naw, they ain't taking us back."

Danby looked first at Ferguson then back at his captain. *"Too much food!"* he sputtered at last. The look in his eyes said it all: too much food for Johnston's Army? How could anyone who wintered in Bridger ever consider there being such a thing as too much food again?

Peck slowly eased himself from the top of the revetment wall back down into the muddy gun pit. He laid a steadying hand on Danby's trembling shoulder. "He means, son, that there are more supplies coming in than we'd ever need if we were simply pulling out."

Peck stopped there, wanting to be kind to the boy. Ferguson, however, had never been sanguine about a soldier's feelings. *"Hmpf,"* the old sergeant snorted. "Too much food to pull back with, and not enough to go ahead with. Not enough by a jugful. Not if Johnston has us make another try down the Echo—not and still have any food left when winter sets in, even if we do push through."

Peck slowly shook his head. "No. Not if the Mormons keep their pledge to burn the city to the ground if we do make it through to Salt Lake."

Ferguson nodded and spat again. "Danby, you remember how much food you brung with you last spring, boy?" Danby had arrived the year before in a procession even grander than the one they watched today. "How many sacks of them beans are left?"

Danby nodded dully. The beans had run out in December, the mules and the oxen that freighted them had run out in February. Corn meal paste mixed with bark and what scarce game they could shoot had been the only food they'd eaten these past few months. A tear trickled down Danby's cheek. He wiped at it with a grimy, bandaged hand. "You mean we—we—oh, Cap'n! *Another winter*, Cap'n?"

Peck turned away. He looked to the west, past the Mesa, toward the Echo where the Mormons waited patiently, hidden, fortified in the narrow sheer-walled canyons, their hands poised on the cranks of their mechanical Browning repeating rifles. "Worse, son. Far worse. Another summer."

•••

Hours later, Peck and his men were still at their post, manning their guns. Drunken laughs and shouts and camp songs echoed from inside the walls of the fort. Mercifully, the bitter west wind kept the smells of the cookfires away from the starving men. The first wagons to arrive had passed out some beef jerky to the men. Peck had kept his men from eating theirs. As starved as they were, the jerky would do little good—only cause their empty stomachs to swell up painfully and render them unfit to man their guns.

Eventually an orderly strolled out to the revetment. The orderly was almost as young as Danby. He saluted Peck clumsily, his hand buried deep inside an oversized tunic sleeve of a crisp new uniform. The sleeve unrolled as he saluted. "General Johnston's compliments, sir, and you're to report to him soonest." The boy's breath hung heavy with the smell of cheese.

Peck returned the boy's salute. He turned to Ferguson. "I was wondering how long before our esteemed Albert Sidney sent for me. Take charge of the battery, Rufus." He glanced at the setting sun. "I imagine you've still time for one more practice drill."

The young orderly looked up from rolling back his sleeve. "Oh, I almost forgot the next part of the message." He screwed his face in concentration. His voice took a sing-song quality as he parroted: "'B' battery is to be hereby relieved from duty until further notice on my—I mean General Johnston's—authority."

"He what—?" exploded Ferguson. Peck motioned him to be quiet. "Relieved? By whom?" Peck asked.

The orderly gulped. "Uh, my guess'd be nobody, sir. Truth is, you're the only ones left at their post. Everybody else is beginning to celebrate, like. All the other men, well, they think you're crazy sitting out here in the wind and not joinin' in the doings."

"Crazy are we? Crazy? Well, someone's crazy around here, and it ain't us," snapped Ferguson. "These guns we're crazy enough to keep manned are the only things keeping the Mormons from swarming over the flats and taking this ramshackle excuse for a fort."

The boy gave an adenoidal snort. "Reckon they'd be fools to try anything now, what with two whole fresh infantry regiments marching in. And nearly as many cavalry troopers as well."

Ferguson took a deep breath and sighed. "Son, when Buchanan started this Utah War, there were only eight regiments in the whole US Army. The Mormons have chewed up four already and lost nary a man doing it. What makes you think they're going to be a-scared of a mere regiment or two?"

"No need to chew at the boy, Rufus," Peck said. "It's not his fault our 'second Napoleon' hasn't an ounce of sense."

"'Second Napoleon,'" Ferguson hooted. "Albert Sidney Johnston ain't nothin' but a sawed-off Texas horse colonel—light colonel at that!—breveted over his head. Curse the day Jeff Davis and the War Department ever saw fit to promote that skunk."

The poor orderly glanced nervously in the direction of Johnston's headquarters. "Excuse me, sir, but the general did say 'soonest.'"

Peck looked at his guns, then at his starving, ragged men. Ferguson followed his gaze. He spat, then pushed back his cap and hitched up his britches. "Don't worry about us, Cap'n. Figger me and the rest of the boys'll join in the doin's sittin right here. Sunset ought to be mighty purty tonight."

Peck nodded a curt thanks.

"'Course," Ferguson said, clearing his throat, "maybe you should send Danby to bring us some of that there grub. And some plug." He grinned. "Oh, an' something stronger than crick water to fill our canteens with—some moral 'suasion to rinse this joe-fired prairie dirt outa our craw. An' some blankets to keep the night chill off'n us. And some new boots. Ones with the soles stitched on, not glued with that Connecticut glue that washes out when it gets the tiniest bit wet. And . . ." his voice trailed off as he grinned even wider.

"Something else?" Peck almost smiled.

"Not unless they brung a Kansas City woman in one of those wagons," winked Ferguson.

A red flush crept up the orderly's face. "Uh, best not wait to get them boots or new uniforms, 'cause they're going real fast."

"Naw." Ferguson spat in the direction of the large cemetery outside the stockade. "I'm thinkin' the War Department planned on a few more of us being here than what there is. There'll be more than enough extra new uniforms to go around." He turned to Peck. "Go on, Cap'n. We can handle things here."

"As soon as I straighten this mess out, Rufus, I'll have a proper relief sent out to you—that is if our Albert Sidney doesn't throw me in irons first, now he most likely has a replacement for me."

Ferguson wiped the corner of his mouth and grinned. "Haw. That ain't too likely, what with you being the chief of staff's godson. Johnston's too promotion happy. He'll gum a bit, but he ain't gonna bite much." He frowned. "Can't say the same about them trucklin' pea wits around him, though." Ferguson stared down at his boots and scuffed them around in the mud. "Best watch yer back, Cap'n, just the same. And your temper. You're worse'n I am sometimes," he grinned.

Peck smiled and clapped the old sergeant on the shoulder. "Only around Johnston." Peck climbed out the revetment and followed the orderly toward the fort.

•••

Peck pushed his way through the camp, possibly the only man inside the fort sober, and possibly the only one not singing some camp song or another at the top of his drunken lungs. The most popular, of course, was that Brigham Young song some reporter from Back East had brought out a couple years ago with the '58 expedition.

I drug the Saints to the desert here
    (A profi'ble prophet am I!)
Just crickets and seagulls, no 'baccy or beer.
    (A profi'ble prophet am I!)
I grew a beard to cover my face
    To hide the shame of choosing this place.
I'm building a Temple to cap the whole case.
    A profi'ble prophet am I!

Peck headed for the crude adobe cabin slumping against the low stone wall the Mormons had built when they'd bought the fort from Bridger himself. The cabin served as Johnston's headquarters. The closer Peck got to it, the thicker the drunken mob he had to push through. Next to the cabin, however, the crush of singing, shouting men abruptly thinned. A picket of armed guards, new arrivals from the look of their full, beefy faces, had cordoned off the cabin and the northeast corner of the fort as well. Peck shook his head. Most likely Johnston didn't want any of the enlisted rabble disturbing him while he and his bootlickers sat smoking cigars as their dinners cooked.

A peculiar gun carriage sat in front of the cabin. Prairie mud, cracked and dry, coated its wheels a goodly way up to the hubs. The mud shouldn't have been that deep, thought Peck. Then he noticed both wheels and carriage were too small by half. Small, but heavy. The canvas tarp draped over the gun bulged oddly, not the shape a cannon should bulge at all. Peck had never seen the like of this gun before.

Peck wondered what new deviltry President Buchanan's munitioneering cronies had foisted upon him. Hopefully, the strange gun would be of more use than those white elephantile Parrot guns the War Department had tried sending them last year. The huge five-ton siege guns had been abandoned somewhere near the North Platte. The Indians—assuming they could ever budge them—were welcome to them as far as Peck was concerned.

Imagine trying to drag those siege guns down Echo Canyon once they'd made it to Bridger, Peck snorted to himself. What was the War Department thinking anyway? "Blast the doors off the Mormon Tabernacle" indeed. No doubt whatever was under that tarp probably would turn out just as useless as the Parrot guns.

If only the Army would send something practical, like a couple dozen mountain howitzers. Peck could throw one on the back of a mule and its carriage on another mule or two—or if necessary, his men could carry them up mountain slopes and flank the Mormons' positions. That would be the only way they'd ever break through to the Salt Lake Valley. They certainly weren't going to do it going up against Brownings with only muskets.

One wife's a horrible, mortible sin
  (A profi'ble prophet am I!)
Us Mormon tomcats, we spread ourselves thin.
  (A profi'ble prophet am I!)
So come join my harem, it's not a bad place;
  I send off to Europe for converts and lace.
If the devil wants sinning—"This-is-the-Place!"
  A profligate prophet am I!

A sentry posted at the door of Johnston's cabin snapped to attention as Peck stepped up on the flimsy wooden porch. The porch swayed and groaned with the added weight, but held somehow. Peck pulled on the door's crude rope latch and stepped inside.

The Army is coming to learn us a lick.
    (A profi'ble prophet am I!)
Johnston's a sly one, but I'm Brigham Slick.
    (A profi'ble prophet am I!)
I'll block off the canyons and dig up the dirt,
    Jump in a big hole and then lie there inert,
And just hope my harem don't gossip and blurt.
    A pitiful prophet am I!

Inside the cabin, the air hung heavy with the homey smells of cigar smoke and coffee as General Johnston and his gathered staff gratified vices denied for far too long. Gathered around Johnston were his various toadies "come to teach the Mormons a lick": Ben Butler, the Massachusetts politician somehow still corpulent after a Fort Bridger winter; spit-and-polish George McClellan, the Napoleon of the dispatch paper; Texan cavalry cronies from Johnston's earlier days; and several scruffy Missourians out to avenge the Francher party.

Three new faces sat to one side of the room. A colonel, a youngish major and a fat greasy-looking civilian in a butternut jacket. The blue tobacco smoke was so thick, Peck could hardly see their faces.

General Johnston bent low over his dispatch papers. His face was all frown and moustache, a weasel face jutting out from beneath a head of hair borrowed from

Stephen A. Douglas. Too bad Johnston hadn't borrowed the rest of Douglas' shrewd head as well. When the Creator had fashioned Albert Sidney Johnston, He'd set a pigmy-sized head atop a massive torso. Ferguson once said the reason Johnston hadn't had a new idea in years was on account of there being no room for one to squeeze inside his tiny skull.

Peck latched the door behind him, stepped forward and saluted. "Captain Peck, reporting as ordered, General."

Johnston looked up from his papers. A glass of brandy and cigar sat in one hand, a copy of his new orders in the other. "Ah, gentlemen." However pedantically precise Johnston's speech was, his Texas drawl was red clay thick. "Our illustrious, if somewhat tardy, Captain Peck has arrived. Captain Peck, actually Lieutenant Peck, has been acting as artillery commander since Johnny Phelps' unfortunate demise. Brevet captain, I should say. His promotion is only temporary. Very temporary."

The major, an artillery major Peck now noticed, turned sharply to stare at Peck. "I shouldn't wonder. A *lieutenant* commanding a battery?"

"Hobson's choice, I'm afraid," smiled Johnston. "Until your arrival, Major Willis, Peck here was the only artillery officer I had in my command, regardless of what, ah, irregularities exist up his family tree. Oh, how careless of me. I forgot introductions. Peck, Major Willis here is your new artillery commander—"

"Major," Peck said stiffly.

"—and this is Colonel Stuart, Second Cavalry. Colonel Stuart will be keeping the lines of communication back to Ft. Levenworth open for us."

Peck's face brightened. Stuart had been a classmate at the Point. Class of '54. Peck started to step forward to shake hands, slap his old friend on the back, but a cold, icy glare from Stuart caused Peck to step back. "Colonel," he said stiffly.

Stuart didn't answer.

Johnston chuckled. He pulled a quick draw off the cigar. "Now, Colonel Stuart. No need for that. When I mentioned those family irregularities, I didn't mean the kind that would rightly shame any son of the South. No, Peck here has a sister that went and ran off with the Mormons a few years back. Tends to make him here a bit softheaded towards them."

"I do my duty."

"Perhaps—after a fashion. You *do* your duty—but only that." Johnston drew on the cigar again. "Colonel, we've much to discuss tonight. Shall we act like gentleman and finish the introductions so we can get on with it?"

Stuart looked at Peck. "I think I'd sooner his family had the *other* kind of irregularities."

Smoke curled from Johnston's smirk. "Come, Colonel. You're a better man than he."

Stuart's eyes flicked toward Johnston and back. "*Lieutenant.*"

Johnston nodded, satisfied. "Now then, Peck, this distinguished-looking civilian gentleman is Mister Agar. He's connected with the War Department, you might say."

Peck eyed the man's silk shirt and well-fed middle. "*Well* connected, I should say."

A broad grin snaked its way across Johnston's face. He turned to the major. "You see, Major Willis, what I've had to endure from our Captain Peck? Major, the most pleasant aspect of your arrival—and that includes fresh victuals and these wonderful cigars—is that I no longer have to pay any heed to Hobson or his horse at all—or to Peck's high horsery, either."

Peck stiffened. Johnston held up a hand, sloshing his brandy a bit as he did so. "I believe our captain is about to protest my ordering his men from their posts, an order I'm sure he's already ingeniously circumvented. Peck here is quite conscientious about his duty. At least, conscientious with what he *feels* his duty to be. Sometimes—rarely—his self-assigned duty even manages to match my direct orders."

"General," Peck said slowly. "I must indeed protest. Those wagons lined up like ducks for the shooting, my men to be pulled off their guns, that drunken brawl outside. Surely you know the Mormons can see everything that goes on in this camp from the Mesa."

The Mesa was really three small mesas clumped together about four miles from the fort. It jutted up from the prairie like an inverted "T," giving any spyglass-carrying Mormon atop it a commanding view down into the camp. Old cantankerous Jim Bridger had died trying to chase them off it. He'd been found face down, a Mormon Bowie knife stuck in his gut. Camp rumor held that the knife had belonged to none other than Porter Rockwell himself, but Peck knew better than to believe in that supernatural Danite nonsense. That was for fools and Back East reporters. Mormons were only human—once you took away their Brownings.

Johnston smiled and nodded. "Of course the Mormons'll see it. And they'll also see the two regiments of fresh infantry troops that arrived today. And that strong cavalry screen of Colonel Stuart's. Peck, the camp is in no danger whatsoever from a couple of Porter Rockwell's boys sitting up on that mesa with homemade spyglasses."

An empty bottle shattered against the outside wall of the cabin. A large whoop from a drunken group of soldiers accompanied it.

Peck jerked a thumb at the noise. "If the rest of camp is as drunk as that, a couple of men is all it'd take to overrun the fort."

Johnston leaned back and laughed. "Peck, stop your fretting. Major Willis' men will take over your guns tonight."

The major squirmed. "Ah, General, with all due respect, Peck and his troops do know the local situation better than I do. Wouldn't it be better if his men got together with mine and—"

Johnston fixed his eye on Willis, his voice suddenly low. "Don't you *ever* question my orders again, Major Willis. Understand?" He stubbed his cigar out and smiled sardonically. "Now, some reporters Back East have also questioned me, asked why haven't I tried to go around Echo Canyon. This only demonstrates their vast ignorance. The Rocky Mountains are part of a great mountain chain that stretches from the Arctic to Panama. We're on this side of that chain, the Mormons on the other. Here, and only here, is a gap—a cone-shaped gap that narrows down to only one small mountain ridge between the Great Plains and the Great Basin: Echo Canyon. We can't go north to get at the Mormons. We can't go south. We have to go through that canyon."

He tapped a forefinger at the dispatch papers. "Gentlemen, my orders are to march down the Echo and take Salt Lake City and crush Brigham Young's vile rebellion against the Union. To do so, it is my duty—our duty—to put the drive, the determination, the fire in the belly that will enable the men of our army to do so. I aim to do just that using every and any means possible. That drunken scene outside, as distasteful as it is to we gentlemen of proper breeding"—his men around him smiled and nodded to themselves—"is necessary to raise the common soldier's common spirit. Gentlemen, you have my word that tonight's celebration and my liberal disbursal of spirits will prove the key to inspire our army to victory." A cold smile crossed his face. "The key. My solemn word."

Johnston pushed himself out of his chair. "And now, gentlemen, shall we retire outside? I believe Mister Agar has something to show us."

•••

Agar proudly whipped the tarp off the strange-looking gun. It wasn't a cannon—that much was certain—but Peck, for all his years as an artillery officer, had never seen a gun quite like it. A long, slender gun barrel protruded from a gear-filled mechanical box with a hand crank on its side and a tin hopper on its top. Through a complicated gear arrangement, the gun could swing side to side as well as up and down.

McClellan brushed his moustache with the back of his finger and sniffed. Butler grunted, "Looks like a coffee grinder with a gun barrel sticking out of it." Of course Butler would compare it with something edible or potable.

Instead of being offended, Agar took that as a compliment. "Precisely," he beamed. He patted the tin hopper on top. "Gentlemen, may I present the War Department's answer to the Mormon's miracle gun: the Agar Rapid-Fire—or, as we like to call it, the Agar 'Coffee Mill.' The world's finest mechanically operated repeating rifle." He had to shout a little over the yelling and singing nearby.

Johnston examined the end of his cigar. "Major Willis, I must confess that you were at least partially correct: Peck, here, is the closest thing to an expert on the Mormon's Brownings I have." He jammed the cigar in his mouth. "Peck, inspect the weapon."

Peck stepped over to examine it. He ran his hand down the slim barrel. It looked so delicately attached that the slightest touch would snap it off, but it held firm. "Only a single barrel?" he asked Agar. "The Mormon gun has six barrels; the barrels rotate as the handle's cranked."

Agar frowned. "Richard Gatling out of North Carolina tried that approach, Captain. Alignment problems in trying to synchronize feeding in the cartridges caused him to have to scrap the design."

"Funny, the Mormons don't seem to have that problem. Or if they did, they solved it."

Agar's face reddened. "The War Department judged my uncle's design superior."

"Try lasting a winter on the sort of rations Secretary Floyd's cronies sell the Army and then see what you think of the War Department's so-called 'judgment.'"

"*Captain Peck!*" snapped General Johnston. "You're appraising the weapon, not the War Department. My apologies, Mister Agar." Agar signified gracious forgiveness with a flutter of his hand.

Peck peered into the open crank mechanism. "How do you keep the grit out?" Agar hemmed and hawed. Peck ran his finger across the hopper's interior and extracted gritty black grime. "Just as I thought: you don't. Ammunition?"

Agar handed him a steel-cased cartridge from his pocket. "Uses a .58 caliber. Dump a whole box into the hopper. Fires one hundred and twenty rounds a minute."

"If it fires."

"Oh, it fires. Indeedy it does." Agar snapped his fingers. A private nervously approached with a small wooden box of ammunition. He pried it open and dumped the cartridges into the hopper.

Johnston pointed at the charred east wall of the stockade where the planked logs had started to tumble down. "Aim there," he ordered. They wheeled the carriage into position. Johnston had the milling troops shooed out of the way. Agar removed his butternut jacket and rolled up his silk shirt sleeves with a showman's flair. He spun the elevation and traverse wheels furiously to aim the gun.

"Never mind that," barked Johnston. "Just fire."

Agar cracked his knuckles and grabbed the crank handle. He stood waiting for Johnston's signal.

Johnston nodded at McClellan who drew his Navy Colt and began firing into the air. As if on cue, the drunken men in camp cut loose with their own weapons, firing volley after staggered volley, whooping and yelling. Above it all, however, a deafening racket arose from the Agar as the fat man cranked it: a steady *clack-clack-clack* of the machine gears and the *chug-chug-chug* of the shells. A stream of bullets traced a pattern on the log wall, throwing flame-blackened splinters flying. "Has a range of a thousand yards," Agar yelled over the din. While he cranked steadily, methodically, the private keeping the hopper full. A small pile of expended steel cartridge shells formed at Agar's feet.

Agar cranked a full minute, a minute and a half, then suddenly there was a clang and a crash of metal parts grating on each other and the Agar stopped firing. The intoxicated random firing by the men in camp dwindled away. Agar nursed a set of bloody gear-chewed knuckles in his mouth. With his good hand he slapped the private away from meddling with the hopper. "Keep away, you fool! Want to blow your fool hand off? It could be another hang-fire."

"*Another*—?" Peck shook his head. "How often does this happen? And how long does it take to clear the weapon when it does?"

"An hour or two," admitted Agar. "Have to take the gear box apart." He wrapped his bloodied knuckles with his frilly handkerchief. "You have to understand of course that the weapon really is still in the prototype stage. We *were* rather rushed. Another year or two—"

"Another year or two and Jonathan Browning may well design a weapon as light and as easy for a single man to carry as a Sharps' repeater." The thought of each Mormon rifleman carrying the firepower of a Browning made Peck shudder.

Johnston ordered the tarp replaced over the gun. "We're not here to worry about the future. Mister Agar's weapon seems to work well enough for our purposes, limited though it perhaps is. Peck—your analysis?"

Peck rubbed his chin. "It's unreliable, General. No way to keep it from fouling with grime, not with that open hopper. The single barrel design *is* lighter, though—easier to carry up and down the Wasatch." He looked back at the gun. "And if the Mormons don't suspect we have them . . ."

"And now you know precisely why I *ordered* this celebratory din, Peck: to drown out the noise of the test firing. And they can't see down into this part of the camp from the Mesa. My cabin blocks the view. The Mormons will never even know we have that weapon until the next time we fire it. And next time we fire it will be in Echo Canyon, down their rebellious throats.

We'll see how they like being surprised for a change." He smiled again. "As I said, Peck. My solemn word."

• • •

Peck sat in the dark, alone, slowly eating his food.

He'd walked back to the revetment, only to find that Major Willis had taken over command of the guns. None of the new men seemed to know a caisson from a cascabel. Well, that was Willis' worry.

So Peck had wandered down by the creek to eat alone. He sat there on a small white stone hidden in the rushes and young cottonwoods listening to the creek babble. Better by far than listening to Johnston or his cronies babble.

After a while Peck heard someone blundering through the underbrush toward him. "There you are, Peck," Jeb Stuart called. "I *knew* you'd be somewhere off by yourself." He unslung a bottle of whiskey he had cradled under his arm and tossed it to Peck. "Catch." The bottle plonked in Peck's outstretched hands.

Stuart sat down on a rock next to Peck. He gestured at the bottle. "Figured I needed to make amends for the way I treated you back there in the cabin. Didn't want you to think I wasn't talking to you anymore."

When Peck didn't answer, Stuart clapped him on the shoulder. "You still riled over that crack 'bout your sister? You know that doesn't make a lick of difference between us. Didn't at the time she run off. Doesn't now."

"Then why the whole routine?"

Stuart shrugged. "Obvious even before you showed up that Johnston hates your guts." He smiled. "I wasn't about to go agin him back there for the sake of your ugly Yankee hide. Thought I'd come pay my respects on the quiet later on like."

Peck uncorked the bottle with his teeth and took a healthy swig. He wiped his mouth with the back of his hand and passed the bottle back to Stuart. "You always were the ambitious one, Jeb."

Stuart laughed. "Not like you. Funny. Third in our class—any commission you wanted was yours for the asking. Cavalry. Infantry. Something with promotion attached to it. And what'd you ask for? Artillery." Stuart took a slug. "That's where they put the bottom-of-the-barrel cadets. Why, the top artilleryman in the whole Army's only a colonel. What ailed you, son, to go asking to be put with all the misfits?"

Peck reached for the bottle. "Artillery misfits like Braxton Bragg, Ulysses Grant, Thomas Jackson—even our old West Point Commandant Robert E. Lee? Seems to me it was artillery that decided most of the battles in the war with Mexico. So maybe I just prefer serving where I can do the most good to where I can collect the most gold braid."

Stuart looked down at his shoulder and laughed. "Don't be fretting over these oak leaves too much, old son. I've seen one of those orders Johnston got today, the one confirming your brevet rank, *captain*. Johnston was just stickin' it to you one last time in front of Willis before he had to acknowledge 'em."

"It's still a long ways from captain to light colonel," Peck said as he took another drink.

"Only brevet. Sole reason I got it was that there wasn't another ranking cavalry officer left to give them to besides me. Same deal as you—Hobson's choice."

Peck lowered the bottle and looked sharply at Stuart. "The Army can't be *that* low of men, can it?"

"Why, *thank you*. I have a high opinion of you, too."

"You know what I mean. We've taken a lot of losses here, but not *that* many. Surely they're recruiting the

Army back up to strength, aren't they? What's happening back there?"

Stuart reached for the bottle. "I sorely wish I knew, old son. Yup, they've been recruiting up a storm back home. Just that our old commandant Granny Lee took an' marched them and just about what's left of the entire US Army onto the entire US Navy and sailed off for who-knows-where."

"California," nodded Peck. Coming at the Mormons from the west, the flatter ground wouldn't favor their Brownings as much.

"That's my guess too. Sailing around the Horn. They ought to be arrived a short space back." Stuart snorted. "Johnston wasn't happy when he read *that* set of dispatches! I don't think he wants anyone beating him into Salt Lake City. He's trying to keep it a secret, but it won't last long."

"I don't think Johnston has figured out that the problem isn't so much getting to Salt Lake—it's what's to be done after he gets there. Shoot all the Mormons on sight? Pardon them all? Shoot some, pardon some? What?"

Stuart grunted. "That's more thought than *he's* given the matter—and more than the politicians back home, either."

Peck sat quiet for a moment. "Jeb, what's it like back home? Three years. Three years now—us marching down the Echo and getting slaughtered. How long can this keep going on?"

Stuart sighed. "Not too much longer. Oh, the newspapers and the politicians are still carrying on, but plain folks are pretty sick of the whole mess. Especially down South. The Republicans up North of course yelling about rootin' out them 'twin barbarisms—polygamy and slavery.' It's making us Southerners start worryin' that if the Yankees can twist things so that the entire US Army gets sent to put down one 'barbarism,' what's to stop them from trying to do the same with the other? Fact is, lots of folks down South are beginnin' to hope the Mormons win."

"Are you one of them?"

Stuart forced a laugh. "Just like a Yankee to go and ask that! You know me, old son. Long as it's the one 'twin barbarism' we're putting down, and not the other 'un."

"You didn't answer my question."

"No, I guess I didn't." Stuart put his hands on his knees and slowly got up. "I don't think much of the Mormons. The way they live in Utah is a sin before God and man—but I imagine you know all about that with your sister and all." Peck said nothing. "No, old son, what I like even less than Mormons is the idea that folks from one state can call in troops to make folks of another behave."

"Utah isn't a state."

"Only because your Missouri Compromise wouldn't let them into the Union."

"*Our*—? You Southerners rammed that monstrosity down the nation's throat—"

"Our quarrels with you Northerners have always been as much about States Rights as they ever was about slavery. You're the ones who insist the Federal Government can limit what the states can do inside their own borders. This whole war sets a very dangerous precedent."

Peck stood. "Dangerous for whom? For the Mormons, certainly. The only reason Buchanan started this war was to try to get the country's mind off slavery."

"Well, it hasn't exactly worked, has it?" snapped Stuart. "Let me ask *you* a question: Are you the kind of Northerner who'd be as glad to tackle the second barbarism as you seem to be the first?"

Peck hesitated. "I'd obey my orders, the same as I'm doing now, regardless of my feelings."

"You didn't answer my question."

Peck looked at him. "No," he said slowly. "I guess I didn't."

Stuart swung the whiskey bottle back, ready to strike at Peck. Then he realized what he was doing and slowly lowered his arm. He poured what was left of the whiskey on the ground. "Congratulations on your promotion, *Captain*," Stuart said through clenched jaws. Peck mumbled thanks. His former friend turned his back and walked into the night.

•••

Mormons sneaked into the drunken camp during the night and torched the supply wagons. The fires leapt from one canvas wagon top to another. A giant fireball, noonday bright, exploded high up in the night sky. Orange tendrils of flame showered over the canvas-topped wagons. Then another and another wagon erupted as kegs of powder went up in flames.

Drunken men streamed from their tents to form bucket brigades. Through the choking sulfurous smoke they manhandled the unhitched wagons out of the path of the flames with sheer brute force.

The Mormons escaped unscathed in the confusion, disappearing as if they'd never been there at all.

The sun rose before they'd put the last fire out. As the last bucket of water was thrown on the smoldering wagons, Johnston ordered the troops to assemble.

The men gathered. Peck went up to Johnston to report that the Mormons had spiked two of the cannons in the raid. A penny's worth of iron driven into a gun's vent, and a half-ton bronze cannon was useless.

"Never mind about that now, Peck. They're Willis' problem," snapped Johnston who was preening himself in a mirror held by the young orderly as his cronies, old and new, gathered round. Peck was glad that at least Stuart wasn't there. The cavalry was off chasing Mormons.

An aide handed Johnston a pair of scissors to trim his beard with. "Peck, I'm putting you in charge of the Agar guns. Guard them. Nothing is to happen to them, understand?" He gestured at Agar with the scissors. "Take him along, too. He can be explaining the mechanism during our march to the Echo."

Agar looked up startled. "'During the march?' With all due respect, General, I'm a civilian. I may deliver the weapons, but I don't go off to war with them. I shall be starting back to South Carolina today."

Johnston paused from trimming his beard. He lowered the scissors and smiled like a crocodile. "Ah, but with all due respect, sir, you shall not. Rather, you shall be marching down the Echo right along with the rest of us. Now whether you march as a temporary lieutenant and technical advisor or a twenty-year private mucking out cavalry stalls, makes no never-mind to me."

The fat Agar goggled. "You can't do this!"

Peck pulled Agar aside. "Quiet, you fool."

"But he can't! He can't do this!" Agar insisted, mopping his sweating face.

"He can do anything he pleases. He's military governor. Buchanan's declared the Utah Territory under martial law and suspended *habeas corpus*."

"My uncle—"

"—won't be able to do a thing. Out here, Johnston's judge, jury and executioner—answerable to no one but himself."

"By all that's holy, he's answerable to God!"

"That," Peck grimaced, "is precisely what the Mormons have been saying." Peck laid his hand on Agar's plump shoulder and led him back to Johnston.

"Well, Mr. Agar?" asked Johnston, while he casually snipped at his beard. "I trust Peck's explained the situation to you. What shall it be?"

Agar's jaw trembled, his double chin wobbling like a turkey gobbler, but before Agar could or would answer, Johnston looked up sharply from the mirror, not at Agar, but at the troops behind him forming up by companies. "McClellan!" he barked. McClellan approached and saluted. Johnston ignored it, handing the scissors to his aide. "Did I say to form them up? We haven't time for that nonsense." He motioned a half-circle with his finger. "I said I wanted them gathered around like this. A horseshoe. A mob. That's what I want. A milling mob."

This brought a snort of derision. To Peck's surprise, it came from McClellan. "A mob?" sputtered McClellan. "That's precisely what you've got! A ragged, starving mob!"

"You forget yourself, Major. I am your commanding officer."

"Exactly—the commanding officer responsible for losing almost our entire food supply the very day we get it!"

"Are you saying that I am to blame for this? That's treasonous talk, Major."

The crowd around Johnston suddenly fell quiet and began edging away from McClellan.

"That's *precisely* what I'm saying," said McClellan, the cords in his neck taut, his face leeched white. "I think you all but arranged for the Mormons to burn our wagons on purpose."

"*My own men?* Sir," hissed Johnston through gritted teeth. "I *demand* satisfaction."

A friend grabbed McClellan's arm to try to pull him away. "You fool, he'll kill you." McClellan shook him off. "You shall *have* satisfaction," he spat.

Johnston smiled. "As challenged party, you have the choice of weapons."

"Pistols shall be entirely acceptable."

Johnston's smile grew wider. "And I have the choice of time and place—*and I choose here and now!*" The Texan drew his Navy Colt. In one smooth motion, he swung the barrel up, then down and fired-point blank into the chest of the astonished McClellan.

Johnston reholstered his gun even as McClellan's dead body fell to the ground. "A traitor's death for a traitor. Drag him away and bury him with those two other traitors, Cummings and Kane," Johnston said coolly. He pointed to two men. "Bring a wagon over here. An uncovered one. Pile some crates up in the bed. I want a sort of tower I can stand on to speak to the troops, otherwise they'll never all hear me."

He looked sharply back at Peck. "Peck! Unless you want to join McClellan, get to those infernal Agar contraptions and *stay* there. And take your rabble with you." He looked at Agar. "You, too, *Private* Agar."

•••

From the Agar guns, Peck and his men could plainly see both Johnston and the mob of troops circled around him. Johnston clambered up the rickety makeshift platform in the wagon bed and stood facing his troops. Wisps of smoke still curled from the burned wagons. The glow of sunrise haloed behind him. Johnston drew his sword and held it high. The sunrise glinted blood red on the blade. So silent was the crush of the gathered men that the scraping of the sword against its scabbard could be plainly heard.

"Men," Johnston began, his voice a clarion in the chilly prairie air, "you're too cold, tired, hungry, sick at heart at what has happened during the night for speeches. I know that. I am too. But we must put aside our weariness. The Mormons have burnt most of our food, most of our ammunition. They think that in one night, they have defeated us. But they have not!"

There was a ragged cheer. Peck noted it came mostly from Johnston's cronies.

"Our new Agar guns survived intact," continued Johnston. "With these new weapons and with the strong right arm of God behind us, we shall take back what they have taken from us!"

This time the assembled men erupted in a true cheer.

"The Mormons have proved they will submit to no government but their own. It is a usurpation of the people of the Union to have to endure the erection of a government in their midst neither loyal nor acknowledging any allegiance to the Federal Government. We must either stand by and allow this to happen, or compel them to submit. I say compel them! Compel them with the sword and the cannon and the torch! We shall march down that canyon, we shall march into their city, we shall march into their temple and pull their counterfeit Kingdom to the ground. They wanted rebellion, we shall give them repression. They wanted war, we shall give them *hell!*"

The assembled men frenzied. They surged toward the wagon. They began chanting Johnston's name, over and over. Johnston stood before them, arms raised high, sword outstretched. The crush of sobbing, shouting troops crashed and broke against the wagon like a living ocean wave with no other thought but vengeance. *Vengeance on the Mormons!*

Johnston lowered his sword. At the signal, buglers blew "roast beef," the call to assemble the troops for meals. Cold corn mush, after yesterday's promise of decent abundant food, served to recast their heated anger into cold, hard rage.

• • •

The column wound for miles back through the narrow switchbacks of Echo Canyon. There were few wagons, even fewer spare oxen. Johnston had ordered them slaughtered, butchered, and salted down. There simply wasn't enough forage; it'd all been set to the torch by the Mormons. Most of the horses had been sent back with Stuart to Ft. Levenworth. Johnston saved a few for a small number of cavalry vedettes and a few more to pull the artillery pieces, but none to pull the carriages of the Agars. Peck and his men pushed and pulled the gun carriages toward Salt Lake City like some grotesque parody of the Mormon handcarts.

Ferguson eyed the walls of the canyon suspiciously. The south face was green with brush and scrub and

Illustrated by Steve Turner

deceptively smooth and sloping. You didn't realize until you tried climbing how steep it really was. The barren north face was different entirely. The north face rose in a sheer vertical line. It seemed almost as if the rough blocks of yellow sandstone formed the battlements and ramparts of a castle wall.

"I don't like it, Cap'n," Ferguson grunted as they heaved the gun carriage out of a muddy rut. "I don't like it at all."

"You think I do?" Agar mopped his brow with the filthy remnants of his once-frilly handkerchief. Sweat stained and soaked his dirty, ill-fitting blue tunic. We're sitting ducks down here—and Mormons all around ready to let fly any moment now."

Ferguson spat. "No they ain't—that's what I don't like!" He jerked his head toward the north cliff wall. "This is where we ran into an ambush the last time down—and so far, nothing. Not so much as a peep from the Mormons."

"*Hmpf.* How can you tell? I can't tell one part of this canyon from the next," Agar asked.

Ferguson spat again. "Simple." He pointed to the next bend in the canyon. "See up ahead where the canyon narrows. See how the yellow sandstone turns reddish." Agar nodded. Ferguson's eyes narrowed. "Every time it narrows, every time there's a spot in the canyon that's good for settin' up an ambush, the canyon turns red. Red as blood. If'n I was a superstitious man, I'd say it was a sign for us to do the smart thing and turn back."

"Reckless talk, Rufus," cautioned Peck. He was pushing along with them, as tired and sweaty as the meanest private. "Johnston could have you shot for less."

Ferguson's parched throat gave a dry cackle. "Happens I ain't a superstitious man, Cap'n. Besides,

Uncle Albert won't get the chance to shoot me—the Mormons'll get me first. They're up to something, I tell you. I can feel it. We're most of the way down the canyon now. We haven't seen hide nor hair of 'em." He eyed the canyon walls again. "I don't think there're any up there. And I don't like that at all."

Agar huffed. "I, for one, *do* like it a lot better that way."

The carriage wheel hit a rock and the gun almost toppled over. Only the quick action of Peck and his men saved it. It took several tense moments of grunting and heaving to right it. One man collapsed after the effort. Peck detailed another to carry him until he revived. Johnston had given orders to leave all fallen men where they lay and press on regardless, but this Peck refused to do. He didn't believe much in the camp tales about what the Mormon Danites did with prisoners, but he wasn't going to take a chance in leaving helpless men alone after the sun set.

They struggled on with the gun carriage, short two men now. On they pushed, trying to keep up with the rest of the column.

"As—important as—these guns—are to Johnston," puffed Ferguson, "you'd think—he'd assign us—more men to—*uhng!*—push!"

Shortly the grade sloped a bit more downhill, not enough to cause more work trying to keep the carriage from running away, but enough to ease the load.

Ferguson was still nervously eyeing the canyon walls. Agar, having caught his breath a bit, said, "Maybe we caught the Mormons by surprise. I dare say the thing they least expected Johnston to do after they burned our wagons was for us to make a mad dash down the Echo."

Ferguson grunted. "Might be some truth in that." A corner of his mouth found the energy to turn up slightly. "I know it took me by surprise. Usually our Second Napoleon's a bit more plodding in his reckless abandon. Cold molasses is a fair way of puttin' it." He hocked and spat. "This is the fastest forced march I've ever been on. If it weren't for the wagons an' our artillery, I'd swan we'd be making this trip at a dead run all the way. Faster, ev'n, than the last time we run back up the Echo with our tails between our legs." He eyed the canyons, his face suddenly grim. "Do or die, I can tell you one thing. I ain't running agin. I'll stand and die like a man 'fore I let the Mormons chase me back to face another Bridger winter."

Peck raised his head and looked down the canyon, noting landmarks. "You'll get your chance soon, Rufus. At this rate, we'll be to the Breastworks in two days."

"Two days ain't soon enough to suit me an' my aching back." Ferguson grunted as the wheel fell into another rut. "Agar," he growled, "next time your uncle builds a gun, tell him to make it lighter, eh?"

•••

Johnston halted the troops in broad daylight just around the bend from the Breastworks. The Mormons had fortified that very narrow stretch of canyon back in '57, before the shooting had started, and they'd had three years to improve on those fortifications. Twice before Johnston had fought his way down the Echo, and twice before the Mormon's defenses at the Breastworks had stymied him. The mouth of Echo Canyon was just beyond the Breastworks, however—tantalizingly close—and if they could just win through, they could march down what looked to be a wide valley beyond and follow the Weber River to the Great Salt Lake itself.

There was still no sign of the Mormons.

Peck had his men make camp, which meant very little, as they didn't dare start any fires for fear of Mormon snipers on the walls of the canyons, nor had they any wood to do so if they dared. The men could only unroll their bedrolls, chaw dejectedly on their salted horsemeat strips, and soak their sore feet in the crisp water of Echo Creek.

Peck left them there, soaking their feet, and walked over to the canvas tent being set up for Johnston. The tent flap was open.

Johnston bent over his collapsible table poring over a map of the canyon. His cronies, those of them left—Butler, Francher and Willis—were also standing around the table, grim-faced. The half-rations and tomorrow's planned attack had them all on edge—enough so that they were actually arguing with the general. ". . . It's impossible," Ben Butler was saying, mopping his shiny bald head with a handkerchief. "We've less men and cannon than the last time we tried, and look what happened then."

Seeing Peck standing there, Johnston motioned him inside the tent.

Butler pointed a pudgy finger at Peck. "Instead of a frontal assault by my infantry, why doesn't Peck use his new miracle guns to break through?"

"All three of them?" asked Peck. "Their only real worth to us is their shock value—if we can surprise the Mormons with them. Wheeling them out in front of the Breastworks in plain sight isn't much of a surprise."

Butler turned red. "You're a coward, that's all."

"Oh? And who stayed at the Napoleons and covered the retreat last year? And who was the first one to run back up the canyon?"

"Mormon-lover!" spat Butler. "Just like the rest of your family!"

"That will be enough," Johnston said. He stretched upright and rubbed his tired kidneys. "Much as it pains me to admit it, Peck happens to be right about the Agars. Throwing them in front of the Breastwork would be like shoveling snow into a furnace."

Butler snorted. "Then I repeat: what good are they?"

Johnston didn't answer. Instead he pointed to the map of the canyon. "Gentlemen, why is it we are having such difficulty getting down this canyon?" There were a few snorts and chuckles. "I asked a question, gentlemen. I'd like an answer. We have two and a half regiments of Army regulars. A well-drilled artillery battery, and even a fair amount of cavalry. All that's stopping us is an untrained Mormon rabble. Why can't we get down this canyon? Ben?"

"If it *pleases* the general," Butler said sarcastically, "because the cussed canyon's too narrow."

Johnston nodded. "Exactly. We may have the edge in both quantity and quality of troops, but a few men armed with a mechanical repeating rifle can hold off an entire army."

The glum-faced Missourian spat on the floor. "You ain't telling us nothin' new here, General."

"Ah, Francher, but I am. If the Mormons can use the canyon against us, why can't we use it against the Mormons?"

Francher laughed sourly at that. "They ain't the ones anxious to git down the canyon—we is."

Johnston pulled a cigar out of his pocket and lit it. "But what if they were. What if we were to make them 'anxious'?" He blew a smoke ring. "Gentlemen, the Mormons are only human. Echo Canyon's as narrow for them as it is for us. It's high time we started using that little fact of nature."

He pointed at the map to a spot just around the curve from his Army's camp. "This long straight stretch of canyon here is the Breastworks. Just beyond that is this small hill the men call 'the Plug' because it sits in the middle of the canyon and plugs it like a cork in a bottle."

Francher hooked his thumbs in his suspenders and spat on the ground again. "Tell us sumptin' we don't already know. Me an' my boys, we's the one who scouted out that map for you." He jabbed a thick callused finger at the map. "Yup, that's the Plug. An' just a mite ways past it the canyon ends, on account of the Echo flowin' into the Weber. We knew that three years ago. Thems Mormons got a whole camp around that Plug: stables, kitchens, magazine bunkers. All the comforts of home—everything they need to keep them Breastworks manned agin us. Nothun's changed, 'cept maybe the Mormons have built a few more outbuildings around the Plug, maybe dug in a little better. Even if we did get past the Breastworks, the Plug'd still stop us cold."

"So a few Mormons with Brownings sitting on the Plug could still bottle us up, is that what you're saying?"

Francher stretched his suspenders and let them snap. "That's just exactly what I'm saying, General."

Johnston smiled. "And what if a few of *our* troops with Agar guns were sitting on the Plug instead?"

A stupefied look slowly crept over Francher.

Butler's fat chins gobbled up and down. "Why, the Breastworks would be completely cut off!" he exclaimed.

"They couldn't fight their way down the canyon any better than we could. Pretty soon, they'd run out of food—"

"—and, what is more important, ammunition for those 'miracle guns' of theirs," finished Johnston. He snapped his fingers. "And that would be that."

Butler frowned. "But . . . how are we going to get the Agars on the Plug? It's impossible."

Johnston just smiled like a canary-fed cat and hooked a finger at Peck.

Peck stepped up to the map table. "The Austrians thought it was 'impossible' for the French to haul heavy artillery up St. Bernard's Pass in time for the Battle of Marengo in 1800. Napoleon proved them wrong. We can do the same to the Mormons." He pointed to the map. "I've proposed to General Johnston that we haul the Agars up the south wall of the canyon. It's steep, but not nearly as vertical as the north wall. And it has a few trees for block-and-tackle work."

Butler looked unconvinced. "And how will you manage to simply 'haul' the guns up the wall of the canyon?"

"The same way Napoleon did. Disassemble the gun carriages. Hollow out logs, put the guns in the logs, then drag them like sledges up the slope. Carry the ammunition and the dissembled carriages by hand."

He pointed at the map again. "Skirt the ridge of the canyon wall, stay on the other side of the slope to keep out of sight. March to about here. There's a relatively gentle slope to the canyon wall here next to the Plug. Run down the slope, take the Plug by surprise, set up the Agars, and hold out until you force the Breastworks and join up with us."

Johnston nodded. "A classic textbook military maneuver, gentlemen."

Butler was unconvinced. "*Textbook* maneuver? What's to say the Mormons are reading the same text? What's to stop the Mormons from preparing themselves against another Marengo? They've planned for just about everything else."

Peck shook his head. "Brigham's a shrewd old bird—I'll give him that—but 'prophet' or not, there's one thing we have that he hasn't: a West Point military education. I'll match my *de Jomini* against his *Book of Mormon* any day of the week—and twice on Sunday."

"Butler's right. Seems to me like they'd be a-waiting for us to flank them like that," said Francher. "Seems to me like they'd put some lookouts up on the hill or something like that. I know I would."

Johnston took a long drag on his cigar and blew another smoke ring. "Not if they were convinced we were planning to make another frontal assault."

"Which we ain't stupid enough to do."

"Which is *precisely* what we are going to do—and make our preparations for it quite obvious. Butler, I'll expect you to lead that."

"Suicide!" Butler almost screamed. "I tell you a frontal assault is suicide!"

Johnston fixed his cold stare at him. "And it's suicide—slow suicide!—if we don't get past the Echo and into Salt Lake before our food runs out. It's either take the Breastworks now while we still can or starve to death. This is the only plan that will work."

"If it's so great a plan, why didn't we try it last year? Or the year before that?"

Peck snorted to himself. That's precisely what he was asking himself. He'd presented this same plan two years ago when he'd first requested for mountain howitzers. Johnston, however, insisted on attacking his way: straight down the canyon like a steer heading down the chute to the stockyards.

Johnston took his cigar out of his mouth and stared at the smoldering end. "Without these new Agars it simply wouldn't have worked. Couldn't have held the Plug with rifles or cannons. Not enough firepower, not a high enough rate of fire. Between their Brownings and those five-shot slide rifles of theirs, the Mormons would have had us for breakfast."

"Maybe," Butler muttered, "you just weren't desperate enough to try it before."

Johnston studied his cigar. "Maybe." He stuck it back in his mouth. "I'm certainly 'desperate enough' now, as you put it. If the men want food they're going to have to fight their way to it."

"*McClellan*—" Butler whispered. Johnston silenced him with a withering glare.

Major Willis, who'd kept quiet through all this, finally spoke up. "I realize I've not fought the Mormons the way the rest of you have. On paper, it looks as if this plan should work." He looked up at Johnston. "But, General . . . can it? Will it really work?"

A cold smile crossed Johnston's face. "My solemn word."

•••

It was over an hour before Peck could return to his men.

"Rufus, I need you to gather up as many axes as you can find, and men fit enough to use them."

Ferguson got to his feet, grunting a bit from the effort. "That's going to be no mean trick, Cap'n. The axes'll be easy to find; fit men's a whole different fittle of fish." He looked at Agar. "Git up, Agar. You're a fit 'un."

Agar stood up. "I'm not sure how much wood we're going to find around here to cut. Just sage and scrub, and it doesn't burn."

"There's some decent-sized trees up the canyon a ways. I've been keeping an eye out for them. I want trees big enough so that when they're hollowed out, you can set an Agar gun in."

Agar cleared his throat. "Cap'n, in spite of the occasional ruts, broken axles and busted wheels, I do believe that the guns will be easier to haul in the carriages than in those logs."

"Not where we're going." He tilted his head meaningfully up the slope of the south canyon wall.

Ferguson took off his cap and rubbed his hair. "You've got to be kidding, Cap'n. That's impossible."

"That's what the Mormons think, too. And so has Johnston for the last three years. I've finally managed to convince him otherwise." He gave them a rough outline of the plan. "We're leaving as soon as night falls. Johnston wants us in place by dawn."

Ferguson eyed the canyon wall again. "I'm thinking, Cap'n, that Uncle Albert'll need to give us a few more men to lug those guns up *that* slope. In fact, I'd feel a mite better if we had some mules."

"Johnston said he's giving us the Missouri irregulars," said Peck.

Ferguson spat. "Personally, I'd prefer the mules. They're smarter, smell better, and ain't half as mean, ornery, or stubborn as them Missourians."

Agar's stomach growled. "Mules would eat less, too."

•••

They started up the slope at dusk. A thin screen of Missourians scouted the way ahead to watch for Mormon ambushes. The rest of the Missourians and Peck's men grunted and heaved on the ropes fastened to the log sledges. The last few men carried the dismantled gun carriages, axles and wheels, like two-legged pack mules up the slopes behind them.

They managed to drag the logs up to the top. After that, the going got far easier. They skirted summit ridge, just below the crest on the other side, so as to keep just out of sight of any watchers across the canyon on the north wall.

As they reached the spot directly across from the Breastworks, the Missourians all let go of the ropes and flopped down to rest. Peck grabbed their leader up by the scruff of the collar and whispered as loud as he dared, "What do think you're doing? Get back on the ropes and pull." He hauled him to his feet and gave him a shove in the direction of the ropes.

The Missourian tripped and fell. He picked himself up with an insolent air. "Say, ain't this where we're diggin' in at? Them Brownings're right across there, ain't they?" For all his bluster in camp about wanting to avenge his "kinfolk," he didn't seem too eager about it now.

"Quiet, Francher," Peck whispered savagely. "Sure the Brownings are across from us, but if all we wanted to do was directly assault the Breastworks, we could do that from the canyon floor." Peck explained the plan again. Comprehension slowly crept over the man's sullen face. Sheepishly, he got up and picked up his ropes and started pulling again. His men followed.

A few hundred yards later, Peck signaled them to stop. Below them lay the Plug. The place seemed almost deserted, though. No camp fires burned, and there were no sentries apparent at all.

Ferguson said he still didn't like it. It looked like a trick. Peck told him to be quiet.

Peck called his men together. "That," he whispered quietly pointing at the Plug, "is our objective. We take that and the Breastworks are cut off. Then it's only a matter of time before Johnston can punch through past them. Once he does that, the rest of the canyon's no problem at all and we follow the Weber river and march right down to Salt Lake City."

He motioned to Agar and Francher to follow him. They crawled over to the slope and stared down. "Here's the plan: we're going to go down this spur— slope's a bit gentler here. Francher, have a third of your men spread out in front. You're our infantry screen. The rest of your men and mine help drag the guns and carry the ammunition down as fast as we can to that small ridge near the bottom. Meanwhile, your screen will make for those gun revetments as fast as you can. After the guns are down, the remaining two-thirds of your men will join the assault on the Mormon position."

Francher chewed on a twig and thought about it. "Going to make the devil's own noise dragging them logs down. Wake up the whole Mormon camp. I'd feel a sight better if them fancy guns of yours were set up before we made for the Plug."

"Can't be helped," Peck shrugged. "We'll do this just like they do Conastogas going down a mountain pass. I'll have a couple of men on ropes pulling the logs forward and the rest on ropes pulling back to keep the logs from running away on us. We'll set up the guns on that small ridge near the bottom." He turned to Agar, "What I need to know from you is how fast can you unship your guns and get them going once we reach that ridge."

Agar rubbed his chin. "You want me to get all of them in place at once, or just one at first, then the rest later?"

"Just one. I want to be able to pin down any Brownings they may have down there. Set up the others as soon as you can."

"Three minutes for the first one, provided you have Ferguson helping me, but I can't guarantee more than a lick and a promise in setting it up. Can't promise too stable a base to get set up on. Won't be very accurate."

"Just as long as you can spray 'em with bullets and force them to keep their heads down and prevent them from spraying us. Their sheer surprise at being on the receiving end of a mechanical should more than make up for our lack of accuracy. I hope."

"So do I."

•••

Just before dawn Peck's men quietly readied the block and tackles. They lowered the log sledges as far down the slope as they could without making noise. They still were a couple hundred yards away from the small ridge. As the dim light of false dawn lit the mountain tops, Peck signaled Francher's men to creep down the hill.

With everyone in position, the men waited, poised for Peck's command that would send them sliding down the steep slope in a desperate race for the revetments.

Ferguson sidled over to Peck. "I've done some blame fool things in my time, Cap'n, but this is the blamed foolest."

"I was just thinking along those lines myself, Rufus." His voice sounded tight, strained.

Ferguson hacked softly. "Throat's too joe-fired dry to even spit. Figgurin' with all them buildings, there surely has to be several hundred of them down there."

And how many of them would turn out to be friends of his sister? Or family? Peck shook his head clear. He couldn't think about that now. "All the more reason for us to get to the Brownings first."

"Good thing they're all tucked in those buildings fast asleep." Ferguson hunkered down and waited.

Peck waited for the minute hand of his pocket watch to crawl toward the fatal moment. "*Now!*" he whispered, signaling to the men.

Francher's men advanced down the steep slope. Peck cursed. They were starting to run, just what he'd told them not to do. They started sliding and stumbling on the loose rocks, knocking several of the smaller ones free. The rocks started rolling down the slope, creating small landslides and making a devil of a noise.

Fuming, Peck turned back to the Agar guns. The three log sledges began to slide down the hill, picking up speed. Ferguson was trying to get those on the ropes to slow down. He hissed, "Pull, you Mormon-lovin'—"

"She's comin' loose!" cried one of the men. The tackles on the far sledge groaned and popped. There was a sudden snap and the twang of a rope giving way. The sledge, suddenly free, wrenched the remnant end of the rope, yanking to their feet the men still holding on. The sledge began sliding faster and faster downhill, pulling along with it hapless men still caught up in the ropes. Men screamed, huge rocks crashed down the hill, as the sledge rumbled ever faster. Then it hit a small bump and went flying into the air. The sledge landed with a crash and threw the Agar gun out. The metal gun caromed off rock outcropping after outcropping, tumbling over and over. It reached the bottom with a horrible crash and groan of rending steel. The wooden sledge thudded and splintered on top of it.

Peck stood transfixed, horrified. The noise had to wake up the Mormons and Peck's men were nowhere near in position. He had led his men into a slaughter. He started shouting orders for his men to hurry, but Peck knew it was hopeless. The Mormons only had to run to their gun pits before Peck could set up his Agar guns and it would be all over.

Peck waited for the Mormons to boil from out of the buildings, angry ants out of an anthill.

He waited. For the briefest moment, nothing happened.

Then the Mormons started pouring out of their buildings.

"Run!" Peck yelled to the Missourians down the slope. "Run for the revetments!" Francher's men ran, racing the Mormons to the waiting Brownings.

The Mormons may have been groggy with sleep, but they were closer. They dived into the shallow gun pits. The first gun crew to arrive swung the muzzle of their Browning around and cranked its handle.

Francher's men scattered like hens before the fox. They threw themselves flat on the ground. The aim of the Browning could be traced from the blossoms of dust kicked up by the deadly stream of bullets. At first, the aim was wildly off—the gun pits must not have been designed for firing the guns in the direction of Francher's attack. Even so, the spray of bullets forced the Missourians to huddle flat on the ground, preventing them from firing back.

Then, slowly, the Mormons found their aim. The trace of bullets edged closer to the Missourians and began cutting a bloody swath through their huddled masses.

Trapped men screamed, tried to shoot back, tried to crawl away. Tried to beg for mercy. It was no use. The deadly spray continued. A second Mormon crew had readied another Browning. A second deadly arc began crisscrossing the first in a bloody crossfire, leaving no escape at all.

All Peck could do was urge his men who handled the remaining two sledges to redouble their efforts. If they could just set up the Agars in time. If they could just—

The crack of a rifle went off next to Peck's left ear. The Mormon cranking the first of the Brownings suddenly grabbed at his chest as he flew over backwards. Peck turned. Francher stood calmly reloading, as if on a turkey shoot. Another Missourian on the hill took aim and hit the other man in the gun pit. Francher smiled grimly and spat tobacco in the direction of the revetments.

Ferguson, heaving on a rope, grunted, "They're not good for much, but them Missiourians can sure shoot, can't they, Cap'n?"

Francher took aim, slowly and calmly. Peck watched his trigger finger slowly squeeze. *Crack! Thunk!* The man next to Francher went flying backwards, a deepening stain in his chest. Bullets began pinging off the rocks around Peck. Peck dove for the ground. Mormons rifles were picking off the men on the slope one by one. The Mormons seemed to be good shots, too.

One of the Brownings swung from the Missourians toward the hillside. Puffs of dust began to dance in an arc uphill toward the rope crews, but stopped just short of the ridge.

"Looks like they got a limit on how high those guns can be elevated, Cap'n." said Ferguson. "We're safe enough up here till we git down to your ridge." A rifle shot ricocheted off a rock behind him. "Relatively speakin', of course."

Peck roared for the rope crews to speed up. In trying to hurry, a second log sledge gave way.

Losing the second gun may have saved their lives. So totally were they distracted by seeing the second Agar come crashing down, that the Mormons stopped shooting for a moment. Before they recovered, Peck had gotten the third Agar lowered down safely behind the lee of the small ridge.

It was too dark still for the Mormons to see what exactly was going on up the ridge. Still, the Mormons knew somebody was up there doing something they wouldn't like.

Bullets began pinging off rocks. Then, deciding it was pointless, the Browning swung back down to help keep the Missourians pinned. Ferguson used the short respite to yank the gun out of the sledge. Agar had promised three minutes. He set up the gun in less than two.

At that moment, the Brownings fell silent.

"Conserving ammunition?" whispered Peck.

"Shouldn't wonder," Ferguson replied. "They must have gone through several thousand rounds already."

"More likely the gun barrels are too hot," Agar whispered. "Cooling them down."

Peck crept to the crest of the rise and peeked over. The first screen of Missourians were still huddled on the ground between the slope and the revetments, not daring to move. Those of Francher's men who'd been working the ropes were slowly creeping down the hillside, trying not to draw attention to themselves, although almost every step they took sent more landslides tumbling down.

Peck bit his lip, knowing he was about to order men to their deaths. There wasn't any other choice. The Brownings' *fire* must be drawn away from the Agar for that first critical moment of surprise. Without the Agar, none of them were going to make it out of this.

"Francher!" he yelled. "Take the revetments!"

Francher and his men obeyed. Yelling and screaming, the men on the slopes poured down the hillside. The Brownings wheeled and started mowing them down. The men on the ground sprang up and the Brownings wheeled again.

Ferguson heaved the Agar gun up on the ridge. He started loading the hopper. Private Agar began cranking. For a moment, it almost looked as if the Brownings' own bullets began streaming back down the hill toward the Mormons as Agar got his aim. Bullets danced around the rims of the gun pits.

In the breaking dawn, Peck could see the surprise on the Mormons' faces. They stopped firing and dove for the shelter of the revetment walls.

The Agar chose that moment to jam.

Our one chance, groaned Peck. *Our only chance . . . gone.*

Not quite. The shock of a Johnston's Army with their own Browning must have been too much for the Mormons. Stupefied, they peered over the lip of the revetment and stared up at the hill. And in that moment, that precious moment, the muddy, bloody Missourians rose up and leapt at the gun crews. From the slopes, Peck could not see what was happening inside the depths of the gun pit. He heard only the thunk of rifle butts, the clash of burnished steel bayonets and the screams of the dying. There could be no mercy and no quarter in that fight. There could be no prisoners.

The battle went on and on. Then quiet. The Missourians slowly rose from the pit, like the just from their graves, tossing out dead and dismembered Mormons the way a terrier tosses away dead rats.

They had done it. Francher couldn't believe it. After three years, they had taken the Plug.

Echo Canyon was theirs and beyond it, Salt Lake City.

•••

As the sounds of the fighting at the Breastworks echoed down the canyon, Peck set his men to fortifying their position on the Plug. He ordered Agar to see to his contraption and the captured Brownings, to get them in place in the revetments and in working order before the Mormons up at the Breastworks came boiling down the canyon. Most importantly, he ordered Ferguson to make sure the buildings were as deserted as they seemed.

It took only a couple minutes for Ferguson to return and report. "'Cept for the dead, they've gone, Cap'n. Pulled out. Ain't no food, ain't no ammo, ain't no nothin'. Them buildings are picked cleaner than a dog's bone. Completely empty of anythin'."

Peck had just gotten a count on the number of Mormons killed in the small battle. Only eighteen. Hardly any at all. Why had they seemingly abandoned their strongest position?

"Maybe they found out about my uncle's guns," Agar said with a grin.

The battle at the Breastworks suddenly grew silent. Apparently, it hadn't been manned very strongly, either. But why?

Ferguson spat slowly and deliberately as he turned and pointed. "Well, Cap'n, there's your answer," he said, pointing toward the western sky down the Weber River Canyon. "Part of it at least."

The western sky was nothing but a black haze of smoke as far as they could see. White flakes of ash began drifting down, covering them like the first snowflakes of winter. "They've done just like they said they would if we ever made it past 'em. Burn the place to the ground. That's Salt Lake, Cap'n. That's Salt Lake City a-burning." He spat again. "And, I reckon, just about the entire rest of the territory as well."

Francher let out a whoop. "It's Bobby Lee, I tell ya! Just has to be. No other thing it could be. Bobby Lee and the rest of the Army marched in from California and gave it to the Mormons but good. The war's over, I tell ya. It's over. We won!"

Peck looked at Francher. "Have we? When we get to Salt Lake and it's burnt to the ground and there's no food to be had for a thousand miles, tell me again about how we've won." He looked back at the smoke. "It's not over, Francher. It hasn't even begun."

•••

Johnston lost no time celebrating his Echo Canyon victory. He marched his men through the Echo and down the Weber Canyon toward the Great Salt Lake. As they marched, one thought echoed over and over in Peck's mind. No army in the world could have forced their way past Brownings down the crag-lined walls. The Weber was the Echo all over again, only longer and steeper.

They passed through, out of the Weber, past the huge rock formation called Devil's Slide, and into the Great

Basin, within sight of the north shores of the Great Salt Lake. And the land between the lake and the mountains was as lifeless as that dead, dead sea.

Up and down that thin corridor of land, as far as the eye could see, there was nothing but black soot and ashes. Not one home stood, not a barn or building. Not a foot of lumber, a stick, a tree, a single blade of grass or hay—not one thing had been left to Johnston's Army that would burn.

They could see below in the lower Weber valley entire towns, each nearly identical, each neatly laid out in the same grand sweeping design of perfect grids, streets broad enough to easily turn a wagon and a full team of oxen round—all of them empty. Devoid of a living soul. Burnt to the ground until only the brick chimneys stood, and even most of those pulled down. Farms and fields surrounding each town were just as dead. The intricate web of canals and irrigation ditches destroyed.

The men staggered on for a few pitiful yards. Dead ground crunched under foot. Each step loosened puffs of gray ash. Soot and smoke filled the air. High up on the slopes of the Wasatch, the forests still burned.

Most eerily of all, there was no life in that land. No livestock, no animals in the blackened waste. Only the lonely, mocking cry of the gulls circling above the dead lake gave any sign of life.

Johnston called a halt to a column that could go no farther. He summoned his officers. As they gathered around him, Johnston's old Texan cavalry buddies brought him his horse. Johnston mounted up and looked down on his officers to address them. "Men, I will be leading our cavalry south into Salt Lake City as fast as possible, where I hope to secure what foodstuffs remain before the Mormons can burn them all."

Amid the muttering, Butler snorted. "I'd say you're too late by half."

"That may be, but it's less a fool's errand than you may think. As some of you are aware, Buchanan has sent the rest of the Army to attack the Mormons from California: Ulysses S. Grant is marching up from the south, aided by a squadron of gunboats up the Colorado; Robert E. Lee is marching over the Sierras, through Donner's Pass and straight across the salt flats. My plan was that those diversionary attacks would draw off troops from the Echo; they've succeeded beyond my wildest hopes. They've panicked the Mormons, allowing us free passage into their heartland; now we must finish them off by securing their capital."

He paused as if he had expected applause. The men didn't want a city. They wanted food.

"And what if there isn't any Mormon food left?" Butler demanded.

"Then we will link up with the two diversionary columns, each one of which will have plenty of food to see us through."

"Carrying it over the salt flats?" demanded Butler.

Johnston ignored him. "As I am doing this, you will continue your march on foot to Salt Lake City, foraging for food along the way."

"What food?" came the cry. The knot of officers tightened around Johnston's horse. His horse skittered back.

Overhead, a seagull cried. A flock of the birds wheeled past.

Johnston pointed up at them. "There's your food." He said, "That should see you through to Salt Lake City." He spurred his horse forward. His cavalry officers rode after him, kicking up the soot-blackened dust in their wake.

Wearily, Peck and the other soldiers could only follow on foot. There was simply nothing else they could do.

•••

They were just a few miles north of Salt Lake City now. Peck's crude maps called the area Davis. Salt Lake City lay just around a mountain spur to the south. Peck and a handful of his men were tramping wearily toward it. Agar was a bit farther back with his two remaining guns. Other small clumps of soldiers, scattered up and down the valley, vainly looked for something to eat as they staggered south.

Ferguson hacked, his mouth too dry to spit. "Cap'n," he said, "remember when I said I wasn't a superstitious man?"

Peck nodded.

"I think I'm beginning to git that way." Ferguson raised his face to look up at circling seagulls. "Them's the birds that saved the Mormons from the crickets. It's beginning to get to me. Reckon we look to them like another rampaging horde of crickets, the way we're scattered about foragin' off the land. I'm dreamin' of them at night, Cap'n. Huge seagulls that carry me off like a cricket."

Peck laughed, then coughed at the effort. His throat was just as dry. "This time, we 'crickets' are eating the gulls."

"Cap'n!" called Danby from up ahead a way. "Come quick!"

Peck shuffled over as fast as he could, drawing his Navy Colt as he ran. Danby was standing on the edge of a small gully that had been washed out by the spring rains. Down in the gully, hidden from sight, was a horse that had fallen in. The horse had broken its neck in the fall; it was quite dead. Still alive, however, was its rider, his legs pinned under the horse's dead weight. The man was barely conscious. He looked up and saw Peck and his men and stretched his arm, trying to grab the rifle that lay in the sand just beyond his reach. Peck imagined that if the man had been able to reach his rifle, he would have shot himself long beforehand.

"No telling how many days he's been down there," Peck said.

"True enough." Ferguson pushed back his cap. "I don't think that horse is going to be good eatin', Captain. Looks mite puffy to me."

Peck shot him a look. "Never mind about the horse. Let's get that man up out of there."

After some heaving, they got the man out. Both his legs were crushed and one was obviously gangrenous from the smell. They gave him some water to try to help him come to.

Ferguson motioned Peck aside. "Cap'n, what are we goin' to do with him? We don't have enough food or water for ourselves to be wasting on some Mormon who's as good as dead anyway. You should have just left him lay there."

"That," said the man chuckling sourly as he slowly opened his eyes, "is an accurate assessment of this entire war." His chuckle slid into a weak choking cough.

Peck looked at the man, then looked at Ferguson. "He seems plenty alive to me. Rig some sort of litter. We'll carry him along as we go."

"Cap'n—the men are too weak to carry around a half-dead Mormon—"

"Then carry only the half that's still alive, but get moving."

"Yes, sir," muttered Ferguson, glaring angrily at the frail Mormon.

•••

The prisoner's name was Reddick. He was an officer in the Mormon's Nauvoo Legion. Peck couldn't question him much beyond that. The man slid in and out of consciousness as they carried him in the litter. Even when he was conscious, much of the time he was delirious with fever.

Peck's men reached the small spur. Wearily, they climbed the rise for their first look at the Salt Lake Valley.

The desolation of the small farming communities to the north had been bad, but nothing Peck had ever seen prepared him for what he saw now. In the middle of a land that grew nothing but sage and knee-high scrub, near the shores of the dead lake had lain a bustling, living, breathing city of twenty thousand souls. A shining metropolis rising from the midst of the wilderness. Nothing remained now but its charred skeleton. Peck could see from the perfect square grids of city and farms the exact demarcation between sterile desert and the lands the Mormons had tamed, lands that now lay torched.

Reddick rose up in his litter and said with a husky voice, "You should have seen it when it was alive."

Peck whispered, his voice raw, "Johnston promised this: this is surely a hell if ever there was one."

Of all things Reddick could have done, laughing was not one Peck had expected. "It's our turn now," Reddick said, "but yours is coming. Mark it well. This is your future, too."

Looking closer, Peck could see troops milling about in the dead city. Too many to be sure for the small number of cavalry Johnston had taken with him. Mormons? "More likely General Lee's," Reddick said, coughing weakly. "He was right on our heels as we evacuated the city. I'm afraid your General Johnston was several days too late to arrive first—if that's what he was trying to do."

Ferguson spat, "That double-crossing Uncle Albert. He knew! *He knew!* That's why he goaded us down the Echo so hard. He was trying to beat Lee into Salt Lake. He didn't want to end up the goat."

Peck nodded, his face grim. "No, Albert Sidney Johnston isn't the kind of man who's about to let someone else have all the glory." He let out a sour chuckle. "Lee's the hero and Johnston's left with nothing to show but three disastrous winters at Fort Bridger." He shook his head. "That's one situation a dueling pistol isn't going to solve for him."

Peck ordered his men to start marching down into the city.

• • •

In the center of the charred city, stood untouched two large buildings where Lee undoubtedly had made his headquarters. "The Lion and the Beehive Houses," Reddick said. "Brother Brigham left his houses intact." He chuckled sourly. "He wanted to leave Johnston something to burn, I guess."

Peck suspected another reason. Young wanted to give the invaders a small taste of what had been here before they came. The clean, neat buildings and lush shade trees stood in stark contrast, a painful oasis in the charred destruction the Army had brought upon the city. Peck shook his head, "'Johnston's a sly one, but I'm Brigham Slick,'" he muttered.

They were walking through scattered clumps of tents now. The smell of Army cookfires tempted them, but Peck was firm in having his prisoner delivered to Lee as soon as possible.

They passed a large column of Mormon prisoners being marched west toward a makeshift prison camp closer to the lake. The prisoners were as footsore and ragged as Peck's men, but despite everything their spirits seemed higher.

"Boys from St. George," Reddick said as they passed, "I recognize some of them. Your General Grant must have marched in from the south, as well."

The prisoners seemed to recognize Reddick. Some of them saluted him. As Peck passed one group, they straightened their shoulders and held their heads high and began to sing.

• • •

At the hands of foul oppressors,
We've borne and suffered long;
Thou hast been our help in weakness
And Thy power hast made us strong;
Amid ruthless foes outnumbered, who seek our
  mountain sod;
For the strength of the hills we bless Thee,
Our God, our fathers' God.
Thou hast led us here in safety
Where the mountain bulwark stands
Thou hast made Thy children mighty

In the hills shaped by Thy hands;
Thou hast led Thy chosen Israel to Freedom's last abode.
For the strength of the hills we bless Thee,
Our God, our fathers' God.

Peck turned to stare after them. "I know that song," he said. "My family's Swiss Lutheran. That's not a Mormon song; that came from Switzerland."

"The Saints are not the first people persecuted for their beliefs," Reddick said. "Nor shall we be the last." He started to cough weakly, then closed his eyes. When Peck's men arrived at the makeshift hospital a few hundreds yards farther into the city and set the litter down, Reddick was dead.

•••

Ferguson held out the plate to Peck. "Cap'n, you best eat something," he said, nodding at the hardtack and spoonful of beans. "Won't be too long before there won't be nothing left."

Peck didn't answer. He only continued to finger the chain of a small gold locket.

"Lee and Grant didn't bring enough for themselves, let alone us. And the Danites still have our supply lines choked off," Ferguson continued. Still Peck didn't answer.

If only he hadn't seen to Reddick's burial himself. If only the chain hadn't broken and the locket come loose from Reddick's neck as they had rolled him off the blanket into the shallow grave. If only Peck hadn't picked up the locket and opened it and seen the small photo inside.

Ferguson set the plate down. "Maybe they was only sweethearts. Maybe..." His voice trailed off. "Be kinder that way, anyhow," he said gruffly. "'Cause if he was married to her, chances are he was married—"

Peck leapt to his feet, knocking the tin plate over with a crash. The plate wobbled to a stop near his feet. "Don't say it. Don't you dare say it!"

Ferguson took a large chew from the last of his tobacco. "What you're thinkin' is crazy. You didn't kill him, son. You did everything you could to save him. Sight more than me. But even if you had killed him— you're a soldier an' he was the enemy. That's your job."

"Enemy? He was an American. He was my brother-in-law. Is that what the Army is for? Brother against brother?"

Ferguson lifted up the flap of the tent and spat outside. "He was a Mormon, and that's good enough for me."

Peck looked at Ferguson, really saw him for the first time in days. "You really hate them, don't you?"

"Back in the Echo, it was just soldierin'. But once we'd won, and once they'd *lost* . . . they should have given up. But no, they're still fighting, and we're starving, Cap'n. We're starving. We're starving when we oughta have won." He lifted the tent flap again. "It's become right personal now."

Peck fingered the locket. "Yes it has."

"Don't you see, Cap'n? We're gonna have to hunt down every last one of them before they'll give in. Hunt 'em down like dogs. An' that ain't solderin'. Not at all. They've taken my trade, my whole life . . . my honor and made me kill it, the same as they made you kill—" He bent over and picked the hardtack out of the dirt. "Cap'n, I'm ashamed of myself. Ashamed I hate any man because of *this*. If I can learn to hate his kind, then maybe I'm capable of hating my own kind, and that scares me, hatin' and fightin' my own. That Reddick feller and I, we should have been friends the way you and me are, 'stead of the way I feel t'wards him now. You can do something about it, Cap'n. You're a good talker. They'll listen to you. Both Lee, on account of he's a fair man, and maybe the Mormons, on account of your sister." He nodded toward the makeshift graveyard and the newly planted cross. "That's what *he* would have wanted." He scuffed his boot over the beans splattered on the dirt floor. "Not this."

•••

Robert E. Lee sent for Peck the following day. Sentries standing outside the porch of Brigham Young's Lion House saluted Peck and he entered. An orderly ushered Peck straight into Lee's office. The large room must have been Young's study. Once elegant furnishings were soot-stained. Books and mementos of the former owner lay haphazardly pushed aside to make room for the general's charts and maps and other implements of command.

Lee was behind his desk, trying to catch up on the never-ending Army paperwork. His heavy dark blue tunic lay draped over the back of a chair. He wore a plain gray vest over a white shirt. With his pair of reading glasses perched on the end of his nose, the gray-haired Lee looked every bit the nickname he'd picked up from his students at West Point: Granny Lee.

Peck stepped into the room. Before Peck could salute, Lee rose from his chair and walked quickly around the desk, taking Peck by the hand and pumping it up and down. "Good to see you, 'Cadet' Peck." Lee's eyes twinkled warmly. "Good to see you."

"Good to see you, too, General."

Lee waved him to sit down. "I was sorry to hear about . . . " He looked at Peck then cleared his throat. "I imagine," he said breezily, "this feels a might bit better than the last time I had to call you into my office. You could have been first in your class if you'd have just learned to get along with your superiors." He frowned. "Albert Sidney tells me . . . well, to put it politely, that you're impertinent and, shall we say, argumentative?"

"Only," said Peck, flushing, "when he's wrong."

Lee snorted. "Which, I'd wager, is probably most of the time." Lee rifled through some papers and extracted a sheaf. "I have here Albert's Sidney's plan he sent to Washington to use the Agar guns to flank the Mormon's position in the Echo." Peck's face darkened. "Secretary Floyd has suggested Johnston be given some sort of decoration for his brilliant plan." Lee dropped the sheaf noisily on the desk and sat back in his chair. "Sometimes justice is not just blind, but mulishly wrongheaded as well. I know about Johnston's 'brilliant plans': they consist entirely of repeated hasty frontal assaults on the center of a fortified position. I also know which of my former cadets received superior marks on his paper on artillery tactics at Marengo."

Lee scooped up the papers and shoved them into a desk drawer. "Johnston will get his commendation, nothing I can do about it. No sense fighting a war you can't win. But you're getting something that I think you'd appreciate more. I'm transferring you out of Johnston's command and assigning you to my personal staff, Major."

"Th-thank you, General."

"I should thank *you*. We used your plan at Donner's Pass. We couldn't have broken through any other way." A hardened look came over him as he remembered the battle. "A horrible business, that," he said softly. "Our Agars against their Brownings. It is well war has grown so terrible, else we should be too fond of it." His voice became firm again. "At any rate, I'll be needing men on my staff who understand these new weapons. I don't mind being told I'm wrong when I'm wrong"— Lee looked at Peck sharply—"provided it's done judiciously."

"I understand, General."

"Don't worry; you'll get plenty of chances to learn judiciousness." Lee leaned back in his chair and rubbed the bridge of his nose. "I thought I understood war. Meet the enemy, grapple with his armies, defeat him. We've crushed the Mormon army, captured their capitol, and we're no closer to winning than we were when we started."

Lee shook his head. "Heaven knows I don't understand these Mormons at all. I doubt anybody does. Did I tell you we found their half-built temple?" He pointed out the window at a large walled square nearby. "They'd torn it down, buried the granite blocks, then plowed over them to make it look like some sort of big cornfield inside an adobe wall. We'd put up tents and were camping on top of it until Johnston finally forced a prisoner to tell us where it was." He snorted. "More of Johnston's idea of how to pacify the natives. He's got the temple blocks dug up now and on display like some game trophy."

There was a loud knock at the door and an orderly burst inside. He wheezed as if he'd been running. "Begging the general's pardon," the orderly said, "the Mormons have sent someone in under a white flag to parley."

"White flag?"

"Yes, sir." The orderly paused to catch a breath. "And, sir, it's *Porter Rockwell*."

Lee reached for his coat. "Go and find General Grant," he said to the orderly. "Bring him here at once. And General Johnston, too, if he's not off riding after Mormon stragglers."

Peck stood to leave. "You've work to do—"

"You're staff now. You stay put," Lee said as he slowly began to fasten the buttons on his tunic. He looked up and smiled wryly. "I may need someone to tell me I'm wrong. Judiciously, of course."

• • •

The room seemed to shrink when Porter Rockwell strode into it. Smelling of buckskins and sage and sweat, Rockwell filled the entire room. He was large and barrel-chested. His unkempt hair flowed down his back and twined around his front to tangle into his beard. But it was his booming voice and piercing eyes Peck noticed first. No wonder those who met him ascribed supernatural powers to him. He seemed less a man than an elemental force.

Grant, seated in a chair to the side of Lee's desk, mumbled a curt greeting to Rockwell through the cigar clenched in his teeth. Johnston simply glared. Rockwell paid no more attention to them both than he did to Peck. It was Lee he'd come to see.

From the tales Peck had heard about the so-called Danites, Peck had half-expected Rockwell to swagger in with a clutch of bowie knives and flintlock pistols thrust through his belt like some backwoods highwayman. The only visible weapon Rockwell had brought in with him was his unholy self-confidence. The Mormons had been whipped as thoroughly as any people ever had, and still they acted as if they'd won. From his stance, one would have guessed that it was Rockwell who was issuing terms here today.

Was this what had attracted his sister to the Mormons? Did they all have this utter certainty of their place in the universe? Peck thought of old Jim Bridger boasting of stopping Rockwell at the Mesa. Bridger might as well have tried holding back the Mississippi with a wave of a hand. Peck looked at the others. Only General Lee seemed unmoved, unperturbed.

Lee wasted no time in initial pleasantries, which seemed to suit Rockwell just fine. "You realize, of course, Rockwell, that I cannot allow your people to reach Canada. Washington will insist that you be stopped before you reach the border. You know I have the troops to run you to ground. It would be better for your people—better for all concerned—if your people would come back on their own, peacefully."

Lee rose out of his chair and walked over to the window. "The papers back East say we're out here putting down a rebellion." He turned to Rockwell. "We both know otherwise. This war was never about you Mormons or Utah. You know that; I know that. It's about slavery and Kansas and trying to take the nation's mind off of the problem that is tearing us apart. You Mormons were only a scapegoat. This war was fought to buy time so the auction blocks could continue."

Johnston drew himself up from the velvet-cushioned chair he had sprawled in. "General Lee, your being a Virginian and all, I must say I am shocked to hear you say that. The states have a perfect right to self-governance. They have a right to their own peculiar institutions."

Rockwell laughed, his voice booming off the walls. "But we don't ours? At least us Mormons enter our 'peculiar institution' by free consent—we don't require chains or whips. We have no auction blocks."

Johnston sniffed. "Utah isn't a state."

"Not from our lack of trying. For thirteen years we've asked Washington for statehood. Met the requirements for statehood a dozen times over. Three separate statehood petitions were before Congress the very day Buchanan declared us 'in rebellion' and ordered your army here. Twice the number of troops sent in to quell 'Bleeding Kansas,' I might add."

"You're rebels. Stinking treacherous Mormon rebels."

"'Rebellion?' We're begging Congress for statehood while half of Congress is talking secession themselves!"

"*Enough!*" Lee paused and gazed out the window. "Tell Brigham Young, tell your people to surrender, return and rebuild. Please." He pointed at what lay outside. "This valley—you can't let it be left like . . . like *that*."

Rockwell chuckled sourly. 'You want it rebuilt, old man? Find somebody else. You've seen our canals and dams. You've seen the desert they're holding back. Takes an entire community, working as one mind, one heart, to make a desert blossom like that. Something you'll never understand. Us Saints were the only people alive who could've worked this land. Nobody else wanted this basin. So we took it. And then, after we made something of it, suddenly you folks all want it. Same old story for us. Well, we're shut of it. We won't have it. This basin was dead when we got here. It'll stay dead 'til we come back. If we ever do."

"You may not be given a choice."

Rockwell laughed. "You may not be in a position to bully us around." He pulled a folded-up newspaper from under his buckskin jacket. "My outriders have choked your supplies off so tight, you probably haven't received the word yet, have you?" He looked at Johnston. "No, you haven't. Thought I might bring it to you myself, seeing as how Brigham's just a little too busy right now to entertain all the company staying in his house."

He tossed the paper over to Lee. It landed on the desk, face down. Lee started searching his pockets. "I'll save you the trouble of reaching for your spectacles, old man," Rockwell announced. "South Carolina has seceded. The Union is dissolved."

Like marionettes all connected to the same jerked string, Peck and the three generals rose from their chairs. Lee scrabbled for his reading glasses.

"The shooting hasn't started yet," Rockwell added. "But it will. The Federal Government will send its troops, just as it did here. You folks are going to be too busy shooting at each other to worry about us."

Lee read rapidly, his lips moving in shock. Finishing, he dropped the paper to the desk and put his face in his hands.

Johnston snatched the newspaper and read for himself. Grant walked over to a small side book cabinet that once must have held *Book of Mormon* and the like and pulled out a bottle of whiskey and a set of glasses. He poured himself a drink and stiff-wristed it in one gulp.

Peck remembered the dead Reddick's words to him: *It's our turn now, but yours is coming.* That day was already here.

"You realize, of course, that it won't be just South Carolina," Johnston said, positively buoyant. "If the North forces her back into the Union, then states rights won't be worth *that*." He snapped his fingers. "No, sir. The rest of the South will have no choice but to join alongside of her. Hand me some of that, Sam," he said to Grant. Johnston poured himself a glass of whiskey. "It's a glorious day, Bobby Lee." He hoisted his glass. "Here's to the South and a glorious new nation!"

"*This?*" roared Grant. "*This* from the man who not two minutes ago was taking such a high moral tone against 'treason' and 'rebels'?"

"This is *the South* we're talking about!"

Rockwell burst out laughing. "So. All this high-sounding talk about loyalty and rebellion! Turns out this entire war was really only about hatred and bigotry and the fear of anybody different from yourselves."

Lee sighed. "I'm afraid, Mr. Rockwell, that this parley is ended. My men and I have matters to discuss that don't concern you."

"Oh, but they do, General Lee. They do," said Rockwell. "It was the fight we put up that put the backbone in your secessionists—and it was our defeat that panicked them. More important, we hold the key to your future as much as you hold ours. I imagine your troops will be recalled back east to fight your new war. But do you really think you can march back home, back through the Echo, if we decide not to let you? We can let you be, or we can bottle you up and let you fight here among yourselves."

"There's a third choice," Grant growled. "You claim you've always been loyal. Prove it now. Come to the aid of the Union."

Rockwell only laughed. "We tried that route back in the Mexican War. You promised us statehood then. We've since learned better."

"The South can offer you better than that," Johnston said. "Complete independence! The independent nation of Deseret—with the original boundaries you petitioned Congress for."

Grant glared at him.

"You see," shrugged Rockwell. "It does concern us." He stood up. "But you're partly right. You folks have things to discuss among yourselves." He paused at the door, and turned, grinning. "Let Brigham know what you decide." He paused again. "Oh, and General Johnston—how did that speech of yours go? We could hear you quite plainly from up on the Mesa. Something about 'the erection of a government neither loyal nor acknowledging any allegiance to the Federal Government?'" He laughed again and left.

•••

Johnston ground a fist into his other hand. Grant snorted. "Rather galling, is it? Finding out you're both the same stripe of traitor?"

"It galls me only to have to give the Mormons what they want."

"Perhaps," Lee said simply, "if you hadn't shot Governor Cummings in that pointless duel, this war here would have been prevented and the new one we face would never have happened."

Johnston thumbed his chest. "Don't lay this at *my* feet, Bobby Lee. It was only a matter of time before the South had to break away. The North keeps pushing and pushing 'til they get what they want. Just like the Mormons did. Just like Kane and Cummings tried to do."

Grant drained his second glass. "And you, Robert? What is it you plan to push for? Have you made your choice yet?" He pointed at the paper. "The newspapers are calling for you to take command of the Federal Armies, you know."

Johnston's mouth fell open. "You can't be serious. You're a *Virginian*, Bobby Lee. Virginia's bound to side with us, not with the Yankees. You wouldn't fight against Virginia?"

Lee bowed his head. "No, I could never raise my hand against Virginia."

"Don't you see, General Lee," Peck burst in. "That's just what you'd be doing if you join the rebellion."

The generals all turned to look at the mere major they had all forgotten about. Peck was out of line, and knew it, but he didn't see the faces of three scowling generals, he saw the faces of Ferguson, and young Danby and Reddick. "You told me to tell you when you're wrong. Well, sir, you're wrong. You're the hero of Donner's Pass. You don't have to follow the choice Virginia makes; Virginia will follow *yours*."

"You overrate my influence, son," Lee said gently.

"And you underrate it, sir."

Lee pursed his lips. "How would I betray Virginia by defending her?"

"The South isn't going to invade the North, but the North *has* to invade the South to win. If Virginia sides with the South, the battles will be fought in Virginia. In the Shenandoah. In Richmond. In Arlington."

Johnston laughed. "Bobby Lee, you can't prevent Virginia from choosing the South, no matter what this Yankee says. My solemn word on that, Bobby Lee. My solemn word."

"Your word isn't worth quite what it was five minutes ago," snapped Grant.

"General Lee," Peck pleaded, "do you want Virginia to end up looking the way it does outside that window? Do you want a war of brother against brother, father against son?"

Grant nodded at Peck. "Robert," he said slowly, "you've seen now what making war with guns like the Agar means. Imagine an Echo Canyon or a Donner's Pass across the width and breadth of the nation. Is that what you want for Virginia? For the nation? It's your choice."

Lee was silent for a long time. "You all seem to think I should be allowed a choice." They nodded. "If I am to be allowed a choice, then the men must be allowed their choice as well."

"And the Mormons?" Peck asked.

Lee turned to him and sighed. "The South cannot claim self-governance in one breath and deny it to the Mormons in the next. Nor can the North afford to continue to fight one war here and one with the South. I imagine they'll end up with whatever they decide they want—statehood or independence."

Grant flung his cigar on the floor and crushed it under his boot. "They can stew in their own juices for all I care."

"I think that's what they've wanted all along," Peck said softly.

Lee got up and walked again to the window. "I feel as if I have the fate of a nation resting on my shoulders. Or the fate of three." He sighed. "This new war we're about to fight will still be over the same questions this unfinished war here is being fought over. Who holds the higher allegiance: one's people or one's nation? Do you have the right to live in a manner your neighbor finds morally repugnant? Does he have the right to prevent you from doing so?"

"Depends on which side is right," said Johnston.

Grant knocked back another whiskey. "Depends on which side is wrong."

"In a war where both sides have Agars and Brownings," Peck whispered, "does it matter?"

From outside the window they could hear the Mormon prisoners begin singing again, not a hymn this time, but a mocking song of defiance:

> The Army is leaving, they've got a new fight.
> > (A profi'ble prophet am I!)
> The South has seceded, slunk off in the night.
> > (A profi'ble prophet am I!)
> They've stopped chasing Mormons since Sumter's been shot.
> > It's hard not to laugh at the troubles they've got.
> We'll watch here from Utah and hope they all rot.
> > A propitiative prophet I'm not!

Lee fell silent. At length he asked Peck to help him on with his jacket. "Walk with me, Peck, to that temple lot. Perhaps I can decide whether those granite blocks lying there are the unfinished foundation of a new nation; or the tombstones of a foolish, lost cause."

And outside the window, flags were flying, brass bands playing. Boots were tramping, boots that soon would be tramping off to another war.

ABOUT WRITERS OF THE FUTURE

Written by
Dave Wolverton

About the Author

As the Coordinating Judge for the Writers of The Future Contest, *Dave Wolverton reads each contest entry before choosing which to pass on to the other judges. In addition, he edits the anthology and teaches writing workshops.*

Dave's novels have placed high on a number of bestseller lists, including the New York Times *and* London Sunday News *bestsellers lists. He has won awards for his short fiction, novels and poetry.*

Wolverton's seventh novel, Lords of the Seventh Swarm, *recently appeared in hard cover from Tor books, completing the "Golden Queen" series. Though Wolverton has won awards for both his mainstream writing and his science fiction, his first love has always been fantasy, so he is happy to announce that he has just finished his first fantasy novel,* The Sum of All Men, *and that it will be published by Tor in 1998.*

Fourteen years ago, L. Ron Hubbard founded the Writers of The Future Contest, the world's largest program designed to help discover, train and promote new writers of science fiction, fantasy and horror.

Nine years ago, a sister contest, the Illustrators of The Future Contest, was initiated with the same goal.

The fine writers and illustrators of tomorrow are alive today, aching to be discovered. Some of the names you see in this anthology may well rank up there with Tim Powers or Bob Eggleton in five years. We've found winners on five continents, in dozens of countries.

The Writers of The Future and Illustrators of The Future Contests are sponsored by Author Services, Inc., which pays prize money to contest winners. In addition, Bridge Publications, Inc., pays generously for the right to print the winners' stories and illustrations in this anthology.

The *Writers of The Future Contest* offers three quarterly prizes for our writers: $1,000 for our first-place winner, $750 for our second-place winner, and $500 for our third-place winner. In addition, each year our judges evaluate the four first-place winners and bestow a grand prize of an additional $4000.

Each author published in the volume is given the opportunity to attend an awards ceremony where he or she gets to meet contest judges and participate in a week-long writing workshop designed to help launch writers in their chosen profession.

This year, we have added one new writer to our illustrious panel of judges. Doug Beason has joined our ranks. Doug has worked with Kevin J. Anderson on a number of projects, including the blockbuster novel *Ignition*, which will soon appear from Tor and which is being made into a major motion picture. In addition to being a fine writer of hard science fiction, mysteries and adventure, Doug is also one of the nation's top scientists.

Our writing judges for this year are Kevin J. Anderson, Doug Beason, Gregory Benford, Algis Budrys, Anne McCaffrey, Larry Niven, Andre Norton, Frederik Pohl, Jerry Pournelle, Robert Silverberg, Tim Powers, Jack Williamson and Dave Wolverton.

•••

All of our illustrators also receive prize money, payment for publication and workshops of their own.

Each illustrator submitted three works of illustration in the competition. Based on those entries, three winners each quarter received a $500 prize and the opportunity to compete at a higher level. The three winning illustrators were then each assigned one of the prize-winning stories from their quarter and were given a limited amount of time to complete an illustration. Bridge Publications paid the illustrators for the right to publish the illustration for the story in the upcoming anthology and the assigned illustration was then entered into the final round of competition.

The illustrator judges evaluate the twelve finalist pieces at the end of the year, then select the grand prize winner.

Our illustrator judges for this year were Edd Cartier, Leo and Diane Dillon, Vincent Di Fate, Bob Eggleton, Will Eisner, Frank Frazetta, Frank Kelly-Freas, Laura Brodian Kelly-Freas, Shun Kijima, Paul Lehr, Ron and Val Lakey and H. R. van Dongen.

We would like to heartily thank all our contest judges for their time and support.

Below you will find a list of all our winning authors and illustrators for the year. We wish them great good fortune:

Writers of the Future Prize Winners in this Volume:

First Quarter

First Place: Morgan Burke, "A Prayer for the Insect Gods"
Second Place: Alan Smale, "Wings"
Third Place: David L. Felts, "Troder"

Second Quarter

First Place: Kyle David Jelle, "Black on Black"
Second Place: Malcolm Twigg, "Altar"
Third Place: Heidi Stallman, "The Winds"

Third Quarter

First Place: Bo Griffin, "The Scent of Desire"
Second Place: Janet Martin, "White Jade"
Third Place: Sara Backer, "Orange"

Fourth Quarter

First Place: Lee Allred, "For the Strength of the Hills"
Second Place: Ken Rand, "The Gods Perspire"
Third Place: S. Seaport, "Recursion"

Published Finalist

Cati Coe, "The Garden"

Illustrator Winners

Karen Pollitt
Eric Williams
Arthur Roberg
Nathan Hale
Jack Hines
Mia Hopper
David T. Hubbard
Igor Baranko
Ulia Semenenko
Steve Turner
Partrick Haslow
Victoria Dunayeva

NEW WRITERS!

L. Ron Hubbard's
Writers of The Future Contest

A Contest for New Writers & Amateur Writers

OPPORTUNITY FOR
NEW AND AMATEUR WRITERS OF
NEW SHORT STORIES OR NOVELETTES OF
SCIENCE FICTION OR FANTASY

No entry fee is required.
Entrants retain all publication rights.

ALL AWARDS ARE ADJUDICATED BY
PROFESSIONAL WRITERS ONLY

PRIZES EVERY THREE MONTHS: $1,000, $750, $500.
ANNUAL GRAND PRIZE: $4,000 ADDITIONAL!

Don't Delay! Send Your Entry to:

L. Ron Hubbard's
Writers of The Future Contest
P.O. Box 1630
Los Angeles, CA 90078

CONTEST RULES

1. No entry fee is required, and all rights in the story remain the property of the author. All types of science fiction and fantasy are welcome; every entry is judged on its own merits only.

2. All entries must be original works of science fiction or fantasy in English. Plagiarism will result in disqualification. Submitted works may not have been previously published in professional media.

3. Eligible entries must be works of prose, either short stories (under 10,000 words) or novelettes (under 17,000 words) in length. We regret we cannot consider poetry, or works intended for children.

4. The Contest is open only to those who have not had professionally published a novel or short novel, or more than one novelette or more than three short stories.

5. Entries must be typewritten and double-spaced with numbered pages (computer-printer output okay). Each entry must have a cover page with the title of the work, the author's name, address and telephone number, and an approximate word count. The manuscript itself should be titled and numbered on every page, but the author's name should be deleted to facilitate fair judging.

6. Manuscripts will be returned after judging. Entries must include a self-addressed return envelope. U.S. return envelopes must be stamped; others may enclose international postal reply coupons.

7. There shall be three cash prizes in each quarter: 1st Prize of $1,000, 2nd Prize of $750, and 3rd Prize of $500, in U.S. dollars or the recipient's local equivalent amount. In addition, there shall be a further cash prize of $4,000 to the grand prize winner, who will be selected from among the 1st Prize winners for the period of October 1, 1997, through September 30, 1998. All winners will also receive trophies or certificates.

8. The Contest will continue through September 30, 1998, on the following quarterly basis:

October 1–December 31, 1997   January 1–March 31, 1998

April 1–June 30, 1998   July 1–September 30, 1998

Information regarding subsequent contests may be obtained by sending a self-addressed, stamped business-size envelope to the above address.

To be eligible for the quarterly judging, an entry must be postmarked no later than midnight on the last day of the quarter.

9. Each entrant may submit only one manuscript per quarter. Winners in a quarterly judging are ineligible to make further entries in this or any future Contests.

10. All entrants, including winners, retain all rights to their stories.

11. Entries will be judged by a panel of professional authors. Each quarterly judging and the grand prize judging may have a different panel. The decisions of the judges are entirely their own, and are final.

12. Entrants in each quarter will be individually notified of the results by mail, together with the names of those sitting on the panel of judges.

This Contest is void where prohibited by law.

© 1997, L. Ron Hubbard Library. All Rights Reserved.

L. Ron Hubbard's

ILLUSTRATORS OF THE FUTURE CONTEST

OPEN TO NEW SCIENCE FICTION
AND FANTASY ARTISTS
WORLDWIDE

All Judging by Professional Artists Only

$1,500 in Prizes Each Quarter
No Entry Fee   Entrants Retain All Rights

**Quarterly Winners compete for
$4,000 additional ANNUAL PRIZE**

L. Ron Hubbard's
Illustrators of The Future Contest
P.O. Box 3190
Los Angeles, CA 90078

1. The Contest is open to entrants from all nations. (However, entrants should provide themselves with some means for written communication in English.) All themes of science fiction and fantasy illustration are welcome: every entry is judged on its own merits only. No entry fee is required, and all rights in the entries remain the property of their artists.

2. By submitting work to the Contest, the entrant agrees to abide by all Contest rules.

3. This Contest is open to those who have not previously published more than three black-and-white story illustrations, or more than one process-color painting, in media distributed nationally to the general public, such as magazines or books sold at newsstands, or books sold in stores merchandising to the general public. The submitted entry shall not have been previously published in professional media as exampled above.

If you are not sure of your eligibility, write to the Contest address with details, enclosing a business-size self-addressed envelope with return postage. The Contest Administration will reply with a determination.

Winners in previous quarters are not eligible to make further entries.

4. Only one entry per quarter is permitted. The entry must be original to the entrant. Plagiarism, infringement of the rights of others, or other violations of the Contest rules will result in disqualification.

5. An entry shall consist of three illustrations done by the entrant in a black-and-white medium. Each must represent a theme different from the other two.

6. ENTRIES SHOULD NOT BE THE ORIGINAL DRAWINGS, but should be large black-and-white photocopies of a quality satisfactory to the entrant. Entries must be submitted unfolded and flat, in an envelope no larger than 9 inches by 12 inches.

All entries must be accompanied by a self-addressed return envelope of the appropriate size, with correct U.S. postage affixed. (Non-U.S. entrants should enclose international postal reply coupons.)

If the entrant does not want the photocopies returned, the entry should be clearly marked DISPOSABLE COPIES: DO NOT RETURN. A business-size self-addressed envelope with correct postage should be included so that judging results can be returned to the entrant.

7. To facilitate anonymous judging, each of the three photocopies must be accompanied by a removable cover sheet bearing the artist's name, address, and telephone number, and an identifying title for that work. The photocopy of the work should carry the same identifying title, and the artist's signature should be deleted from the photocopy.

The Contest Administration will remove and file the cover sheets, and forward only the anonymous entry to the judges.

8. To be eligible for a quarterly judging, an entry must be postmarked no later than the last day of the quarter.

Late entries will be included in the following quarter, and the Contest Administration will so notify the entrant.

9. There will be three co-winners in each quarter. Each winner will receive an outright cash grant of U.S. $500, and a certificate of merit. Such winners also receive eligibility to compete for the annual grand prize of an additional outright cash grant of $4,000 together with the annual grand prize trophy.

10. Competition for the grand prize is designed to acquaint the entrant with customary practices in the field of professional illustrating. It will be conducted in the following manner:

Each winner in each quarter will be furnished a Specification Sheet giving details on the size and kind of black-and-white illustration work required by grand prize competition. Requirements will be of the sort customarily stated by professional publishing companies.

These specifications will be furnished to the entrant by the Contest Administration, using Return Receipt Requested mail or its equivalent.

Also furnished will be a copy of a science fiction or fantasy story, to be illustrated by the entrant. This story will have been selected for that purpose by the Coordinating Judge of the Contest. Thereafter, the entrant will work toward completing the assigned illustration.

In order to retain eligibility for the grand prize, each entrant shall, within thirty (30) days of receipt of the said story assignment, send to the Contest address the entrant's black-and-white page illustration of the assigned story in accordance with the Specification Sheet.

The entrant's finished illustration shall be in the form of camera-ready art prepared in accordance with the Specification Sheet and securely packed, shipped at the entrant's own risk. The Contest will exercise due care in handling all submissions as received.

The said illustration will then be judged in competition for the grand prize on the following basis only:

Each Grand Prize judge's personal opinion on the extent to which it makes the judge want to read the story it illustrates.

The entrant shall retain copyright in the said illustration.

11. The Contest year will continue through September 30, 1998, with the following quarterly periods (see Rule 8):

April 1–June 30, 1997   July 1–September 30, 1997

The next Contest will continue through September 30, 1998, on the following quarterly basis:

October 1–December 31, 1997   January 1–March 31, 1998

April 1–June 30, 1998   July 1–September 30, 1998

Entrants in each quarter will be individually notified of the quarter's judging results by mail. Winning entrants' participation in the Contest shall continue until the results of the grand prize judging have been announced.

Information regarding subsequent contests may be obtained by sending a self-addressed business-size envelope, with postage, to the Contest address.

12. The grand prize winner will be announced at the L. Ron Hubbard Awards events to be held in the calendar year of 1998.

13. Entries will be judged by professional artists only. Each quarterly judging and the grand prize judging may have a different panel of judges. The decisions of the judges are entirely their own, and are final.

14. This Contest is void where prohibited by law.

© 1997 L. Ron Hubbard Library. All Rights Reserved.

FINAL BLACKOUT

London 1975. As the great World War grinds to a halt, a malignant force more sinister than Hitler's Nazis has seized control of Europe and is systematically destroying every adversary...

In the heart of France, a crack unit of British soldiers survive, overcoming all opposition under the leadership of a hardened military strategist highly trained in every method of combat—known only as "the Lieutenant"...

Ordered to return to British Headquarters, the lieutenant is torn between obeying his military code and satisfying the politicians in London or doing what he knows is right for his country, regardless of the price.

Hardcover: $16.95
Paperback: $6.99
Audio: $11.95
(2 Cassettes, 3 hours)
Narrated by Roddy McDowall

"Compelling... riveting..."

Publishers Weekly

**Order Your Copy Today! http://www.bridgepub.com
or Call 1-800-722-1733**
or mail the tear off card with your order to: Bridge Publications, Inc.
4751 Fountain Ave., Los Angeles, CA 90029

TRAVEL 1000 YEARS INTO THE FUTURE TO MANKIND'S LAST FIGHT FOR FREEDOM

Written by L. Ron Hubbard, supreme storyteller and an absolute master of the genre, *Battlefield Earth* is one of the biggest and most acclaimed science fiction books ever published.

The story is set in the year 3000, when most humans have been destroyed and Earth is ruled by the Psychlos, a cruel, tough, alien race of invaders whose only interest in the planet is its mineral resources and wealth, which they continue to plunder. But when one lone man, Jonnie Goodboy Tyler, decides to break away from a small band of survivors to challenge the power and might of the Psychlos, the scene is set for a fast-moving, thrilling adventure of suspense, intergalactic warfare, intrigue and romance which will keep you gripped for hours. Read this book and find out for yourself why *Battlefield Earth* was voted by a survey of thousands of fans as one of the best SF novels of all time.

"Battlefield Earth is like a 12-hour 'Indiana Jones' marathon. Non-stop and fast-paced!"
—Kevin J. Anderson

Hardcover, $25.00, paperback $6.99
Audio narrated by Roddy McDowall, 6 cassettes, $29.95

ESCAPE THROUGH A GATEWAY TO ANOTHER WORLD...

Mike de Wolf, friend of the popular pulp fiction writer Horace Hackett, finds himself transported through a freak accident into the pages of Horace's swashbuckling work-in-progress. But to his horror, he finds himself cast as the villain with only one end in sight — his own...

ORDER YOUR COPY TODAY! CALL 1-800-722-1733
or mail the tear off card with your order to: Bridge Publications, Inc.
4751 Fountain Ave., Los Angeles, CA 90029

"A classic tale of creeping, surreal menace and horror... one of the really, really good ones." — Stephen King

"Of all L. Ron Hubbard's stories, this is my favorite."
— Isaac Asimov

FEAR

Professor James Lowry didn't believe in spirits, or witches, or demons.

Not until a gentle spring evening when his hat disappeared, and suddenly he couldn't remember the last four hours of his life.

Now, the quiet university town of Atworthy is changing — slightly at first, then faster and more frighteningly each time he tries to remember.

Lowry is pursued by a dark, secret evil that is turning his whole world against him while it whispers a warning from the shadows: "If you find your hat you'll find your four hours. If you find your four hours then you will die..."

Hardcover: $16.95
Paperback: $5.99
Audio (2 cassettes, 3 hours): $15.95
Narrated by Roddy McDowall

Order Your Copy Today! Call 1-800-722-1733
or mail the tear off card with your order to: Bridge Publications, Inc.
4751 Fountain Ave., Los Angeles, CA 90029